Sign up for our newsletter to hear
about new and upcoming releases.

www.ylva-publishing.com

BOOKS IN THE SERIES
CHRONICLES OF ALSEA

The Caphenon
(Book #1)

Without a Front: The Producer's Challenge
(Book #2)

CHRONICLES OF ALSEA

WITHOUT A FRONT

THE WARRIOR'S CHALLENGE

Fletcher DeLancey

For all the tyrees.

TABLE OF CONTENTS

PART ONE:
- Chapter 1: *Burned* ... 1
- Chapter 2: *Incompetence* ... 9
- Chapter 3: *Non-interference* ... 11
- Chapter 4: *Restriction* ... 15
- Chapter 5: *Window to a bond* ... 22
- Chapter 6: *Release* ... 27
- Chapter 7: *Publicity* ... 30
- Chapter 8: *Freedom* ... 33
- Chapter 9: *An unlikely source* ... 44
- Chapter 10: *State House quarters* ... 46
- Chapter 11: *Little spy* ... 51
- Chapter 12: *Breaking the boundary* ... 58
- Chapter 13: *Warrior types* ... 78
- Chapter 14: *Herot's message* ... 84

PART TWO:
- Chapter 15: *Investigations* ... 93
- Chapter 16: *The whole truth* ... 95
- Chapter 17: *Picking up pieces* ... 99
- Chapter 18: *Micah speaks* ... 103
- Chapter 19: *Salomen's strategy* ... 109
- Chapter 20: *True terror* ... 113
- Chapter 21: *Skimming Ebron* ... 118
- Chapter 22: *To Herot's health* ... 123
- Chapter 23: *Lead Guard Vellmar* ... 125
- Chapter 24: *A different way* ... 130
- Chapter 25: *Sharing a search* ... 133
- Chapter 26: *Oath of service* ... 142
- Chapter 27: *Group Sharing* ... 145
- Chapter 28: *Traitor* ... 148
- Chapter 29: *Game of tiles* ... 151

PART THREE:
- Chapter 30: *It's still magic* ... 159
- Chapter 31: *The payoff* ... 161
- Chapter 32: *Plan of action* ... 162
- Chapter 33: *Fear and failure* ... 165
- Chapter 34: *Extraction* ... 172
- Chapter 35: *Team blue* ... 182
- Chapter 36: *Path of the Return* ... 186
- Chapter 37: *Counting heartbeats* ... 193
- Chapter 38: *Redmoon* ... 196

Chapter 39: *Prisoner waking* 206
  Chapter 40: *Scope of betrayal* 209
  Chapter 41: *Isolation* 218

PART FOUR:
  Chapter 42: *Loyalty test* 225
  Chapter 43: *Herot's education* 232
  Chapter 44: *Morning in Redmoon* 240
  Chapter 45: *Family* 243
  Chapter 46: *Bondlancer* 247
  Chapter 47: *Strategy session* 261
  Chapter 48: *Stuck in the web* 272
  Chapter 49: *Dream job* 274
  Chapter 50: *Siblings* 279
  Chapter 51: *A breed apart* 289
  Chapter 52: *Sparring* 292
  Chapter 53: *Bedside visit* 296
  Chapter 54: *Awake in the dark* 300
  Chapter 55: *Looking for the Lancer* 301
  Chapter 56: *The warrior's challenge* 303
  Chapter 57: *Fahla's champion* 313

PART FIVE:
  Chapter 58: *First run* 325
  Chapter 59: *The return* 328
  Chapter 60: *Sentence* 336
  Chapter 61: *The Chosen* 340
  Chapter 62: *Autumn feast* 343
  Chapter 63: *Damage control* 349
  Chapter 64: *Inclusion* 356
  Chapter 65: *Flames in the temple II* 363

Glossary 375

About Fletcher DeLancey 383

Other Books from Ylva Publishing 385

ACKNOWLEDGMENTS

I could probably make this section very short and simply say, "Please read the acknowledgments from *Without A Front: The Producer's Challenge*," since the same team supported me through both that novel and this. But that's a bit of a cop-out, because who is going to get out of their comfy chair and go pull another novel off a shelf to check the acknowledgments page? Or close this file and open a different one on their e-reader?

So let's give these people the recognition they deserve for all their hard work and support.

As always, the greatest thanks go to my tyree, Maria João Valente. She taught me the difference between contentment and happiness, and inspired me to pursue the latter. She also makes really, really excellent gin and tonics.

Karyn Aho was indispensable when it came to analyzing characters and plot lines, and kindly pointed out when I dropped a detail or two while juggling a few hundred of them. I am particularly grateful for her expertise in psychotherapy, which came in especially handy in two chapters of this book.

In addition to general beta reading, Rick Taylor made sure that any references to swords or sparring carried the weight of realism and provided the impetus for me to turn a throwaway mention into several paragraphs of world-building. It never occurred to me to think about whether a sword was single-edged or double-edged until he asked.

Rounding out my list of expert consultants are Saskia Goedhart for martial arts and S. N. Johnson-Roehr for astronomy. Thank you, ladies, for making sure I didn't guess wrong.

Rebecca Cheek hired on for the beta-reading and fact-checking job without the slightest idea of what it would require, and though I'm certain it involved far more time than she had anticipated, she dove in with the focus and drive for which she is famous. (And also with a good dose of acerbic Southern commentary, which I understand is good for me.) I completely rewrote one chapter in response to her feedback, and it is so much better for it.

Erin Saluta wrapped up my beta reading team, acting as the proxy for readers who lead with their hearts. Since I lead with my head, I need that alternative viewpoint.

In the production department, I'm grateful to Glendon Haddix of Streetlight Graphics for the atmospheric cover, and Astrid Ohletz for being both publisher and friend. My editor Sandra Gerth is a joy to work with, as is my copy editor Cheri Fuller, who is not averse to cussing me out in the margins because she got emotionally involved while scanning for errors. Lisa Shaw is possibly the fastest proofreader in the West, though I'm still grumbling about the amount of work she caused with a single observation.

Finally, thank you to Daniela Huege and all of the folks at Ylva Publishing. You're a great team.

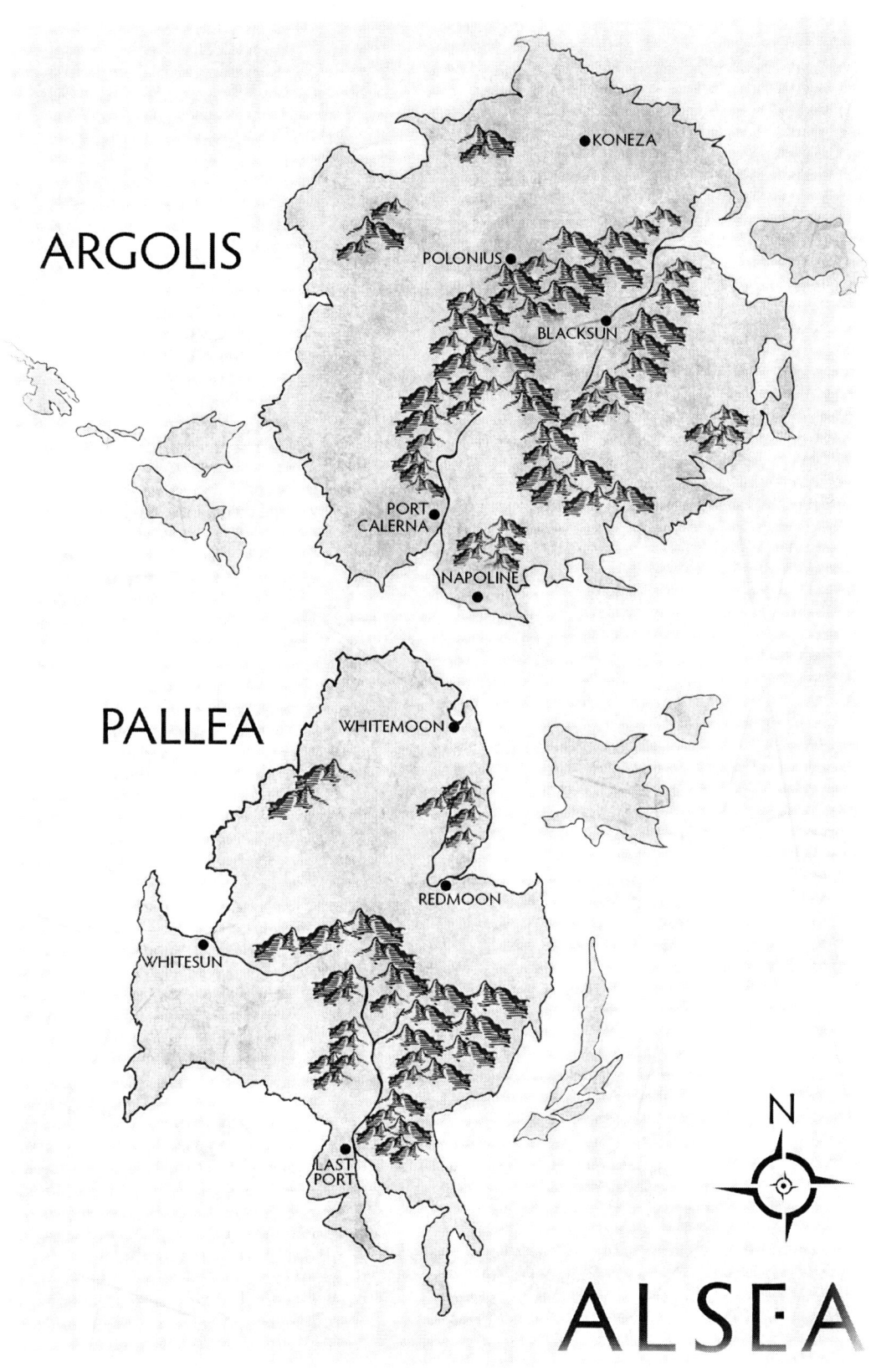

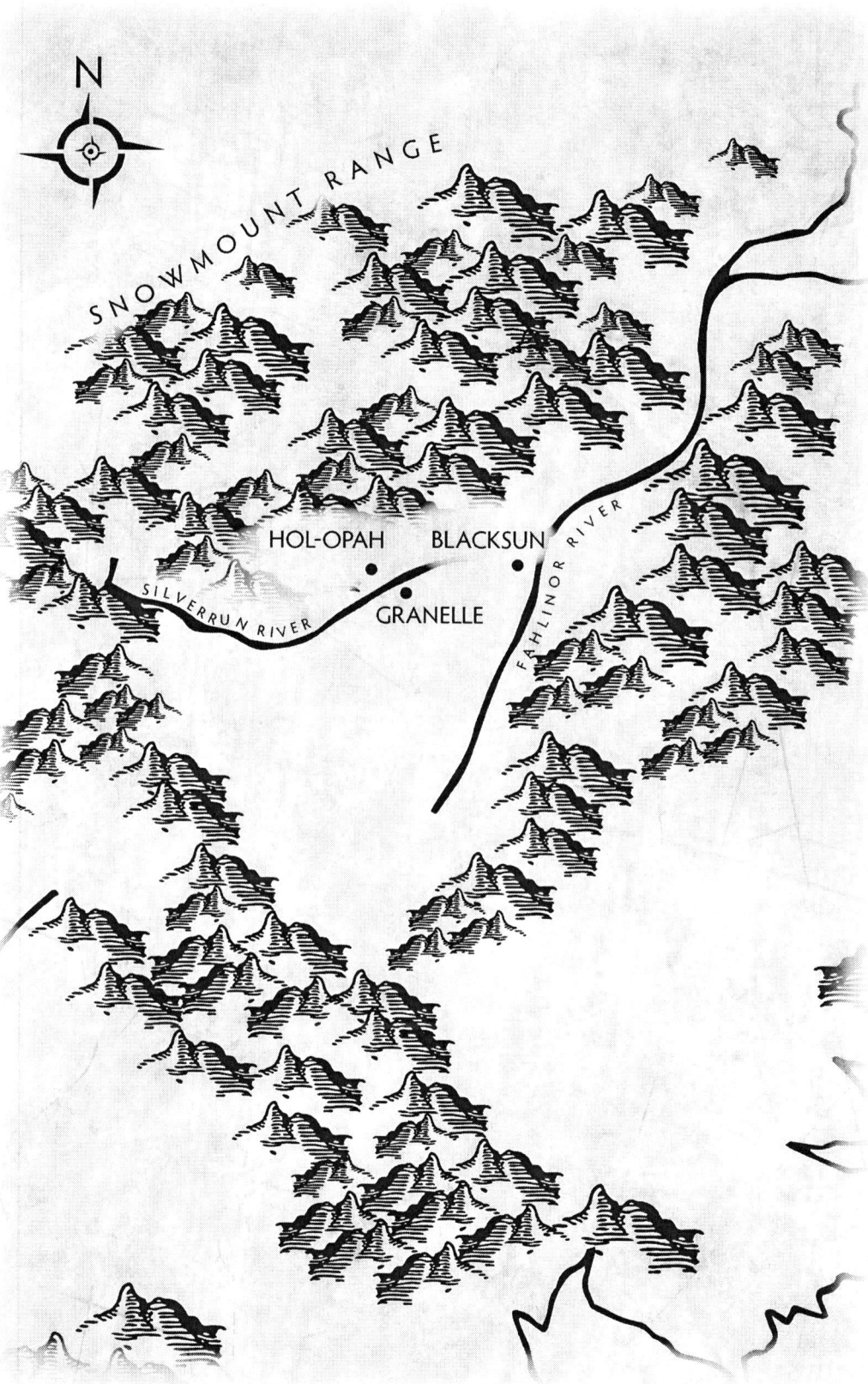

PART ONE:

CONFLAGRATION

CHAPTER 1
Burned

"Andira...wake up."

"I can feel you. You're almost there."

"Please, tyrina. Come the rest of the way."

"No change?"

Tal heard Salomen's voice, but the words made no sense, not until the deeper tones of Micah registered. She wanted to assure them that she was all right, but everything seemed so slow.

"No." Salomen's voice again. "I can feel her; she's just under the surface. Thank the Goddess I at least have that. If we hadn't Shared, they would probably have sedated me by now."

"She'll be all right. Healer Tornell is the best in her field. If she says the damage can be repaired, then it can."

"I know. It's just so hard to see her like this."

"Like what?" Tal mumbled.

A gasp sounded above her as someone touched the back of her neck.

"There you are!" Salomen's voice was in her ear. "You frightened me most of the way to my Return!" Soft lips kissed her neck, and Tal managed to open her eyes. She quickly shut them again; the room was far too bright.

"Sorry." It hurt to speak, but she felt an urgent need to tell Salomen that she hadn't meant to frighten her.

Salomen's laugh was halfway to a sob. "Don't you dare apologize to me."

Another kiss was pressed to the same place, and Salomen lingered there before pulling away with a reluctance that Tal could barely sense. Her mind seemed to be wrapped in feathers.

And her throat felt as if she had been chewing on cinders. "Thirsty..."

Footsteps hurried on a hard floor, away and back, and Salomen's voice came from a different direction. Below her, somehow. "I have some water here if you'll open your mouth."

She did, expecting that water would be poured in, but then something bumped against her lower lip. Instinctively, she closed her lips on it and sucked. Cool water filled her mouth, and she held it for a moment, marshaling the courage to swallow when she knew it was going to hurt.

Oh, but it was worth it. The hot coals in her throat were quenched, and she imagined wisps of smoke coming out of her nostrils. She sucked up a lake's worth of water, then cleared her throat and tried her voice again.

"How bad is it? What do I look like?"

Much better. Her voice was rough, but she could speak normally.

"Like something the fanten stomped over and refused to eat," Micah said.

"Thanks, Micah. I can always depend on you."

"Can you open your eyes?" Salomen asked.

"I think so." Tal carefully opened her eyes a bare slit, testing the brightness and finding it tolerable this time. She widened the slit and blinked several times, confused by the fact that she saw nothing but the blue of the ocean on a summer afternoon.

Oh. It was a floor.

"No blue floors in Hol-Opah. Are we in Blacksun?"

Salomen's face appeared at the edge of her vision. "Yes. We're in the healing center. How are you feeling?"

"Like something the fanten stomped over and refused to eat. Though a good deal better than before."

Micah's face appeared next to Salomen's. "I was joking. You don't look bad, considering what might have been."

"Healer Tornell says you'll be on your feet in half a nineday," Salomen said. "Your back is badly burned, and you have a few burns on your legs as well. But she says the damage can be repaired. The hard part will be staying on this restriction bed for five days while the gel packs are working."

Tal shifted her head in the padded ring supporting it, wanting to look at them more directly. She frowned when she found them crouched down in order to see her. "Do they not have chairs?"

Salomen sat cross-legged on the floor, and Micah soon followed, though with far less grace. "None low enough for this," Salomen said. "It's so good to see you awake."

"It's good to see you, too. But I can't feel you. I can't feel anything."

With a trembling smile, Salomen caressed the part of her face that she could reach. "That's the medication. It blocks your empathic senses as well as your pain receptors."

Tal remembered now. She had required that medication on other occasions, with the same result. It was the worst thing about being under the care of a healer. She stared at Salomen, trying with all her might to break through, but all she could pick up were whispers of emotions. When Salomen dropped her hand, even those vanished.

"I would almost prefer the pain. To go from a Sharing to this…"

"I know. I've been trying to tell myself that this is more of Fahla's sense of humor."

Tal looked at her more closely, seeing the signs of past worry and fear. "Are you all right?"

"Thanks to you, yes."

"That's not what I meant." She was beginning to feel a little more in command of herself. "You were Sharing my pain."

"It's gone, Andira. It was gone as soon as I let you go. I'm tired, but all right."

"Thank the Goddess." There was so much more to say, but not with Micah there. "What time is it?" she asked instead.

"Night-two."

"So it's only been a few hanticks." She looked at Micah. "Did you get him?"

"He's in custody on the base. Colonel Razine has already questioned him. I asked her to take care of it personally."

"And the weapon?"

"It was a plasma gun. He claims it's been in his family for three generations, and Gordense and Iversina confirm it."

That made no sense. "Nobody uses a plasma gun for a long-range sniper shot. They're not accurate enough."

"We think this was an isolated action. Cullom is on the very low range of mid-empathy; Colonel Razine had no difficulty with him. According to her report, he was acting entirely of his own volition. It wasn't exactly a well-planned or well-equipped mission."

He watched her too steadily, and Salomen's gaze was on the floor.

"My senses may be blocked," Tal said, "but I know there's something you're not telling me. I want to see that report."

"Perhaps you should wait until you're feeling a little better," he suggested.

"I'm feeling well enough. Give me the report."

Micah looked at Salomen, who nodded.

Tal narrowed her eyes. "I don't recall abdicating my authority to Salomen. My brain is still functioning quite well, thank you. What are you two hiding?"

Without a word, Salomen got up and left the room.

Tal watched as far as she could crane her neck, looking back at Micah when she heard the door shut. "What is going on?"

He sighed. "This hasn't been easy for her."

"I...I know that." Damn, but she hated feeling like this. "Micah, I'm blind as a sonsales and I don't know what's happening, but something obviously is. Just tell me the truth. I can handle it."

Even now he hesitated, and she began to worry. Something was seriously wrong.

"Cullom had help," he said at last. "Plasma guns may be inaccurate, but they're good enough if all you need to do is hit a large window."

She stared at him, trying to see what he was leading to. "So he knew that was my room? But..." A shock ran down her spine. "He knew I sat in that seat, didn't he? At a regular time each night. He had inside information." There was only one person it could have been.

Micah nodded. "We're still looking for Herot."

"Oh, no," she groaned. "Salomen…"

"She has the bearing of a warrior. You would never guess to look at her that she nearly died because of her own brother."

"I'll kill him with my bare hands. That fantenshekken! He'd best run long and far, because when I find him I will *tear him apart.*" She already knew which of his bones she would break first.

"And you will lose Salomen," Micah said sharply. "This isn't you talking. You have some powerful drugs in your system, and one of them is interfering with your emotional control. Healer Tornell told us to expect it."

Tal closed her eyes. Perfect. Maybe she really should abdicate temporarily. No empathic senses, no emotional control, and no ability to do anything except lie in this damned bed and let everyone else deal with the crisis. "All right. At least knowing that allows me to recognize it. Just tell me everything. I promise to be reasonable."

"Don't make promises you cannot keep." He settled himself more comfortably. "There isn't much to tell. Cullom was intercepted on Hol-Opah, thanks to your information on his location. The three outer Guards were at different areas on the holding, and he timed it just right so that none of them were in empathic range. We can thank Herot for that. If Cullom hadn't been told that all he had to do was hit the window, he would have required a much closer approach and would have been well within range of our empathic net. He would never have gotten off a shot."

"But Herot told him that I sit in the window seat every night after evenmeal, so all he had to do was wait until he could see a shape in the window through the targeting lens. Which is easy at night when the room is lit."

"Actually, he didn't wait at all. As I said, this was not a professional mission. He was drinking at the tavern with Herot and left after Herot told him that you…well, that you thought you were untouchable with your Guards, but anybody could kill you without half trying. When Cullom pressed him on it, Herot was apparently very forthcoming, explaining that you could be taken out with a simple shot through the correct window from the west side of Hol-Opah. He also informed him that only three Guards were patrolling the outer ranges of the property."

Tal could hardly believe it. "He may as well have taken the shot himself. How could he hate me that much and hide it?"

"I don't know. Neither does Salomen. She doesn't believe he did, but right now we're all questioning our assumptions about him."

Tal hoped that wherever Herot was, he was terrified out of his mind. He deserved that and so much more. "So Cullom left the tavern, probably worse for the spirits, and decided to act out a little fantasy."

"Yes, after stopping by his house to pick up the plasma gun, which his father kept in a case in their parlor."

"And Gordense didn't question his son running off into the night, drunk and carrying their heirloom plasma gun?"

"He says he never saw Cullom return from the tavern. I wouldn't have believed him, but I took Gehrain with me and he confirms that Gordense was telling the truth."

"Ironic," Tal said. "We've always been so concerned about a professional attempt by someone in the warrior or scholar caste wanting to create an opening for themselves. Or something arranged by the fringe that wants me dead because I broke Fahla's covenant. And when it finally happens, it's a young, spoiled producer who gets drunk and decides to go out and kill the Lancer before bedtime."

"With considerable help from his drinking partner, Herot Opah," Micah said in disgust.

"Does the rest of the family know yet?"

He shook his head. "They're shaken up enough as it is, what with half the room being destroyed by the plasma blast. Salomen spoke with Nikin a hantick ago. They were still cleaning up the mess. I told them to send any bills to me."

"Good. Do we have any leads on Herot?"

"Not yet. The tavern owner says he left half a hantick after Cullom did, but none of the Opahs ever saw him. I'm still trying to guess his state of mind. Did he have no idea that Cullom would act on his information, and that's why he stayed at the tavern? Or did he know what Cullom planned, and stayed precisely for that reason?"

"And Cullom can't tell us that."

"No. We need to find Herot."

Tal processed that for a few moments, then asked, "What about the media?"

"It hasn't been publicized yet. Miltorin is making an announcement in five hanticks. He'll say there was an attempted assassination, that you sustained minor injuries from which you will fully recover—we didn't think it wise to advertise just how badly you were actually hurt—and that the criminal has been identified and detained." For the first time in his report, Micah hesitated. "In the absence of instructions to the contrary, I told Miltorin to keep Herot's name out of it."

"You did right. He doesn't deserve the consideration, but his family does. But we'll need to prepare them for the inevitable. Herot's absence won't go unnoticed for long."

"No, it won't. But at least we can give them a little room to breathe."

"Very little. What a mess. It couldn't get much worse, could it?"

"Oh, yes," he said quietly. "It could have been far, far worse."

Tal's imagination brought up a vivid illustration of just how bad it could have been, so horrifying in its intensity that for half a piptick she could hear the screaming.

"Is that all of it?" she managed.

He nodded. "At this point it's mostly a matter of waiting."

"Then would you ask Salomen to come back in?"

"Certainly. Salomen!" Micah called.

Tal glared. "I could have done that myself."

"You could have, but you asked me to."

The door opened, and Salomen settled down next to Micah. Just seeing her alive and in one piece was an enormous relief, but when she looked up, Tal's heart stuttered. She had been crying.

"Now you know," she said softly. "I'm so sorry, Andira. I have no defense for my brother; he's brought dishonor to our name even if this wasn't intentional. And I can only pray that it wasn't."

Tears were rising in Tal's eyes as well, just from seeing her misery. Damned medication!

"Micah, I need to see Salomen alone."

To her confusion, Micah turned to Salomen and said, "Will you aid an old warrior?"

"You're not old. Just slightly dented." She wrapped her hands around Micah's upper arm and helped him to his feet.

Tal gasped. "Micah! Your hands!"

He crouched down again, back into her field of view, and looked at his hands as if he hadn't noticed they were encased in gel gloves. "As she said, I'm slightly dented."

"He burned nearly all the skin off his hands trying to get the molten glass off you," Salomen said.

The realization sent shivers all the way to Tal's toes. "That was Fahla's sign. At Whitemoon Temple."

They looked at each other, then at her. "We hadn't thought of that," Micah said.

Salomen nodded. "Too much else to think of."

"It was never about me. It was about you."

"Perhaps it was about both of you," Salomen said.

"Perhaps." Micah looked at his hands again. "Or perhaps it was about more than that. I believe I'll have a cup of shannel and give this some consideration. Call me if you need me."

As he walked toward the door, Tal said, "Micah, thank you. You're one of the reasons it wasn't worse." He would say it was merely his duty, but truly it required a special kind of courage to voluntarily put one's hands in fire.

He stopped with his back to her. "You owe me no thanks."

The door shut behind him, and Salomen returned to her spot on the floor. "He's very upset. He feels responsible."

"He's not responsible for the fact that Cullom Bilsner was given privileged and very specific information." Tal barely stopped herself from adding *by your own shekking excuse for a brother*. "Nobody can guard against that."

"Maybe not, but that's what I'm sensing." Salomen scooted closer. "I've been waiting and waiting for you to wake up, and now that you have, I don't know what to say. You have every right to your anger."

Tal closed her eyes. The bond. Salomen could feel everything now, but thanks to the drugs, it only went one way. "I'm sorry you felt that. Yes, I'm angry, but I don't know how much is me and how much is the medication. Mostly, I'm worried about you."

"I'm not the one in the restriction bed."

Tal carefully moved her arm, found it functional, and slipped it off the support. As soon as Salomen felt the hand on her cheek she reached up to hold it there, her face crumpling.

"I'm so sorry," she choked. "So sorry. You were hurt so badly! I tried to help you, but even that little bit that I could Share was unbearable, and I couldn't hold it…"

"Shhh, Salomen, please. None of this was your fault. And it wasn't a 'little bit' that you took from me; it was a great deal. I saw what it did to you. It broke my heart."

"How do you think I felt when I let go? You were in agony because I wasn't strong enough."

"Oh, tyrina. If you were any stronger, you would not be Alsean. I've never seen anything like what you did. It humbled me."

Salomen's laugh was bitter. "*I* humbled *you?* If you could feel me, you'd know how ridiculous that is."

"And if you're feeling me right now, then you know this is the truth. I love you." She would not let one more piptick go by without saying it, not after such a brutal reminder that time was finite. "I'm sorry I didn't have the courage to say it earlier. I felt it; I just couldn't…speak it out loud. And now I don't even remember why."

A fresh surge of tears streamed from Salomen's eyes as she turned her head and kissed Tal's palm before lacing their fingers together. "I told you not to say it until it came from your heart."

"It does," Tal whispered. "You know that."

Salomen nodded. "I've known it for a while. Probably longer than you did. That's partly why I put off our Sharing. Most people need it to see into a heart, but those flashes…I saw yours. For me, the benefit was far outweighed by the consequences."

"Is it still?"

"Oh, Fahla, no. If I hadn't had this connection with you, I would have gone insane the moment you passed out on top of me. I thought you were dead at first; you were so heavy and limp, and Colonel Micah—I've never seen him like that. I was starting to lose my mind, but then I felt a tiny little thread that had never been there before. It was holding us together, and it never broke all these hanticks

I've been waiting for you to wake up." Her mouth twisted. "I could hate Herot for taking this from us. Because of him, our first Sharing was torture. And because of him, I'm alone in this bond. All this time I put it off, and now that I want our full connection—Great Mother, I want it now—but it's not there. You're sonsales."

Tal would have given anything for that connection as well. For a moment she wondered if this was a punishment for the way they had delayed their Sharing and denied the divine spark.

"I'm only sonsales for a few days," she said, trying to convince both of them. "After that, you won't be able to get me back out of your mind again. And you don't hate Herot. He's your brother."

"If we find out that he did this intentionally, he is not my brother. I won't share our mother's name with him, and I doubt Father would share his, either."

Retraction of a family name was one of the greatest punishments that could be incurred outside the justice system, and Tal could not believe Salomen would actually do it. "Then for all our sakes, I hope he was just a drunken fool."

"So do I." Salomen used her free hand to wipe the tears from her cheeks. "I'm also extremely angry that after all this waiting, we're finally at the point of being able to touch each other without fear and I still can't have you. You're so—" Her breath shuddered in her throat. "Hurt," she finished in a whisper.

"But you said the damage can be repaired, yes?"

She nodded.

"Then in a few days I won't be hurt anymore. And I can tell you right now that thinking about our joining is going to make me heal twice as fast."

Salomen gave her a watery smile. "At least we're both still here. I'd have been very upset if one of us went to our Return before we ever got a chance to join or Share properly."

"Fahla would never let it happen. Not even she would incur your wrath lightly."

"You wouldn't let it happen, either. I know you're going to tell me this isn't necessary, but I believe it is. Thank you, Andira. First for saving my life, and then for saving my body."

Tal opened her mouth before realizing that she was about to say exactly what Salomen had predicted. "Well, I had to get you out of that window seat one way or another. I told you it was mine."

Salomen kissed the back of her hand. "Next time, you can have it."

CHAPTER 2
Incompetence

Spinner stabbed his finger on the encrypted message, deleting it forever, and threw the reader card on the desk.

"Fahla-damned *idiot!*" he shouted. Furiously he grabbed the first thing that came to hand, a statuette that had stood on his desk for fifteen cycles, and threw it as hard as he could. It shattered against the far wall with a satisfying crash, destroying four thousand cinteks of value in an instant.

It didn't make him feel better.

How could Withernet have been so stupid? A shekking assassination attempt on the Lancer? It was the last thing he wanted! Ten moons he had spent on this plan; ten moons of applying either influence, cinteks, or both as he carefully put all the pieces in place. Tomorrow was supposed to be his day of triumph. It was supposed to be the day he put the final tile in place and it all began to fall apart for Lancer Tal. Instead, she was in Blacksun Healing Center in Fahla only knew what shape. The plasma blast had taken out half the wall of her room; there was little hope she would come out of that intact enough to keep her title—if she was even alive. Either way she would be of no use to him.

And now he had lost his leverage with Challenger as well. He had just gone from triumph to disaster, all because of the flaming incompetence of a grainbird who had the bright idea of exceeding his instructions. In his message, Withernet had the horns to suggest Spinner would be pleased at the news.

At the moment, Spinner thought darkly, the only thing that would please him would be news of Withernet's demise. That man was too stupid to live.

He spent the next two hanticks pacing his study, trying to find a way to salvage the situation while waiting for the inevitable announcement on the news. When Communications Advisor Miltorin finally appeared onscreen, his face grave as he addressed the people, Spinner's heart rate doubled.

Two ticks later, a broad smile creased his face. Minor injuries? She had escaped that with minor injuries? Either Fahla herself was looking out for that woman, or Miltorin was lying through his teeth. One of those was far more likely than the other. But Miltorin wouldn't have promised her full recovery if that much weren't true. Somehow, Lancer Tal had managed to survive in good enough shape for the healers to put her back together.

The game was still on.

By the end of Miltorin's announcement, Spinner's mood had rebounded to near euphoria. Cullom Bilsner was in custody, but no mention had been made of

Herot Opah. If they had Cullom, they knew about Herot. And if they weren't mentioning Herot, there could only be two reasons. One, they were covering up his involvement. Two, he had run and they would not admit they had lost him. Either of those options gave him excellent leverage.

Humming an old ballad, he retrieved his reader card and began sending out orders.

CHAPTER 3
Non-interference

THE SUN HAD JUST CLEARED the horizon when Gehrain arrived with Tal's gear bag. "I picked up everything that seemed important," he whispered as he set the bag on a chair. "Or that was salvageable. How is she?"

Micah looked at the unmoving figure in the restriction bed. "She's…" *Torn apart,* his conscience helpfully informed him. *Alive only because of her own instincts, and no thanks to you.* "On the mend. But the drugs have knocked her out. You can speak normally; you won't wake her."

Gehrain studied her. "I can hardly believe she's still breathing. That room… the whole window seat is gone. And the bookcases, and half the wall. But Raiz Opah is walking around with hardly a scratch. Fahla must have been in the room with them."

"And a good thing, too," Micah said bitterly. "We certainly weren't any help." He held up a hand as Gehrain turned toward him. "No. I don't want to hear it. But you were right, and I was wrong. We should have moved the net farther out."

"He had inside information, Colonel."

"And I should have accounted for that possibility. Take a lesson from this. Always, always plan for the worst scenario."

Gehrain nodded, though he clearly wanted to say more. "I've set up the Guard rotation for the next five days," he said instead. "And pulled in more warriors from the base. Blacksun Healing Center is officially a fortress."

"Good. If I had my way, she wouldn't put a boot anywhere on Alsea without fifty warriors around her."

"She would never allow that."

"I know." Micah glanced back at Tal. "Fahla save us from brick-headed warriors."

It was exactly what Aldirk would have said. They looked at each other and then snorted with laughter. It felt disloyal and wrong, with Tal so grievously injured, but he couldn't stop and neither could Gehrain.

An odd chime broke into their stress release, and they gazed around the room for the source.

"Is that…?" Gehrain pointed toward the status displays on the far wall.

"I don't think so." Another chime brought Micah's head around to the gear bag. He took a step forward and reached for the tabs, then cursed at his useless gel-gloved hands. "It's coming from there."

Gehrain opened the bag and rustled around. "Ah. It must be—" The chime sounded again just as he held up a familiar pad. "There's Gaian script showing, but I can't read it."

"It's Captain Serrado." Micah couldn't read it either, but there wasn't a doubt in his mind. "They talk about once a moon, and it's been a moon since the last one."

The pad chimed again, and Micah weighed his options. "I can't activate it with these damned gloves," he said, gesturing toward the counter at the side of the room. "Set it up there so I can stand in front of it, and then tap the screen."

Gehrain did as requested. The moment his finger touched the screen, the alien script vanished and Captain Serrado appeared. Her smile faded when she saw the two men looking at her. "Colonel Micah, Lead Guard Gehrain. I would say well met, but you don't seem—" Her gaze moved over their shoulders. "Those are status displays. Are you in a healing center? Is Lancer Tal all right?"

"Thank you, Gehrain," Micah said. "That's all I need for now."

"Yes, Colonel." Gehrain nodded at the captain. "It's good to see you again, Captain Serrado."

"And you." She waited silently while Gehrain exited the room, but her expression spoke volumes.

As soon as the door shut, Micah said, "She's not all right. But she will be."

The horror showed clearly on her face as he explained, but by the end she had put on a professional mask. "Are you certain this was an isolated action? I know she's still facing censure for her decision at the Battle of Alsea."

"I'm as certain as we can be, given our current knowledge. That's not to say that an attack might not materialize from a different quarter, but this one had nothing to do with Fahla's covenant."

"This one," she repeated, her eyes narrowing. "I am not reassured. If you need any assistance at all, tell me. I can have the *Phoenix* there in sixteen of your days."

"Didn't you just get that ship?" Tal would never want Captain Serrado to risk her career again, and the last thing she needed was for her lost love to show up now.

"I did, and we just finished our shakedown cruise." The captain leaned forward. "The Protectorate is very invested in keeping Lancer Tal in power. We know there are voices on Alsea calling for an end to this treaty, and we know who those voices belong to. One of them is on the High Council. It wouldn't take but a word from me to have orders in hand, directing me to burn my engines all the way to Alsea. I can help."

Micah swallowed his surprise. It had never occurred to him that the Protectorate would be tracking Alsean politics that closely. But it made sense—why else have an ambassador living in Blacksun?

Tal probably knew all about it. He wished she were awake to handle this delicate moment.

"We're never without a Protectorate ship close by," he said. "If we had to call in help, it would be here sooner than you could be. And I really don't think we'll need the assistance, though I'm grateful for the offer." There, that sounded like something Tal would say.

"You do have a closer ship," she agreed. "But not one with the resources of the *Phoenix*. And not one with a captain who understands Alsean culture and knows when to help and when to let you take the lead."

"Captain Serrado—"

"Why don't you want me there? She's my friend. And I can see exactly how worried you are about her."

He sighed and reached up to scratch the back of his neck, then swore when the gel glove touched his skin. He was never going to get used to these damned things. "I didn't tell you everything. It's really her story to tell."

"Well, she doesn't seem capable of it right now. And I only have this call. Personal quantum com time is a limited resource, especially when it's being routed through this many base space relays."

Serrado could stare a hole through a person when she wanted to. No wonder she and Tal had become friends so quickly.

Micah gave up. "The woman she saved last night—Salomen Opah—she and Tal are tyrees."

"Andira found her tyree?" A warm smile transformed her face. "In the producer who challenged her?"

He chuckled. "I don't think Salomen will ever stop challenging her."

"That's wonderful news, Colonel. I'm thrilled for her. But it doesn't explain why you don't want me there."

"They've been bonded for less than one day," he said, hoping desperately that she would understand.

She tilted her head with a slight frown. "What terrible timing. But I'm not a threat, if that's what you're worried about. A tyree bond can't be broken from the outside."

Now that was strange, hearing an alien lecture him on Fahla's gift.

"No, it cannot. But Tal is…a special case. This isn't her first tyree bond." He hoped Tal would forgive him. "Her first one was with you."

Serrado stared at him, speechless. At last she cleared her throat and said, "You need to explain that."

"I know about her Sharings with you and Lhyn." As the mask fell over her face, he added, "She had no intention of telling me. I forced her into it, because she was…not doing well. Captain, what she did with you was unprecedented. And very dangerous, because neither you nor Lhyn had any way to control the power of your bond. Every time Tal linked you, some of it spilled over into her brain. When you left, it was…well, you severed a partial tyree bond. In truth, she should have been under the care of a healer. But she was stubborn and never told a soul until I gave her no other option."

Serrado closed her eyes and shook her head. "Damn her. Why didn't she—?" She stopped and exhaled softly. "Never mind, I already know the answer to that question. Is she all right now? I mean, regarding that?"

"Yes. It took several moons, but she recovered."

"Colonel Micah, I know this comes too late, but if I'd had any idea—"

"I know. So does she. Though I think she would have done it even if she had known the risk."

"She probably would have. So…you're saying I'm a threat after all."

"Salomen only consented to their bond last night. Two ticks after they Shared, Tal passed out on top of her from the pain and shock. Since then, Tal has either been unconscious, or awake but sonsales because of the drugs they're giving her. Their bond is so new it hardly even qualifies as a bond yet. And it's Salomen's brother we're looking for. This is a very delicate situation."

Serrado's shoulders went back. "I see. Then I'll stay out of it for now. But I meant it when I said the Protectorate wants Andira in the State Chair. If you can't resolve this threat internally, you're going to see me whether I ask for it or not. I'll run interference as long as I can, but my influence only goes so far. And I'll be Shipper-damned if anyone gets sent there other than me." Her posture softened. "But more importantly, if something happens to her and I could have prevented it, then neither you nor I are going to be able to live with ourselves."

He nodded in perfect understanding. "From one warrior to another, Captain, I swear I'll keep her safe."

"I hope you're bringing in reinforcements to bolster that oath."

"I am." *In more ways than she realized.*

"Good. Tell her to call me as soon as she can. I'll arrange for a priority call status."

"It will probably be several days."

"As soon as she can," she repeated.

They ended the call a few ticks later, leaving Micah looking at a pad that he had no way of deactivating. He turned to the bed, where Tal lay immobile and nearly invisible beneath her pile of gel packs.

"Between your friend and your tyree, you are never again going to hold the upper hand," he told her. "But I'll enjoy watching you try."

CHAPTER 4
Restriction

T<small>AL SLEPT THROUGH THE MEDIA</small> announcement and most of the first day, and when she woke up, she met Healer Tornell.

Blacksun's premiere burn specialist was an older woman whose stature made Tal look like a giant. She had hands like the wings of fairy flies and the voice of Fahla herself. She also had the most intractable, overbearing personality that Tal had ever come across.

At the first opportunity, Tal told her that she would no longer be taking the paincounters, and Tornell informed her that she might be Lancer outside the dome of the healing center, but inside she was just another patient and would be best advised to leave the healing to the experts. When Tal stated that she would rather be uncomfortable than empathically blind, Tornell suggested that she hadn't a dokker's idea of what discomfort meant in this situation. Tal pointed out that she most certainly did, having experienced a rather high level of it recently, and Tornell noted that the result of that particular experience had been unconsciousness, at which point she was empathically blind anyway, so what was the difference?

Tal greeted her next visit as a personal challenge, but fared no better.

The third time she summoned all her powers of intimidation—which were admittedly limited given her position on the restriction bed—and Tornell merely seemed amused.

But at the end of the second day, Tornell did indeed take her off the paincounters, so Tal felt that a victory had been achieved. The fact that her recovery had progressed to the point where the paincounters were no longer absolutely necessary did not diminish her achievement.

She spent the third day feeling as if an entire swarm of biting flies was walking around on her back, occasionally sinking their barbed mouthparts into her flesh. Tornell explained that this was the result of the accelerated healing process, and if she thought that was bad, she should wait for the itching, which would begin the next day.

She was not exaggerating. On the fourth day, Tal would have scratched all the new skin off her back if she could have reached it. Micah sat in the room with her, gritting his teeth over his itching hands, and they commiserated about unsympathetic and arrogant healers who smiled at their complaints and said the itching was a good sign.

"How can anything that feels this bad be good?" Micah held his gel-gloved hands under his armpits.

"I think they mean in the same way that our parents told us that fanten brains were good for us," Tal said.

"Ugh. I hate fanten brains. It doesn't matter how they're cooked, they're still disgusting."

"I know. But they were right, the brains are good for us."

"I prefer to get my vitamins from a different source, thank you."

"At least you get to sit in a chair," Tal pointed out. "I'm still flat on my face."

"Not quite flat."

Which was true. When Tornell had taken Tal off the paincounters, she had also changed the thick gel packs for the thinner, lightweight versions that could be easily strapped in place. With the new packs strapped on, the restriction bed could be raised into an angled position. Now Tal was upright enough to look straight out through the head support and see visitors in their chairs, a vast improvement over her earlier prone position. She could also rotate the bed at will, enabling her to take the full weight off her front by shifting the bed to different angles. Steep angles required that her arms and legs be cuffed to the bed, a concept she found untenable, so she contented herself with shallower angles and frequent changes. But she couldn't move, not with the skin still growing, and was intensely envious of Micah's freedom.

"By the way, I'm still angry at you," she said for at least the fifth time. "You should have woken me up."

"I couldn't have woken you if I'd tried," he said with damnable patience. "You were drugged out of your mind. We had a perfectly nice conversation, all of which you know about."

"I only talk to her once a moon! You took my call!"

"And she told you to call her back as soon as you could. You seem perfectly coherent now. Why don't you call her?"

She grumbled under her breath.

"What was that?" he asked.

"I don't want Ekatya to see me like this. And you know it. So stop smiling." She had sent a message saying she was all right and promising to call when she felt better, but that didn't mean she wasn't irritated with Micah for his high-handedness in telling Ekatya to stay away.

"Are you certain they took you off the anti-infection agent? Your emotions still seem a bit volatile."

"You try lying in this bed for four shekking days and see how volatile you feel!"

She stopped, having just sensed Salomen leaving the restaurant she had gone to for midmeal. An unbidden smile on her face set Micah chuckling.

"No emotional control whatsoever. Just from that expression I can guess that Salomen is on her way back. Really, she's here so much that I'm not sure what you've accomplished by not moving into a family unit. At least then she could have slept in the room with you."

"I wish we could have, but suspicion is one thing. Overt proof is another. I won't advertise her status until her Guards are ready."

"You might remember that I did tell you to wait."

"Mitigating circumstances." Tal's smile grew larger as she felt Salomen's anticipation of seeing her.

"It must be amazing to sense her from so far away," Micah said wistfully.

"It's the most incredible, glorious thing, and I have no idea why I was ever afraid of it. Truly a gift from the Goddess—all the richness of her emotions as if she were right here in this room."

"No more doubts about sharing every emotion? I still have a difficult time imagining that."

"I know. I thought I would feel naked as a newborn. But Salomen and I had been dropping our fronts with each other for some time already. I don't think I've raised mine with her since the speaking tour. So the only thing this has changed is that I can't raise it again, but the truth is I wouldn't want to. It would hurt her, and I'd be equally hurt if she shut me out. We were afraid of being pushed into a place that we had already walked into under our own power. We were just too panicked to realize where we were standing."

He gave her an approving smile. "Romance really has hit you over the head. I wasn't sure I'd live to see the day, but it was worth the wait."

"Really, Micah, you shouldn't be living vicariously. You should be out finding your own romance. I did offer to help, if you'll recall. You refused, and look what happened. A whole cycle of nothing."

"I don't want your advice. You do it all backward. For Fahla's sake, you're fully bonded and you still haven't joined. Does Salomen even know what you look like?"

"Well, I've been half-naked for the last four days…"

"Doesn't count. All she sees is gel packs."

"But I hear they're very attractive gel packs."

They were both laughing when the door slid open to admit Healer Tornell.

"I see you're feeling better," she said, walking over to unstrap Tal's gel packs. "I'll take that as a testament to our skill in the face of opposition from the patient."

"Take it as a testament to friendship. Micah has been at least as beneficial as these packs. And he irritates me far less."

"Not for lack of trying," Micah said.

"Being irritating is clearly a trait that warriors aspire to. I've treated enough to speak from experience." Tornell gently removed the packs, dropping them into a sterilizing and recharging unit before beginning her examination. "This is looking good," she said with satisfaction. "You're healing well. Barring anything unexpected, your skin will be established enough for movement tomorrow. *Gentle* movement," she added sternly.

"Meaning I can leave?"

Micah smirked at Tal's hopeful tone.

"Meaning you will no longer be gracing us with your presence, yes. And we will miss your sparkling personality." Tornell moved down and lifted the small pads covering the leg burns. "Excellent. These no longer need pads. Another few doses of salve and that should be it." She pulled a small jar from a drawer and began applying the salve with a touch so gentle that it lulled Tal into a state of relaxation.

"That actually feels good," she said.

"Imagine that. It *is* possible to feel good in a healing center."

Tal was saved from a response by Salomen's approach. She looked toward the door, a rush of happiness flowing through her as her tyree walked in. "Hello," she said, barely managing not to call her *tyrina* in front of Tornell. "So I was right, yes?"

"You know you were." Salomen sat in the chair by Micah. "Corsine himself should visit that restaurant. It was sublime. There were too many things on the menu that I wanted to try and not enough space in my stomach."

"Perhaps we can go back tomorrow."

"You're being released, then?"

"More like thrown out."

Tornell had an impeccable front—a necessity for a high-level healer—but Tal thought she could detect amusement. "We shall be sorry to see you leave, Raiz Opah. You've been the voice of reason. I wish you good fortune in your bond with Lancer Tal."

They looked at each other in dismay.

"Is it that obvious?" Salomen asked.

Tornell chuckled as she began applying new gel packs. "Not empathically, no. You both have excellent fronts, and I'm not even going to ask how a producer has a front like that. But a nonranking producer is not normally among those with free access to the Lancer—especially one who has spoken so publicly against her policies. You've been in this room so often that I wondered why you didn't request a family unit."

"Because we need to keep it a secret," Tal said. "At least for now." She felt the tap on her shoulder and raised her torso enough to allow the straps to be passed beneath her.

"Rest assured it will never be revealed by anyone in this center." Tornell tightened the straps and tapped the shoulder again. As Tal settled herself, the healer moved around to stand in front of Salomen and Micah. Even seated, they were as tall as she was. "And how are your legs, Raiz Opah?"

"I can barely even see where I was burned anymore," Salomen said. "I stopped applying the salve today."

"Good. Smaller burns are so much easier to heal. I was certain we could take care of you quickly."

When Salomen had revealed her own burns two days earlier, Tal had nearly gone through the roof. After all her effort to protect her tyree, she had failed? It took Salomen some time to calm her down, pointing out that total protection would have required Tal to balance entirely atop her once she had rolled them over.

Salomen pulled up the loose cloth of her pants, exposing her legs to Tornell's inspection. From her vantage point on the bed, Tal couldn't see so much as a blemish. That helped, but not enough.

Tornell straightened. "They're beautiful. You won't be able to find any sign of them in another few days."

"Thanks to you." Salomen tugged her pants legs down. "I appreciate the care you've given all of us, Healer Tornell. But in defense of my bondmate, I must tell you I'm not the only voice of reason here. Lancer Tal is a good deal more reasonable than you think. It's just...difficult for her to be so restricted in her movements."

"It's difficult for anyone to be restricted. Most people manage it without assuming they know a healer's art."

"I never said I knew the healer's art," Tal said. "I only said I knew what was best for my own healing."

"That is the same thing."

"No, it's not."

"Of course it is."

Salomen looked at Micah. "Do they always argue over who rules the playground?"

He nodded as Tornell strode regally to the door.

"There is no argument because there is no question," she said, opening the door. "The ruler of this playground has been well established."

Salomen chuckled as the door shut behind her. "I do believe you've met your match, Andira. You are Lancer of nothing in here." She sobered. "But her skill has no match either. I cannot believe you will be walking only five days after the damage I saw."

"But she will *only* be walking," Micah noted. "I distinctly heard Healer Tornell say that she could engage in gentle movement only. So you two won't require a private room tomorrow night."

"Weren't you just leaving?" Tal asked.

"Actually, I was." Micah stretched his legs first, his arms more carefully, and stood up. "I'm working with Salomen's Guard unit in a hantick, but I need to check in with Colonel Razine first."

Salomen's mood shifted instantly; her worry was never far from the surface. "It's not looking good for him, is it?"

"The longer he stays out, the guiltier he looks," he admitted. "But we won't know anything for certain until we can speak with him directly. He can't be judged in his absence."

Except that he already had been. After Gordense Bilsner's ill-advised public statement the day before, Herot's name was plastered all over the headlines, and the consensus was in: he wouldn't have run if he were innocent. Salomen had been furious, stating that the only motive Gordense could have had was to spread the dishonor and divert some of it from his son.

"I keep hoping the truth favors him." Salomen rose and rested her hand on Micah's forearm. "Good luck with my Guards. I look forward to meeting them."

He gave her a slight bow. "They have no idea what they're in for."

When they were alone, Salomen pulled her chair closer and sat down. "I finished reading their histories at midmeal. Imagine my surprise when I realized that seven out of the ten have a producer parent."

"Is that right? What a coincidence."

"Really, Andira, I can't believe you even attempt that anymore." But Salomen could no more pretend exasperation than Tal could fake surprise. "Thank you. It was very thoughtful, and it makes me feel more comfortable with the idea of having them. Though I admit I was already somewhat reconciled to the concept after coming a little too close to a plasma blast. What are you going to do about Colonel Micah?"

Tal sighed. "I can't do anything. He's trying very hard to front his feelings about that night, and it would be an invasion of his privacy to ask him about them when he clearly doesn't want me to know. I've told him that I don't hold him responsible and I don't believe the situation could have been foreseen, and that's all I can do right now. He'll talk to me sooner or later. My guess is that he doesn't want to do it in here."

"I always thought one of the greatest things about being open with my talent would be not having to hide what I can sense," Salomen said. "And yet you still hide your knowledge. You just do it to keep other people's secrets instead of your own."

"Only some of them."

"Well, I'm tired of hiding it. When we started my training, the chance to be openly empathic with even one person was a dazzling freedom. Now it's not enough. I want to tell my family." She sighed wearily. "But I don't think this is the time. Damn Herot for that, too."

"Now might be the perfect time, tyrina. Maybe you're exactly what they need right now: a good surprise. Once they get over the shock, that is."

"Hm." Salomen stared off into space, then met Tal's eyes with a hopeful smile. "Maybe *we're* exactly what they need right now."

"Shall we make that our first stop after getting out of here?"

"I'd like that. And Father needs it. Your message didn't convince him that you don't blame our family. I've told him you're seeing no one but your closest advisors right now, but…"

"I know, but I stand by my decision."

"And I agree with you. It's been difficult enough for me to see you like this; I don't think Father or Nikin would soon recover from it. But for Father, truth lies in the action, not the telling of it. He says he wouldn't blame you if you never returned to Granelle or Hol-Opah."

"Oh, no. I have to go back and be seen going back. It's the only thing that will clear the dishonor from your family name."

Salomen didn't answer, but the pulse of warmth hit Tal's senses like a sunbeam in a shadowed corner. She rose from her chair and stepped to the side of the bed, and when Tal lifted her head from the ring to see her, Salomen bent down and kissed her with a toe-curling thoroughness.

"That's for caring so much about my family," she said. "And this is for caring so much about me." Another deep, searching kiss made it difficult for Tal to get her eyes open again. When she did, Salomen was looking straight into them. "And this," she said, "is because I love you."

The third kiss started out more gently, gradually increasing in passion until Tal was surprised her gel packs hadn't melted. "Are you trying to kill me?" she panted.

Salomen's smile was sensual. "More like a sort of mutual annihilation." She trailed a fingertip over Tal's lips, her own arousal soaring as Tal sucked her finger in and ran her tongue over and around it. Slowly reclaiming her finger, Salomen whispered, "Definitely a mutual annihilation."

Tal reached out to caress her face, still not quite used to being able to touch her without fear. "When I think of how close I came to losing you... I've been telling Fahla every day how grateful I am."

Salomen laced their fingers together. "I'll be a lot more grateful when you're out of that bed."

"That makes two of us."

"Then hold this thought: in precisely one day, you and I are going to have all sorts of things to thank Fahla for. I plan to see just how loud your gratitude can get."

Tal whimpered. "You *are* trying to kill me."

"Not at all. Think of it as an incentive to finish up your healing. I've got plans for that body that involve a different sort of bed."

"And no Healer Tornell to walk in on us."

Salomen dropped her hand. "Well, that was a bucket of rainwater."

"Good. Think of it as an incentive."

"For what?"

"For not frustrating the shek out of me when I can't do anything about it!"

Salomen's smile was slow and entirely too knowing. "All right. I promise not to frustrate the shek out of you...until you can do something about it."

Tal gave a resigned sigh. One more day.

CHAPTER 5
Window to a bond

"The Lancer is expecting you. Please go through that arch."

Lanaril thanked the clerk and walked in the direction he indicated, her nose wrinkling at the pungent smell of narnell root. She often came here as part of her duties, but that odor did not improve on acquaintance.

She had barely stepped through the arch before being stopped by an imposing warrior in the uniform of a Lancer's Guard. Offering a palm, she said, "Lead Guard Gehrain, isn't it?"

He had a kind smile. "Well met, Lead Templar Satran. Lancer Tal is waiting for you, but there are a few things you need to know before seeing her."

"Is she going to be all right?"

When Chief Counselor Aldirk had refused access for three interminable days, Lanaril feared the worst. She had been around Blacksun long enough to recognize the scent of political dokshin, and telling the world that Andira's injuries were minor while simultaneously preventing visitors from seeing her meant somebody was shoveling it into a deep pile.

"Yes. In fact, they're releasing her tomorrow."

"Thank Fahla. It wasn't minor, was it?"

He shook his head. "Since you've been approved for a visit, you have clearance to know. She was badly burned and has been in a restriction bed for the last four days. Needless to say, this is privileged information and should not leave this healing center."

She hardly heard his last words through the fog of horror. Badly burned? What had happened?

"She really is all right, Lead Templar. But she can't move, so you'll have to do the moving for her. Please stand or sit where she can easily see you. If she needs to shift her bed, move yourself to stay in her sight."

"Yes, of course. Is there anything else?"

"No, that's it. If you'll come with me?"

Two Guards flanked the door he led her to. Opening it slightly, he said, "Lancer Tal, Lead Templar Satran is here."

Lanaril strained to hear Andira's voice, but she must have given him a signal instead.

Gehrain opened the door fully and stood to one side. "Please enter."

"Thank you." She stepped through and stopped, her hand going to her mouth as the door softly closed behind her. "Oh, no."

Andira was looking at her through a ring at the top of the angled bed. She seemed lost in it, her body buried under gel packs, and it was all so terribly wrong. The only part of her that was recognizably normal was the direct gaze of her light blue eyes, but even they seemed strange, framed in that ring that hid so much of her face. Lanaril's vision swam with tears.

"I'm all right, Lanaril. Didn't Gehrain tell you?"

She groped for the nearest chair. "Yes, but…Great Mother, how *can* you be? What happened?"

"I got in the way of a few hundred pieces of molten glass."

Her voice, so strong and in such contrast to her appearance, helped Lanaril focus. "Don't they teach you to avoid those things in your training?"

Andira chuckled. "Yes, but I was a poor student."

"You were never a poor student at anything. I'd bet a barrel of temple oil on that."

"If I hadn't burned, it would have been Salomen."

"Oh, no—"

"So you can see why I chose me."

She certainly could. Andira's natural protectiveness combined with a tyree bond? Salomen Opah would probably never get so much as a stubbed toe for the rest of her life.

"She's a fortunate woman," she said. "Are you sure you're all right? Because—forgive me, but you don't look like someone who's being released tomorrow."

"It looks worse than it is. I just can't move while the new skin is growing. If I tear it before it's fully formed, I'll be in here twice as long and end up with scars. At least, that's what Healer Tornell threatens me with on a daily basis."

"You must be as frustrated as a child in a candy shop where all the jars are on high shelves."

"As frustrated? Oh, no, it's much worse than that." Andira pressed a button on the bed, and it tilted slightly to one side. "Besides the fact that it itches like a shekker, you have no idea how much I envy every person who walks in this room."

Lanaril moved to the next chair. "At least your room smells better than the corridor. I see someone is keeping you supplied with hyacot. Is Salomen all right?"

"She had a few burns too, but—"

"No, I know she's fine physically. She was photographed in town yesterday. I'm asking if she's all right here." Lanaril put a hand over her heart.

"She's distressed about her brother, obviously. And every time she walks in and sees me, there's a wave of guilt. But other than that, she's wonderful."

"Wonderful?" Lanaril repeated. "Not the word I'd have expected to hear, given the circumstances."

Andira smiled. "Remember when you bet me that once we completed our bond, I'd tell you I couldn't imagine not having it? You already won."

"You did it! Oh, I'm so glad. Surprised, after the way you sounded the last time we met, but very glad for both of you." She frowned. "Wait. Tell me you didn't do that here."

"That would have been an improvement."

She listened with increasing astonishment as Andira told a story that could have been torn from one of her ancient texts. Minus the plasma gun, of course, but that passage about conflagration could have been written for this. Andira and Salomen had burned both inside and out.

"Salomen got the worst of it by far," Andira said. "My senses were too blown out to feel much of anything when we Shared, but she felt the full brunt of the bonding and took on some of my pain as well. I thought it was just the bonding at first, but..." She trailed off. "She was fine as soon as she let me go, but I don't think I'll ever forget hearing her. Or seeing it. I've never felt so helpless."

"Helpless? What do you *expect* of yourself?"

"I was supposed to be protecting her! She should never have been hurt."

"It sounds like she chose to take that on. She was protecting you. That's what a tyree does, you know that. Or do you think the producer can't protect the warrior?"

"That's not—she can't—" Andira closed her eyes. "She's not trained for it. It killed me to see her hurting like that."

"And it killed her to see you hurting. Andira, you're physically connected as well as emotionally. You cannot protect her from that."

"And I hate that. When we first started her empathic training, she told me I wasn't a safe woman. I said I wasn't in a safe line of work. But I never dreamed the choices I made half a lifetime ago would affect someone besides me."

Lanaril chuckled. "Really? You wanted to be Lancer and you didn't think your choices would affect others?"

"That's not what I meant."

"I know what you meant. But Salomen made a choice of her own. She willingly shouldered your pain. Would you take away her power of choice?"

Andira glared at her. "Remind me again why I put you on the visitor list?"

"Because I tell you the things you need to hear."

"Maybe I need a few more sycophants in my life." She sighed. "No, I know you're right. It's just hard to accept."

"That I'm right?"

That made her laugh. "Yes, that's it."

For half a hantick, their conversation was so normal that Lanaril almost managed to forget how badly her friend had been hurt. But it was driven home every time Andira moved her bed, and she had to change chairs to stay in her line of sight.

"I don't know how you haven't lost your mind in that thing," she said after the fourth change.

"I might have, if I didn't have Salomen in here with me." Andira tapped her head. "It really helps to be able to reach for her when I need her. She's always there."

"Last time we spoke, you thought that was a nightmare scenario."

"Last time we spoke, I was a shekking idiot." A bright smile spread over her face. "And speaking of Salomen…"

Lanaril turned at the sound of the door opening.

A tall woman stepped in, water beading off her rain cloak. Her rich brown hair was loose, falling in soft waves past her shoulders and slightly damp around her face where wisps had escaped the hood. Her skin glowed with the color and health that came from a lifetime of working outside, and though she looked tired, she carried herself with confidence. Before she had fully entered, her dark eyes went to the bed, a beautiful smile forming as soon as she saw Andira.

"Hello, tyrina," she said.

"Salomen, I'd like you to meet my friend Lanaril Satran, Lead Templar of Blacksun. Lanaril, this is Salomen Opah, head of Hol-Opah and my tyree."

Salomen offered her hand. "Well met. So you're the Lead Templar that Andira is teaching profanity to?"

"She tries." Their touch gave her the impression of quiet strength, watchful care, and genuine enjoyment in their meeting. "I am beyond honored to meet you, Salomen. I hope I can call you that?"

"Please. That is, if I can call you Lanaril."

"Of course."

Salomen crossed the room and dropped a soft kiss on Andira's cheek. "Nice to feel you enjoying the company of a friend for once, instead of another advisor."

Lanaril watched Andira practically melt under her touch and wondered how these two had survived not joining yet. She wouldn't lay odds on them making it through more than half a day once they left the healing center.

"Lanaril is at least as much advisor as friend. It's one of her more annoying traits."

"Then I'm quite sure I'll like her." Salomen returned to sit next to Lanaril. "What have you been advising her on this evening?"

"How to stay out of trouble. Unfortunately, she hasn't been listening to me."

Salomen smiled. "I've only recently begun studying the warrior's code, but so far I haven't found 'stay out of trouble' anywhere in the teachings. You might be choosing the wrong audience for that advice."

"You're studying the Truth and the Path?"

"Self-defense. I like to know what I'm getting into."

So Andira had just spent a moon learning Salomen's way of life, and Salomen was reading up on Andira's. Interesting.

"Besides," Salomen continued, "if she'd wanted to stay out of trouble, she would never have accepted my challenge."

"Let's not forget who issued the first challenge," Andira said. "One which you still have to fulfill, I might add."

"Oh, you mean my moon-long vacation in your magical dome? I do recall you saying something about that, but instead I'm spending my days and nights in a healing center."

Lanaril listened to their gentle banter and remembered Andira's description of the much harder-edged battles they had fought in the beginning. An old parable came to mind, about a child who found a studded metal sphere in a field and began playing with it, not realizing that it was a weapon of war left from a long-ago battle. But the sphere kept cutting her hands with its sharp spikes, until her father noticed. A metalworker by trade, he showed her how to put the sphere into his furnace, where he heated it until it became malleable. Together they pounded down every spike, and when it cooled, it had changed its nature. Once meant for injury and pain, it now provided joy and pleasure. And it could not be broken.

She smiled. Fahla really did know what she was doing.

CHAPTER 6
Release

"Let's get you off this bed and out of my healing center." Tornell pressed a control pad, and the restriction bed hummed its way from the elevated position Tal had been using to a fully horizontal one. "Roll to this side, please. Now bend your knees... Yes, good, put a hand here..." She took Tal's upper arm in a surprisingly firm grip and helped her into a sitting position.

Tal slid her legs over the edge and thrilled to the touch of her feet on the floor. And what a treat to not be viewing the world through that damned head ring!

"You look a little squished," Micah said.

"Thanks, Micah. You're always good for my self-image."

Salomen moved closer and put a hand on her shoulder. "He's lying, you look fabulous. How do you feel?"

"Odd. It's very strange being able to move." She patted Salomen's hand and stood up, swaying slightly. Her sense of balance was off after so many days. "I'm fine," she said quickly, as both Tornell and Salomen dove in to help.

They stood back, and after a few pipticks she took a step, then another, walking slowly across the room to one of the chairs Micah and Salomen had spent so much time in. She sat down, carefully rested her back against the chair, and let out a sigh of pure happiness. "I cannot tell you how good this feels."

"By the look on your face, I'd say pretty good indeed." Micah had also been smiling nonstop, having had his gel gloves removed half a hantick ago.

Salomen sat down beside her. "Are you sitting because of the novelty or because your legs are tired?"

"The novelty. I won't be running my usual ten lengths tomorrow, but my legs feel fine."

"Excellent," Tornell said briskly. She made a note on her reader card and slipped it into her coat pocket. "I've just signed you out of the healing center. As of now you are a visitor, not a patient. And remember—"

"I know. Gentle movement for the first two days." Tal stood and offered her palm for a farewell touch. "Thank you. I've appreciated your gentle hands. And if you think I'm an irritating patient, pray you never get Colonel Micah in here for anything worse than hand burns."

"Don't believe her," Micah said.

"Oh, I do." Tornell looked up at his imposing bulk. "In my experience, the bigger they are, the louder they whine. Please try to keep her out of trouble, Colonel. Good day and good health to you all." With a wave she was gone.

Micah held out a gear bag. "Don't take too long in the shower, or we'll have to go and check on you."

"What do you mean, 'we'?" Salomen demanded. "If anyone checks on her, it won't be you, warrior."

"This is going to feel wonderful." Tal hefted her bag of clothes and turned toward the bathroom door.

"Do you need any assistance?" Salomen's tone was now one of utter politeness. "Perhaps you shouldn't shower alone."

"Perhaps not, but any assistance from you is not likely to be all that helpful. Gentle movement, remember?"

"I can be very gentle."

"Excuse me," Micah said. "There's someone else in the room."

Tal laughed as she walked into the bathroom. Leaving the bag and robe in the drying area, she stepped onto the tiled shower floor and activated the unit. Warm water poured over the protruding shelf in the corner, creating a wide waterfall that was continually filtered and fed back into the system. She gloried in the feel of it on her skin—particularly the new skin of her back, which was exquisitely sensitive. For a moment she imagined Salomen touching that skin, then reluctantly quashed the thought.

The soap sponge held a floral scent she wasn't fond of, but at this point it could have smelled like an unventilated training room and she would not have cared. After five days of disinfecting bed baths, this was bliss, and she began scrubbing with ruthless efficiency.

It didn't last. As her mind wandered back to a familiar fantasy, she found herself passing the sponge across her breasts in a sensual manner that was rather ineffective for the purpose of cleaning.

The bathroom door opened. Tal continued soaping herself, now moving on to her legs and trying not to smile too broadly.

"Andira," Salomen said in a strained voice. "Stop that."

"Stop what? I'm taking a shower."

"Just so you know, I'm not looking. And I don't want to feel that, either. How can I concentrate on anything else when you're putting these thoughts in my mind?"

"What else is there to concentrate on right now?" Tal put the sponge back and picked up the comb. Now her motions were decidedly sensual as she slowly pulled the comb through her hair, enjoying the sensation of its smooth glide as it distributed a silky hair cleanser. She heard the door slam shut and laughed. It was only fair that they should both be suffering.

She stood under the warm water in hedonistic pleasure, until the soap had long since been rinsed and there really was no excuse to remain any longer. Even then she would probably have stayed, but Salomen and Micah were waiting.

The drying cloths were luxuriously soft, a necessity if they were to be used on new skin. A few passes with the dehumidifier dried her hair, which she could swear was a lighter blonde now that she'd finally managed to wash it. Gathering a few strategic pieces of longer hair from the front, she pulled them to the back and clipped them in place to hide the burned patches. She had considered cutting it all short, but Miltorin had advised against it when they discussed the news coverage. If she emerged into the public view with a radically different look, he warned, people would ask too many questions and their "light injuries" story would come apart.

She looked into the mirror with a wry smile. Amazing how even hair could become an issue of global importance. Miltorin had actually brought in a stylist to determine the best arrangement to cover up the damage, and she'd had to lie there and listen to them discussing hairstyles as if they were planning the next campaign against the Voloth. Thankfully, they had agreed on a simple solution.

Her uniform slid on like an old, comfortable skin, and when she pulled on her boots, she felt ready to take on the world. Strolling out of the bathroom with her jacket in hand, she said, "That was the best shower I've ever taken."

Micah chuckled. "Better than after you had to pull me out of that mud bog?"

"Better even than that."

Salomen simply looked at her, the joy in her emotions warming Tal's senses. "You look…the way you're supposed to."

Tal tugged her in for a gentle kiss. "I feel the way I'm supposed to. Better, actually. The skin on my back isn't the only thing I've acquired in here."

Salomen kissed her again. "Come, tyrina. Let's go tell my family about that other thing you've acquired."

"You're not always going to be kissing now, are you?" Micah asked as they filed out of the room.

"It's possible," Tal said cheerfully.

"I'd better warn Salomen's Guards," he grumbled.

CHAPTER 7
Publicity

They flew to Hol-Opah in a military transport, though Tal would have preferred her private one. At least they didn't have to bring an entire contingent of Guards with them, since half of the original Guards were still at the holding. Tal had kept them there to protect the Opahs from curiosity seekers or possible reprisals, and to ensure the privacy of the family on their own land. But she couldn't do anything about their privacy in town, and Granelle was currently housing a contingent of journalists.

After Healer Tornell's revelation that she had already assumed their bonded status, Tal had called Miltorin to her room for a media strategy session. His suggestion: hit two targets with one throw. They could control the narrative to publicize her good relations with the Opahs and simultaneously hide her bond with Salomen in plain sight. Since few would imagine the Lancer finding a bondmate in the producer caste, introducing her as a lover would satisfy everyone's expectations. "People see what they want to," he said.

Salomen agreed. So did Shikal and Nikin, not realizing that they, too, were seeing what they expected.

Accordingly, the six most-watched journalists on Alsea received a message from the Office of the Lancer, inviting them to send vidcams to the meeting between Lancer Tal and the Opah family. Their equipment now sat dormant in a holding rack near the door. Tal glanced at it, wishing she could prevent what was about to happen. Once the transport landed and those vidcams were activated, life for the Opahs would never be the same.

They passed over the Silverrun River, a landmark she now knew as well as the State Park itself. Looking upstream, she saw the distinctive bend that marked the southeast corner of Hol-Opah land.

Salomen reached for her hand. "I've dreamed of bringing you back home every hantick since it happened. Thank you for making this our first stop. I know you have a few hundred other things to do."

"None of which are as important as you and your family. I know where my priorities lie." Tal indicated Micah, who was watching out his window. "You can thank the good colonel for that. He's the one who taught me that a warrior with a whole heart was a better servant to Alsea than a warrior with only half a heart."

"Colonel Micah is a very wise man."

"Yes, he is. I try not to tell him that too often."

"Perhaps you should tell him soon."

She looked at him again, noting the tension that he was trying so hard to hide. "I know. That's another top priority."

As planned, Shikal, Nikin, and Jaros were waiting at the landing area behind the house, wearing rain cloaks to ward off the light drizzle. Tal could sense their apprehension from inside the transport. As soon as the Guards were in place and the vidcams had been deployed, she walked out with Salomen, stood in the doorway of the transport to give the world a good look at the two of them holding hands, and then sealed the visual by nuzzling her ear. At least, that was how it would appear.

"First performance, tyrina," she whispered into Salomen's ear. "Try to look as if you think I'm the hottest thing walking."

The smile that spread over Salomen's face was completely natural, and Tal smiled back before leading her down the ramp. Walking straight up to Shikal, she raised both of her hands. Though visibly startled at a gesture normally reserved for very close friends or family, he reached out without hesitation. A flood of relief and gratitude poured off him as soon as they made contact and he could sense her.

"Well met, Shikal."

"Well met, Lancer Tal." In a slightly louder voice, he said, "In the name of our family and our honored ancestors, I thank you for your generosity in returning so soon after your healing. None of us can sufficiently express our sorrow, our shock, or our shame for what happened here."

The cadence of his speech was stiff; he had rehearsed it.

"None of you here were responsible," she said, ignoring the vidcams hovering around them. "Your sorrow and shock I understand, but the shame does not belong to you. My greatest regret is that your family has been so shattered by this event. I never once held you, your sons Nikin and Jaros, or your daughter Salomen to blame for the attempt on my life." She wished she could include Herot's name in that list, but her only concern now was damage control for the rest of the Opahs.

"During this past moon," she continued, "you treated me with the utmost honor, respect, and friendship. You made me feel less like a guest and more like part of the family, and I hope you will not allow recent events to change this. I value your friendship no less today than I did five days ago."

He closed his fingers over her hands. "I value your friendship even more after the fear of having lost you. If you felt like part of our family, then you sensed our true feelings. You are always welcome here on Hol-Opah."

"I'm glad you said that, since I plan to be here now and again. Hol-Opah's horten soup is not to be missed."

His smile was unforced, the vidcams momentarily forgotten, and she moved on.

"Nikin, it's good to see you again."

"It's *so* good to see you," he said, clutching her hands in the strongest grip she had ever felt from him. "We were so worried. But you look fabulous." He clamped his mouth shut and looked at her in silent pleading, embarrassment wafting off him.

"Thank you," she said with an easy smile. "My injuries were minor. I suspect the damage to your house was much worse."

"It was a mess," he admitted. "Besides the damage to the room itself, we lost our mother's portrait and all of her books."

Tal was shocked; Salomen hadn't told her that. "I'm so sorry. I didn't know."

"The books can be replaced, at least those whose titles we remember. But the portrait is gone forever." His grief was laced with anger, but he straightened his spine and met her eyes with an even gaze. "Nevertheless, we're grateful. It could have been so much worse. Those are just things, and valuable as they are, they don't compare to your life."

"But their loss hurts just the same, and I grieve that loss with you." She squeezed his hands before crouching down in front of his brother. "Hello, Jaros."

With no warning he threw himself into her arms, nearly sending her over backward.

"I was so scared!" His voice shuddered. "I thought the house was falling down, it was so loud, and then everyone was shouting and nobody would let me see you and then you were gone and you didn't come back!"

"Shhh. It's all right. I'm all right." She stroked his head with one hand while holding him tight with the other, and hoped that his desperate hold on her wasn't pulling the new skin too much. "I know it was frightening, and I'm sorry I couldn't see you until now. But I'm back and good as new. See?" She pulled back, smiling at him.

He promptly buried his face in her neck again. "Please don't leave. Please? I don't want you to go."

"Oh, Jaros." She looked up at the others, seeing her own emotions reflected in their faces. Of all the people who had been affected by this, Jaros had probably suffered the most because he didn't understand.

"I'm going to be coming here for a long, long time," she said in a voice too low for the vidcams to pick up. "Don't worry about me leaving, all right? You heard your father. I have a standing invitation, and I plan to make good use of it."

"Promise?" His voice was muffled.

"I promise."

He loosened his grip but did not let go, and Tal did the only thing she could bear to do, even though she knew it would light up vidcams all over Alsea: she gathered him in her arms and stood up. Looking over his shoulder at Shikal, she said, "I believe Jaros could use a drink of water, and I've been thinking about one of your excellent bottles of spirits for several days. Shall we go inside?"

"That sounds wonderful," he said with relief. Once they went inside, the vidcams would be deactivated and they could all behave normally again. All of them except Jaros, who was himself whether there were vidcams nearby or not.

"I hope there's some horten soup left," Tal said.

Shikal laughed as he led the way up the porch steps. "You're in luck, Lancer Tal. We saved you some."

CHAPTER 8
Freedom

The vidcams were sent back to Blacksun while Tal, Micah, and the Opahs passed a pleasant half hantick in the parlor, catching up on news and avoiding any mention of the most pressing issue. When the conversation faltered and Shikal and Nikin began to look uncomfortable, Tal asked if she could see her old room.

"Do you want to?" Nikin said in surprise.

"Yes, I do. I was…a little less than myself that night. I'd like to see what really happened."

"We didn't think you would want anything to do with it, but…of course you may." Shikal rose from his chair and led a general exodus out of the parlor and up the stairs.

Tal thought she was prepared, but seeing the actual damage was a shock. Nothing of her cheerful, comfortable room remained. The debris and damaged furniture had been hauled out, leaving a bare shell. The plasma blast had thrown molten glass onto every surface, scarring the walls and floor with burn marks, and the area around the window had suffered extensive damage. The window seat was destroyed, as were the bookshelves on either side, leaving a jagged hole in the wall. It was now sealed with a transparent construction sheet to keep out the rain, but the temporary repair could not disguise the wreckage.

Had Salomen been there when the blast hit, there would have been nothing left of her larger than a pastry.

She held Salomen's hand tightly as she took it in. "I didn't realize how bad it was."

"It was bad." Salomen pointed down.

Tal followed the direction of her finger and felt sick. The floor was marked with a scattering of burns, except for one area. One body-shaped area, where she and Salomen had burned instead.

"At least I managed to save part of the floor," she said.

"You saved our family," Shikal said.

"You saved Salomen!" Jaros, always more literal, pointed at the ruined outer wall. "Look! She would have died if she'd still been sitting there. But you pulled her off. How did you know?"

Tal looked at Salomen and received a slight nod.

"I was actively scanning the emotional landscape at the time. Cullom was at the extreme edge of my range. I didn't know who he was, but I knew he didn't belong here—and that he was planning to do something that scared and excited him at the same time. That combination of emotions means danger, and since I sat in that seat every evening…" She shrugged. "The rest was just instinct."

Jaros took her explanation at face value, but she could feel Shikal and Nikin puzzling over it.

"Do you normally scan the emotional landscape?" Nikin asked.

"Not on a regular basis, no. That's what my Guards do."

"What a fortunate coincidence that you happened to be doing it at that moment," Shikal said.

"It wasn't coincidence." Salomen squeezed Tal's hand, her stress spiking as she took the leap. "We had been doing it every night for six nights by then."

He frowned. "What do you mean?"

"We weren't conducting delegate business all those evenings. And we weren't doing what you were all thinking, either. Andira has been training me since shortly after she arrived." She took a deep breath and straightened her spine. "I'm a high empath."

Both Shikal and Nikin gaped at her, while Jaros grinned. "Speedy! You're so lucky!"

"How in Fahla's name can you be a high empath?" Shikal demanded. "When did this happen?"

"It didn't just happen. I've been this way for as long as I can remember."

"Salomen Arrin Opah! Are you telling me that you've been a high empath all your life and never said a word to your family?"

"Yes, I am." Salomen's calm voice belied her distress. "When I was Jaros's age, I didn't know anyone else like me, and I didn't want to be different. And I was afraid to say anything, because if a tester had marked me, they would have taken me away. So I fooled them and made sure that no one ever knew."

Nikin was wide-eyed. "You fooled the testers?"

"I've been carrying this secret forever, and believe me, I never wanted to. But if anyone had found out, none of you would have seen me for five cycles, except for training breaks. And that would have been the positive outcome. The other possibility was too frightening to think about."

"She had a great deal of strength, but no control," Tal said. "On my second night here, she probed me without being able to stop herself."

Shikal and Nikin looked at each other in horror.

"Scared myself halfway to my Return," Salomen said, attempting to lighten the mood. "Luckily, I picked the best person to get caught by."

Tal wanted to kiss her for that one. "Once I knew of her talents, I couldn't allow things to go on as they had been. The law exists for a reason. So I made her a deal: if she would allow me to instruct her in basic techniques, I would waive the full training requirement. That's what we were doing every night in my room, training her to control and focus her senses. She's extremely gifted. And if you could see how hard she's worked and how astonishing her growth has been, you would be very proud of her. I certainly am."

Shikal turned away, shaking his head. "This is too much to take in. We should be discussing this in the parlor over a new bottle of spirits."

"I'm with you." Nikin followed him down the hall, while Salomen turned and rested her forehead on Tal's shoulder.

"It will be fine," Tal said quietly, stroking her dark hair. "You knew they would be shocked. They'll adapt."

"I know." Salomen lifted her head. "That doesn't make it any easier."

"Nothing worthwhile is easy," Micah said. "But when your family has moved through this, you'll be living openly at last. Keep your eye on that."

"That's what I'm telling myself," she said, and set off after her father and brother. Tal, Micah, and a frowning Jaros trailed behind.

"Why is Father so upset? Don't you think it's speedy that Salomen is a high empath?"

"I think it's very speedy," she assured him. "Your father just needs a little time to get used to the idea."

He shrugged. "What idea? It's not like she's any different. She's Salomen."

Tal and Micah shared a smile over his head.

They arrived at the parlor in time to see Shikal opening a second bottle of spirits. The room was silent as he poured five glasses, filled a sixth with grainstem juice for Jaros, then stood waiting while each person took a glass and found a seat.

"This is now a family council," he said. "Start from the beginning, and don't leave anything out."

Salomen sipped her drink, set it on the table beside her chair, and began speaking. For a quarter hantick Tal silently held her hand, until Salomen's tale had brought her family up to the present.

"When Andira caught me probing her, I thought my world had come to an end," she said. "I had probably done that hundreds of times before, but never knew it and never got caught, because there's no one in Granelle who has the skills to detect it. Or at least, no one I come in regular contact with. I had no idea how strong I was. She told me that the Whitemoon Sensoral Institute would take me—"

"Whitemoon!" Nikin exclaimed. "That's the best institute on Alsea!" He looked at Tal for confirmation.

"They would have taken her in a heartbeat. Salomen has an extraordinary gift."

"It didn't feel like a gift to me. It was just something I had to hide. Then Andira came and showed me a whole new world on our first night of training. For the first time, I didn't have to hide, and I was finally learning how to control my powers. It was…magical. This last moon has been magical." A smile wreathed her face. "To truly be myself with someone, to let go of a secret I'd been carrying all my life—every night, I walked up those stairs and shed a burden with each step. That's why I'm telling you now. I cannot bear that burden anymore. I need to be who I am. And I'm so sorry that I couldn't tell you before."

No one spoke, and Salomen shrank against Tal, her courage failing her at last.

Tal wrapped an arm around her and pulled her close. "You did well," she whispered.

Salomen didn't respond. She was focused on her father, who was staring into his glass and looking very stern indeed. But his expression covered a deep pain of disappointment, and she shivered with it.

"I understand your original decision with the testers," he said. "You were ten and you were afraid. And I understand your fear of being different and why you would have kept your secret as a pre-Rite child, though I grieve that neither I nor your mother were given the opportunity to help you. What I don't understand is why you continued to keep this secret after your Rite of Ascension. How could you be afraid of your own family? Why didn't you trust us?"

"It was not about trust." Salomen's voice was shaky. "I have always trusted you, and I've always loved you. Everything I've done, I did to keep my family whole. I know this is hard for you, but please look at it from my point of view. How was I to go to you or Mother and tell you I had been keeping a secret for twenty cycles? How do you start a conversation like that? Would you have been any less hurt than you are now? At twenty-five cycles it was even harder, and at thirty it was harder yet. A secret grows more entrenched the longer it's kept—that's a lesson I've learned far too well."

"It's just..." He stopped, blinked hard, and tried again. "I could have helped you, but you never allowed it. And you still wouldn't, even now. If this disaster hadn't forced your hand, I might have gone to my Return without knowing my own daughter. Herot won't let me reach him, and now I find that you've been holding yourself away your whole life..." His eyes reddened. "Have I been such a poor parent?"

"Father, no..." Salomen was too crushed to say any more. She covered her mouth, fighting her own tears, and Tal had had enough.

"She wasn't forced into anything. She's been wanting to tell you for several ninedays now, ever since she began learning to control her gift. That's when she finally felt normal, for the first time in her life."

"But I could have told her she was normal. I could have told her that when she was ten."

Tal shook her head. "She wouldn't have believed you. Unless you were prepared to send her to training where she could be with other high empaths, your words would have been just words and she would have known it. You cannot reassure when you do not understand."

"Lancer Tal," he said in a stronger tone, "I respect and admire you, but don't tell me I could not understand my child. Unless you have a child of your own, you have no idea how insulting that is."

"I meant no insult. But I speak as one who shares Salomen's gift. It's impossible to communicate what this power is like and impossible to understand if you've never felt it." She cast about for another way to explain. "You know when your children are happy or upset, yes? You can sense the emotions of your kin?"

"Yes, of course."

"Then why did you never know that Salomen was desperately lonely?"

He stared at his daughter, his jaw working. "I...should have."

"You couldn't, because she was instinctively fronting it. You could never feel what Salomen didn't want you to. But her senses allow her to feel anything. *Anything.* Only a very strong and fully trained high empath could maintain a front against her. You could not be expected to know what she was hiding, and she could not communicate what it is that she feels. In a way, you were speaking two different languages."

"We could show him." Salomen had finally found her voice again.

Tal reached for her hand. "Are you sure?"

"Yes. You're right, words will not suffice. I cannot bear the emotions in this room, and I don't think we can resolve them through talking even if we talked the rest of the day."

Shikal looked at them curiously. "How could you show us?"

"In a group Sharing," Tal said.

"But that's only done at bonding ceremonies," Nikin said. "You'd need a bond minister."

"This is part of what you don't understand. We don't need a bond minister. Two of the most powerful high empaths on the planet are here in the room with you."

She waited while they absorbed that concept.

"Salomen is that strong?" Shikal asked.

Tal smiled at her. "I don't know how strong she is. She's never been assessed. But I think she may be as strong as I am, and I have the highest rating on the scale."

"Great Goddess," mumbled Nikin.

"I want to." Jaros spoke for the first time. "I've never been to a bonding ceremony. And I think you're being rather hard on Salomen. Why are you making her feel bad? I'm *glad* she's telling us."

Salomen abruptly rose from her chair, pulled Jaros out of his, and squeezed him in a warmron. "Thank you, Jaros."

"I just don't see what everyone is so upset about."

She laughed and kissed him on the forehead. "And that's precisely why I'm thanking you." Gently, she pushed him in front of her to the center of the room, where she stood with her hands on his shoulders. "All right, I have one person who's ready to join Andira and me in a group Sharing. Are there any others?"

Tal silently took her place next to Salomen, met Shikal's eyes, and waited.

He set his glass down with a click and stood. "I'll do anything to help my daughter."

"Well, I'm not missing out on this." Nikin joined them.

Tal looked over to Micah, the last holdout.

"I'm not a part of this family," he said.

"You're a part of *my* family. Get over here."

With a look of resignation, he pushed out of his chair and walked over. "Where do you want me?"

"Behind me. Would you get a chair for Jaros, and he can go behind you?"

While Micah fetched a chair for Jaros to stand on, Salomen said, "I would like Father behind me."

"I guess I know where I'm going," Nikin said as he waited for his father to get into position.

Tal watched Jaros climb up onto his chair. "All you have to do is put your hand on Colonel Micah's neck."

His eyes were wide as he nodded.

Tal faced Salomen and waited until she felt the warm touch of Micah's hand. "Jaros, are you there?"

"I'm ready."

"Are you in place, Nikin?" Salomen asked.

"Yes."

She smiled at Tal. "We're ready on this side."

Slowly, relishing the moment, Tal reached out to cup her jaw. She rested her other hand on the back of Salomen's neck, her fingers bumping into Shikal's as she found the right spot. Salomen mirrored her position, and with one last look into each other's eyes, they touched their foreheads together.

The first thing she thought was how nice it was to not worry about an empathic flash. Then her senses abruptly expanded as they joined with Salomen's in a molten rush. Her hands grew warm, and she felt that heat travel through to Micah behind her and Jaros behind him. Focusing on Salomen, she lifted their joint emotions and directed them toward the others in the link, waiting as they absorbed the gift. Salomen's pain dissipated into the link, the Sharing relieving her of sole ownership, while she reveled in the unimpeded access to her family.

In a group Sharing, emotions were sent outward from the couple at the center, retaining the privacy of all other participants. But Tal and Salomen were not limited by a bond minister and allowed themselves access to everyone in the link. Tal was pleased to sense Shikal's hurt confusion fading into comprehension. Jaros was a bright point, radiating awe and appreciation for this new experience. Nikin's quiet love for his sister was a steady, strong current, and Micah's emotions carried a warmth that might have surprised those who did not see beyond his gruff exterior. They also carried the weight of failure, and Tal realized too late that she should not have pushed him into taking part. She sent him a tendril of reassurance, but when he didn't react, she knew he had not been able to pick it out from the rest.

She held their link together until she was sure that Salomen's family had received the full impact. A normal group Sharing would have ended there, but this had a greater purpose.

"Let me show you what Salomen has been practicing," she said, and took them beyond the walls of the house to settle on the first individual they found. "That's Varsi. Judging by what we're feeling, I'd guess she lost at tiles last night." She moved on, naming each of the Guards they came across near the house, then found another farther out. "And that's Gehrain. Now we know who Varsi lost to. You would think she'd have learned by now."

One by one, she showed them each of the Guards on their property, including the six who were now at the outer edges of Hol-Opah, creating an overlapping scanning network to be certain that no one came through their empathic net. "Feel the effort they're making?" she asked. "Active scanning is very draining. Guards train long and hard to arrive at a point where they can actively scan for up to two hanticks before needing a break. Normally, they would scan once every few ticks rather than continuously, but they're on the highest alert level now."

She lifted away from the outer Guards and brought them all back in, taking the time to make sure everyone was settled before breaking her link to the others. She and Salomen remained in their position, reveling in their own private Sharing for a few precious pipticks. It took a considerable act of will to break away and stand up straight.

The others had shifted around them and were watching with wide eyes.

"I have never felt the like," Shikal said. "Not even during a bonding ceremony."

Nikin and Micah echoed his sentiments, while Jaros was too awed to speak.

"That would never happen in a bonding ceremony," Tal said. "Most bond ministers wouldn't have the power to do the long-distance scanning that we just showed you. Even if they did, they wouldn't use it during a ceremony."

"And you can do this?" Shikal asked Salomen. "Without Sharing?"

She nodded. "I'm not skilled at it yet. I can't pick out individuals the way Andira can, unless it's one of you. But I can sense them, yes."

He made his way to his chair and sat heavily. "It's as if I've had a winden living right here in my house and never known it. You can reach heights I never imagined." He looked up at Tal. "You were right. Even after experiencing it, I'm not sure I can understand it."

Salomen knelt by his chair. "You don't have to understand. I just needed you to know, and to accept it."

"You're my daughter. I would love you if you were sonsales. Why would I love you any less for flying so high?"

"I never worried about you loving me less. I worried about hurting you."

"And what hurts me most is knowing that I wasn't able to save you from being hurt," he said. "Aren't we a pair?"

Salomen laughed as she took his hand in hers. "We are. And as far as understanding—ask me anything, and I'll tell you as best I can. Now that you all know, I want you to know as much as possible. I'm through with secrets."

"I don't think you are," Nikin said, attracting every eye in the room. He raised his eyebrows at his sister. "There's something you aren't telling us. Or did you just trust the Sharing to make it clear?"

She rose, still holding Shikal's hand, and smiled at him. "Well...I did think it would be nice to not have to confess two things in one day."

Jaros looked from her to Nikin and back again. "What?" he asked.

"Jaros," Salomen said, "our family has grown by one."

"Huh?"

Tal walked over and took Salomen's free hand.

"They're already bonded," Nikin said. "When did you do it? And why keep it so quiet? Because she's the Lancer?"

"Is that what it was?" Shikal asked. "I felt that too, but it's not like any bond I ever felt at a ceremony. I just thought that was because they're both high empaths." He looked at Salomen, the disbelief graying out his emotions. "You had a bonding ceremony without your family? Now I *am* going to be upset. How could you?"

"We haven't had a ceremony. I would never do that without including my family."

"Will someone tell me what's happening?" Jaros said.

"It turns out that tyrees don't need a ceremony to be bonded." Salomen's smile gained a mischievous edge.

There was a moment of silence before it sank in.

"Great Mother!" Nikin exclaimed. "You're tyrees? Is there anything else you need to tell us? Because we're all so shocked now that a little more won't matter."

"Salomen?" Shikal wanted to believe but needed reassurance.

"I finally found my dream, Father."

His earlier pain washed away like dust in a joyous rainstorm, and his smile was so wide it nearly crinkled his eyes shut. "I could not have wished more for you in my own dreams. But how did this happen?"

Salomen looked at Tal and shrugged. "I think you have to ask Fahla that question. We had no control over it."

"None at all," Tal agreed. "We've spent the last half moon trying to keep some sort of hold on it, because we were both frightened by how fast it was moving. For tyrees, the first Sharing seals the bond, so we were doing our best to delay it. But the assassination attempt took it out of our hands."

"Andira's empathic senses were knocked out by the shock. But she saw enough before the attack to know that the assassin was out of her Guards' range. She needed my empathic strength to find him, so...we Shared."

"While the room was burning?" Nikin asked incredulously.

Tal and Salomen looked at each other. "I didn't notice that part," Tal admitted. "Neither did I."

"They weren't in immediate danger," Micah said. "Most of the damage had already been done by then."

"But what a terrible way to have your first Sharing," Shikal said. "I hope you've made up for it by now."

"Well..." Salomen hesitated. "No, we haven't. Andira has been healing, and the circumstances weren't right. What you just experienced was only our second Sharing."

"What?" he sputtered. "No, no, no! This is not right!" He shook a finger at Tal. "You take my daughter somewhere special tonight, and you Share with her the way Fahla meant it to be. She deserves that."

"I promise." Tal couldn't keep the grin off her face. As if she had thought of anything else these last five days! But before she could do that, she needed to make up for her prior breach of tradition.

Still holding Salomen's hand, she knelt in front of Shikal's chair. "Honored Raiz Arrin," she said, "please know that had I been able to do so, I would have asked for the gift of a place in your family before presuming to take it. It was not in my power then, but it is now."

She felt the weight of his expectation as she prepared to speak the words that every Alsean over fifteen cycles knew by heart.

"Under the eye of Fahla, who sees all, I speak so that all may hear. I love Salomen Arrin Opah. Her happiness is my ambition; her well-being is my purpose. All that is mine I place freely at her disposal, including my heart and my life, which I would gladly lay down to protect hers. This I swear in Fahla's name. I am Andira Shaldone Tal, and I ask this gift of you and Nashta and all your ancestors: Will you do me the honor of accepting me into your family?"

The room was utterly still as Salomen knelt beside her. "I know I should have said something earlier, but to speak of anything would have meant revealing everything, and I wasn't ready. I'm ready now." She squeezed Tal's hand. "Under the eye of Fahla, who sees all, I speak so that all may hear. I love Andira Shaldone Tal. Her happiness is my ambition; her well-being is my purpose. All that is mine I place freely at her disposal, including my heart and my life, which I would gladly lay down to protect hers. This I swear in Fahla's name. I am Salomen Arrin Opah, and I ask this of you: Will you speak for Mother and all of our ancestors, and accept Andira into our family?"

Her last words were choked as the tears spilled from her father's eyes, and Shikal needed a few moments to answer.

"It's been a long time since I've seen you as happy as you were this past moon," he said at last. "I worried about what would happen when this challenge was over, because it never occurred to me—well. I just didn't expect this. And I wish...I wish Nashta were here."

"Me too," Salomen whispered.

He nodded, wiping his eyes, then cleared his throat and spoke the formal words. "Salomen, Andira, I hear your petition. Under the eye of Fahla, who connects our past with our future, and in the name of my beloved Nashta and all of our ancestors, I say that Andira Shaldone Tal is now one of our family. May our descendants rejoice in this bond, which enriches our family beyond measure."

Tal's own eyes were damp, and she surreptitiously dried them with her free hand. "Thank you. I will honor your name and that of your daughter."

"You already have. And I think you may be the first petitioner in memory to have fulfilled your vow even before swearing it. You already laid yourself down to protect her. I could wish for no better bondmate for Salomen, nor a better addition to our family. Welcome, Andira."

"Yes, welcome!" Nikin swooped down on them and held up both hands, laughing as Tal met his palms. "What a surprise! We knew you two had something going on, but we had no idea it was this serious. I didn't sense that from Salomen." He turned a mock severe look on his sister. "Now I know why. She was fronting it."

"I'm sorry, Nikin. It was so new and out of control that I could barely deal with it myself. I simply couldn't face any questions from you or Father."

"Don't worry; it's enough that I get to tease you now." He gave Tal an impish grin. "I must say, never in my wildest dreams did I think Salomen's ridiculous challenge would lead to a joining of our families. We were all afraid she might have brought ruin on our heads with her outspoken ways."

"I might yet," Salomen said. "Don't relax too much."

Jaros came over with Micah, his brow furrowed. "Does this mean Lancer Tal is my sister?"

"I'm your bondsister. Not quite the same thing, but close."

He grinned. "Speedy! Wait until everyone at school hears about this!"

Salomen reached around Tal and pulled her brother over. "Jaros, you cannot tell your friends about our bond. Not yet. You can tell them that we're a joined couple, which we've made public as of today. But not that we're bonded and *especially* not that we're tyrees."

"Why not?"

"Because someone might try to hurt me by hurting your sister," Tal said. "Being my bondmate will make her a target. Being my tyree only increases the danger."

He blinked up at Salomen, then wrapped his arms around her. "I won't tell, I promise."

She gave him a warmron as Nikin asked, "How great a concern is that?"

"Great enough that I'm currently training Salomen's Guards," Micah said. "We hadn't planned to go public with this quite yet, but the assassination attempt pushed our schedule forward. Right now I have a unit of Tal's Guards ready to step in. Salomen's own Guards will begin their duties in four days."

"You get your own Guards!" Now Jaros was over the nearest moon.

"Yes, I do. I think you're happier about it than I am."

"Why wouldn't you be happy? This is fantastic!"

"I suppose it is." Salomen couldn't help laughing at his enthusiasm. "But do you know what's even better?"

"What?"

"You're going to participate in your first bonding ceremony, and it will be a state event. You'll be the only boy in school who will get to go."

"That's right," Shikal said. "We have a rather large ceremony to think about, don't we?"

Tal nodded. "And not a great deal of control over the details. Since this will be a state ceremony, I'll have to bring in Counselor Aldirk." She looked at Micah, sharing his mirth at the thought. "I'm sure he'll be happy to fly out here and help."

"Let's go into the dining room and write down a few thoughts," Salomen said. "Besides, you promised Andira horten soup, and you haven't delivered yet."

"True. That *was* the main reason I came back here."

"If I believed that for a moment, I would retract my permission." Shikal rose from his chair and led them toward the dining room.

Salomen slipped an arm around Tal's waist. "Is your back all right?" she asked quietly.

"It's fine." Tal pulled her aside as the others filed into the dining room. She watched Shikal and Nikin continue to the kitchen dome, while Jaros sat down at the table and began peppering Micah with questions. "Do you think Jaros ever runs out of questions?"

"No." Salomen watched him with a fond smile. "You'll get used to it."

Tal took advantage of the moment to study the peaceful expression on her face. "All the time I've known you, there's been something in the background of your emotions, weighing you down. And now it's gone."

"But something else has taken its place."

"I know. An incredible lightness. It's even making me feel giddy."

"No, I think you're feeling giddy about everything else. I'm talking about something you've always had, so you probably don't recognize it as anything unusual."

"What wouldn't I recognize as unusual?"

The beaming smile that Salomen gave her could have evaporated the rain from here to Blacksun.

"Freedom, Andira. I'm finally free."

CHAPTER 9
An unlikely source

"Excuse me, Chief Counselor?"

Aldirk looked up impatiently from the stack of work that threatened to slide off his desk. "What is it?"

His aide stood in the doorway, her brows drawn together. "I, ah…have a rather odd call that I'm not certain what to do with."

He put his reader card down and gave her his full attention. She was the smartest aide he'd had in three cycles and would not ask for assistance unless it was something unusual. "I'm listening."

She took one step inside, letting the door shut behind her. "It's a small boy wanting to speak with the Lancer. I told him that was impossible, but he was very insistent. He said he's been trying for a hantick to get through to her, but no one will take him seriously. He says he has extremely important information for her."

Aldirk huffed. "What information could a small boy possibly have? And why is he calling me?"

"He's calling you because all of his prior efforts have taught him that you're the gatekeeper to the Lancer. As for the information, he won't tell me. But I think you might wish to speak with him."

"And why is that?"

"Because he's one of the boys who bullied Jaros Opah. Which means Lancer Tal really does know him. And if Lancer Tal had punished me for behaving that badly, the last thing I'd ever want to do is seek her out to speak with her again. Whatever is motivating this child, it's powerful."

"Hm. That *is* interesting." He thought for a moment, then nodded. "Very well. Send the call to me and let's find out exactly what this boy thinks is so important."

Half a tick later, Aldirk accepted the transferred call and was looking at a thin, sandy-haired boy. "I'm Chief Counselor Aldirk. And who are you, exactly?"

"Pendar Fall," the boy answered smartly. "I need to speak with Lancer Tal. If you would just tell her it's me, she'll listen. I know her."

"So I hear. I also know why you know her, and it does you no credit. Let me explain something to you, Pendar. This is as far as you will get. Lancer Tal is a very busy woman, and she does not have time to speak directly to every person who wishes to speak with her. However," he continued when the boy tried to interrupt, "if I deem your information important enough, I will share it with her. Personally."

Judging by the scowl, Pendar was unhappy with this offer. He pursed his lips, blinked several times in thought, and finally asked, "Do you promise? To tell her?"

"I always keep my word. Now, what do you think she needs to know?"

He drew himself up, a stern look adding cycles to his face. "Someone in Granelle has been spying on Lancer Tal, and I know who it is."

CHAPTER 10
State House quarters

TAL AND SALOMEN LEFT HOL-OPAH amid many double-palm touches, a few urgent warmrons from Jaros, and a transport full of good wishes and joyous feelings. Micah accompanied them as far as the State House entrance before heading toward his quarters with a final "Remember, gentle movement!" tossed over his shoulder. His chuckles drifted down the corridor as he walked away.

Shaking her head, Tal called over the nearest Guards and asked them to take Salomen's bags to her quarters. She was still learning new things about her tyree, and today she had learned that Salomen had no idea how to pack lightly. Those two overstuffed bags must have contained her entire wardrobe, and Tal wasn't about to risk a return trip to the restriction bed by trying to carry one.

As they followed the Guards, she swelled with unexpected pride at Salomen's awe. She had always preferred her base quarters, but there was no denying that the State House was more impressive.

"Amazing." Salomen swiveled her head this way and that, taking in the rich tapestries on the walls, the small heirloom tables with ancient art and vases of flowers, and the portraits of historical figures and events.

"What is?"

"The decor. The history and opulence, all of it. It's so beautiful. But it's not very homey, is it?"

"Not at all." Tal nodded a greeting to the two Guards standing watch at the entrance to her private hallway. "Except for one part. Thank you," she said as their escorts dropped the two giant bags at her door. "We'll take them from here."

They saluted her, smiled at Salomen, and returned the way they had come.

"Which part?" Salomen asked.

Tal unlocked her door and decided she could chance carrying one of Salomen's bags a few paces. "This," she said, dropping the bag just inside the entrance.

Salomen put the second bag next to it and looked around with a wide smile. "Now this space I would have recognized as yours had anyone asked."

"What gives it away?"

"The feel." She turned in a slow circle, facing Tal at the end. "I can feel you in this room."

"That's one reason I love Hol-Opah. I can feel you and your family and all the people who lived there before. It has a warmth and history that I haven't often sensed in the places I've lived."

Salomen half-closed her eyes. "There's plenty of history here, too, but it's not all warm. And your presence overpowers all of it. Maybe that's because your energy is what I'm attuned to, but this room feels like home to me."

Tal stepped into her. "I'm so glad," she murmured, tucking her face into Salomen's throat.

"Oh…" Salomen squeezed her, careful of her back, then brought a hand up behind her head. "I've missed this."

"Me too. I wish we could stay this way for a few hanticks."

"I know. But you have meetings."

"No, *we* have meetings. Time to start your challenge, tyrina."

"You're serious?"

"When am I not?"

"Often, but let's not get into that. You told me you were meeting with Colonel Razine. Surely you don't want me sitting in on that?"

"If you were still Raiz Opah, the woman who drove me insane in delegate meetings, no. But you're my tyree, and that changes everything. Besides, what else are you going to do? I can't have you getting bored on your challenge moon."

"Somehow, boring is not the word that comes to mind when I think of you."

Her smile was so beautiful that Tal had to kiss her. She still wasn't used to their new ability to touch without danger, to kiss without keeping half her brain focused on the inevitable flash. It took some time to settle in fully rather than waiting for a reason to stop, but when she did, her sense of Salomen suddenly bloomed. Their emotions became difficult to separate, not that she had any desire to sort them out. This was the connection they had both been needing, and this time there were no other people linked to them.

"We have to stop," Salomen murmured against her lips.

"I know."

They kissed again, hands tracing curves and brushing through hair, lips seeking hollows and ridges.

"We really have to stop, Andira."

"Shek." Tal pulled back. "You're a cruel woman."

"Me! I'm not the one who started something we have no chance of finishing."

"You stood there looking lovelier than anything that has ever been in this room. Was I supposed to resist that?"

Salomen shook her head. "I won't argue with you. On *that* topic. But you—I mean, we have meetings starting in about twenty ticks, don't we?"

Tal sighed and stepped away. "Yes, we do. We should have left Hol-Opah earlier, but I couldn't bear to go." She picked up one of the bags and headed for the large bed at the side of the room. "Let's at least get you partially settled."

Salomen followed with the second bag. "This really is gorgeous. Luxurious and elegant, but still…livable."

"Thank you. I like the space, I must admit. Base quarters are never this large."

"No joke. You could fit the top floor of my house in here. I'm guessing base quarters don't have ceilings like this, either." Salomen tilted her head back, examining the carvings adorning a wide strip atop the walls. On the high, arched ceiling, wood strips of different shades formed subtle patterns.

"Not for anyone but the commander. There's a benefit to living on the top floor."

The room was an open design, with living, cooking, and sleeping quarters separated only by visual space. All of the furniture was antique, but also comfortable and useful. When Tal moved in, she had sent quite a few pieces into storage that she was afraid to touch, much less sit or write on.

The door opened into the center of the room, where a richly embroidered circular rug told the story of the Wandering King's discovery of Blacksun Basin. To the right was her desk, placed to have a view out the windows, and beyond that, the kitchen area filled the inside corner. Her desk had a built-in recessed vidcom unit, but the room featured a second, much larger wall unit above the dining table, which sat in the opposite corner from the kitchen and under the first of the windows that marched across the outer wall. Half-height bookcases lined the entire wall below the windows, their polished wooden tops displaying various pieces of art that Tal had picked up in her travels. A sofa and a collection of chairs and side tables made a comfortable place to read or entertain guests—not that she ever brought anyone here besides Micah. She had too few inviolable places in her life, and this was one of them.

The sleeping area took up the left part of the room, with the huge bed facing the windows and set on an equally large, plush rug. A hand-carved clothing organizer was tucked up against the head of the bed, facing toward the inner wall, its glass doors revealing a colorful assortment of clothes and blankets inside.

Tal opened the organizer and cleared linens off two of the shelves. "You can keep some of your clothes here, but there's more room in the closet."

"There?" Salomen pointed toward the arched doorway in the left wall.

"Yes. The bathroom is through there as well." Carrying the linens, Tal started off for the doorway before noticing that Salomen had wandered to the bookcases, where the only plant in the room held court.

"What is this?" Salomen touched one of the orchid's flowers and drew back in surprise when it changed color. "I've never seen anything like it. Is this—?"

"A Filessian orchid." Tal reached her side, still holding the linens. "It's from the *Caphenon*. I have another in my office, with purple flowers that turn yellow. They both came back into bloom again last moon."

"How incredibly beautiful. And it smells divine." Salomen touched the yellow flower again, smiling as the petal under her finger shimmered into a deep blue. "I read that the Gaians had an entire garden on that ship. Are you going to give me a tour when you take Jaros?"

"I'll give you a tour this nineday if you like. As soon as I've caught up on everything."

"I would love that." She picked up the small box propped against the orchid's vase. "Is this from the *Caphenon* as well?"

"That's, ah…" Tal swallowed. "They're medals of valor. They belong to Ekatya."

Salomen looked from the red and silver medals to her. "Why did she leave them with you?"

"She didn't. She didn't mean for anyone to see them. I'm just keeping them safe until she comes back."

Salomen returned the box to its place. "There's a story here, and I want to hear it, but I'm guessing we'll need more time than we have." She turned to face Tal. "And surely you can feel that I'm fine."

"I can, but…part of me is still waiting for the second stone to hit." And she hadn't yet told Salomen the full truth. As irked as she had been at Micah for keeping Ekatya away, she was grateful for his foresight now.

"There is no second stone. I'm not competing with a memory anymore. She has her tyree, and I have mine."

Tal nearly dropped the linens when Salomen took her mouth in the most possessive kiss they had ever shared. She was two pipticks away from canceling every meeting for the rest of the day when Salomen finally pulled back and smiled.

"Hold that thought," she whispered, then added in a normal tone, "So. You were going to show me the bathroom?"

Tal stared at her while her brain scrambled to switch tracks.

"Bathroom…?" Salomen prompted.

Tal shook her head. "If you wanted to kill me, there are easier ways." She turned, smiling at the sound of Salomen's laughter, and led the way into the bathroom. "It's a little larger than I need."

"Goddess above, an entire unit of Guards could use this!" Salomen stood in the center of the cavernous tiled room, looking around with awe. "How many guests does a Lancer usually sleep with?"

Tal stacked the linens on a small table by the door. "There were some large parties in past eras. This one has been rather sedate, I'm afraid."

"Good. Let's keep it that way." Salomen went to one of the tall windows and looked out. "Best view I've ever seen from a bathroom. Is there a privacy screen, like on your transport?"

"You don't want to bare yourself to half of Blacksun?"

Salomen turned her head and scorched Tal with a look. "Don't talk about baring bodies when we have meetings in fifteen ticks."

"Why not? It's only fair. And yes, there is." She indicated the control discreetly embedded in the wall.

Salomen walked past her, brushing an arm along her waist as she did so, and peeked through the doorway set in the wall of the bathroom. "Ah. A closet large enough for that Guard unit as well."

Tal followed her in. "As you can see, there's plenty of room for you. In my younger days, I had entire housing units that would have fit into this closet. I couldn't fill this in a lifetime."

"Oh, but what you do have is top of the pile." Salomen walked over to one of the wall racks and pulled out Tal's most formal suit. "I saw you wearing this at the funerals after the Battle of Alsea. And the one right after the *Caphenon* landed. You looked spectacular."

Tal sidled up to her. "If we didn't have meetings, I could put it on for you… and you could take it off again."

Salomen let the suit swing back in. "Don't tempt me." With a look of warning, she strode past Tal to the main room. A moment later she returned with both bags.

Tal raised an eyebrow at her effortless display of strength and wondered if she was even aware of how sexy that was.

"At least unpacking won't take long," Salomen said. "It's not as if I need to find space."

True to her word, she was fully unpacked by the time they left their quarters for the first meeting. Tal stole sideways glances at her as they walked down the corridor to the lift, marveling that she was actually here. The moon at Hol-Opah had been a complete departure for her, making it somehow easier to accept the radical changes that becoming tyree had wrought. After all, everything had been different then. But now she was back at the State House, settling into what used to be her normal life, and Salomen's presence was a brilliant reminder of just how much had changed. Some of it she could have done without, but the rest…

The rest was a gift so great that no amount of oil could ever convey her gratitude to Fahla.

CHAPTER 11
Little spy

Aldirk checked his wristcom and nodded to himself. Right on time as always. He knocked on the Lancer's inner office door and heard the familiar "Enter."

The chair behind the desk was empty. He turned toward the conference table and stopped in his tracks.

"Aldirk." Lancer Tal smiled at him from her seat. "I would like to introduce Raiz Salomen Opah. Salomen, this is Chief Counselor Sunsa Aldirk."

Aldirk stared at the woman next to the Lancer, hoping his surprise did not show. Of course he recognized her. He knew all about her. Just this morning he had helped arrange today's demonstration of her status to the media.

What he didn't know, and what had startled him into silence, was that she was a powerful empath. He had not detected anyone in this room prior to walking in. While that was normal for the Lancer, it was decidedly abnormal for a producer.

After what felt like an embarrassingly obvious amount of time, he recovered enough to give her a short bow. "Well met, Raiz Opah. It's a pleasure."

"Well met, Counselor Aldirk. And the pleasure is mine." She offered what appeared to be a genuine smile. "I've heard a great deal about you. Andira says she couldn't do her job without you."

"Well, I could," said Lancer Tal, "but it would be much more difficult."

Aldirk had never heard anyone call the Lancer by her first name. "Thank you," he said faintly. "I do my best."

Lancer Tal tilted her head to one side. "Is something wrong?"

"No, no." He forced his legs to move and took a seat. "I hadn't realized we would have a guest at our meeting."

"She's not a guest. That's part of what we'll be discussing."

"Ah, yes. The second phase of your challenge. I was unaware that you planned to include Raiz Opah in all of your meetings."

"She won't be. But circumstances have changed. Salomen will be here for more than just the challenge moon. And she's more than just my lover, this morning's media show notwithstanding." She glanced at the producer, her expression showing a startlingly open warmth. "She's my bondmate."

"Your—" For one paralyzing moment, his brain cleared of all thoughts. "I, ah…I'm surprised. Your bondmate?"

She nodded. "I received inclusion from her family today. And I know you're more than surprised, though your front is perfect as always. But Salomen is the reason I asked you to research tyrees with the divine spark."

"Great Mother. I had no idea." She couldn't have mentioned this little detail earlier? He had never been so off balance in his entire professional life.

"It happened very suddenly. We weren't bonded until the night of the assassination attempt."

"Then I'm even more glad to welcome you back, and to meet you, Raiz Opah. You surely deserve a better place than the healing center to celebrate your bond. Though I'm five days late, may I offer my congratulations?"

"Thank you," they said in unison, and Aldirk felt as if he had dropped into an alternative existence.

"This morning's demonstration was just to throw the gossip mongers off the track," Lancer Tal said. "Colonel Micah needs time to train Salomen's Guards, so as far as the world knows, she's just my lover. I'm sorry I couldn't tell you earlier, but we had to keep this tightly wrapped, at least until I got out of the healing center."

He nodded, feeling slightly better. But still—that meant Miltorin had known about it before him! He must have, in order to work out this morning's public relations stunt. And he was surely going to preen about it, the little zalren.

"In the meantime, we have a bonding ceremony to plan," Lancer Tal continued. "I want you to fly out to Hol-Opah tomorrow and meet with Salomen's father and brother. They have no idea what to expect in a state ceremony and will benefit from your expertise."

"Very well." Aldirk whipped out his reader card, taking refuge in the calendar. "What is your timeline for this ceremony?"

"First decision," the Lancer said to Opah. "What would you prefer?"

"My preference is probably not going to be popular. The best time of the cycle for me to be focusing on a big event is right now. This is the quietest moon for us. Next moon we begin planting the winter crop, so that wouldn't work at all. But the moon after is a possibility."

"This moon is impossible. Aldirk can work miracles, but even he couldn't manage that one. We'll be bringing people in from all over Alsea, and quite a few of them have schedules planned a cycle in advance. We'll have to give more notice than just a few ninedays."

"Then it will have to be the moon after next."

"You're sure that will work for you and your family?"

Opah thought for a few moments. "Yes, it would."

Lancer Tal looked back at Aldirk. "Looks like we can plan it for two moons from now."

Aldirk was torn between relief at the two-moon reprieve and utter horror that he was being compelled to schedule a state bonding ceremony around a crop planting. "One moment," he said briskly as he pulled up that moon. "Rosslin is the final moon before bringing the matter printers online; you have a number of appearances scheduled. But…" He shifted a few appointments around. "If we move two meetings and one appearance off the twenty-seventh day, we can—"

"Wait," Lancer Tal interrupted. She had a strange look of excitement as she pulled out her reader card and began tapping away. "Ah! I knew there was one that moon. Make it the twenty-third."

"That's not a good day. You have five—"

"Make it a good day," she said firmly. "That's the day I want."

"What makes that day so important?" Opah voiced Aldirk's thoughts.

"It's a red moon."

"Oh, that's perfect," Opah and Aldirk said together, and now he was certain he had dropped into an alternative existence. Still… "It's an excellent choice," he added. "An ideally symbolic occasion. Of course, the ceremony would have to be at night."

"My thoughts exactly." Lancer Tal turned to her bondmate. "How would you feel about a bonding ceremony at Whitemoon Temple?"

Before Aldirk could object to the venue—Lancers were always bonded at Blacksun Temple—Opah unleashed a dazzling smile, and he knew that argument was already lost.

"I would love it. Mother always wanted to go there, but she never made it before she got sick."

"Nashta will be there." Lancer Tal rested a hand over Opah's heart. "You carry her here, every day."

Aldirk was startled to witness such a gentle gesture from the woman he knew only as an impenetrable leader. Her front was as strong as ever, but anyone with a grain of ability to read body language could see her feelings for Opah. He couldn't begin to understand how it had happened, but it was clear that Lancer Tal was actually in love.

He redirected his attention to his reader card, stifling a smile. Lancer Tal in love! He would have to reassess his lifelong cynicism regarding Fahla's attention toward individual Alseans. Apparently, she was still producing miracles after all.

When they had worked through the bonding ceremony details, he turned his attention to the first item on his own list.

"I had an interesting call earlier today, from someone I think you'll wish to speak with. His name is Pendar Fall."

"Pendar called you? Here?"

Aldirk nodded. "It appears there is a spy in Granelle."

"A spy?" Raiz Opah asked incredulously. "Who is spying on whom? It's Granelle! Everyone knows everyone else."

"And you will know this man, I'm fairly certain." Aldirk checked his notes. "His name is Nessil Withernet."

Though her front was still perfect, Opah looked shocked. "I've known Withernet half my life. He's no spy. He runs an equipment store in town."

Aldirk hadn't intended to do this with Raiz Opah in the room, but it seemed nothing was going according to plan today. "Lancer Tal, I suggest you hear what Pendar has to say. He's at home now, waiting for your call."

"Very well."

Pendar was indeed waiting, and his eyes widened when he saw who else was in the room. "Lancer Tal! Thank you for calling. And, um…Raiz Opah, well met."

"Well met, Pendar," said Raiz Opah in an even voice.

Pendar shifted in his chair. "I'm, um…I'm really sorry. About Jaros."

"Are you ever going to do anything like that again?"

"No! I don't even know why I did it then. It was just… It just happened. And I wish I could go back and fix it. I apologized to Jaros at school."

"I know. He told me. That was very well done, and I accept your apology as well. But I don't think that's why you wished to speak with the Lancer, is it?"

Visibly relieved, Pendar turned his attention to Lancer Tal. "No. Did you hear about the spy?"

"Only that there is one. I'm told you have a story for me."

He nodded vigorously. "I was in the Golden Scythe with my aunt and uncle for midmeal today—"

"A family tavern in town," Raiz Opah murmured to Lancer Tal.

"And the vidcom was showing the news about you coming back to Granelle. They kept showing that scene with you and Raiz Opah in the transport doorway and then you talking to the family, over and over. And then I had to go to the toilet, and when I came out, I heard someone saying your name. So I stopped to listen, and it was Withernet and his bondmate. They were having midmeal in the back room, and they thought they were alone, and they were arguing. His bondmate—I don't remember his name—"

"Balen," said Raiz Opah. "Balen Tellamor."

"Yes, that was it! Withernet called him Balen. Anyway, Balen was saying 'She is our Lancer, I don't care how much you hate her,' and Withernet said 'It's not about hate, it's about our livelihoods,' but then he said he wished now he hadn't done it."

"Done what?" Lancer Tal asked.

"Told Cullom Bilsner to kill you."

There was a dead silence in the room.

Lancer Tal leaned forward. "They were talking about this with you standing right there?"

Pendar made a huffing sound. "I pretended to be playing with a toy on the floor. Adults are so stupid. I'm *twelve*; I'd never play on the floor, but they didn't even notice me. They just thought I was a little child."

"Pendar," said the Lancer in a too-calm voice, "I need you to tell me everything you heard."

Pendar shot Aldirk a glance that said *See?* and straightened his spine. "Withernet was getting paid by somebody named Spinner to spy on you and the Opahs. Balen was angry with him, and Withernet said 'You didn't have a problem with it before,' and Balen said 'That was when it was just information. You went too far.' And Withernet looked sad and said yes, he knew that. He said the worst part was that he thought Spinner would be happy with it, but he wasn't."

"This Spinner person had nothing to do with the assassination attempt?"

"I guess not? I mean, it sounded like he ended his arrangement with Withernet because of it."

"Do you know what sort of information Withernet was sending?"

"They didn't say anything specific. I just know it was anything about what you were doing on Hol-Opah or in Granelle, and anything to do with the Opahs if you were involved. And then they argued about Cullom Bilsner. Withernet said it wasn't his fault that Cullom actually went through with it, and Balen said 'You don't get to hide behind that idiot producer when you were the one feeding his delusions,' and that was when my uncle came looking for me."

Lancer Tal sat back. "So Cullom Bilsner had encouragement, from someone who was spying on us for the benefit of someone named Spinner."

"Yes. Oh, and Spinner is in Blacksun. I remember Withernet mentioning that. He didn't know his real name, but he's someone big in Blacksun."

"Anything else?"

"No. I'm sorry. I wish I could have listened longer, but they stopped talking when my uncle came in. And I couldn't think of a reason to stay."

"Of course not. It would have looked very suspicious if you had. But you've done me a service, and I appreciate it. Tell me, how did your fathers react when they heard about your recent…adventure at the Pit?"

Pendar looked as if someone had let the air out of him. "They didn't even get mad. But they said they were disappointed in me, and that's so much worse."

"Do you think they might feel better if you could show them a personal letter of thanks from me?"

He sat up straight again. "You mean it?"

"As I said, you've done me a service. And I'm guessing you had to work rather hard to get as far as Chief Counselor Aldirk's office. I think that deserves a letter with the Seal of the Lancer on it."

A smile split his face. "That would be speedy! Thank you!"

When they ended the call, Lancer Tal turned to Aldirk. "Have you spoken with Colonel Razine about this?"

"She expects to have the warrant ready tomorrow."

"Good. I'm suddenly very interested in hearing what a Granelle merchant has to say. And who is this Spinner?"

"I'm wondering the same thi—" Aldirk stopped when Lancer Tal swiveled to her bondmate.

"Salomen?"

"How *could* he?" Opah burst out. "How much did it take to buy his family name and honor? Did it ever occur to him that people might die because of him? His family won't be able to hold their heads up in town. Herot may have smeared the Opah name, but at least he didn't do it for *pay*." She stopped in mid-rant, her anger winding down to uncertainty, then rested her head on one hand. "Fahla, I hope he didn't."

"We'll figure it out," Lancer Tal said. "And Withernet will pay for it, I promise. Selling publicly available information isn't illegal, but inciting murder certainly is. Though to be honest, I'm less interested in his encouraging Bilsner than I am in his spy activities."

Opah raised her head again. "Is this your life? People spying on you wherever you go?"

Lancer Tal actually looked pained. "Not usually. I live such a public life that there's normally no need to spy on me. But I dropped out of the public eye when I went to Hol-Opah. Miltorin wanted me to take advantage of our challenge—vids of me with the field workers, photo sessions, carefully crafted quotes about the things I was learning—but I wouldn't allow it."

"Why not?"

Lancer Tal opened her mouth, then shut it again.

Aldirk leaned back in his chair, startled and amused by what was unfolding in front of him. This was not the Lancer he knew.

"I thought it was because I wanted a vacation of sorts. To be out of reach of the usual image-conscious politics. But looking back now…I think it was because I didn't want to share you with the world."

They smiled at each other, lost in their own little universe, and Aldirk cleared his throat. "Then the question becomes, was this Spinner threatened by the fact that you dropped out of the public eye, or was it specifically your activities on Hol-Opah that interested him?"

Lancer Tal straightened and turned, her visible emotion vanishing behind a familiar façade. "From what Pendar says, it was specifically my activities on Hol-Opah or with any of the Opahs. So why were they so interesting? What was the motivation?"

"Maybe he's running some sort of gambling scheme," Opah suggested. "Based on what you did during the challenge. People were betting on the outcome."

"Micah did mention that." Lancer Tal raised an eyebrow. "As I recall, the odds were four to one in my favor."

"Not in my caste, they weren't. Five to one against you."

"Really? I hope you didn't throw away your cinteks on such a bad bet."

"They wouldn't let me bet on myself, but I had Nikin put down a few cinteks for me. And I still plan to win." Opah's expression held a slight challenge before she continued, "Anyway, we know there was worldwide betting. Maybe someone saw this as a way to make a quick profit, by hiring someone local to give him an advantage."

"That's a possibility," Aldirk said. He wouldn't have thought of it, but who knew?

"An advantage…" Lancer Tal repeated distantly. "An advantage…" She looked at Aldirk, her light blue eyes focused now. "Yes, but not over other gamblers. Over me. Someone is playing a game. A spymaster who was upset about the assassination attempt? He has a vested interest in me. Pendar said it was someone big in Blacksun, and that smells like politics. This Spinner needs me to do something that I probably have no intention of doing, so he wants to know how to maneuver me into it."

Aldirk nodded, happier with this explanation. "I think you're hunting the right trail."

"What kind of game involves paying someone to spy on you?" Opah looked disgusted.

"An expensive one," Lancer Tal said. "And you might be right about the gambling aspect, but it's not for some kind of betting ring. It's for himself. He's placing a big bet on what I'll do when the right moment comes."

"Colonel Razine will be questioning Withernet tomorrow morning," Aldirk said. "I'm sure we'll have some answers by then."

CHAPTER 12
Breaking the boundary

"How often do you sit through those?" Salomen asked.

"I debrief with Aldirk at least every other day." Tal stretched her arms overhead and then dropped her hands into her lap, slumping in her chair. "Even when we don't meet, he has a report waiting for me every morning. As for Colonel Razine, we're meeting more often these days, for obvious reasons. She has a great deal on her desk between the search for Herot and her investigation into the task force, and now she's added our mysterious Spinner to her list. I'm seeing Counselor Miltorin more often as well. This was a short day, Salomen. I see an average of three to five Council members every day, and advisors as well, in addition to the planned group advisor meetings, the remaining delegate meetings, and of course the Council and High Council sessions when we have them."

"Great Goddess. That's not even sane. Your life is meetings!"

"You learn fast. Ready for an entire moon of this?"

"Not in the slightest. But I'm ready to go back to our quarters." Salomen stood and extended a hand. "May I escort you home?"

Tal allowed herself to be pulled up. "Do you remember the way?"

In answer, Salomen led them out the door, pausing long enough for Tal to palmlock it before resuming their trek through the corridors. It was late and there were few people left on the fourteenth floor, a circumstance for which Tal was profoundly grateful. She did not relish the idea of being stopped now and doubted that she could carry on a civil conversation. She and Salomen had waited too long for this to be delayed by anything less important than a Voloth invasion.

They bypassed the lift in favor of the stairs, both of them running up two steps at a time, and barely slowed their pace as they trotted down the corridor. If the Guards in her private hallway were amused by the Lancer practically running to her quarters with her lover, they had the sense to front it. Offering crisp salutes, they stared straight ahead and kept silent.

Tal didn't even acknowledge them as she dashed past. She slapped her palm on the pad by the door and only then realized that she needed to program Salomen in.

"Shek," she muttered, hurriedly tapping the commands. "If I don't program you, I'll probably forget—"

A hand closed around her wrist, stopping her progress.

"Not now," Salomen said firmly.

Tal laughed as she was nearly yanked off her feet, but her merriment was abruptly halted by a pair of soft lips. The door hadn't finished closing before they were lost in each other, picking up where they had left off three hanticks earlier. For several ticks there was nothing in their minds but the sensations of lips and skin and curves, each of them absorbing the other's excitement in an empathic connection that they were finally allowed to enjoy.

"You feel wonderful." Tal ran her hands down Salomen's sides, settling briefly in the gentle curve of her waist before sliding up her back.

Salomen's hands were wandering as well, unable to stay in any one place for long. "So do you," she whispered between kisses. "And how is it that you still smell like you just stepped out of the shower?" She nibbled her way down to Tal's throat and sucked gently.

Tal dropped her head back. "Because I did nothing today besides sit on my backside."

Salomen chuckled into her ear, then pulled on the lobe with her teeth. "That's about to change," she breathed.

Tal shivered. With an effort, she broke away and held Salomen at arm's length. "You have too many clothes on. And I can't concentrate on undressing you when you're doing that."

"Then undress me quickly."

Never in her life had Tal been so happy to obey an order. She pushed Salomen's jacket halfway down her arms and began unbuttoning her shirt. Salomen lowered her arms, letting the jacket fall to the floor, and stood waiting as Tal finished the last button at her hip. It was a wrap shirt, designed to present a smooth crossover front while buttoning at the sides, and Tal held her breath as she slowly pulled the top layer away. The layer beneath still covered half of Salomen's torso, but as creamy skin and a perfect, full breast were revealed, she thought it was a good thing she wasn't seeing everything at once. Her heart might not survive the experience.

She kissed the skin just above the bottom edge of the shirt, then traced the diagonal line it made across Salomen's torso. As her mouth brushed the curve of a breast, she heard a sharp intake of air.

"This isn't quickly."

"I tried," Tal murmured against the softness. "But I cannot rush this."

She kissed her way around a pliant nipple the color of a just-ripened panfruit, then took it into her mouth and caressed it with her tongue.

Salomen pressed a hand against the back of her head. "That feels…amazing."

Tal released the nipple, no longer as pliant as before. "Yes, it does." She drew it back in, not quite ready to leave it. Besides the sensual thrill, there was the added incentive of the hand holding her in place. It appeared that the prior order had been rescinded; Salomen was no longer in such a hurry to be undressed. Nor was Tal in a hurry to move, not when Salomen's chest rose against her with every sigh.

But there was much still to explore, and with a final kiss, she resumed her journey. Just above the breast on which she had lavished so much attention was a lovely chest ridge, exposed in all its glory. Tal had only seen it once before, when Salomen had worn that beautiful dress with the tiny shoulder straps and deeply diving neckline. Now she nibbled along its length, reveling in the conflicting sensations of soft skin over the hard ridge. When the ridge ran out, she moved inward and upward, seeking the source of the spicy scent that had tantalized her ever since Salomen had come downstairs at her house, packed and ready.

Here, at the base of her throat. As Tal pressed a kiss to the fragrant, warm hollow, it vibrated beneath her lips. Salomen was making a sound of pure pleasure, and it was enough for Tal to pull back, wanting to see what she looked like when she did that.

Salomen's eyes opened, her pupils dilated with the desire singing between them, and Tal's breath caught in her throat.

"You look like a sculpture," she said, tracing one finger back down the line of the shirt. "Feminine perfection, exposed just enough to tantalize the viewer, but not enough to reveal her full beauty." She reached for the last buttons. "It feels like I've waited forever for this."

"At least one of us is getting what she wants."

Tal looked up to see the quirked eyebrow and half-smile that she had come to love. Returning her attention to the buttons, she undid the last one and reverently pulled the cloth away, her eyes glued to the loveliness beneath her hands.

Salomen's skin glowed in the low light, its smooth expanse unmarked except for a long, thin scar at her waist. Tal brushed a fingertip over it, then leaned down and touched it with her lips. "When?" she asked.

"I was eight. Fell out of a tree and caught a branch on the way down. Not with my hands."

"Were you supposed to be in that tree?" Her fingers were moving of their own accord, mapping the contours of this new treasure.

"Of course not. That's why I have the scar, because I didn't let anyone see that I was hurt until it was too late for a clean healing."

"Which does not surprise me at all." She gently cupped Salomen's breasts, reveling in their soft weight. "I'm still not quite believing that I can touch you like this without flying halfway across the room."

"I'd like to find out how that feels myself." Salomen caught and held her hands. "And I'm not standing here for inspection while you're still wearing a full uniform." She reached for Tal's jacket and made no pretense of patience as she unzipped it and pushed it off her shoulders. Tal barely managed to get her arms out of the sleeves without losing her balance as Salomen pulled the jacket toward her, holding it up with a triumphant expression.

"I love you in this," she said. A predatory smile weakened Tal's knees as she added, "But I love you even more out of it." She dropped the jacket in an untidy heap and began undoing the shirt buttons at the side of Tal's throat. Tugging out the bottom of the shirt, she hastily pulled it over Tal's head and stopped, her mouth partly open. "Goddess above," she whispered, the shirt slipping unnoticed from her grasp. "Andira…"

The sense of urgency was gone, replaced by an awe that had Salomen reaching out tentatively. She touched Tal's shoulders, tracing the curves, then slid her hands down her arms and laced their fingers together. Pulling Tal toward her, she leaned in to nibble her way across the collarbone, then the chest ridge, and finally settled on her breast.

Tal closed her eyes as warm lips gently tugged her nipple, then forced them open again. She had waited too long for this to miss seeing any of it; she wanted it to last forever while she took in every detail. But the sight of Salomen at her breast, combined with their mingled arousal, was such a potent mix that she could barely hold herself still. She stood it for as long as she could, but all too soon was pulling Salomen up again.

Their lips met with a mutual hunger neither of them had allowed themselves until now. Tal threw aside all of her prior self-restraint and felt Salomen do the same, their movements growing frantic as they abandoned any semblance of gentleness. Salomen bit Tal's lower lip hard enough to draw blood, and the salty taste drove Tal even higher. She left marks on Salomen's neck, searching for the ridges that were rising to the surface but still just beneath the skin. She had wanted to take it slow, to make this first time mean more than just a satiation of their hunger, but her body had other ideas and she didn't think she could stop—

Strong hands wrenched her head back, and she gasped as she stared into wide, half-glazed brown eyes. This raging need was not entirely her own. Their emotions had merged; they were driving each other.

"Bed," Salomen said in a choked voice.

Tal swallowed hard and nodded. They held on to each other as they stumbled toward the large bed beneath the windows, and Salomen gave her a forceful push backward.

Tal caught herself just in time. "No."

Brought up short, Salomen frowned, lust clouding over with dazed confusion. "No? What—?"

"My back."

"Oh." Her distress was sharp, cutting effortlessly through the sexual haze and pushing them both back to sanity. "I'm so sorry. I wasn't thinking—"

"No, Salomen, I'm fine." Tal caught her shoulders and held her. "I'm fine. Just don't throw me on the bed."

Salomen looked into her eyes for several pipticks, absorbing what Tal was sending her. Her self-castigation abated as the tension left her shoulders. "All right, I won't throw you on the bed. This time."

Tal watched in fascination as she flashed that predatory smile again. "I've never seen you smile like that. And a good thing, too, because if I had I could never have kept my hands off you. We'd have fried all of our empathic senses."

"You fried yours anyway." Salomen urged her into a seated position on the edge of the bed. "Much as I love this look, you still have too much clothing on."

"I'll get those," Tal protested as Salomen began pulling the tabs on her boots. Salomen looked up. "You're uncomfortable with this?"

"I'm just…not accustomed to the idea of you doing that. It doesn't seem right."

Salomen rose, gently nudged Tal onto her back, and crawled right over her. "Why?"

Tal found concentration elusive as she focused on the breasts hovering within a mouth-watering range. "I…ah…" She gave up and reached for her prize, only to find them pulled away. Salomen sat astride her hips, taking advantage of her position to caress all sorts of sensitive places while Tal shivered and twitched.

"Why isn't it right?" Salomen persisted.

"Because…" Tal closed her eyes. "If you really want me to explain, you'll have to stop what you're doing."

"Oh, but it's such fun to feel you trying so hard to think." Salomen skimmed her fingertips across Tal's stomach and chuckled softly at the reaction.

Tal opened her eyes again to see a smug grin on her face. "You realize that you're only getting away with this because I'm under medical orders."

"And I plan to press my advantage as far as I possibly can." Salomen crouched down and slid forward, brushing her breasts along Tal's torso and nearly sending her airborne. "Now tell me," she said, propping herself on her forearms.

"I cannot believe you want to talk about this now." Tal sighed in theatrical resignation. "When I was a fresh trainee, new in my unit, I went through all the usual rites inflicted on young warriors. Most of them were designed to teach humility. And one of them was an obligation to remove the boots of any older trainee who demanded it."

"So taking off your boots is the behavior of a subordinate."

She nodded. "And you are not my subordinate in any way."

"No, I'm not." Salomen seized Tal's head in an unbreakable grip, the strength in her hands reinforcing her point as she leaned down for a passionate kiss. They were both breathing hard when she finally pulled away.

"I will take off your boots because I want to, not because you demand it." She released her hold and ran gentle fingers through Tal's hair. "Power works both ways. Did it never occur to you that while you held the bare foot and leg of an older trainee in your hands, you had an advantage?"

Not once had Tal thought of it like that. "Have you been talking to Micah?"

Salomen chuckled. "Quite a lot, actually, while you were in the healing center. You slept much of the time, so I read up on the Truth and the Path and asked the colonel a lot of questions. I understand you better than I did before."

"I think I'm nervous now."

"No, you're not." Salomen kissed her again. "I'm sensing many things, but nervousness is not in the mix." Gracefully she slid off the bed and returned her attention to the boots.

Tal sat up and watched. This was an act of humility, one that she had learned to hate from her first days as a trainee, yet Salomen's own strength of character had changed it into something completely different. It was caring and seductive all at the same time.

"Just when I thought I could not admire you more," she said quietly.

Salomen pulled off the second boot and tossed the sock after it. "And we really haven't gotten started," she said, her fingers busy at the trouser fastening. "Let's see how you feel by the end."

Tal lifted her hips and allowed her pants to be tugged off, along with her underwear. As Salomen stood up and stared, Tal felt a resurgence of her normal self-confidence. Relaxing onto her back, she propped one foot on the edge of the bed and ran her fingertips up and down her thigh. "Do you plan to stand there all evening?"

"Oh, no," Salomen said in a low voice. "I definitely do not plan to stand here." She kicked off her shoes and had her own pants off in record time. Tal took the opportunity to pull herself the rest of the way onto the bed, and Salomen joined her a moment later, stretching out beside her with her head propped on one hand. Their faces were separated by less than a handspan, and Tal studied the beauty that was so tantalizingly close.

"I was wrong in that field," she whispered. "You *are* my dream."

"Fahla knew what she was doing after all." Salomen traced a line down her jaw. "You're mine as well."

Tal caught her hand, pressed it to her lips, and pushed up onto all fours. Then she was astride Salomen, smiling as dark eyes instantly focused on her breasts. "Is this what you wanted?" she asked, lowering herself until her breasts were barely out of reach of Salomen's open mouth. Just as Salomen lifted her head, she pulled back. "Not yet. I have some catching up to do."

"And I don't?" Salomen's voice cracked as Tal began kissing and gently biting her waist, sides, and the ridge just above each breast…and then reversing direction before coming within range of a certain questing mouth. "Andira, this is cruel. Just give me one tick, please."

Tal made no answer, but the next time she worked her way upward, she did not stop at the chest ridges. Her movements became more urgent as their arousal merged again, and she left marks on Salomen's throat without meaning to. She bit her on the jaw before taking her mouth in a fiery kiss, then positioned herself where Salomen wanted her.

"Finally," Salomen murmured, reaching out and lifting her head.

Tal closed her eyes at the sensation of warm lips on one breast and a firm hand on the other. Her nipples seemed to be attached directly to her groin, and every tug of Salomen's lips and tongue sent liquid heat coursing through her veins.

She gave herself over to pure sensual enjoyment and might have stayed there for a hantick had an urgent desire of her own not taken precedence. Ignoring Salomen's groaned complaint, she pulled out of reach.

"You said one tick," she admonished.

"I didn't think you'd time it!"

Tal nibbled a chest ridge. "I didn't. We have all night." Just to make her point, she abandoned Salomen's torso entirely and moved down to her legs, running her fingertips along their length. Though the burns were faint, she was looking through the eyes of a new lover and saw them all too clearly. Her sorrow rose again, but Salomen was there instantly, smoothing her emotions with her own acceptance. Tal bent to kiss the marks, touching them with all the tenderness in her heart, then wrapped her hands around one smooth calf and lifted it.

"There are no burns on that side," Salomen said.

"No, but there's this." Tal ran her tongue across the back of Salomen's knee and had to tighten her grip as it was almost jerked from her hands.

"I didn't even know—" Salomen's breath hitched when Tal began sucking. "Oh, good Fahla."

Smiling, Tal let go and licked the spot. "That you were sensitive here?"

"Yes! How could you know that when I don't?"

"Apparently, I'm better trained than your prior lovers." Tal took considerable pride in that.

Salomen laughed. "You are so smug. I did have some good lovers, you know."

"They couldn't have been that good if they ignored these legs," Tal murmured between kisses. "I've been watching them for a moon." She set the leg down gently and touched the other, smiling when Salomen quickly lifted it up.

"You've been—oh—staring at my legs? I had no idea."

She loved the way Salomen's breath kept catching, and chased that moment again and again with her lips and tongue. "How could I not? Besides the fact that you look better than anyone has a right to in muddy work boots…" She ran her tongue across the crease and listened for the gasp. "…every night you came into my room, sat in that chair, and crossed these long legs in front of me. You flaunted them."

"Now you're just making it up. I never flaunted my legs. My breasts, maybe."

Caught by surprise, Tal laughed too hard to continue the light touch she needed. She held Salomen's leg against her neck and rested her cheek on it, smiling down at her tyree. "I knew you chose that dress for a reason."

"And it worked. Your eyes nearly fell out of your head."

"I never quite got them back in again." Tal kissed her leg and brought it down, then crouched to touch her lips to a soft inner thigh. She followed a steady path upward, moving from one leg to the other, and studiously ignored the way they shifted apart to invite further exploration. Instead she focused on the tender skin of her stomach and sides, noting all of the sensitive places and revisiting them several times just to be sure. At last she straightened, watching Salomen's flushed face and half-closed eyes with a mixture of awe and pride. She was the reason for that expression; it was her hands and mouth that had left this amazing woman limp with pleasure.

Salomen reached up to brush the backs of her fingers against Tal's cheek. "I knew you'd be like this," she whispered.

"Like what?" Tal leaned into the caress.

"Considerate. And bossy."

Tal chuckled. "You haven't seen bossy yet." She caught Salomen's hand and sucked in one finger, deliberately recreating a moment they both remembered. By the time she released it, lust had chased levity from their emotions.

"Now, there's the matter of these breasts you were flaunting." She bent to take a nipple into her mouth. The gasp was arousing enough, but when Tal pushed the nipple out and then forcefully sucked it back in, Salomen's cry sent a wave of heat surging through her.

Salomen bucked, her hands coming around Tal's head and twisting almost painfully into her hair. "Whatever you're doing, don't stop."

"I won't."

Tal lost all track of time, unable to tell how much of her white-hot arousal was her own and how much was Salomen's. She had never experienced this before, not in a mere joining. When a Sharing and a joining were combined, yes, but she and Salomen weren't there yet. This was simply their normal tyree connection, ratcheted up several levels by their physical contact and excitement.

When she reached down with one hand to caress skin she hadn't yet explored, Salomen could take no more.

"Andira, please…I need you inside," she said hoarsely.

Tal lifted her head. "Now?"

"Yes!"

"But I've just gotten started." It was a cruel tease, but she couldn't help herself. An aroused and frustrated Salomen was a sight to behold.

Salomen closed her eyes. "If you don't go inside right now, I will hurt you."

Tal nibbled the lobe of her ear, then whispered, "If you hurt me, do it for a better reason than that."

"I don't—"

"Shh. Spread your legs."

She slid to one side, giving her room to shift, then knelt between her legs. Salomen's stomach was flat enough to show the full length of the pelvic ridges, and Tal followed their converging lines with her fingertips, finally allowing herself to go where they both wanted. Her fingers met on the curve where the pelvic ridges joined, just above the entrance into Salomen's body, and she gently slipped one finger inside.

"Oh, sweet Goddess," she groaned. The inner ridges had already pulled back, opening the passage. Salomen was so far gone that she wouldn't even feel one finger; her body was ready to complete the act. Of course Tal had known she was that aroused, but feeling it this way, from the inside, was like throwing accelerant on her own fire.

"Not enough," Salomen managed.

"I know." Tal added a second finger, watching in awe as Salomen's hips rose to meet her.

Two fingers fit perfectly, guided on their path by inner ridges that seemed to be made just for her. She reveled in the ease of it, slipping inside with almost no resistance. She understood the biology—when the inner ridges pulled back, they released a powder that filled in both their micropores and those of the penetrating fingers, reducing the friction to nearly zero—but as far as she was concerned, it was simply magic. There was no feeling on Alsea to compare to this effortless, smooth slide, to the sense of being welcomed inside a body.

She pulled her fingers nearly out, then pushed them back in as far as she could, thrilling at the touch of her fingertips to the pouch at the back wall. With any other lover, she would have asked if such a depth was all right, but with Salomen there was no need. She felt the explosion of pleasure and began moving her fingers in and out in a slow, controlled motion that stimulated the inner ridges.

Salomen's hands clenched in the sheets. "Yes, just like that." She could barely get the words out.

"Just like this? Because I was thinking about trying this instead." Tal increased her speed.

Salomen brought up her knees and dug her heels into the bed as her back arched. "Goddess…"

Tal had never seen anything so beautiful as Salomen's body moving under her hands. She watched avidly, trying to commit every detail to memory, wanting this first time to be something she could recall for the rest of her days. She varied her motions, never letting them get too much into a rhythm, drawing out the pleasure for both of them. It could not get any better than this, she thought—until Salomen reached down and began rubbing the curved ridge just above Tal's fingers.

Alseans of both sexes had this curve. It was called by many names, but she had always preferred molwine, a reference to the sacred tree of Fahla. It was the source of the most exquisite sensations of a joining, often leading to a quick finish, which was why she had avoided it until now. Watching Salomen rub her own molwine threatened to finish her on the spot.

Swiftly, she seized Salomen's wrist and slammed it onto the bed, then pulled out her fingers and caught the other hand that was making its way down.

"You're not doing that. I am," she said.

"Then shekking do it!"

Tal wasted no time following that order. She pushed up and covered Salomen's body, both of them gasping as their molwines made contact.

Salomen wrapped her up in a tight embrace. "It has never felt like this."

"For me either." Nothing had even come close. Tal's hips were moving without conscious thought, and she rose up on her forearms, wanting to see Salomen's eyes in this most intimate of connections.

A muscle in her back protested the new angle, sending a sharp spike of pain through her. Tal took a breath, looked down at Salomen—and froze.

It was the position. The last time she had been here, lying atop Salomen, braced on her forearms with pain in her back, her world had been coming apart. She knew what was happening, but her breath still quickened and the fear drove everything out. The air reeked with the stench of burning hair and charred flesh.

She dropped her head and nuzzled into Salomen's throat, seeking that warm, spicy scent and desperately telling herself that she wasn't there, her back was not on fire, Salomen was fine…

Hands touched her back, and she went rigid, bracing herself for the excruciating pain when Micah tore her skin apart.

But the hands vanished again without causing damage, and Salomen's voice was in her ear, saying things like *safe* and *home*. She pushed her hands beneath Salomen's shoulders and held on, needing the comfort. The voice repeated words that meant nothing, because all she could hear was the tone. That calm tone didn't go with the terror that had paralyzed her limbs and left her panting for air. It also didn't go with the deep concern swamping her senses, pouring out of Salomen and taking on its own shade of fear.

They couldn't both be afraid. Her protective instinct surged up, ready to do battle with whatever had Salomen feeling that way. She tensed her muscles in preparation, then gasped as a new reality slammed into her. For a moment she was in two places at once, utterly confused until one reality faded and the other solidified. She was in her dimly lit quarters…on top of a very worried Salomen.

Her terror drained away, leaving behind the oily residue of humiliation. It was a relief to breathe normally again, but she could not bring herself to lift her head. For Fahla's sake, she was the leader of her caste and she'd just had a flashback in the middle of their joining. That sort of overwrought dokshin happened to warriors in weepers, not to her.

But as much as she wanted to move past it, she didn't dare put herself in the same position. She tightened her grip, preparing to roll them over so she could look up at Salomen instead of down. With any luck, she wouldn't have to ask. Salomen would know, and she would drive them the rest of the way through this.

Except…shek. Her new skin couldn't handle her being on the bottom. She had no choice. She almost wept in sheer frustration.

"Andira. I need you to tell me something."

And now her time had run out. With a deep breath, she raised her head and met Salomen's expectant gaze. "What?"

"That business of you not letting me touch myself—are you really that possessive? Because if you are, we're going to fight about it."

Tal stared, not understanding the words that were so far removed from what she had anticipated. Then it all clicked, and she let out a strangled laugh.

"No," she said, and laughed again. "No, I'm not."

"Then that was a one-time thing? For future reference, the correct answer is yes."

Salomen knew exactly what she was doing, and Tal loved her for it. She wanted to thank her, but saying the words would acknowledge what had just happened. She kissed her instead, pouring out her gratitude in a different language.

The next time she lifted her head, everything was as it should be. She was in the same position, but in full control. And now that her brain was operating properly, she shook her head at her earlier stupidity. This was not her only option; they could finish in any number of positions. Not that she would, of course. She had something to prove.

"I cannot say it was a one-time thing. Because I might have to do it again—for both our sakes," she added, stopping Salomen from speaking. "Watching you do that was the sexiest thing I have *ever* seen. If I'd let you continue, I would have finished in three pipticks."

"Good answer." Salomen's gentle smile took on a different shape. "The sexiest thing you've ever seen, hm?"

"You have no idea. I want you to do that again, believe me. Just...not this time."

"Well, if I'm not allowed to touch myself, then do you think you could take care of me?" Salomen brushed her hands through Tal's hair, ran them down the sides of her neck, then moved to her breasts, where she lightly tugged the nipples. "We don't have to—"

"Yes, we do." Those fingers were stirring a spark back to life, and as Tal looked at her tyree, flushed with arousal and achingly beautiful, she felt a fierce sense of victory. They had survived. Salomen was here, right now, vibrantly alive and watching her with so much love that a sonsales could have seen it from fifty paces. "Yes, we do," she repeated, her smile broadening.

It was the easiest thing in the world to move her hips now. They both jolted at the sensation, their molwines nearly as sensitive as they had been before their unscheduled break. Tal kept their rhythm slow, easing them back to their prior level, and took the opportunity to cover Salomen's throat and jaw with grateful kisses. In a surprisingly short time, she was far enough away from her embarrassment to say it.

"Thank you, tyrina," she whispered. "I don't know how you knew what to do, but you were exactly what I needed."

A golden surge of love and pride burst from Salomen as she held Tal's head between her hands. "That's all I ever want to be," she said.

Something in her unwavering gaze shifted the air between them, but Tal had no time to consider it before Salomen began sucking on the ridge along her neck.

All higher levels of brain function ceased immediately. Tal had never known she was *that* sensitive there, nor had she known that her control could be ripped away so easily. By the time she was released again, her hips were moving faster than she intended, stimulating their molwines in an agony of building pressure.

"May I—is this...?" Salomen couldn't finish her sentence, but her hands were tentatively at Tal's sides, not moving and far too light.

Tal huffed out an impatient laugh. "Yes. Please."

The hands slid around her back, and Tal felt nothing but what she should. She kissed Salomen in elation, wanting more, wanting every part of their bodies connected. The closer Salomen held her, the happier she was. This was no longer just a joining; it was an affirmation of life and survival and triumph over anything that tried to come between them.

Salomen tucked her face into Tal's throat. "Don't stop," she said desperately. "Tyrina—" A wave of sensation rippled through her, bringing her shoulders off the bed, and she tightened her grip.

Tal was beyond any concern about her new skin, but despite Salomen's plea, she didn't want this to end so soon. Somehow she dredged up enough willpower to slow her motions, trying to tamp down their need, but after a few pipticks Salomen would have no more of it. She gripped Tal's head, forced it to one side, and bit down hard on her neck ridge.

The power of that bite would have shocked Tal at any other time, but right now it sent her into the atmosphere. A second bite made her gasp, and without conscious thought she buried her fingers in Salomen's hair, wrenching her head back. For a moment she paused, looking at the ridges running down each side of Salomen's throat. They were a potent signal of passion, invisible at any time except during a joining. Now they stood out in sharp relief, begging for attention, and Tal closed her teeth on the nearest one. The half-scream she heard would have told her precisely how good that felt even if she hadn't been able to sense the sharp rise in Salomen's arousal.

"Andira..." Salomen groaned.

Her head was still trapped in Tal's grip, and the sight of her exposed throat, swollen ridges, and open mouth were making Tal dizzy. Her hips moved of their own accord; slowing down was not an option. She had used up all her willpower.

She bit the other throat ridge harder than the first, letting up on the pressure only to work her way down the entire length of it and nearly getting herself bucked off in the process. Salomen's hoarse cries drove her to a whole new level, where control ended and only instinct remained. When she lifted her head, she saw the same wildness in Salomen's eyes. They had become creatures of pure passion, moving together in a glorious storm of sensation as they gasped for breath and strained for the moment they wanted so desperately.

Salomen reached for her, and Tal expected to have her head pushed to the side again. She realized her mistake when one of Salomen's hands settled on the back of her neck. As the other touched her cheek and jaw, she matched the positions with her own hands and rested their foreheads together.

The Sharing was explosive. Had she not been so deeply lost in her sexual haze, she might have pulled back from the sheer shock of it. Of course it would be different from their previous two Sharings, but she hadn't expected anything like this.

Her empathic awareness rocketed outward, surpassing her normal range in the blink of an eye. She was aware of every Alsean in the entire State House complex, as well as those living in the streets nearest the city hub. The sense of so many people all at once was overwhelming, but before Tal could even begin to make sense of it, the explosion reversed itself and she fell directly into Salomen's mind. Everything else was shut out as they became a single entity, aware of every emotional nuance and physical sensation shared between them. It was like inhabiting two bodies at the same time—and both of those bodies were exquisitely close to physical release. The sudden wash of Salomen's love and passion, experienced from the inside with no barriers, pushed Tal to the ragged edge. She was Salomen as much as she was herself; they were the same person, the same body, the same gripping need—and then they were there, minds and bodies frozen as everything crashed around them. It seemed to go on for half a hantick, draining every bit of energy from both of them. When their bodies were finally released from the spasms that had held them so rigidly, it was all Tal could do not to drop her hands and break their connection. Somehow she held on even as her head pounded and her lungs ached for air, and for a few pipticks she felt as if a thick blanket had been thrown over their senses.

"It's gone," Salomen said breathlessly. "I can't feel you!"

Hadn't she experienced the blackout before? But she had said as much, Tal remembered, when she confessed to never really letting go in a Sharing.

"It's not gone. We're just burned out for a moment. Wait, it will come back."

By the time they caught their breath, their senses opened up again. This time it wasn't so explosive, seeming more like a dawning of light over a familiar landscape. They reveled in the exquisite intimacy of their emotions, feeling each other as they felt themselves.

"It was never like this," Salomen murmured. "There's no division between us—I can hardly tell the difference between you and me."

"This is how it's supposed to be. This is a true Sharing, tyrina."

But she was wrong. It wasn't like any Sharing she'd had before, a fact she realized as soon as they turned their attention outward. The welcome familiarity dropped away; this was an entirely new world. They felt the presence of *every* life-form in the area, from the people still in the State House right down to the smallest bird searching for insects in a tree by the gates, and their range seemed to cover several lengths without even trying.

By unspoken agreement they expanded their reach, searching for the limits of their combined senses. They soared over Blacksun, taking in millions of lives in their myriad states, and flew past the western edge of the city into the fields beyond. They felt predators and prey playing out their lives in the dying light of the day, while nocturnal creatures began to stir from sleep. They felt the primal satisfaction as a nightwing snapped its beak on a large moth, filling its belly for another few ticks while it searched for the next bite. The density of life all around them was bewildering, and in an instinctive reach for something familiar, they found themselves at Hol-Opah.

"We're ninety lengths away!" Two ticks ago, Tal would have said this was impossible.

"There's Father and Nikin, in the parlor as usual." Salomen's joy at sensing her family had overwhelmed any disbelief in their extreme range. "Oh, and Jaros is getting in trouble."

The youngest Opah was by himself, probably in the kitchen based on the location of the other two emotional signatures. And if his guilt and fear of discovery were any indication, he was stealing a sweet snack. Salomen's laugh brought Tal's eyes open, and she jerked her head back in shock.

Their hands were glowing.

Salomen's eyes snapped open as well, and she gasped. "Andira!"

It should have ended then. Without their foreheads touching, they no longer had a full connection. But their minds were still wrapped together, and they were still impossibly aware of Jaros sneaking upstairs with his prize. Tal tried to take her hands off the energy points, but it was as if they were no longer attached to her body.

"This is what happened at Whitemoon Temple," she whispered. Her initial surprise had turned to fascination; Fahla's sign hadn't been symbolic at all.

"How can this be?"

"I don't know." Tal watched the glow increasing. Her hands were on fire, a sensation that should have been terrifying given her recent injuries. But there was no pain in this heat, and she seemed in no danger of another flashback.

"It happened at home, too. When we Shared with my family. My hands felt warm when I touched you; it almost burned. But not like this." Salomen's eyes widened. "Great Mother! I can see my bones!"

Tal was staring at hers as well and saw the glow of Salomen's hand in her peripheral vision. "If this is like before, it will pass on its own."

They waited, their minds hovering over Hol-Opah, but the heat in their hands did not abate.

"I have to know," Salomen said.

Tal understood. As one they pushed away from Hol-Opah, heading west. If they could not break this connection on their own, then they might as well find out how far it could take them.

Their shared consciousness flew over the remaining fields in Blacksun Basin, reaching the fingers of forest that marked the first change in elevation. A complex web of life was all around them, in the air, on the ground, in the trees; the smallest mouse and the largest treecat alike in basic needs and desires, all of it registering on their enhanced empathic senses.

In their long-distance training, Tal had begun to teach Salomen to mentally navigate the landscape using the life glow of organisms living atop or rooted in the surface of the soil. All life made itself apparent on the empathic plane, but never had Tal seen it so clearly mapped. This was not just the background glow of active cells feeding and producing energy. It was textured, layered, dense in pockets where vegetation grew in thick profusion, patchy in areas of rocks and poor soil, and constantly crackling with flares produced by more complex organisms.

With no effort they soared up the steepening slopes of the mountains, covered with the tall, slow-pulsing life of trees. They burst past the top of the nearest range and arced over the deep valley behind it before letting themselves slide down the back side of the next peak, where they located a stream by the brilliant flares of complex life-forms confined within it. On the other side of that valley they climbed up once again, finding and following a herd of winden that were making their unhurried way along a ridge top.

"So beautiful," Salomen whispered, voicing Tal's own thought. To feel a winden! Not to glimpse them running from the shadow of a transport, but to feel them and know that they were heading for a safe place to bed down for the night…it was beyond anything she could have dreamed.

They stayed with the winden until the animals stopped, milled around, and then began fading in consciousness. Tal thought her perception had reached its limit, but understood a moment later. "They're going to sleep," she said in delight.

"Amazing." Salomen was just as entranced. They hovered until most of herd was sleeping, though a few scouts remained wide awake as they watched out for the rest of the herd.

Finally they moved off, soaring over ridge after ridge until they reached the final mountains in the range. Just as they flew over a peak and began descending to the plains below, their perceptions dimmed. Tal looked at her hands and saw their glow dimming as well, and in another piptick the incredible vision was gone.

"Great Mother." Salomen lifted her hands and watched them tremble. "What in the name of all that grows was that?"

"I don't know." Tal pushed off, carefully turning onto her back and relaxing her strained muscles with a gusty sigh. "But it was incredible. Like we multiplied our powers instead of just adding them together."

"It must be part of the tyree bond." Salomen rolled onto her side, and Tal turned her head to meet her eyes.

"I don't think it's part of a normal tyree bond."

"We're not normal tyrees."

"Yes, well, I'm not sure that's normal even for our kind of tyree."

They fell silent, their hands finding each other in the quiet dimness.

"We must have covered four hundred lengths," Salomen said after a long pause.

"At least. We were nearly to Pollonius, and that's five hundred by transport." Another pause.

"I wonder—" they began simultaneously, then laughed.

"Only one way to find out," said Tal.

"Are you up to it?"

"Tsk. When will the producer learn to stop asking the warrior such questions?"

"When the warrior learns she does not need to be invincible with her tyree. Soon, I hope."

Tal smiled and turned onto her side. "I'm up to it."

They scooted closer together and reached out, connecting their energy points. A slight hesitation betrayed their uncertainty.

"I'm half afraid we won't be able to," Salomen said, "and half afraid we will."

"I know."

They watched each other a few pipticks longer, then closed their eyes and touched their foreheads together.

This time the shock was not so pronounced, but Tal was still jolted by the outward explosion of their awareness. They hovered in place and soon realized that their immediate range had a radius of nearly thirty lengths. It was bewildering to feel so many lives all at once, but the different emotional levels enabled them to screen out Alseans from other life-forms. After a few ticks they found that they could choose not to be aware of anything but Alseans, much like tuning out a constant background noise. With that filter in place, the emotional landscape came into sharper focus.

Tal opened her eyes to find their hands glowing again. Now the sight seemed reassuring rather than shocking, a measure of the energy flowing between them and enabling their newly expanded powers.

Salomen's eyes opened as well, flicking from her hands to Tal's face, and she smiled. "Where shall we go?"

"How about south? Port Calerna is one thousand and four hundred lengths; shall we see if we can reach it?"

"You want to triple our distance? You *are* a warrior. Always pushing it."

"Don't tell me you don't want to know."

Salomen laughed quietly. "Of course I do."

They sped over the valley floor, each small producer community shining like a beacon with the glow of so many lives concentrated together. Other Alseans dotted the countryside, riding in transports, walking in fields, and on a few occasions, joined together in an emotional blend that could only be a Sharing in progress.

"I feel a bit like a voyeur," Salomen whispered as they passed over another Sharing couple.

"Is it voyeurism if we're not actually looking?"

Salomen was too distracted by their rise over the mountains to respond. She was reaching out, looking for other forms of life now that they had left the inhabited lands behind. They found no winden this time, though they were highly entertained by a family of treecats. The mother's exasperation with her kittens, who refused to come down from their tree, was surprisingly similar to the same emotion in an Alsean parent.

Tal was curious as to whether they could influence other life-forms, so she gave one of the kittens an empathic nudge. It promptly skittered down the tree and was received by its mother with a mixture of affection, relief, and irritation. Soon the other two came down as well, and the entire family moved off as the mother's brain shifted into hunting mode.

"That was incredible," Salomen said. "The emotions are the same. Not nearly so complex as ours, but undeniably the same general feeling."

"Are you ever going to be able to slaughter a fanten again?"

"Oh, no. Not like this, to be sure. Suddenly I'm relieved that we have to Share to reach this level."

"Me, too."

They passed the final peak and found themselves soaring over the rain forest that stretched from the southern mountains to the coast. With experimentation, they discovered that if they did not use energy focusing in on specific life-forms, they could move across the emotional landscape more quickly. They were already farther than they had flown the first time, but Tal's hope of reaching the ocean was dashed. Their awareness faded along with the glow of their hands, and they dropped their tired arms to the bed.

"It's so strange," Salomen said. "What was normal now feels…confined, somehow. Like being in a skimmer with the doors and windows shut, so you can't hear anything outside."

"And just think, we've been in that skimmer our whole lives and never even known there was anything to be heard outside." Tal rolled onto her back and stared at the carved ceiling. "What a gift."

"We need to know more about it."

"Agreed. But I'm not sure where we'll find the information. Aldirk did an entire literature search and didn't come across anything like this."

"But he wasn't looking for it."

"No, but he would have mentioned it had he seen it. I'll talk to him tomorrow. I'll call Lanaril, too. She might have something in one of those ancient texts of hers."

Salomen's hand curled over hers. "And what will you tell her?"

Tal rolled over again, taking in the features of a face that had become precious to her. "Every detail, of course," she said, just to elicit one of those lovely smiles.

It worked. "In that case, I want to be there for that call. Because I don't think you could do anything of the sort without blushing." Tracing soft designs on Tal's arm, Salomen added, "That was wonderful. All of it. Even without the unbelievable Sharing, this joining wasn't like any I've ever had."

"Part of it was because we were so connected. I felt everything you felt." Tal began her own caresses. "But that wasn't all of it. The rest was just you. You're incredibly beautiful."

Salomen caught Tal's hand, brought it to her mouth, and kissed it. "So are you, tyrina."

"It was worth the wait, then?"

"You know it was. Even though you made me wait much longer than necessary."

"I have no idea what you mean. We were joining almost before the door shut. How much faster do you want it? Oh—did you want to join in my office? You should have said something."

"Don't be obtuse. You dragged things out until I had to ask for what I wanted."

"And you have no idea how sexy that was. I suspected you would have no difficulty telling me what you wanted. You did it often enough in the fields." Tal yelped and grabbed for Salomen's wrists as fingernails raked up her ribcage. "No!" she laughed. "Stop it!"

"I swear you're a grainbird sometimes." Salomen was fast, her hands seemingly everywhere while Tal batted them away. "I think the true lie of the Lancer is that you're grown up at all." She surged up, grabbed Tal around the shoulders, and rolled herself on top. Smiling down, she added, "And I love that you show that to me."

Tal wrapped her arms around her back. "You and Micah, you're the only ones. You've singlehandedly doubled the number of Alseans I'm truly comfortable with. Though I'm getting closer with Lanaril."

Salomen's smile faded. "I thought I was the lonely one. How could I not have seen it in you?"

"Because we were lonely in different ways. And you weren't looking for it. I didn't see yours either, not at first. Both of us are very good at hiding it. We've had a lifetime to practice."

"I suppose that's true," Salomen said after a moment's thought. "I never considered that there would be different varieties."

"Of course there are. And you aren't the only lonely one in your family. Not since Nashta's Return."

"No, we've all been lost without her. Mother was the glue that held our family together. We had our own relationships, some better and some worse, but Mother was always the center of it all." A spark zipped through her emotions, and she rolled them onto their sides. "I'm sorry, I keep forgetting about your back. Is it all right?"

"It's fine. You'd feel it otherwise. Don't worry."

Salomen raised an eyebrow. "You realize that I'll be worrying about you until the day of my Return, don't you? That comes with the deal."

"I know." Tal brushed a strand of hair off Salomen's cheek. "That's part of your character. And I suspect it was part of Nashta's as well."

"It was. She worried about all of us. Herot most of all." The thought brought a shard of regret. "I wish he could have known you like this."

"I don't!"

Salomen chuckled. "You know what I mean. I wish he could have seen you as you really are, instead of just the Lancer. It would have made all the difference."

"Perhaps. But I didn't trust him from the moment I met him. And where there's no trust, there's very little of me beyond the professional."

"Believe me, I know that." Salomen slid her fingertips across Tal's shoulder and down her arm. "I'm not saying you should have done it any differently or that he didn't create this mess all by himself. I'm just…sad that it happened the way it did. And sad to think that if he knew you the way I do, he'd like you. At least, the Herot I used to know would have."

Tal watched her in silence, absorbing her shifting emotions. She felt the tears rising before the first one slipped free, and her finger was there to catch it. "I'm sorry, tyrina," she whispered.

"I know." Salomen sniffed and wiped her cheek. "And I'm sorry to be so maudlin on this night of all times."

"Come here." Tal shifted onto her back and tugged her over.

Salomen came willingly, nestling her head on Tal's shoulder and sniffing again.

Her heart aching in sympathy, Tal stroked her hair and kissed her forehead, projecting love and support until she felt it taking hold. "You don't ever need to apologize for your emotions," she said. "Not to me. They are what they are. And if you could write off your brother without a second thought, you would not be the person I love."

Salomen pulled up the sheet and used it to dab the tears from her cheeks. "I hate this. Half the time I want to kill him myself, and the other half I'm worried sick." She wrapped her arm around Tal's torso. "And I'm angry that he's interfered with so much of our time together."

"Not to mention worried about Colonel Razine's report." Which, unfortunately, had been twenty ticks of outlining where Herot was not, rather than where he was. They had traced him as far as Napoline, a port city on the southern coast of Argolis, and after that he had vanished. Searches of all the northern ports of Pallea had shown no sign of him.

"Yes. How is he doing this? Herot doesn't have the skills to evade high empaths. He doesn't know anything about staying out of the system. I don't understand how he could still be out there after five days. That more than anything else makes me question my belief in him."

"We'll find him, tyrina. One way or another, we'll find him, and then we'll know."

"That's what I'm afraid of."

Tal kissed the top of her head. Relaxing into her pillow, she ran her hand up and down Salomen's back, firmly pushing Herot out of her mind and focusing on the woman she was holding right now. As her fingertips traced patterns along soft skin, a memory surfaced and she smiled.

Salomen stirred in her arms. "What is it?"

"I was just remembering a fantasy I had about you the night of our first date."

"Oh, really? This I have to hear."

"It's not what you're thinking. Actually, it was relatively innocent. I was walking across the field to my transport, and I had a sudden vision of you in bed, covered by a sheet. You were waiting for me, smiling up at me, and your shoulders were bare, which was the most alluring thing I could imagine. And then I picked you up for our date—"

"And I was wearing a dress that left my shoulders bare," Salomen finished. "No wonder you were stumbling all over yourself."

"I was not stumbling."

"You were. I'm sorry, o great Lancer, but you were. And it was impossibly endearing."

"Humph." Tal tried to pretend annoyance, but Salomen laughed.

"So bare shoulders turn you on?" she asked, pushing up on one elbow.

Tal's gaze slid from her shoulders to the shadowed breasts visible beneath the sheet. "Yours do. Among other things."

"Tell me about those other things." Salomen nuzzled the side of her throat. "Tell me what it takes to make these ridges come out again."

The mere words had Tal shivering. "With you, not much." She closed her eyes as Salomen pulled gently at her earlobe while sliding a suggestive hand down her pelvic ridge.

"Come, my Lancer. I know you can be more specific than that."

It was difficult to think with that voice in her ear. "Are we going to get any sleep tonight?" she asked, stalling for time.

A soft chuckle sent more shivers down to her toes. "Not if I have anything to say about it."

As it turned out, Salomen had a great deal to say.

CHAPTER 13
Warrior types

THE MORNING DAWNED GRAY AND rainy, a perfect day for staying in bed. Tal wished she could do just that, but unfortunately, she and Salomen weren't on a bonding break. Since no one knew they were recently bonded, they had no excuse for not going about their days as normal. And Tal's day had quite a bit packed into it.

But she still had time to indulge in her current favorite activity, and accordingly, she propped herself on one elbow and gazed at the slumbering form next to her, taking the opportunity to study Salomen in every detail.

She had never seen her asleep before. In a way, it seemed an even greater vulnerability than a Sharing. When they Shared, they were in it together, but a sleeping Salomen was alone and without defenses. Lying on her side facing Tal, her dark hair spread on the pillow behind her, she appeared innocent of all knowledge of an imperfect world. This relaxed face could not belong to someone who had nearly died at the hands of an assassin. Nor could it belong to the experienced and professional head of one of the largest holdings in the district, a woman responsible for more than fifty field workers as well as her own family. This face belonged to a different woman altogether—one whom the rest of the world would never see.

She reached out to caress Salomen's arm, half wishing she would wake and half hoping she wouldn't. She was enjoying the protective intimacy of the moment. Salomen had shown time and again that she could take care of herself, but right this moment she could not, and Tal felt a guilty pleasure in her guardianship.

When she brushed back an errant lock of hair, Salomen twitched slightly. Her eyes blinked open, taking a moment to focus. Slowly, her face lit with the most beautiful smile Tal had ever seen.

"Good morning, tyrina," she said in a sleep-roughened voice.

"Good morning." Tal continued her caresses. "Has anyone ever told you how lovely you look when you're sleeping?"

Salomen shook her head. "Never heard it before."

"Then your past lovers were fools, every one of them."

"Not all of them woke up with me."

"Ah. You don't care to share your bed when the joining is done."

"Not usually." Salomen rolled onto her back and stretched luxuriously before turning to her side again, looking far more awake. "Sleeping is a whole different game than joining."

"I know what you mean. Joining doesn't necessarily involve any intimacy at all. Sleeping does."

Salomen nodded. "Besides the fact that I don't sleep well with another body in my bed."

"We have that in common, then." Tal leaned down to kiss her shoulder. "But I slept like a rock last night. It might have had something to do with being so worn out."

A smile of pure satisfaction crossed Salomen's lips, dissipating any image of her as a slumbering innocent. "I did notice that the warrior had a hard time keeping up with the producer."

Tal pounced, tickling her mercilessly in all the sensitive spots she had discovered the night before.

Laughing, Salomen tried to squirm away. "Stop! This isn't fair, I just woke up!"

"That didn't stop you from making nasty aspersions before your eyes were even all the way open. Why should it stop me from an appropriate response to them?"

"Because I'm your tyree, and I had a very hard night."

"That's a pathetic excuse. You're lucky I'm so in love. That will wear off, you know, and then you'll have to do a lot better."

"By then I'll be more in practice," Salomen said unrepentantly.

Tal leaned down to kiss her. "Juice?"

"Is that a hint?"

"Not at all. But I need it, so I'm happy to bring back a glass for you."

"Yes, please. Don't you have staff to wait on you hand and foot?"

"No," Tal said as she threw back the covers. "Not in my own quarters. This is one of two places on the planet where I have any real privacy, and I don't want anyone coming in here unless I invite them. Especially not when I'm asleep."

She padded through the living area into the kitchen, pulled several pre-cut fruits from the bin in her cooler, and tossed them into the juicer. A tick later she was making her way back to the bed, surprised to see Salomen out of it. "What are you doing?"

Salomen straightened from where she had been rummaging in the clothing organizer. "Looking for this." She held up a small wrapped package and climbed back onto the bed.

Tal joined her, handing over one of the glasses as she sipped her own.

"Thank you," Salomen said. "Oh, that's good." She gulped down half the glass, then nudged the package toward Tal. "This is for you, in case you needed something to do some evening when you aren't swamped by your duties...or by me."

"Thank you, tyrina. I didn't expect anything like this."

"I know. That's the point."

"May I open it now? Or do I have to wait?"

"Would I be so cruel as to give you a gift and tell you that you have to wait to open it?"

Tal looked at her, and they both burst out laughing.

"All right, don't answer," Salomen said, still chuckling. "Just open it."

Tal gleefully tore off the paper, then went still. With a far more careful touch, she opened the elegantly bound book to the first page and read the inscription in bold handwriting.

I always did have a soft place in my heart for strong, adventurous warrior types.
~ Salomen

She looked up, her throat tightening. "I never finished it."

"I know." Salomen brushed a hand across her cheek. "I wish I could have given you the one you were reading. Mother would have liked that. But it burned along with your bed, so this was the next best thing."

"Thank you." Tal turned the book over, running her fingertips along the beautifully tooled binding. "This is a gorgeous edition."

"I wanted it to last a long time."

"It will." She caressed the binding again. "I don't know what to say. I don't think I've ever received a more thoughtful gift. You've taken something from that night and made it...special."

"The most special thing about that night is sitting right here," Salomen said softly.

"I could argue that." Tal put the book and her glass on top of the clothing organizer, then plucked Salomen's glass out of her hand and set it aside as well. "But I'm too busy." She pushed onto all fours and indulged in a slow, deep kiss before pulling back just enough to say, "Mm. Juice."

Salomen chuckled. "I knew you had an ulterior motive."

"Of course." Tal went back to those soft, smiling lips, breaking off to nibble her way down an equally soft throat. "What a wonderful way to start my day."

Salomen made a purring sound of agreement, but then her mood turned serious. "I meant what I said about that night. As horrible as it was, it also brought me the gift of understanding just what I have in you. Remember our first night of training?"

Tal nodded as she sat back. "Do you think I could forget it?"

"You told me about your parents, and that you avenged them, and it frightened me. I saw you as a creature of violence, and for a while I thought I'd made a big mistake bringing you under my roof."

"I know." Tal felt a pang at the memory of Salomen calling her a "terrible enemy." But it was true; that was part of her nature. She would not bear the title of Lancer without it. She could not have saved Alsea without it.

"And you said you were also a good friend and ally. I didn't understand then how those different identities could exist in harmony. And though I've never seen the warrior part of you in true violence, I have seen the other side of it now. I saw it when you saved my life." She picked up one of Tal's hands and examined it, running her fingers over the palm as she spoke. "You've said that was pure instinct, as if you deserve no credit for it because you didn't think about it in advance. But I know you would have done the same thing for my father or Nikin or Jaros. Colonel Micah, too. He may be your Guard, but I think you guard him just as much as the other way around."

"Don't tell Micah," said Tal, trying to lighten the mood.

"I won't." Salomen gave her a knowing look. "Sorry to be embarrassing you, but I need to say this. It may have been instinct to pull me off that window seat, but you made a deliberate decision to roll us over. You chose to burn so I wouldn't. You cannot dismiss that as some sort of warrior-trained reaction, Andira. It's simply who you are. And that's what I mean when I say that night gave me a gift of understanding. I have never in my life felt so loved and so protected. I once feared you as someone with blood on her hands, but now…" She reached out for Tal's other hand. "…these make me feel safer than I ever thought possible."

Tal squeezed her hands. "Thank you. That means everything to me."

"I know. I'm sorry I ever hurt you by saying otherwise."

"It's all right. That was before. This is now, and I just want to savor the fact that you're here."

"In your bed?"

"In my life." She pulled their hands out to the sides and pressed her body forward, nudging Salomen onto her back. A moment later she remembered and rolled them over.

Salomen pushed up onto her forearms, her hair falling over one shoulder. "I hope I can make you feel that safe."

"You already did, last night."

"Then why am I suddenly on top?"

"Because I've realized that I very much enjoy this view," Tal said, her gaze traveling lower. She was treated to an even lovelier view when Salomen chuckled.

"I had no idea you were so single-minded." Salomen leaned down for a leisurely kiss, but came back up with a more serious expression. "You need to speak with someone."

"I know. I'm sorry—"

The gentle finger on her lips stopped her.

"No apologies. This is a battle wound, like the wounds you bore on your back. Would you apologize for those?"

Tal stared up at her. She hadn't thought of it that way. She wasn't sure she *could* think of it that way with anyone other than Salomen.

"I'll talk to Lanaril," she said. "She's been counseling battle veterans; I'm certain she's seen this before."

Salomen nodded. "She's good for you. I'm glad you can speak with a friend." She began a slow exploration of Tal's jaw and throat, coming up now and again to tug a sensitive earlobe.

Tal hummed happily. She could hardly believe this discussion had been so short and easy, but it was clear in Salomen's emotions—the topic was dismissed for now. "I love our bond," she murmured.

Salomen made a noise of agreement, then kissed the hollow of her throat.

"I hate the way you were forced into it," Tal continued, "but I cannot be sorry for what we have now."

Salomen lifted her head. "I wasn't forced."

"What?"

"I Shared willingly, Andira. I was ready."

"But…you were terrified of it just the night before."

"I was terrified of it that night, too." Salomen smiled at her confusion. "I was getting closer to it every day. Every hantick, actually. I loved you, I knew you loved me and you were ready…everything I wanted was there, except one thing. And I kept telling myself that it wasn't important; I'd have it eventually. But apparently I wasn't convincing myself."

"What thing?"

"Knowing that you saw me as an equal."

"Salomen—"

"Don't tell me you already did, because I know better. In some ways you still don't see it even now, but it doesn't matter anymore. I know you'll get there. It's just going to take a while for you to overcome a lifetime of training to be the Lancer."

A prick of familiarity flitted through Tal's mind—she'd used almost the same words in her prayer to Fahla at Whitemoon. It seemed Salomen knew her as well as she knew herself.

"What changed your mind?" she asked.

Salomen brushed Tal's hair back from her forehead, then began running her fingers through it in a soothing motion. "You said you needed me. You were burning; I don't even know how you could be coherent. But you looked at me and said you needed my strength to find the assassin."

"You're not going to tell me you wouldn't have Shared if I hadn't said that. I know that's not true."

"Of course not. A herd of winden couldn't have kept me from giving you everything I had no matter what you said. What I'm trying to tell you is that in that moment I was no longer afraid of it. I was afraid of everything else, but not that."

Tal remembered all too well the look of terror in her eyes. "I'm guessing you've figured this out after the fact."

"I did a lot of thinking while you were asleep in the healing center."

"Then how can you say you Shared based on that, when you didn't even understand it until afterward?"

"Do you understand everything you do when you do it?"

"No," Tal admitted after a pause.

Salomen smiled. "Thank you."

"For what?"

"Your honesty. You gave that to me from the very first day. It's one of the things I love about you. So tell me this, tyrina: How would you feel if you had never been able to do anything for me? If you hadn't been able to train me or help with Herot or teach those bullies a lesson? How would it feel to know that I never needed or wanted your help?"

"I'd feel like I had very little to offer. I'd probably be looking for a chance to prove myself to you."

"Precisely."

"Salomen..." The thought was painful. "You never had anything to prove to me. I cannot even recall how many times I watched you and thought to myself how proud I was of you. Fahla, I admired you even when I was arguing with you at our delegate meetings. Did I never show you that?"

"You did. Well, not at the delegate meetings." Salomen ran her fingers along Tal's cheekbone ridge. "But admiration and pride do not add up to equality. It meant everything to me that I could be there for you when you needed me. It still does."

Tal turned her head into the caress and remembered thanking her for being what she needed after the flashback. *That's all I ever want to be,* Salomen had said. It had seemed out of character for someone so independent, but now it made sense.

She wrapped her up and held her close. "My tyrina," she whispered. "I hope I never need you that way again. But I'll always need you. You're a part of me now."

Salomen made no answer save to squeeze her more tightly.

CHAPTER 14
Herot's message

With a hantick left before the first meeting, Tal and Salomen finally dragged themselves out of bed, showered, and sat down to enjoy the breakfast Tal had ordered earlier.

"I could get used to this," Salomen said as she broke open a steaming biscuit. "You make a call, the food magically appears, and when we're done the dishes magically disappear, yes?"

"Rank does have its privileges. I have enough memories of kitchen duty to never take this for granted."

"The idea of you peeling panfruits all day just doesn't go with my image of you as the glamorous warrior."

"That's because warriors peeling panfruits don't make it into those stories," Tal said, indicating her book on the clothing organizer. "Or nights guarding a warehouse in the rain, or sleeping while sitting on a cold boulder to train your body to ignore its environment."

"The part about the boulder gets in there," Salomen said. "Mmm. Whoever makes these biscuits knows their business."

"So physical privation is glamorous?"

"Of course. Because it's all part of training yourself to be a ranking warrior. Now, producers working all day in the rain or rubbing salve into their screaming muscles because they spent a day forking horten into a transport, and then going out to do the exact same thing for another day—none of that is glamorous physical privation. It's just hard work. So we don't get our own stories."

"You are a snob, did you know that?"

Salomen popped another piece of biscuit into her mouth and smiled. "To be a snob, I'd have to be convinced that my caste is better than the others."

Tal raised an eyebrow as she lifted a cup of shannel to her lips.

"I'm not convinced of that. But I know my caste is just as good as the others, and that's a perception I find in rather short supply among some castes. Particularly scholar. Now there you can find some true snobs."

"My mother was scholar caste, thank you very much."

"So is Darzen."

"Ouch. You really do have a warrior's heart. You have an unerring instinct for where to land a blow."

"That wasn't meant to be a blow. Just a point."

Nodding her acceptance, Tal reached for her own biscuit and was sprinkling grainstem powder on it when Salomen asked, "What was your mother like? You've never spoken much about her."

Tal took a thoughtful bite. How could she describe her mother in a few words?

"She was driven by a thirst for knowledge. Mother loved to learn new things; she collected information like other people collect souvenirs or memorabilia. I've never known anyone so informed in my life. I could go to her for anything at all, and she always knew the answer. And it was always right. But more than that, she had an understanding of life, a wisdom that I always thought was just part of being a mother. It wasn't until I was grown that I realized her wisdom wasn't the norm for adults or parents. It was unique to her."

"What a wonderful resource. It must have been very hard to lose that."

"It was. But oddly enough, I found it again in the strangest place." Tal watched Salomen's expression change as her meaning sank in.

"She sounds remarkable," Salomen said, valiantly ignoring her rosy cheeks. "I wish I could have met her."

"She would have loved you." Tal knew that without a doubt. "You would have kept her challenged forever. Once she knew all about something or someone, she tended to lose interest. The challenge was gone. Simple people bored her, but she enjoyed people with depth and complexity."

"You carry some of that tendency. I've seen the way you absorbed the workings of Hol-Opah; you soaked up every detail. And you certainly love a challenge in any form."

Tal nodded. "True, though I can't say that came entirely from Mother. Father loved a good challenge, too."

"Why were you so much closer to your father than your mother?"

"I was close to both of them. But Mother was a little more unreachable for me, I think. And I don't mean that in any negative way; it's just that she was a parent first and a friend second. But Father was more of a friend first. He was my playmate. And Mother could get lost inside her head. She taught me a great deal, but I don't think she understood that for me, especially when I was young, learning something just for the sake of knowledge wasn't all that important. I wanted things to mean something. When Father taught me, it was because the knowledge was practical, or he felt I needed to know it, or because it was just fun." She smiled. "We had a lot of fun together."

"Doing what?"

"It seems like we were always playing when I was a girl. Looking back, I see that he was teaching me even then, but at the time it just felt like a game. We played Hunter and Prey, and I became very good at closing myself down so he couldn't find me empathically. I remember being devastated the first time he opened the door of the closet I was hiding in, only a few pipticks after the game started. I was so certain he would never find me, and when I asked how he had, he told me he could feel me. Then he told me what I could do to keep that from happening, and I sweated for a couple of moons practicing the technique with him. I'll never forget the day he found me by accident instead of by my emotions. He was so proud of me."

"Goddess, I'm envious."

"I'm sorry, tyrina. I wish you'd had the same kind of childhood."

"Well, I'm only envious about that." Salomen plucked a second biscuit from the bowl. "Other than hiding my powers, I had a wonderful childhood. And I was allowed to keep my parents for longer than you. If I could change anything about your life, it would be that."

Tal suddenly found it difficult to swallow and had to chase her panfruit down with some shannel. "Thank you. I know you would."

Salomen reached across the table and clasped her hand. "I think your parents would be enormously proud of you right now. You've brought so much honor to their names."

"Fahla knows I've tried. I had to make their sacrifice mean something."

"You've done more than try. You succeeded in a very big way." She tilted her head. "May I ask you something that might be sensitive?"

"Of course."

"Are you Lancer because you want to be or because you owed it to your parents?"

"Micah asked me that a long time ago. The answer is both, but mostly the first. I've wanted to be Lancer all my life. Now if you asked whether that was truly my dream or whether my parents instilled it in me, I'd have no response. I'll never know that. Nor do I need to."

Salomen squeezed her hand before releasing it and picking up her shannel cup. "I'm glad. And now I have another question."

"Clearly I didn't tire you out enough last night." Great Mother, but she loved the way Salomen's eyes crinkled when she smiled.

"How odd. I seem to recall that you were the one pleading for rest." The cup clinked back to its saucer. "Who can I petition for inclusion into your family?"

Tal sat back in her chair. "No one, really. My father was the youngest child; his parents and both of his siblings preceded him to his Return. One of my maternal grandmothers died when I was still a baby. And we lost Grandmother Neltowin just after my Rite of Ascension. She was a sharp blade right up to the end—I wish you could have met her. The only living elder relative I have is my Aunt Sima, but she and Mother weren't close, and I never really knew her. The last time I saw her was at my parents' funeral pyre. I wouldn't give her the power of granting you inclusion; she's not truly my family."

"You really were alone," Salomen said. "I didn't realize that you didn't even have family."

The self-castigation felt acrid to Tal's senses, especially after the ease they had just been enjoying. "I do now. And how could you have known when I never told you?"

"I could have asked earlier."

"I could have asked you a thousand things earlier. You're a producer—your life is entwined with your land, and I don't even know what your favorite flower is. Or tree. Or where you go on Hol-Opah when you have time to walk just for the enjoyment of it."

The acrid sense faded as Salomen's smile reappeared. "Windstars. I love windstars. They're so small and brave, blooming when nothing else will because it's still too early and the winter winds are still too harsh."

Of course she would love a flower that was both beautiful and tough. Tal rested her chin on her hand. "And the tree?"

"Cinnoralis."

"Because of the scent?"

Salomen nodded. "Sometimes, when there's no one around, I'll pick a leaf and crush it just to fill my nostrils with that scent. And sometimes I find those crushed leaves in my pockets even after my clothes have been washed."

For some reason, this tiny domestic detail made Tal love her even more. She saw it in Salomen's eyes a heartbeat before it hit her senses, a reflection of emotion met and matched that made her breath catch. Her voice was husky as she said, "Your special place…"

Salomen leaned forward. "On your runs, did you find the place near the southeast corner where the Silverrun drops half a body length?"

Indeed she had. It had been a small waterfall when Tal first found it, which swelled to an impressive torrent once the rains had begun. "It's a beautiful spot. There's a big boulder on your side of the river with a perfect saddle on top—"

"Yes, exactly. That's it. Did you sit on top?"

"Only once. I don't… It's not very relaxing to do things like that with five Guards waiting for me."

In the silence, Salomen ran her fingers over Tal's wrist. "Tell me where your favorite places were when you were a child and there were no Guards."

They traded childhood stories over the rest of the meal, and Tal nearly choked on her last bite of panfruit at Salomen's tale of climbing into the composting bin as a little child, then crawling onto her parents' bed for a nap afterward. Her parents had not been pleased at the disgusting mess she had made of their sheets.

"I would have tossed you into the wash right along with the sheets," Tal said. "You were a problem child!"

"That's not the half of it. Mother and Father weren't that upset about the dirt. They were upset about the smell."

"What smell? It was just field compost, wasn't it?"

"Oh, no. That was the *special* compost bin. The one where we process what the fanten leave behind."

Tal roared with laughter, then gasped, "Did the sheets grow after you fertilized them?"

Salomen broke up too, and they sat helplessly in their chairs, clutching their stomachs.

"Goddess, don't make me laugh so hard right after I've eaten!" Salomen snorted again, then groaned. "Ow. My sides hurt."

"Mine too." Tal wiped a tear from her eye. "I can just see you toddling up the stairs with fanten glop falling off you at every step."

Salomen laughed again. "That compost bin magically sprouted a child-proof cover the very next day."

"I don't doubt it." Tal's chuckles dwindled to a sigh when her vidcom unit chimed. "Well, that's the end of our morning. I thought Aldirk might have the decency to leave us alone, but it appears he couldn't resist." She pushed back her chair and walked over to activate the wall screen. The face that filled it was not Aldirk's.

"Good morning, Lancer Tal," said Colonel Razine. "I apologize for disturbing you so early, but this could not wait."

"Is it about Herot or one of our other investigations?"

Razine glanced over Tal's shoulder. "It's about Herot Opah."

"Have you found him?"

A chair scraped back, and Salomen arrived beside her.

"No. But he made contact with Hol-Opah a few ticks ago. The message was sent on a two-day time delay from Napoline."

"Has my family seen it?" Salomen asked.

"They're most likely viewing it right now. A copy has been downloaded to your unit, Lancer Tal. I'm available to discuss it whenever you wish."

"Thank you, Colonel. I'll be in contact."

Razine nodded once before the screen went dark.

Tal turned to Salomen, who was already tense with dread. "Are you ready?"

"No." Salomen tried to muster a smile. "But that doesn't matter."

"Then let's see what he has to say." She wrapped her arm around Salomen's waist and activated the file.

Herot's face appeared, stress showing in every line and in the dark circles under his eyes. He was in a vidcom stall with significant background noise; Tal guessed it was in Napoline's public transit station, where the high traffic flow would give him anonymity. He looked as if he hadn't taken a shower since the night of the assassination attempt.

"Hello, Father," he said in a hoarse voice. "Salomen, Nikin, Jaros...before anything else, I need to say I'm sorry. Really, really sorry. I never meant for this to happen. I was stupid and a fool, and if I could have five ticks with that fantenshekken Cullom, I'd tear his throat out. It was just talk, for Fahla's sake! It wasn't real. I mean—"

He paused at a loud knock. "Occupied!" he called, then turned back to the screen. "I went home that night, but before I even got to the river, the medical transport flew past me. It scared the dokshin out of me—I thought something had happened to Father. I chased after it and saw it landing in our yard…and then I saw the plasma glow. I've never felt so sick in my life. I thought she was dead. You have no idea how glad I was to see the news report that it was only a minor injury. Shek, I may not have liked her, but I never wished her dead! Please, you have to believe that. I know that dokker Gordense has been blaming me too, but it wasn't a plot. I was just angry…about everything, I guess, and she was a good target. Cullom was angry too. He and his family were looking like fools now that public opinion was turning back to her, and he believed everything Gordense said about her destroying our caste. So yes, we were both angry, and drunk, and saying stupid things, but it didn't mean anything! It was just—" He took a shuddering breath. "My face is all over the news. I don't know how much longer I can hide. But I can't go back. It doesn't matter that I didn't mean for this to happen; I told Cullom how to kill the Lancer and he tried to do it. I'm not going to the Pit. I can't. I'd rather die."

Another knock sounded. "Shek off!" he shouted in sudden fury.

Tal watched carefully, recognizing a man who was in deeper than he could wade and very close to drowning.

"I wish I could see you all again," he said. "I know I've been an ass, and I'm sorry about that too. You'd be amazed at how clear everything became all of a sudden. I thought I lost everything when Mother died, but you were all right there, waiting for me to notice I still had a family, and I never did. And now—" His face twisted into a bitter smile. "Now I'm glad Mother went to her Return. I'm glad she's not here to see this. It would have broken her heart, and that's the worst thing of all, knowing I've broken your hearts."

A more insistent knock made him close his eyes. "Dammit. I have to go." He looked as if he wanted to say something else, then shook his head. The screen went dark.

The tension in Salomen's body had climbed with every word, and now she was almost humming with suppressed energy. "I need to sit down," she said faintly.

"I know." Tal projected calm as they walked to the living area. Salomen sat stiffly, staring straight out the window. As Tal lowered herself onto the cushion next to her, she reflected that only a few ticks ago this same woman had been helpless with laughter.

"It's the best news we could have heard," she said. "When we find him and corroborate his story with an empathic scan, the charge will be direct enabling, not attempted assassination. He won't go to the Pit."

Salomen looked haunted. "But he'll still go to prison."

"Yes, he will. But the sentence will be far less."

"I can't think of Herot in prison. I was praying so hard that he hadn't done it intentionally, but I never let myself think beyond that."

There was nothing Tal could say. She couldn't help Salomen because she couldn't help Herot. He had well and truly put himself beyond aid.

They sat in uncomfortable silence, Salomen's body still rigid while her emotions roiled both of their minds. Tal rested a hand on her thigh, occasionally stroking it, letting her know she was there through the most unthreatening physical touch she could think of.

"I hope you won't think less of me for saying this," Salomen said. "But I want Colonel Razine to be unsuccessful for a good long time."

"I don't think less of you. I think you love your brother."

Salomen slumped back, put her face in her hands, and wept at last.

PART TWO:

SPINNER IN THE WEB

CHAPTER 15
Investigations

Tal felt like a traitor when she met with Colonel Razine later that morning. She had reluctantly left Salomen in her quarters, having called off their challenge for a day, and spent the morning catching up. So far she had spoken with Miltorin about the latest media coverage, met with her economic advisors about the market impact of the last moon and specifically the assassination attempt, and was now seated opposite Colonel Razine at her conference table. And it was only hantick ten.

"Raiz Opah must have been tremendously relieved," Razine said. "Assuming Herot is speaking the truth."

"I think he is. Everything he said tracks with what I know of him—a selfish young man who acts without thinking of the consequences."

Razine made a hum of agreement. "After watching that vid, I'm more convinced than ever that he cannot be doing this on his own. That was the demeanor of a man who knows he will soon be caught. Yet he's vanished with the ease of a well-trained covert investigator. Something is not adding up. At this point I would not be surprised if he made that appearance in Napoline just to throw us off the trail, and has now backtracked north again."

Tal rubbed her forehead. "I really did not need any more mysteries. Did you get anything from that Granelle merchant?"

"Unfortunately, no. He's a low-level tool. He was very cooperative, but it didn't help much. All of his communication with Spinner was done via messages sent to a temporary account based in Redmoon. His last message is still sitting there, uncollected. We have a trace on it now, but I doubt Spinner will ever access that account again."

"So it's a stone wall. Great. Do you have any good news for me?"

"In fact, I do. Last night our smuggler friend Hallwell finally met someone worthwhile."

"In Whitemoon?" Tal sat up straight, all attention.

"Barely. He went to a dirty little inn on the outskirts of the city. The sort of place where blindness can be bought. Fortunately, it was only a temporary affliction, easily cured with a handful of cinteks."

"What did we buy?"

"A room number. To a top-floor room with no direct line of sight into the window."

"Someone is experienced at avoiding observation," Tal said.

"Yes, but most observers don't have the latest cambot. My team sent one to the window and watched the vid feed. I wish we had sound, too, but at least we enjoyed an excellent look at Hallwell's contact. And we thought it very interesting to watch a smuggler meeting with a warrior from the Anti-Corruption Task Force."

Anger coiled in her stomach. "So now we have both a merchant *and* a warrior using their task force positions to pick up some extra credit. This just keeps getting better. Who is it?"

"Her name is Alanor Salir." Razine pushed her reader card toward Tal, its screen showing an image of a warrior who looked to be around Herot's age.

Tal examined the image and the data beneath it. "She's not our target. Too young and not enough power."

"Agreed. But she's sworn to Councilor Ehron. May I?" She tapped the reader card, changing the image to one of a much older warrior.

"Ehron…" Tal muttered, staring at the face. "He's been on the Council for what, three cycles? I don't know him well. He's not one of the shouters." She scanned the data below. "Almost four cycles now. Fairly undistinguished career; he's not on any of the powerful committees. Well, if this is our target, he's done an admirable job of hiding his ambition."

"We're doing a search on his financial records right now, and I have a team following both him and Salir. I wish we could bring Ehron in for an empathic scan and save ourselves the time and trouble, but if he's not the one, that would put the investigation right down the sewage pipe."

Tal drummed her fingers on the table. "I could ask him to meet with me. Some sort of new program I'm implementing, of getting to know the Councilors I don't ordinarily interact with. All it would take would be the right question."

"That seems a bit transparent."

"You're right." Tal drummed her fingers more rapidly, then stopped. "However…I just happen to have a producer on site who is famous for having the horns to challenge me. It wouldn't be out of the ordinary for me to want to introduce her to a cross-section of Councilors."

A slow smile spread across Razine's face. "No, I don't believe that would be out of the ordinary at all."

CHAPTER 16
The whole truth

Just before midmeal, Tal finally found a spare moment to make the call. The pad notified her that the *Phoenix* had received her communication, and she waited longer than usual before Ekatya finally appeared. One look at her robe and disarrayed hair and Tal felt like an idiot.

"It's the middle of the night there, isn't it? I'm sorry. I forgot to check the time converter."

Ekatya looked at her silently for a moment, then smiled. "Stars and Shippers, it's good to see you. And I don't care what time it is. I've been waiting for seven days, Andira. What took you so long?"

"It's been five and a half of my days, and most of that time I spent in the healing center. They just released me yesterday afternoon. Then it was nonstop obligations until evenmeal, and after that…well. You're my closest friend besides Micah, and I've been wanting to talk to you for the last moon, but not even for you would I have interrupted last night."

Ekatya's smile turned knowing. "A little coming-home gift? Then I guess you're fully healed."

"I am. And it was our first time."

"Really? Colonel Micah said you'd been bonded for less than a day, but I thought…well, Lhyn said…" She trailed off.

"Normally, we would have. You have no idea how much we wanted to. But a joining would have killed us."

Ekatya leaned an elbow on the desk and rested her head on her fist. "Tell me everything. How did you learn she was your tyree? I always thought you would just…know, somehow, the moment you met the right person."

"Maybe that's how it works for others. Apparently, I'm stubborn. I look back now and there were so many clues, but I was a grainbird." Tal started at the beginning of the challenge, and in the telling it sounded almost too fantastical to believe. Ekatya interrupted frequently, asking for clarification, and on several occasions her questions set them both laughing.

"I can't even imagine what that must have been like. Every time you linked Lhyn and me, it stayed with us for hanticks afterward. The sex was incredible. And for you it's built in. How are you even walking today?"

"With difficulty," Tal said, setting off another round of chuckles. "Only Salomen could make me want to climb back in bed after spending five days and nights wishing I could get out of it."

"I'm so happy for you," Ekatya said warmly. "You've no idea how much I wished for something like this. Well, not exactly like this—I had something a bit less stressful in mind. But you're special to both of us. It always hurt to think of you just being the Lancer, with no one to see who you really are."

"Salomen sees me more clearly than I do. Sometimes it's a little alarming."

"Good. That's what you need." Her expression shifted. "Colonel Micah told me what happened after we left."

"Micah wags his tongue like a bored merchant."

"I pushed him. He was trying to find a diplomatic way to warn me off, but I wasn't having it. At first I wanted to apologize to you. Then I realized you'd have done it even if you knew the risk. Then I got mad at you."

Tal crossed her arms and waited.

"I'm already in debt to you, and you managed to increase it from four sectors away. I hate being in debt."

"You are not—"

"You suffered for *moons* because of something I asked you to do. Don't tell me I'm not in debt. Yes, you offered the first time. But we asked after that. Now, what's going on with your missing slime worm of a bondbrother, and how can we help?"

"You can't pay off your imaginary debt that way. It's internal, and I am not going to be seen running to the Protectorate for something so trivial. Besides, we received a message from Herot this morning. He says he didn't mean for it to happen, and I believe him. Which means he's already done all the damage he can do to me."

"I'm going to ask you the same thing I asked Colonel Micah. Are you certain about that?"

"The worst that can happen if we don't find him is that my administration will look incompetent. If the Protectorate sends its newest warship out to help, we'll look even more incompetent."

Ekatya didn't seem happy, but she nodded. "All right."

"As for that debt—I wanted to do it. It was the closest I'd ever come to touching the face of Fahla, and I thought I'd never have another chance. And I wasn't entirely honest with you when I did it."

"That's because you're a master of lying by omission. You would think I'd learn. But I notice that regardless of your feelings, you kept yourself out of it until the last time, when we specifically asked you to come in with us. We have to do something about that self-sacrificing kink of yours."

"I'm a warrior," Tal said with a snort of laughter. "We don't think sacrifice is a kink."

"Ask Salomen how she feels about you sacrificing yourself to save her."

"I don't have to. She told me just this morning. She feels safe…and loved."

After a long pause, Ekatya said quietly, "So did I."

Tal looked into her eyes and wished once again that they weren't speaking over a quantum com. She missed being able to feel the richness of Ekatya's emotions.

"I haven't told her the whole truth about you. She knows what you were to me, but…she doesn't know about the Sharings and what they did. It shouldn't be that threatening, because what I absorbed from you and Lhyn was a small dose compared to what I have with her, but I can't even begin to imagine how I could start that conversation."

"Then don't."

"I have to at some point. We based this relationship on honesty."

"So be honest. But that doesn't mean you have to be the one to bring it up, and why would you want to? She recently lost her mother, and now she has effectively lost her brother. And her tyree is the one hunting him. Her family is in flux, and she's only just bonded with you. Do you really think she needs to hear about me and Lhyn right now?"

Tal sighed. "Why am I always keeping secrets for somebody else?"

"Because sometimes that's what you have to do for the people you care about."

The biggest secret of all loomed between them, unspoken.

"She thinks I'm the greatest warrior of our generation," Tal said. "She was afraid of me in the beginning—said I had blood on my hands. And she's never asked me for details about the Battle of Alsea. At first it was because she didn't want me to coast on my celebrity, but then it became more of a kindness to me. Or so she said. But I wonder if she just doesn't want to know, because she's certainly asked me everything else." She rubbed her forehead. "Hol-Opah is the one place on Alsea where I can forget what I had to do. What I almost had to do. I'm afraid that if I ever tell her the whole truth, she won't feel safe anymore."

Ekatya reached offscreen, and the sound of pouring water came through the com. She sipped at her glass with a thoughtful look, then set it off to the side and leaned forward. "If there's one thing I wish I could go back and change, it would be my decision to obey my orders and leave Alsea. You were open with me until the moment you realized my intentions, and then you had to strategize. If I hadn't had my head up my ass about duty and military order, you would never have had to make that choice."

"Yes, but—"

"I'm not finished."

Tal gestured for her to go on.

"I've had a lot of time to think about it. And I've realized that one of the reasons I respect you so highly is precisely because you were willing to sacrifice not just your honor, but your Shipper-damned *afterlife* for the benefit of Alsea. You're a true leader, Andira. The fact that Lhyn almost got caught in the middle of that is not your fault. It's mine. And I hate to think what kind of person I'd be today if I had let the Voloth take Alsea and then found out it was all a scam. Bitter and angry wouldn't begin to describe it. Not to mention alone and grieving. So when the time comes for you to tell Salomen the truth about how you saved Alsea, tell her the whole truth, not just the part that makes you look bad. Or better yet, call me first and I'll tell her."

"I wish I could feel you," Tal said. It was so hard to accept mere words, without the emotional confirmation.

"If you could, you'd know I'm telling the truth."

"I believe you here." She tapped her temple.

"But your heart is a different story. I know how that works. Just chew on that for a while, please? You need to forgive yourself."

Tal glanced at the clock. "I truly hate to end this, but it's time for midmeal and I have to get back to my quarters. Salomen isn't doing well today."

"Because of her brother's message?"

"Damn thing was on a two-day delay. I swear he timed it to cause the most impact."

"Hades of a morning after, eh?"

"Great Mother, yes. I'd like to throw Herot into a deep, dark hole. What he did to me pales in comparison with what he's done to Salomen—and to our bond. He's tainted every single facet of it. This morning Salomen could hardly finish mornmeal, she was laughing so hard, and then his message arrived and I had to hold her while she cried."

"Then why are you talking to me? Go take care of your tyree."

"I'm talking to you because Micah had the distinct impression that if I didn't, we'd find the *Phoenix* in orbit next nineday. And as much as I would love to see you, I don't need that political wrinkle."

"Well, it's true that I live to complicate your life. But I'm reassured now, so you can tell Colonel Micah that he's fulfilled his duty and can relax."

Tal hesitated.

"What?"

"Micah's not going to relax for some time, I'm afraid. Speaking of people who need to forgive themselves. But that's for another call. I have to go."

They said their good-byes, and Tal held the darkened pad in her hand, marveling once again that she could have a real-time conversation with someone so far away. So much had changed since the *Caphenon* had crashed.

Unfortunately, Alseans still had all the same failings. And one of them was hurting her tyree.

CHAPTER 17
Picking up pieces

Tal hadn't even touched her palm to the lock when the door opened.

"I missed you," Salomen said.

Tal stepped inside and drew her into a warmron. "I missed you, too. But you were with me all morning." Salomen was soft in her arms, her body draped over Tal's in a way that bespoke mental exhaustion. "I'm sorry I had to leave you. It was damn hard feeling you hurting in here while I was in meetings out there."

"It would have been harder for me to be in meetings, and you couldn't possibly skip them all." Salomen lifted her head, her face showing signs of a difficult morning. "Thank you for understanding."

"It doesn't require understanding. You needed time."

Salomen dropped her head back to Tal's shoulder, squeezed tightly, and stepped back. "So," she said too briskly, "I want to know what it was that had you so pleased with yourself earlier."

"When?"

"Around hantick ten, I think."

Ah. The meeting with Razine. "Interesting that you should ask." Tal shed her jacket on the way to the kitchen, stopping when she saw the dining table. "You already ordered midmeal?"

"Not exactly." Salomen led her to the table and lifted the lid of a serving bowl. "It's not in my nature to sit around doing nothing, so…I made this. The kitchen worker was somewhat startled to get an order for ingredients rather than a finished meal."

Tal chuckled. "That's probably an understatement." She sniffed happily, recognizing soarfish with sweetfruit even before she saw it. "It smells fantastic. I don't suppose you have any horten soup to go with it."

"You're joking. Aren't you tired of that yet?"

"Are you serious? I've never had anything like the soup you fed me on our date. I'd eat it every day if I could."

"Then I suppose it's a good thing I had this brought from home." Salomen lifted another lid, a satisfied smile on her face.

"I think I love you," Tal said. "Will you bond with me?"

"Already did. Got anything else to offer?"

Tal plucked the lid out of her hand, placed it carefully on the serving bowl, and spent a good five ticks showing her what she had to offer. When she finally pulled back, Salomen's eyes fluttered open slowly.

"I'll take it," she said.

Tal kissed her one more time for good measure before letting her go. "Who brought the soup?" she asked as they pulled out their chairs.

"Nikin. He called and asked if he could visit. I called Colonel Micah, and he took care of it." She picked up a bowl and began serving the soup as Tal poured water for both of them. "We met in one of the conference rooms."

Tal almost overfilled a cup while looking at Salomen in surprise. "Why didn't you bring him here?"

"Because these are your quarters and I hadn't asked you." She put Tal's bowl down and reached for her own, but Tal stopped her with a hand on her wrist.

"Tyrina, these are your quarters as well. Your good breeding is showing, but in this case it's not necessary. The moment we bonded, my home became yours."

"Is that how you feel about Hol-Opah? That you can bring anyone you want there without asking?"

"No," she admitted. "But you cannot compare the two. Hol-Opah is as much your family's as it is yours. My quarters are just mine."

Salomen acknowledged the point with a nod. "Thank you. I'll need some time before I'm comfortable with that concept, though. I don't even know the procedure for getting access for a guest."

"I guess we did skip over quite a bit."

"Such as the entire pre-bond period? Yes, we did."

"Then the first thing we should do is put you and Aldirk in a room together. He knows absolutely everything about protocol and procedure." Seeing that Salomen was ready to eat, Tal took a sip of the soup and closed her eyes. She felt Salomen's amusement before hearing the laugh.

"I think I saw that same expression on your face several times last night," Salomen observed with a lift of her eyebrow.

"Can I help it if I appreciate good food?"

"I hope not. I like that expression." Salomen sipped her own soup. "I'm going to be sorry when this is gone. It's never the same after it's been vacuum stored. Anyway, I can speak with Counselor Aldirk while we're flying out to Hol-Opah."

"I wanted to ask you about that. Do you still want to go? Perhaps today isn't the best day to discuss a bonding ceremony."

"Today is a better day than ever. That's one of the things Nikin and I talked about this morning. Our family needs something positive to focus on. Herot's message doesn't change that."

"How are they doing?"

"Father is putting up a brave front, but Nikin says he's just covering up. In a way, it was harder to know that Herot did this out of stupidity and anger than to think he did it intentionally. At least if it had been intentional, it would mean he made this mess because he actually believed in something." Salomen stopped with her spoon halfway to her mouth, looking at Tal in alarm. "I didn't mean that the way it sounded."

"I know."

She nodded once. "We're all furious that he made such a dokshin pile of his life and our name, destroyed things we can never replace, and hurt you so badly—but at the same time, we're relieved that he's finally snapped out of that self-pitying stage. He finally realized that he has a family, but it took losing us to get him there. And that hurts in so many ways. Especially for Father, because he feels responsible. He thinks he should have been able to break through."

Tal was certain that Shikal wasn't the only one feeling that way, but she knew enough not to say so. "How is Nikin doing?"

"Better than Father. He's more angry than anything else, and it's easier on the heart to be angry than sad. Right now he's more concerned about the rest of us than about Herot. He says Herot planted this crop and he'll have to harvest it, and the rest of us need to go on with living our lives. Herot will have to pay for his actions regardless of what we do. Suspending our lives while worrying about him will accomplish nothing."

"Nikin sees very clearly."

"He always has."

"And Jaros?"

Salomen held up her hand in a *not good* gesture. "He doesn't understand how any of this happened. He has no idea why anyone would want to hurt you, least of all Herot. So he's floating off the ground about being your bondbrother and simultaneously upset and bewildered about Herot. Nikin says he goes up and down like the ball at a wallball game. He's up when we're talking about the bonding ceremony, so bringing Counselor Aldirk to Hol-Opah will help. For a few hanticks, anyway."

Tal curled her fingers around Salomen's free hand. "Then I'll look forward to hearing about Jaros's impressions of Aldirk."

"And vice versa."

"Good luck with that. Aldirk is the definition of discretion. He doesn't usually give personal opinions."

They finished their soup in a comfortable silence, holding hands until Salomen needed hers to serve the soarfish. "You never explained what I sensed this morning," she said as she handed Tal's plate back. "You just said it was interesting that I should ask."

"Sorry, I was too overcome by the horten soup." As they ate, Tal gave her an overview of the meeting with Colonel Razine. "Your presence here gives us the perfect pretext," she concluded. "Would you be comfortable taking part in a little clandestine skimming with me?"

"Isn't that illegal?"

"I said skimming, not probing. We're just going to ask him a question that will make him think about corruption in the task force. According to his file, he's not a strong empath and he's never been through any formal training, so he won't be able to front well. If he really is our man, he'll have strong emotions when thinking about the task force. Maybe smugness, maybe concern about being caught. Maybe even guilt; we could only hope. Those will be right at the surface and easily detectable in a legal skim."

"And you trust me to be able to keep it to a skim?"

"Of course. Why would I not?"

"Because I haven't had much practice at it."

"You've had enough. You've worked on it consistently for a moon."

"Yes, but only with you."

"Are you telling me you've never skimmed anyone besides me in the last moon? While restraining yourself from going further?" She felt the answer and added, "You have the control. I've seen it growing like a hornstalk. But more importantly, you have the discipline. I never had to teach you that; it's always been a part of you. I just taught you how to apply it to your gift."

A tiny smile appeared on Salomen's face, a small reflection of the larger shift taking place in her emotions. Though Tal hadn't intended it, the request seemed to be just what she needed.

"Then I'll be glad to help," she said.

CHAPTER 18
Micah speaks

Micah paused just outside the office and straightened his spine before rapping his knuckles on the open door. Tal was standing behind her desk, shuffling things into piles with the haste of a person on her way out. Her distraction was clear—normally, she called for him to enter long before he had an opportunity to knock.

"Micah, hello, enter," she said, barely looking up. "I was just going back to my quarters. Salomen is on her way from Hol-Opah."

"I heard," he said. "I was hoping you might have a few ticks before she gets back. It won't take long."

Her hands stilled as she raised her head. "For you, always." She crossed the room and closed the door behind him. "Sit with me?"

He followed her past the conference table to the more comfortable chairs beneath the bank of windows, doing his best to keep up a good front. Based on her body language, though, she already knew what he had to say.

"I've been trying to find the right time to do this," he said, watching her carefully and seeing a subtle shift in her expression. Yes, she had been waiting for it.

"When you were in the healing center it was impossible," he continued. "And yesterday I wanted you to have your time with Salomen. But I cannot keep delaying, as tempting as it is, and I know you understand why this is necessary." With a deliberate movement, he pulled his disruptor off its clip and laid it on the small table between their chairs. His wristcom and earcuff followed. "I'm resigning my title as Chief Guardian due to failure to perform my duties."

Whatever she was waiting for, it wasn't this. She didn't even try to hide her shock.

"What? Are you insane?"

As bad as he felt, her reaction made him smile. "I'm going to miss that attitude."

"Micah! What in Fahla's name are you thinking? I've been wanting to *discuss* that night with you, yes, but not because I thought you failed. You did no such thing."

He hadn't expected her to argue. He thought her silence on the matter was simply a courtesy; a way of allowing him to resign on his own terms.

"The fact that you spent five days in the healing center is ample proof to the contrary," he said. "And if you hadn't been as quick as you were, Salomen would be dead. You don't call that a failure of security?"

"I call it the result of a betrayal that none of us could have expected. You had the empathic net set for an appropriate distance to catch a sniper. You anticipated the possibility of a professional attack and doubled my Guard after the demonstrations. You did everything right, so how can I hold you responsible for not considering that my own tyree's brother might be handing out instructions on how to kill me?"

"Because I knew he was a danger. He was arrogant and open in his dislike of you. He resented you and everything you stood for, and he especially resented your relationship with Salomen."

"This I know. Now tell me how that added up to anything other than him taking a swing at me."

"He also drank with the dregs of Granelle almost every night. Drunkenness, bad company, youthful indiscretion, anger, and arrogance make a volatile combination. The signs were all there. I should have put them together."

Tal shook her head. "You're not convincing me. All I've heard so far is that Herot was likely to get himself in trouble, which we all knew. You haven't explained how that translates to Herot getting me killed. I do not and cannot believe you could have foreseen this. Failure to do the impossible is no failure at all."

"I'm not here for a debate." He watched her eyes narrow and gentled his tone. "Your words do you credit as a compassionate friend. But in this, you are not my friend. You are my Lancer, and your compassion can only result in tragedy. You know the truth. If I feel that I've failed and that you would be better served by another Chief Guardian, then you cannot argue. My own conviction disqualifies me from serving you."

She eyed him for a moment, unable to counter that statement. "Every single one of us has failed at some point or another. That doesn't end our careers. It's what we do after the failure that counts. Are you telling me that you won't live what you taught? You're going to let this dictate your actions, instead of acting to overcome it?"

"I've seen sixty-two cycles," he reminded her. "My days of striving to overcome are behind me. At this point in my life, I should not be starting over. I should be taking this as a warning that I've reached the end of my abilities and that I need to retire before any real damage is done on my duty shift."

"Dokshin," she snapped. "Total, unadulterated, steaming dokshin. If I had suggested retirement a nineday ago, you would have been horrified. If I'd suggested that you were nearing the end of your usefulness, you would have set some sort of ambush for me to prove that you still have a few tricks up your sleeve. I'm not buying this one. Try selling me something else."

His throat tightened. He loved this stubborn woman, and leaving her service was the last thing he wanted. But it had to be done, and she was making it so much worse. "Can you not just let me go? Don't make me fight for this. It's hard enough as it is."

Her expression softened, but she shook her head. "I cannot. And not because of the security issue. Do you think that a Chief Guardian is all you are to me? You're my advisor and my closest friend as well. You know that; you admitted as much when you said you didn't resign yesterday because you wanted me to have some time with Salomen. You knew that your resignation would be personally upsetting for me, and you were right. I don't want this." She laid her hand palm up on the table between them, inviting a connection.

He looked at it, part of him not wanting to feel her, knowing it would make an already difficult task close to impossible. But to ignore such an invitation was a personal affront.

Carefully, he laid his hand on top of hers, closing his eyes as he sensed the very things he would have given anything to prevent. She was hurt, worried, and afraid, and instinctively he tightened his grip.

"I can't function nearly so well as a Lancer without you," she said, "nor would I be as happy in my personal life. I depend on you for far more than security. If you resign, you'll leave a hole that I cannot fill. Denying your services is detrimental to me, to this office, and to Alsea by extension. You *know* this."

"But you've already filled that hole. You have Salomen now. She's proven her worth, and she certainly makes you happy—more so than I ever could as your friend."

A sharp edge cut through her emotions. "I see. So now that I finally have two people on Alsea that I can trust completely and be myself with, you think that's one too many? Good of you to make that decision for me."

They stared at each other in a shared pain. "I have always been honored to be your friend," he said. "And I will gladly keep that particular title for as long as you want me. But I cannot keep this one." With his free hand he took his reader card from its holder, tapped it open, and slid it across the table toward her. "I've been training Gehrain with an eye toward his eventual promotion. You could do no better for a Chief Guardian."

She didn't even glance at the file on display. "Yes, I could, and I already am."

"He advised me to move our empathic net farther out."

Tal had been about to say something else; now she closed her mouth. This she had not expected.

He nodded. "You say it was impossible to anticipate Herot's betrayal, but in a way, Gehrain and I both did. We knew that if we were going to spend an entire moon in one place, we should account for the possibility of inside information on your movements reaching someone with malicious intent. I was more concerned with you being in the middle of fifty field workers; I thought if there was any danger, it would be closer in. So I focused inward. Gehrain said we should also focus farther outward. But even with twenty Guards I couldn't have set the net that far out and simultaneously maintained my watch closer in. I made a judgment call, but it was the wrong one. The only reason Salomen didn't die is because you had the capacity to look farther out than the rest of us."

There was an uncomfortable silence while Tal processed this new bit of information. At last she said, "You've trained him well."

He inclined his head. "He already had good instincts. I've just worked with natural talent."

"Nevertheless, he wouldn't be as good as he is without your instruction. In time, I think Gehrain will be an excellent Chief Guardian. But not today."

"Tal, I—"

"I want you to continue training him," she interrupted. "With the understanding that he's in line for a promotion when you retire from active service. But I'm not comfortable with Gehrain in that role just yet. Give me a compromise. Stay in my service for a while longer while you finish his training. Promote him to Head Guardian and start delegating some of your duties to him. I'll have the benefit of two sharp warriors looking after my security, and you'll have more free time for your new duties."

"I'm sensing a trap. What new duties?"

"Chief Counselor to the Bondlancer."

"No." He shook his head emphatically. "No, no, no. I don't think—"

"She needs you, Micah."

That stopped him. "What do you mean?"

"I mean she's here in the State House with absolutely no idea of what it means to be a Bondlancer. She's here because of a two-moon challenge that just turned into a lifetime, and I haven't prepared her. No one has. She had to call you today to get clearance for Nikin's visit; how appalling is that? She shouldn't be feeling like a guest. She's the second-highest title on Alsea, or will be once we hold our bonding ceremony. Someone has to guide her."

She was right, of course. When Salomen had called him that morning, he had been ashamed that she found it necessary. In the chaos of the assassination attempt and its aftermath, no one had remembered that Salomen didn't have State House protocols etched in her brain like the rest of them.

"Wouldn't Aldirk be a better choice?" he asked, even though the very thought made him cringe.

"Aldirk is my Chief Counselor. I did ask him to start working with Salomen, but that can't be a permanent solution. He doesn't have time, and I don't think he and Salomen will mix all that well. He's a snob, and if I know her, she's already put him in his place once or twice today."

"She probably has." Micah couldn't help smiling as he envisioned the scene. "I would have paid to see that."

"And I don't mean that you should be taking over the organizational aspects," she continued. "We'll bring in a scholar for that. But Salomen needs someone she can trust, someone she likes, someone she can find comfort in while she's learning a whole new life. And someone who can protect her. That's you."

She was pulling the ground from beneath his feet, and he didn't know how to stop it. "How can you say that when I've already failed you once?"

"Because I still trust you with my life. More importantly, I trust you with *her* life." She raised her eyebrows, letting that sink in before adding, "If you force me to accept your resignation, fine, but give me this much. Don't make me do without you now. Of all the times you could leave me, this is the worst. Stay with me, train Gehrain, advise Salomen, and plan your retirement with a little more forethought. And if you don't trust yourself, then trust your backup. Gehrain will make an excellent Head Guardian of both Salomen's Guard unit and mine. You can work around this, Micah. Walking away hurts both me and Salomen. Please don't do it."

She was sincere; their palm touch made that clear. He could hardly believe that she still trusted him that much, but it was there in the emotions that she was freely sharing. He wanted to say no, to protect her from his limitations, to do the right thing…but her counteroffer was seductive, and he didn't seem to have enough strength to fight it. Perhaps he'd never had that much strength to begin with. Fahla knew he didn't want to leave. What if he could work around his limitations? Then he could stay in her service. He could still be of use. He could help guide Salomen through the pit of zalrens she was now living in and keep her from becoming a tool to those who would attempt to use her naiveté. Salomen was intelligent and tough; she would soon understand the machinations that were always taking place beneath the surface, but in the meantime, she needed advice and protection. Those were things he could provide.

"If I delegate some of my duties to Gehrain," he said slowly, "I'm going to need a new Lead Guard for you."

Tal made a show of thinking about it, but her relief flowed through their touch. "There's no one qualified for that position in my unit yet. We'll have to look outside."

"Agreed. And I already have." He shrugged at her expression. "I was planning to retire. I had to find someone to take Gehrain's place anyway."

"Who did you find?"

He tapped his reader card to activate the next file. "I looked up her record after our trip to the Pit. She has the experience and the leadership qualities. And you liked her, which is a recommendation all by itself."

Tal smiled as she read the file, topped by an image of Lead Guard Vellmar staring out with a stern look in her dark blue eyes, shadowed by the black hair falling over her forehead. "But can she run?"

"Yes, she can. And her empathic rating is as high as yours."

She thumbed the reader card and read to the end before looking up with a raised eyebrow. "Impressive. She certainly does have the qualifications. I think she'll fit in very well." She squeezed his hand. "Do we have a deal?"

After a slight hesitation, he nodded. "We have a deal."

"Good." They released their palm touch and clasped forearms to close the negotiation. "Thank you, Micah. And I want to be there when you give Gehrain his promotion."

"That's a given." He released her arm. "I just hope you won't live to regret this."

"I know I won't. Now if you'll tell Lead Guard Vellmar that she's just received a promotion and a transfer, I'll tell Salomen about her new Chief Counselor. She'll be thrilled."

"She's been with Aldirk all afternoon. She'd be thrilled if you assigned her a talking grainbird."

"Oh, I think I made a better deal than that." Tal pushed the disruptor, wristcom, and earcuff to his side of the table. "I assigned her the one man in all of Blacksun that she likes and trusts."

He clipped the disruptor to his belt and replaced the earcuff. Picking up the wristcom, he said, "From Salomen Opah, that means something."

"Yes, it does."

"It means something from you, too." He settled the wristcom in place and met her eyes. "I'll do my best to earn what you're giving me."

"I expect nothing less. But it's not my gift you need to earn. It's yours."

He nodded, appreciating her quiet understanding. She caught his arm as he began to rise, pinning him with an intense gaze.

"Fahla is the only perfect one among us," she said. "Everyone else makes mistakes. And everyone else must learn to forgive."

Sometimes, he thought, Tal showed a wisdom that seemed to have been conferred at birth. Usually he saw her father in her, but at moments like these, she reminded him very much of her mother.

"True," he agreed. "But not all mistakes are equal, nor do they have equal results. My mistakes carry greater consequences both because you gave me greater responsibility and because I accepted it. And I accept this new responsibility you offer, but with great care. There is a limit to forgiveness."

He rose and saluted her, bid her good night, and left.

CHAPTER 19
Salomen's strategy

Tal stood on the landing pad, watching the transport settle to the ground and appreciating the role reversal. How many times had Salomen stood behind Hol-Opah's main house, waiting for her?

The engines hadn't yet spun down when the ramp extended. As soon as it touched the ground, the door opened, revealing Salomen. She waved at Tal and strode down the ramp like a warrior on a mission. Aldirk was a few steps behind her, moving more sedately, and behind him came two Guards.

Salomen walked straight up to Tal and enveloped her in a warmron. "What happened? You went from happiness to dread in two ticks. I don't like feeling that when I can't get to you."

"Not here." Tal held her tightly, closing her eyes as she soaked up the comfort. It was hard to remember that she had spent her entire adult life without this until just last moon. How had she functioned?

"Lancer Tal." Aldirk offered a minimal greeting as he walked past.

Tal let go of Salomen but retained her hold on one hand. "Aldirk. Did it go well?"

He stopped and turned. "It did. We were able to deal with a number of details, and I believe the Opahs have a better understanding of the demands of such an event."

A very diplomatic answer. Tal thanked him and led Salomen down the path into the park. One of the Guards followed, keeping a respectful distance.

"How did it really go?" she asked.

"As well as can be expected when you bring a scholar caste snob into the parlor of a bunch of uneducated producers," Salomen said. "If he and I spend much more time together, one of us is going to get his ego pruned, and it won't be me."

"He did not say you were uneducated."

"Oh, no, he neither said it nor did he let his front slip even a finger's width. But I swear he looked for dirt on the chair before he sat down."

Tal laughed. Poor Aldirk; he must have thought he was being punished for something.

"And as much as I appreciate your manners, my time with Aldirk is not what's on your mind. What is?"

"Micah tried to resign."

"He *what?*"

"My reaction exactly." They reached a fork in the path, and Tal pointed left, toward the fountain. "I thought I was prepared for a serious talk, but I wasn't ready for that one."

"You refused, of course."

"I don't have right of refusal. He can leave my service any time if he feels it's best. You know that from studying the oath ceremony: service is a gift, not a contract."

They reached the fountain and sat on its smooth stone edge. The gentle plash of falling water soothed Tal's nerves as she told Salomen about her meeting with Micah.

"I don't understand," Salomen said when she finished. "It sounds as if you found the perfect solution for a bad situation. Why are you so afraid?"

"Because it's not a perfect solution. I just put a skin sealer onto a deep wound, and all I can do now is hope it holds long enough to stop the bleeding." She dipped her hand into the small waterfall flowing over the fountain's edge and tried to think of a way to explain. "All Micah agreed to was probation. But he's his own judge, and he'll be unforgiving. If he decides he's failed his probation and resigns anyway, he'll lose everything."

"He'll lose his *job*; that's not—"

"It is, Salomen." Tal gestured at the State House, looming through the trees. "This is his life. He never bonded, and he has no family of his own. I think he adopted me instead, back when I was a child. And he's a father figure to most of the Guards. He doesn't just train them; he mentors them, and they love him for it. If he retires due to failure of performance, he'll lose his chosen family and all his sense of self-worth." She swallowed hard and added, "I've attended funeral pyres for warriors who thought they'd lost everything and had nothing more to offer. I'll be damned if I'm attending Micah's."

"That's a real risk?"

"It is," she said grimly.

They sat in silence, each wrapped up in her own thoughts, until Tal realized that the droplets hitting her skin were not coming from the fountain.

Salomen looked up at the approaching squall. "Time to go in. That looks like a heavy one."

They jogged back to the State House, their Guard close behind. The breeze picked up, rustling through the fallen leaves, and when they opened the door, it pushed them through with a sudden urgency. The rain was already pouring down in sheets before the Guard shut the door behind them.

When they reached their quarters, Salomen went straight to the shannel dispenser while Tal walked to the windows and watched the rain-shrouded city. A flash of lightning was immediately followed by thunder; the squall was directly overhead.

Salomen arrived with two cups of shannel and an air of determination. "We have to make certain Colonel Micah never feels that he's lost everything."

Tal accepted her cup with a nod of thanks. "I wish it were that easy."

"Part of it is. We may not be able to directly help him with his sense of self-worth, but we can offer him a family that would still be there even if he retired."

"Are you talking about us?" Tal shook her head. "It's not the same. Without his daily duties, the connection wouldn't be there."

"It would be if we made it a different connection."

Tal watched her, trying to figure out what she had in mind. "All right, I give up. You have something in your pocket. Let's see it."

A smile spread across Salomen's face. "If Colonel Micah has adopted you, that makes him the only elder family member you're currently in touch with. And I need an elder to petition for inclusion into your family. I think you and I should petition him."

Tal stared at her. "You're serious?"

"You know I am."

Yes, she did, but she couldn't quite believe it. What Salomen was proposing was highly unorthodox, but...

"That could work," she said.

Salomen nodded. "I've only known him for a moon, but that's long enough to see what kind of a man he is, and how special you are to him. I would be honored if he accepted me. And I'd have no difficulty in petitioning him, because I've seen for myself that he's family to you. There's no rule that says the family connection must be by blood."

"No, there isn't." Tal was thinking furiously. Would Micah accept it? Or would he see it as a well-meaning ploy? "We cannot petition him now," she decided. "He'll know why we're doing it. We need to wait a few ninedays. And it's to our benefit that he'll be working directly with you; that will help him build his own relationship with you and—"

"Stop that. Listen to me very carefully."

"I'm listening." Tal stifled a smile at her fierce expression.

"Family is sacred. It is the thread that holds our entire world together. I would never use it as part of a strategy, so get that out of your head. Yes, it might help Colonel Micah, and I hope it will, but even if it were the only thing between him and an early Return, I would not petition him if I did not believe he's your family. This is a real proposal, not a trick."

Ashamed, Tal said, "I didn't mean to imply that it was. I was just—"

"Working out a strategy," Salomen finished. "Don't. I know that's part of your nature, but you cannot kneel before Colonel Micah with that on your mind. It must come from your heart, or it won't work."

Tal shifted her gaze to the windows. "He mentioned you when he was trying to convince me that I didn't need him anymore. He said you had already filled the hole he might leave by retiring. I couldn't believe how much that hurt—the idea of him stepping aside because I have you." A warm hand enclosed hers, and she looked into Salomen's eyes. "He *is* my family. He has been for as long as I can remember. We just don't talk about it. I've been so happy these last few ninedays, but not because I have you instead of Micah. It's because I have you in addition to him—and the rest of your family, too."

"Most of it, at least."

Tal squeezed her hand; there was little she could say to that. "I can petition Micah with a clear heart. And I'm grateful that you can as well. It's a wonderful idea, tyrina."

"It will be my pleasure, believe me." Salomen slipped an arm around her waist.

"When would you like to petition him?"

"I think we should wait a few ninedays. Otherwise he might think he knows why we're doing it."

Tal laughed. "Excellent advice."

They sipped their shannel and watched the rain stream down the glass.

"I love that sight," Salomen said quietly.

"Do you? I only love it when I know I don't have to go out in it."

"I love it because it means I'm free for a whole moon. It means harvest is over and I can focus on other things. And it means the autumn feast."

Tal had nearly forgotten about that. "Have you set a date?" She hoped she would be able to schedule it in.

"Don't worry, I already spoke with Aldirk. He found a free afternoon."

"You scheduled your feast around my obligations?"

"Yes, I did. Do you have a problem with that?"

"Ah…" Tal hesitated as Salomen loosened her arm and looked at her. "No, of course not. I'll be delighted to attend, and I'll try to forget that a feast honoring your field workers has been planned around my calendar."

"You were a field worker too," Salomen said. "And you're my bondmate. But you're not quite used to thinking of yourself as part of Hol-Opah, I see."

"Not yet," Tal admitted.

"Then we're even. I'm not quite used to thinking of myself as Bondlancer, either."

There was another long pause as they watched the rain.

"I really do like the sound of that," Tal said.

"The rain?"

"No. Bondlancer. It's a lovely word, don't you think?"

"I'll let you know in two moons."

CHAPTER 20
True terror

Lanaril often used the act of pouring shannel as a means of concealing her facial expression or giving herself time to think. It was not effective when neither she nor her guest had their fronts up.

"What?" Andira demanded. "Why are you so surprised?"

Lanaril handed her a cup and sat down with her own, looking out her study window for a moment as she took her first sip.

"Because it took you nine moons to tell me anything about your experience in the Battle of Alsea," she said. "Yet here you are, talking about something even more personal just a few days after the fact. It's a good kind of surprise. I'm honored that you feel you can speak with me about this."

"Hm." Andira wasn't convinced. "Are you sure it's not surprise that the leader of the warrior caste had a shekking flashback?"

"Being the caste leader doesn't preclude being Alsean," Lanaril said gently. "You're less than one nineday from a significant trauma. It takes time to move past that."

"But that's what I don't understand. What trauma? I've been hurt before. Pain doesn't frighten me. It doesn't make sense, and I need it to make sense so I can make sure it doesn't happen again."

She couldn't help her smile.

"Lanaril, I swear, if you don't—"

"I'm smiling because I've just realized that you could never be in any other caste. You're doing battle with it, aren't you? Most people would put off dealing with this for as long as they could, or just hope it never happened again. You want to find it and tear it apart."

"Of course I do. For Fahla's sake, we're afraid to use the traditional joined Sharing position with me on top. I don't want to be that restricted, and I especially don't want Salomen to be worrying."

"All right." Lanaril set her shannel on the small table beside her chair and leaned forward. "Let's do battle with it. I need you to tell me every detail, no matter how small. What you felt, what you thought, what you saw and smelled—"

"How did you know that?" Andira shook her head. "Never mind. That's why I came to you. I hate to think how many times you've done this with veterans."

"Too many. But this is different. You're my friend, and we will fight this together."

Andira's defensive prickliness softened. "Thank you. I cannot imagine talking about this with anyone else." She sat straight in the chair, her posture perfect, and began speaking in a clinical tone about love interrupted by abject fear.

But her attempt at detachment didn't last, and Lanaril could certainly see why she wouldn't share this story with anyone else. This was Andira at her most vulnerable, and she felt humbled by such a display of trust.

"Remarkable," she said when the story ended. "You pulled yourself out of it. Most people need training to do that."

"It wasn't really me. It was knowing that Salomen was afraid. I just responded to that."

"It's a powerful motivator, isn't it? Wanting to protect her?"

"I don't think there's anything more powerful."

Lanaril nodded. "Well, here's the good news. I'm fairly certain the position was not the trigger. At least not by itself. You were experiencing a great deal of kinesthetic sensation at that point, none of which was remotely similar to the sensations of being burned. The position itself and the visual stimulus of looking down at Salomen—those were necessary ingredients, but they wouldn't have been enough. It was the muscle twinge in your back that combined the ingredients and set off the reaction."

"I wondered about that."

"Which you might have avoided had you not joined mere hanticks after being released from five days of immobility." She didn't try to hide this smile.

"Ha. We did well to wait that long." Andira's answering smile reflected her loss of tension; just addressing this was improving her mood. "Salomen thinks it was about the burns. She tried to rub my back to comfort me, but when I went stiff as a staff, she realized what was happening."

"For Salomen, it probably would be about the burns. She doesn't have your regrettable history with injuries, nor your training for compartmentalizing pain. And she Shared your pain when it happened. But as you said, pain doesn't frighten you."

"Then what did?" Andira asked impatiently.

"Tell me again, what brought you out of it?"

"Worrying about Salomen."

"What is your most powerful motivator?"

"Protecting Salomen. What does this—?"

"What is your greatest fear, Andira? What terrifies you more than anything else?"

Andira stared at her, the understanding blossoming in her emotions. "Losing her. Oh, Fahla, of course. That makes so much more sense." She sat back in the chair, her wrists dangling limply over the armrests. "I almost lost her that night. When I woke up in the healing center, Micah and I were talking about what happened after I passed out, and I said it couldn't have been much worse. He said yes, it could. And when he said that, I had a vivid vision—" She cleared her throat. "I could actually hear it, Lanaril. What I would have sounded like if I hadn't pulled her out of that window seat. All I could think of then was seeing for myself that she was all right."

"And when you did save her, you had almost no time to process that fact before passing out. Nor did you take much time to consider it in the healing center, did you?"

"After that vision, I didn't want to think about it again."

"But it's still inside your mind. Were you afraid when it happened?"

"I didn't have time. I just reacted, and then I burned, and that took up all of my attention. Well, along with finding that fantenshekken and realizing that Salomen was sacrificing herself for me."

Thankfully, Lanaril had enough experience with this to hear what Andira was not saying. "You reacted. To what?" She saw Andira's brow furrow, felt the too-quick answer coming, and held up a hand. "I know, you reacted to a threat. But what did you feel when you recognized that threat?"

Andira's gaze grew distant. "I felt...a sense of putting a puzzle together. I'd been trying to determine who that emotional presence was, and then it all came together and I was..." Her eyes focused. "Shekking terrified," she whispered. "She was going to die because of me. Because she was sitting in my seat."

Lanaril let her sit with that for a moment.

"That's the fear in my flashback. Goddess above." Andira picked up her shannel, a slight clink of the cup against the saucer betraying her unsteady hands. "How do I fight that? It's not as if I can tell myself I was wrong to be afraid. I was right."

As she drank, her gaze went to the window, where the top of the State House rose over the trees.

"Salomen was afraid of the wrong thing," she said, replacing the cup in its saucer. "The day I came to you to ask about our empathic flashes—that was the day she told me she was afraid. Of my Guards and what they represent. She was afraid of *me* being killed."

Her head turned, and Lanaril was held by the intensity of her light blue eyes.

"You told me she would be a proxy assassination target. You understood the true risk. So did I, so did Micah...but Salomen didn't. She was focused on the risk I live with, and her loss of privacy, and all of the expectations that come with being Bondlancer. But loving me almost killed her before we even bonded."

Lanaril shook her head. "I think we need to separate that. Loving you did not almost kill her. If anyone else had been sitting in that seat, they would have been the target. If Herot Opah had been there, he would have been the target, and I'm reasonably certain he's not very fond of you."

"Herot would never have been in that seat."

"If he had, would you have been able to save him?"

That brought her up short. "I...don't know. I don't know if I would have been fast enough if it were anyone but Salomen."

Ah. Here it was. "What made you so fast? When you told me about it in the healing center, I really couldn't picture it. You were sitting in a chair, and then you leaped halfway across the room? How did you do that without a running start? Or at least a standing one."

Andira's confusion was a gray fog in her emotions, covering the landscape and blocking her understanding. "It wasn't halfway across the room; I was closer than that. But...I didn't think about it. I just did it."

"How?"

"I don't *know*. What are you asking? You want something." Irritation thickened the fog.

"I want you to put yourself back in that chair and tell me how you got from there to the window seat, and pulled Salomen out of it, in what sounds to me like a physically impossible feat. What fueled that?"

Andira watched her with narrowed eyes, and the fog grew thicker still. They were going in the wrong direction.

"I know this is difficult," Lanaril said. "And I'm sorry to be asking all of these questions about a time you don't want to remember. But I wasn't there; you were. You're the only one who can solve this. Let me ask you a different way. What were you feeling when you made that leap? Determination? Anger?"

"Utter terror," Andira said without hesitation. She stopped then, as if she had just heard herself, and the fog lifted.

"Loving you did not almost kill her." Lanaril repeated her earlier words and watched them take root this time. "It saved her. You would not have been that terrified for anyone else. You did the impossible for her."

Andira's eyes were wide. "Fear is a weapon," she said. "Practically the first lesson we learn."

"And you used it."

"I did." Her features relaxed. "So that's what I need to remember if I have another flashback."

"That's how you fight it," Lanaril agreed. "If it ever happens again, and I don't think that's very likely, because the set of circumstances that led up to it were very specific. But don't shy away from remembering what happened that night. That kind of fear, the kind that comes out in flashbacks—it lives in shadows. In the unexamined parts of your memory. It maintains its strength only as long as it can slink along unnoticed, with no light shining on it. But you can think about that night without flinching. You know that fear saved Salomen. You used it. It's not your enemy. It's your weapon."

Andira dropped her head, then looked up with a smile of relief that transformed her face. "Lanaril...thank you. I don't know what to say. You are—"

She stopped, gave one quick nod, and then did something Lanaril had never expected: she held up both palms.

"You are a treasured friend," she said simply.

The gesture meant so much more than that, as did the solid warmth of her affection, and Lanaril blinked back tears as she raised her own hands. "As you are mine. Fahla blessed me the day you overrode my quiet time and walked into this study."

They wove their fingers together and stayed that way for some time, smiling at each other. At last Andira released their hands and reached for her cup. "But you have got to get a better shannel dispenser."

Lanaril laughed. "Any time the Lancer wishes to put that in the temple budget, she should feel free to do so."

CHAPTER 21
Skimming Ehron

It was two days before Tal and Salomen could meet with Councilor Ehron. In the meantime, they met with Councilors from four other castes to throw off suspicion. Tal had thoroughly enjoyed watching Salomen put them at ease, asking questions about their work in the State House and listening with an air of active interest that invariably resulted in a final invitation for her to please call them if she wished to know anything else.

"I must congratulate Micah on his instruction," Tal said when Councilor Treslen from the builder caste had shut the door behind him. "You already know how to play the role of Bondlancer. They're eating out of your hand."

"They're meeting me with you sitting beside me," Salomen pointed out. "It would hardly be to their benefit to treat me rudely."

"Believe me, if they wanted to be rude, my presence wouldn't stop them. There are ways to do it while appearing polite and respectful."

"And you think that's a skill limited to Councilors? Come to a producer caste house meeting in Granelle some time. No one can throw a polite insult like a small-town producer. Especially when we all know each other's business."

"Or not-so-polite insults, in the case of Gordense Bilsner."

"He doesn't know how to be polite. He thinks it's beneath him."

"Actually, I was thinking of you telling him that the only reason your name was still good was because you'd turned down his bond offer. I still wish I'd been there to see that."

Salomen chuckled. "Compared to what I wanted to say to him, that *was* polite."

An approaching presence alerted them to their next appointment, and soon Tal was introducing Councilor Ehron and Salomen to each other. He was an average man in both height and appearance, and unable to completely front his nervousness at being asked to a private audience with the Lancer. Sitting straight-backed in his chair, he touched Salomen's palm and said, "I'm honored to meet the producer who had the horns to challenge our Lancer."

"And look where it got me," Salomen said. "An entire moon of meetings. So much for the glamour of rank."

Ehron visibly relaxed at her response, and Tal watched in fascination as Salomen worked her magic once again. She could be extremely charming when she wished to be. After yesterday's meetings, Tal had teased her about the vast difference between how she behaved now and how she'd acted in their delegate meetings. Salomen had given her an arch look and commented that her behavior was entirely reactive. If treated courteously, she responded in kind; if treated with arrogance and condescension... Well, a certain Lancer had seen the results of that.

Tal had made her pay for that later.

With some effort, she pulled her thoughts away from the pleasant memories and focused on the present. For ten ticks, Salomen asked questions on several topics and listened keenly to the answers, creating such a casual atmosphere that even though she was expecting it, Tal was still surprised when the real question came.

"I know you're not part of the Anti-Corruption Task Force, but perhaps you can give me a warrior's point of view on it. How do the merchants and warriors work together when their value systems are so different? If half the members value honor and the other half value profit, isn't there a potential for corruption within the task force itself?"

Ehron shot an uncomfortable glance at Tal, who nodded encouragingly. "We're in a private conversation, Councilor. There's no need for politicking here."

Shifting his gaze back to Salomen, Ehron said, "It's my understanding that the merchants on the task force were chosen for their known integrity. Corruption hurts the merchant caste more than any other, I think, because it's already expected of them. They have to work harder to achieve the same level of respect that the other castes have by default. So most of the merchants on the task force are just as committed as the warriors to stamping out any corruption they find." He radiated nervousness as he continued, "That said, I believe your question is very perceptive. One of my own warriors works with the task force, and she's heard rumors about favors being exchanged. But is it possible to completely avoid dishonor in a situation of this type? I don't believe so. And I believe that the task force is doing an excellent job overall. It's better to have it with some minor issues than not to have it at all."

While he spoke, Tal skimmed him with an intensity that was just this side of a probe. She could not detect anything approaching what they were looking for, and knew that Salomen hadn't felt anything either. Ehron was not their man.

But he had just given them the perfect justification for bringing in the next best thing.

"I agree," she said. "Some internal corruption was probably unavoidable, and the accomplishments of the task force overshadow it. However, I would be very interested in hearing about these rumors. Which of your warriors is working with it?"

"Her name is Alanor Salir. She's an honorable warrior, Lancer Tal. She only spoke of these rumors to express her distaste for the possibility. I'm certain she would be happy to speak with you, though her information may not be of much help. Rumors are rarely accurate."

"Sometimes they are. And information from someone on the ground level is often more valuable than the reports I get from my normal sources. Please instruct your warrior to report to Chief Counselor Aldirk. He'll schedule a meeting."

"Yes, my Lancer." Ehron showed no unease at the prospect, but Tal suspected the order would unsettle Salir to the extreme.

"Thank you." She looked at Salomen. "Was there anything else you wished to ask Councilor Ehron?"

"There is, yes. I've been studying the Truth and the Path these past few ninedays, and I wonder if you might give me your thoughts on a few of the teachings."

"With pleasure, though my thoughts are just that. The Truth and the Path can be interpreted in different ways, so my opinions may vary from those of other warriors."

"I'm counting on it," Salomen said with a smile.

The discussion that followed was so lively that Tal found herself drawn into it despite their original purpose. By the time Ehron made his departure, she quite liked him. Too bad he had poor taste in the warriors he chose to serve him.

"Not what you hoped for," Salomen said when the door closed behind their guest.

"I'd have been sorry if he turned out to be our traitor." Tal crossed to her desk and pulled up the vidcom code. "And this was more profitable than you think. You were perfect, tyrina."

Her call was picked up immediately; Colonel Razine had been waiting.

"It's not him," Tal said without preamble. "But he volunteered the information that Alanor Salir had spoken of 'rumors' of corruption in the task force. I asked to speak with her, and he seemed to think she'd be happy to assist."

Razine smiled. "Somehow, I don't think she'll be nearly as happy as he believes."

"Nor do I. He should be passing on the instruction soon."

"Then we shall hope Salir will be nervous enough to seek advice. Both her personal and her office vidcoms have redirects installed, and her wristcom code has been tapped. If she contacts anyone, we'll be watching."

"Good. Let me know as soon as you hear anything."

"Of course. Is Raiz Opah still with you? I have an update regarding her brother."

Salomen was next to Tal's chair in an instant. "What is it?" Though her voice was calm, her tension hummed through their link.

"We located a witness at the public transit station in Napoline. She commutes through the station on a regular basis and recognized the footage of Herot. She remembered him because she thought it odd that someone so dirty and unkempt would be walking with two well-dressed warriors. At first she thought they were escorting him out, but he was smiling."

"What? Herot doesn't know any warriors! I mean, other than Lancer Tal and her Guards."

"Are you certain of that?"

Salomen's posture slumped. "I'm not certain of anything anymore."

"At least this moves us one step forward," Razine said. "Before, we only suspected that Herot had help. Now we know it. We have descriptions of the two warriors and an entire team of investigators looking for them. We'll find your brother, Raiz Opah."

Salomen gave her a tiny nod. "Thank you."

"Was there anything else?" Tal asked.

"One more detail that you may find interesting. The warriors wore the uniform of Lancer's Guards. Someone was planning ahead. They wanted to make sure no one asked them any questions."

"What is he doing?" Salomen looked from the screen to Tal. "That sounds as if the whole thing was prearranged. But Herot's message was real."

"With respect," said Razine, "we can no longer accept that as fact. It's possible the message was meant to raise your sympathies and possibly influence the Lancer through you."

"Herot is not that good an actor!"

"At this point in the investigation, we cannot assume anything. The truth will only be known when we can subject him to an empathic scan."

"Good work, Colonel," Tal said. "This puts us in a far better position. Two fake Lancer's Guards can't have strolled through that station unnoticed."

"Agreed. It will be easier to find people who saw the warriors than people who saw Herot. That may have been a mistake on the part of whoever planned this."

"I hope so. Keep me apprised of any change, no matter the time."

"Yes, Lancer." The screen went dark.

Tal stood up and reached out, only to let her arm drop when Salomen turned away. She understood, but the rejection still stung.

Salomen walked to the window and stared out at the city, her arms wrapped around her torso. It made her look much too alone, and Tal's resolve to give her space evaporated. Carefully, she moved up beside her, keeping her hands to herself while she monitored Salomen's churning emotions.

"It's hard to hear you say that." Salomen didn't take her eyes off the view. "Congratulating Colonel Razine on hunting down my brother."

"Colonel Razine is doing her job. And Herot betrayed a trust. I'm sorry, tyrina, but you know that's true."

"I have no idea what's true. The only thing I know for sure is that Herot won't be coming home."

Tal dared to slip an arm around her waist, feeling the stiff bearing give way slightly. "If his message was real, he'll be coming home. Not right away, but he will."

With a sigh, Salomen turned and burrowed in for a warmron. "I'm sorry. I know this is difficult for you as well."

"The most difficult part is feeling what it's doing to you."

"You must be very confused, then. My feelings change from one moment to the next. And who are those warriors? Does Herot have a secret life that none of us ever knew about? Is he even who I thought he was?"

Tal held her silently. Two of those questions were unanswerable with their current information, but the third had evoked a suspicion she was not ready to share.

Warriors as a caste did not take kindly to assassination attempts on their highest-ranked member. It was possible that those two warriors were not there to help Herot at all.

And if that was the case, she had a much bigger problem on her hands.

CHAPTER 22
To Herot's health

"That is not good news," Micah said.

"I know." Tal looked at him from across the table, the stress evident in her face. "I didn't even think to put out a directive. It never occurred to me, and now—" She didn't finish, but she didn't need to.

He had been surprised to find Tal knocking on his door. By this time of evening, he would have expected her to be enjoying Salomen's company, not his. But the moment she voiced her suspicions, he understood the urgency.

"You've sent it now?" he asked.

"Yes, but it's been eight days. Eight days, Micah! If Herot turns up dead, I have no defense. Not a believable one, anyway."

"Five of those days were spent in the health center," he pointed out, but his heart was sinking. He had failed her again. She had been in no condition to be worrying about a vengeance killing; this was not her fault. He should have seen this possibility and prevented it. Because he hadn't, no directive had gone out to the warrior caste warning against unauthorized action. For any warrior bent on avenging the Lancer's honor, a lack of orders to the contrary was tantamount to permission. Such a killing would have been legal had Tal died in the attack, but now the rules were very different. Tal would be held partially responsible for Herot's death, and the ramifications were enormous.

"Yes, and the other three were spent at the State House in full health and visibility," she said. "I even had my first run yesterday morning. I don't think the new lover excuse will fly in the face of a public outcry. And given the fact that I've only just recovered public opinion after the economist debacle and the war criminal contingent has never stopped biting at my ankles, I think my chances of surviving Herot's death are small. Even if I had put out a directive, I'd lose respect for not being able to control my caste. The fact that I failed to send one makes it worse." She put her head in her hands. "Shek, shek, shek! I could lose my title *and* Salomen, all at the same time."

"Nothing has happened yet," he said. "And it may not. The important thing is that you've sent the directive now."

"No, the important thing is that we shekking find Herot! There *must* be a way. I can't afford to wait any longer." She gave a short, unamused laugh. "What an irony. Eight days ago, I wanted to kill him myself. And now everything depends on him being alive."

"I'm sorry," Micah began, but Tal held up a hand.

"Don't you even start with that. I don't want to hear it. Gehrain didn't think about it either, so don't try to convince me that this is one more failure on your part. We all created this pile of dokshin." Her spine slumped as she added, "And now I have to go back to my quarters and explain to Salomen why I'm so upset. She's already upset herself, just feeling it."

"Even if the worst happens, you will not lose Salomen. She'll understand. She won't judge you."

"No, but every time she looks at me she'll know I'm at least partially at fault. And that will change everything."

Not knowing what else to do, Micah rose, pulled two short glasses from his sideboard, and filled them with grain spirits. He set one in front of Tal and said, "Then let us drink a toast to Herot Opah's vibrant health. He's the only man I know who's an even bigger pain in the backside dead than alive."

Tal's frown turned into a wry half-smile. "True words. May Fahla witness them."

They drained their glasses and smacked them back on the table, and when their eyes met, he could see that some of her normal fight had returned.

"I needed that," she said. "Damn him anyway." She pushed herself out of her chair and turned toward the door. "I'm open to suggestions, Micah. Anything at all."

The door closed behind her, and Micah was left staring at his bottle of spirits. He poured a fresh glass and held it up, peering into the dark brown depths as if the answers might appear there.

"Where are you, you little fantenshekken?" he murmured.

CHAPTER 23
Lead Guard Vellmar

Fianna Vellmar dropped her travel bag on the floor of her assigned housing and looked around with an appreciative smile. "Nice."

"Bigger than your old quarters, eh?" Head Guardian Gehrain stood near the front door, the top of his head almost brushing the frame. He was as fit as he was tall, with a charming smile that lit up his hazel eyes and creased his cheeks, and she guessed he had no shortage of lovers. "The pay is better, too."

"Who cares about the pay? I'm just happy to have somewhere to spend it. Koneza isn't exactly a shopping metropolis." She poked her head into the bedroom. Fahla on a funstick, it was huge! Curious, she trotted toward the bathroom. "Are your new quarters even bigger than these?"

"They are. But take good care of this unit, all right? I have a special attachment to it."

"How long were you here?" she called. Goddess above, the bathroom was big enough for herself and two or three friends.

"Six cycles."

She walked back into the living room and eyed him with increased respect. "Then you've been with the Lancer since her election."

He nodded. "I joined her Guard eight cycles ago and made Lead Guard right after her election."

"I can't imagine being in one place that long." She felt a twinge of envy. His career had been very different from hers.

"Show her loyalty and respect, do your job well, and you'll be here as long as you want to be. Lancer Tal keeps good warriors forever. But she has no patience at all for warriors who don't live up to her expectations, so make sure you keep discipline tight."

"That won't be a problem. Discipline was the only thing that stood between my unit and utter boredom at the Pit. We used to pray for an escapee, just so we could have a little excitement."

"I believe it. That's not exactly a prime action spot, but it's high prestige. And your post there is what brought you to the Lancer's attention."

"I know." She still couldn't believe her luck. "When she stopped in front of me and told me to explain my sword grip, I had just one thought in my head."

"What was that?"

"Don't shek this up."

He laughed. "You really impressed her. She mentioned on the flight home that she wished she could have seen you do it a second time."

Vellmar could practically feel her head swelling. "I'll be happy to show her any time she asks. I could even train her if she's interested." For a moment she entertained a dizzying fantasy of actually teaching the Lancer something, but sternly told herself to get realistic.

"She might be," Gehrain said, promptly kicking her fantasy back into full flight. "She's better than any of us with throwing blades; I can easily see her wanting to expand into something bigger. Do you spar with that sword as well, or just throw it?"

"I'm pretty good at sparring."

He narrowed his eyes. "Pretty good, eh?"

"Mm-hm. I've had a few sessions here and there." She met his gaze with all the innocence she could muster, but he grinned and shook his head.

"Your front is perfect, but your confidence is leaking out through your skin. If you're just pretty good, then I'm Fahla's latest lover."

"What's she like in bed?" she asked, and enjoyed his deep chuckle. "My birthmother trained me in blade handling. Anything sharp, she loved. It was either learn it or lose body parts."

He looked her over in frank appraisal. "Everything still seems to be attached, so I'd guess you learned."

"Eyes elsewhere, Gehrain. I'm not your type."

"No, you're not. I like them less curvy."

"Perfect." The best of all possible situations, she thought. It was always easier when you could get the sexual issues out of the way right from the start.

"And even if you were my type," he continued, "I'm taken."

"Is he local?"

He nodded. "A crafter. I was going to his house as soon as I got you settled in."

"Consider me settled. Go see your lover."

"Are you sure? There's a lot we need to discuss yet."

"Does any of it need to be discussed tonight, or can it wait until tomorrow when I'm actually on duty?"

"Oh..." He pretended to think, then flashed her a smile. "I suppose it can wait."

"In that case—" She stopped and stared over his shoulder. "Lancer Tal!" Stiffening, she thumped her fists to her chest and bowed her head.

Gehrain turned to face the figure in the doorway. "Lancer," he said more calmly. To Vellmar's surprise, he did not offer a salute.

"Gehrain." The Lancer's gaze flicked to Vellmar. "Welcome to Blacksun, Lead Guard. And congratulations on your promotion." She made no move to cross the threshold, and Vellmar's initial excitement faded as she saw the tension in her bearing. Not only that, but—what in the name of the Goddess was she wearing? That shirt looked like it had eight holes in it.

"I'll get changed," Gehrain said.

Lancer Tal nodded as he walked to the door. "My apologies, Vellmar," she said. "I forgot Gehrain doesn't live here anymore. And for future reference, I don't require salutes in the living quarters. This is your home, and you're off duty. We'll leave you to get unpacked and relax. I'll see you tomorrow at the oath ceremony."

"Wait," Vellmar said before she had a chance to second-guess herself. "Are you on some sort of training mission?" She gestured toward the ragged shirt.

To her embarrassment, both of them looked amused.

"That's her running outfit," Gehrain said. "Colonel Micah and I have tried to convince her to wear something a little more dignified, but she refuses."

"I wear dignified clothes all day long. When I run, I want comfort." Lancer Tal gave Vellmar a mock glare. "So don't even think about trying to pick up where Gehrain is now leaving off."

"I won't," said Vellmar, who found even that mock glare intimidating. "But may I accompany you tonight instead of Gehrain? I've spent the day in transit; I'd love the chance to stretch out my legs."

Gehrain gave her a surprised, grateful look, while the Lancer's expression was much harder to read. She nodded once. "Get changed. But be warned that I'm not in the best of moods."

"Yes, my Lancer." Vellmar picked up her bag and hustled into the bedroom, leaving her enigmatic new oath holder at her door. Realizing her lapse, she poked her head back out and saw Gehrain and the Lancer in quiet discussion. "Please, Lancer Tal, come inside. I'll just be two ticks." She swore softly to herself as she pulled off her tunic and threw it onto the bed. Leaving the Lancer outside…great way to make a first impression.

But she'd already made a good first impression, she reminded herself while digging out her workout clothes. That was what got her here. Now she just had to make a second one.

She was back out the door in the promised two ticks, though there hadn't been enough time to pull on her running shoes. Gehrain was gone, and Lancer Tal was leaning against the now-closed front door, arms crossed over her chest.

"Slow down," she said. "You'll end up with your shoes on the wrong feet."

"Yes, my Lancer." Vellmar sat on the nearest chair to put on her shoes.

"And stop with the 'my Lancer.' Just Lancer is fine."

Vellmar nodded as she focused on her shoe straps. "Yes, my—I mean, Lancer." She flushed with embarrassment, though she fronted it instantly. "I'm ready," she announced a few moments later, standing up and bouncing a little in place.

Lancer Tal watched with a half-smile. "Thank you."

"For what?"

"For making me feel better already. Let's go." She hit the palm pad and walked out into the corridor with Vellmar one step behind her. They strode through the unfamiliar halls of the State House in silence, eventually emerging from a side door into the cool night air. The rain had diminished to a mist, for which Vellmar was grateful. She wasn't used to the constant autumn rains of Blacksun Basin. Koneza was much drier.

The Lancer didn't even wait for the door to finish closing before breaking into a jog, heading down a path toward the center of the park. Vellmar was momentarily surprised, but caught up quickly with her longer stride.

"Lancer Tal, we're staying on the State House grounds, correct?"

"Yes. Don't worry, I learned my lesson quite some time ago about leaving secure areas without a proper escort."

Vellmar sensed a story there, but she didn't know the Lancer nearly well enough to ask. Instead, she concentrated on taking in her surroundings in as much detail as possible. Her mothers were both warriors and had taught her from childhood to use all of her senses. So she watched, listened, took in the scents, and felt the air currents as they swirled through the fine mist. The sooner she established a familiarity with what was normal for this environment, the sooner she would be able to do her duty properly.

They passed a fountain splashing quietly in a small clearing, then turned into a path overhung by tall trees spaced at regular intervals. The tiny droplets of moisture gathered at the tips of the leaves, grew too fat to hold themselves up any longer, and fell to the ground with a heavy splat. With the constant sound of falling drops, Vellmar kept expecting to feel rain on her face and was slightly discomfited when nothing touched her skin but mist.

Perhaps Fahla heard her. An enormous drop splatted on her head as they passed beneath a tree, and she smiled at the absurdity of it. The clouds weren't raining; the trees were.

She breathed deeply, reveling in the multilayered scents that were so different from the high, dry plains of Koneza. Here she could smell decaying wood and leaves, freshly cut grass, loamy soil that had been recently raked, and all manner of trees and plants that she didn't know yet. But she would learn them.

After half a length, they joined another path near the encircling wall and picked up speed. Lancer Tal might be short, but she moved quickly. Vellmar had to extend her stride to match her.

A length later, the Lancer was running in a flat sprint and Vellmar's long legs were no longer helping. She was up to her aerobic limit and desperately hoping that this was as fast as they would go, because she had no more speed left in her.

After nearly half a hantick of nothing but hard breathing, she had figured out a few things. One, Lancer Tal used running as a stress release. Two, something had her very stressed tonight. Three, there was clearly not going to be any need for awkward conversation, which was a great relief given that Vellmar could barely get enough air as it was. And four, a circuit of the State House grounds was about two lengths. They were now on their fifth circuit, and she silently pleaded for it to be the last one. She wasn't used to running full speed for such a distance, and it would be embarrassing beyond belief to drop out. She would rather die. Then again, at this rate, death might be a real possibility.

As if in answer to her prayers, the Lancer slowed from her all-out run to a more relaxed jog. Vellmar tried not to whimper in relief, but her lungs were planning to hold a celebratory dance as soon as they recovered.

They had gone halfway around their fifth circuit when Lancer Tal finally spoke.

"Are your legs stretched out yet?"

"Shek, yes," Vellmar blurted before she could stop herself.

The Lancer laughed so hard that she had to stop and put her hands on her knees. "Oh, Fahla," she gasped, and laughed again. "I needed that. Thank you. I'd apologize for doing that to you, but damn, it was worth it. I feel so much better."

"I'm glad I could help," Vellmar said dazedly.

"Oh, you did." Lancer Tal straightened and began a cool-down walk, still smiling.

Feeling emboldened by what was so far turning out to be an extraordinary first day, Vellmar said, "If you want to talk about what's bothering you, I'm a good listener. And I don't know anyone here, so I can't make any judgments."

Lancer Tal gave her a keen glance, then looked forward again.

When a full tick of silence passed, Vellmar knew she had put a foot wrong. She wanted to apologize, but thought it might make her sound even more stupid than she already did.

"Tell me something," Lancer Tal said unexpectedly. "If you wanted to find someone who couldn't be found, how would you go about it?"

This had to be about Herot Opah. Everyone on the planet knew that the Alsean Investigative Force was looking for him as the accomplice in the assassination attempt. And they had the best investigators on Alsea at their disposal, so if they couldn't find Opah, he was well and truly hidden. How in the name of the Goddess was a newly promoted Lead Guard supposed to come up with a different angle than the AIF?

A breeze blew Vellmar's hair off her face, and she absently noted that the wind had backed around. Then she remembered her parents' training.

"I'd find out how everyone else had looked and then look a different way," she said. "Sometimes it's not where you look, but how."

Lancer Tal came to an abrupt halt, staring straight ahead. "Great Mother. I wonder if that would work?"

Vellmar kept quiet, watching while the Lancer gazed at nothing. The mist thickened and turned to rain, spattering off their uncovered heads and beginning to soak through their shirts, and still they stood there.

At last Lancer Tal turned her head. "Vellmar, I require your services."

"I'm at your disposal."

"Good. Then I'd like you to meet someone."

CHAPTER 24
A different way

Tal led her new Lead Guard through the State House and up to her personal quarters. For just a moment, as the door opened at her palm touch, she thought perhaps she should have given poor Vellmar a chance to shower. But then Salomen was in front of her, looking at her with fear in her eyes, and Tal forgot how sweaty they were. She hadn't meant to leave Salomen alone this long.

"I'm sorry, but five lengths turned into ten," she said. "I just needed some air."

"I know." Salomen stood an arm's length away, clearly wanting more but too aware of their guest.

"Salomen, may I introduce Lead Guard Fianna Vellmar. She's just arrived from Koneza, and I'm afraid I didn't even give her time to unpack before dragging her out with me. Vellmar, this is the future Bondlancer of Alsea, Raiz Salomen Opah."

"Well met," said Vellmar politely. "Ah, I'm a bit sweaty, but…" She tentatively held out her palm.

"Well met." Salomen touched her palm without hesitation. "And I could wish that you'd had a more leisurely arrival, but I'm glad Andira had your company."

"So am I," said Tal, moving them all into the living area. "Vellmar, would you like some water?"

"Yes, please."

"Sit down. I'll bring it over."

Tal drank her glass while filling a second one, which she handed off to Vellmar before taking a seat next to Salomen. "Vellmar gave me an idea about finding Herot."

Salomen paled. "You mean if he's alive."

Sometimes, Tal thought, honesty wasn't always the best thing for a relationship. But Salomen had known something was very wrong when she returned from Micah's quarters, and lying wasn't an option. The truth had not been much better.

"I think he is," she said gently. "While I was running, I remembered that vengeance killings aren't usually done in secret. The whole point is to advertise that honor has been reclaimed. If someone killed Herot, they would want the world to know. So I don't think it's happened."

"Yet," Salomen said.

"Excuse me." Vellmar was watching them with a frown of concentration. "Are you worried that a warrior might exact a vengeance killing in your name?"

"Yes, I am. You just arrived, so you're a little out of touch. I sent out a directive today, forbidding all warriors from vengeance actions on my behalf. The problem is that it took me eight days to realize that the directive might be necessary."

"But it shouldn't be necessary. You didn't die; there's no vengeance to be gained. It's not legal."

"You and every normal warrior know that, but it's the fringe I'm worried about. Herot Opah has stayed out of sight too long to be doing it on his own. Today we learned that he was seen leaving the transit station in Napoline in the company of two warriors wearing the uniform of Lancer's Guards."

"My Guards!" Vellmar paused before continuing in a quieter voice. "So someone is using our uniform for their gain, and you want to find Herot Opah before anything can happen."

"Exactly." Tal met Salomen's eyes again. "I asked Vellmar how she would go about finding someone who couldn't be found. She said she'd look a different way. And that made me think about what Lanaril found in her literature search."

"You didn't tell me you heard from Lanaril." After this afternoon's debacle, Salomen was sensitive about anything being kept from her.

"She called just before I closed down my office. I was…distracted by other concerns after that. Anyway, she found a reference in a very old history. It said that the divine spark acts as a lens, magnifying the bearer's natural abilities. When we said it was as if our powers were multiplied, we were right."

"I don't—"

"What if it's not just our powers that we can magnify? Vellmar's empathic rating is the same as mine."

Salomen looked from her to Vellmar and back again, a sudden excitement marking the moment she understood. "Yes," she said. "I want to try, if Lead Guard Vellmar agrees."

"Agrees to what?" Vellmar asked.

"A Sharing with Salomen and me." At her wide-eyed shock, Tal added, "Listen, Vellmar. This is important. When Salomen and I Share, we have the ability to extend our empathic senses a very long way. But there are limits to our range. I think your empathic strength might help us extend and focus that range, and we could use it to search for Herot. If you're willing to join us, that is."

Vellmar stared at her. "Exactly what kind of range are you talking about? I can sense out to six lengths with line of sight, but that's it. I've never heard of anyone going farther than that. I don't see how this is going to help you."

"We've sensed well over a thousand lengths," Tal said.

Vellmar was speechless, and Salomen took pity on her. "I know this must feel surreal to you," she said, "especially since you just arrived and you don't know us. But somewhere out there, my brother might be in mortal danger, and you may be able to help us find him. Nothing else has worked so far, and I'm worried that our time is running out."

After a few pipticks of uncomfortable silence, Vellmar straightened in her chair. "I came here to serve," she said firmly. "I will do so in any manner you see fit. If that means Sharing, then I will be honored to link with you and Raiz Opah."

Tal had already decided she liked her new Lead Guard when the poor woman hadn't uttered a single word while Tal ran them into the ground. Now she found her respect notching up several levels. "Thank you," she said.

"Yes, thank you," Salomen added. "But I have one thing to ask before we begin this."

"Of course," Vellmar said.

Salomen sniffed delicately. "The two of you really need to take a shower."

CHAPTER 25
Sharing a search

Vellmar looked around the Lancer's bathroom in awe. She had seen entire barracks that would fit into this space. If someone turned off the lights while she was showering, she might never find her way out.

She walked across what felt like an entire wallball court to the shower. There were several settings to activate the water, one of which turned on a dual waterfall in a smaller cubby off the main shower. "Holy shek," she whispered. She had to try that one.

Warm water sluiced over both her front and back, the effect luxurious beyond belief. She wished she could stay and enjoy it, but the knowledge that Lancer Tal and her bondmate were waiting made her take an even faster shower than normal.

As she toweled off, she thought about the mystery of Raiz Opah. When Lancer Tal had introduced her as the future Bondlancer, Vellmar had barely been able to front her shock. All of the news stories had referred to Opah as the Lancer's producer lover, and like everyone else on the planet, Vellmar had assumed it was a relationship of convenience. Opah was a fine-looking woman, the Lancer had spent a moon on her holding… It made sense that they would enjoy each other's company. But Lancers did not choose their mates from the producer caste. That hadn't happened in at least ten generations, maybe fifteen.

Opah was obviously something out of the ordinary. That had been verified while the Lancer had taken her shower, leaving Vellmar with her bondmate. Opah had treated her with complete respect and courtesy, making conversation, putting her at ease…the second most–powerful person on the planet, acting as if they were equals! And all at a time when she must be stressed beyond measure. Vellmar had lived her entire life in constant awareness of the hierarchy of rank, but she had never met anyone like the new Bondlancer.

She hung up the towel and wrapped herself in the thick, warm robe that Lancer Tal had provided. Padding across the vast tiled floor, she paused in the arched doorway to watch the two women in the living area.

They were huddled close together on the wide seat, facing each other with knees touching and hands clasped. Lancer Tal was saying something in low tones, and Opah was nodding, the stress and fear evident on her face. But she was fronting it perfectly.

Vellmar took one step out and stopped when the realization hit. A *producer* was fronting perfectly. What in Fahla's name was a producer doing with a front like that?

Both women turned, catching her staring.

Cursing the flush that warmed her face, she continued into the living area. "The shower was wonderful, thank you."

"You're welcome." Opah's tone was a little cooler than it had been earlier, and Vellmar felt it keenly.

She sat in the chair opposite them and leaned forward. "I didn't mean to stare. I just never expected to be in the Lancer's personal quarters on my first night." Damn, that sounded even worse. "I mean, ever," she amended, and closed her mouth in frustration. She was making a complete dokker of herself.

To her immense relief, Lancer Tal smiled at her. "Nervous?"

Not trusting herself to say anything intelligent, Vellmar simply nodded.

"So am I," Opah said. "I'm afraid this won't work."

Vellmar forgot her own worries in the face of this admission. "If my empathic strength can help make it work, then you have all of it I can give."

"We appreciate your willingness to serve," said Lancer Tal. "Especially on such short notice and in a rather unusual situation. Have you done a triad Sharing before?"

"No. So I don't know how this works." And she really didn't want to do anything wrong.

"Salomen and I will make the core connection. You'll extend it with a hand on our necks. So get close enough for an easy reach; you may be holding up your arms for a while."

As they crossed their legs beneath them, Vellmar stood up and moved her chair over until it touched the front of their seat. She slipped into a cross-legged position and hesitated, unwilling to make the first move.

Opah brushed her dark hair to one side and forward over her shoulder, baring the base of her neck. "Go ahead."

Vellmar tentatively reached out.

"I won't break, Fianna."

Startled by the use of her first name, Vellmar let the full weight of her hand come down.

"Better." Opah gestured toward Lancer Tal.

It took more determination to put her hand on the Lancer's neck. Vellmar half-expected a defensive block, but Lancer Tal merely gave her a sidelong glance and a quick nod of approval.

"Ready?" she whispered.

"As I'll ever be," Opah said. They lifted their hands toward each other.

"Vellmar," said Lancer Tal without looking at her, "don't worry if you see something unexpected. Just remember that for us, it's normal."

Before Vellmar could ask, their hands slipped into place and the connection was completed. She slammed her eyes shut against the explosion of sensation, barely managing to keep her hands in place. What in the name of the Goddess…?

She could feel *everything*. Not just the emotions of other Alseans in the building, but the life force of all the creatures around her, from the mice in the walls to the nightwings hunting on the grounds outside. Even as she gasped at the impossibility of it, her awareness expanded further, until she felt the whole city throbbing in her senses, a cacophony of life bombarding her with empathic noise that she could not separate into its component parts. She was overwhelmed and frightened, until a soft calm enfolded her as the other two soothed her entrance to their Sharing. She floated in a gossamer web of the most intimate emotions, her individuality lost in the entity their Shared feelings had created. Here were emotions she had never experienced before, and she marveled at how flat and featureless her own life had been compared to the brilliance of this. She had taken part in enough Sharings to know that some part of this was normal, but what she felt now could not be compared to any prior experience.

"Don't try to control it," a voice said, and it took her a moment to identify it as Lancer Tal's. "Just relax, Vellmar. Let us do the work. We won't let you fall."

"I know." It was impossible to be a part of their minds like this and not be certain of her own safety. Right now she trusted them as much as her own mothers.

"Salomen, try the test."

They took flight, soaring over an emotional landscape that was strange and exhilarating and oddly familiar, covering an impossible amount of distance, and yet Vellmar knew it was normal. She had seen this before, or some part of this Shared entity had. They came to a stop, hovering over a place packed with Alseans, and from the largely unguarded emotions pouring out, she guessed it was a tavern full of drinkers getting relaxed.

"There he is, that damned little zalren." Opah's triumph cut through the self-doubt like a knife severing a knotted rope. "Andira, we can do this!"

"*You* can do it. I don't know Gordense well enough to recognize him emotionally."

The pleasure that came through their connection made Vellmar feel warm all over. She didn't know the history of this, but she was certainly enjoying the ride.

"We had to test our focusing ability," Lancer Tal explained. "We wanted to see if Salomen could locate someone other than her family. We're too familiar with them. Our minds go to Hol-Opah almost automatically, so it's not a good indicator. We had to look for someone our minds would not normally be drawn to."

"Who did you choose?"

"Gordense Bilsner. The father of the would-be assassin."

"Damn," Vellmar said. "That's not the first mind I'd go looking for."

"But it's proof of concept," Opah said. "Let's find Herot."

They left the tavern behind, soaring over fields and villages, and Vellmar soon realized that they were flying a search pattern.

She didn't know how much time they spent searching Blacksun Basin, but a selfish part of her hoped it might never end. The sensation of soaring on their senses, of feeling impossible things, was far too glorious to give up. When they showed her how to filter out the emotional presence of life-forms other than Alseans, she was simultaneously exhilarated by the knowledge and power, and disappointed to be losing her awareness of all those creatures. Sensing a hunting vallcat had been thrilling, and she hated the thought of actively shutting out her awareness of any more such encounters. But this was a mission, not pleasure, and she gave the Lancer and her bondmate as much of her focused strength as she could.

When they had covered the entire floor of the Basin, they made a great circuit and scanned the inner mountain slopes as well.

"He's not here." Opah's disappointment was heavy.

"We didn't think he would be," said Lancer Tal. "We just had to rule it out. Now we move on."

In the pause, Vellmar opened her eyes for the first time, wanting to see these two extraordinary women with her normal vision. What she saw made her gasp, and she snatched her hands away without thinking.

"It's normal," Lancer Tal said. They hadn't moved, sitting there as if their glowing hands were nothing out of the ordinary.

"Not for me!" Vellmar tried to will her heart rate down. Great Mother, that had scared her halfway to her Return! But now that the shock had worn off, she looked closer, fascinated by the sight. "Doesn't that hurt?"

"Did you feel any pain before?"

"No. Was that happening before?"

"It happens every time. You didn't see it earlier, but it was stronger than usual before you broke the connection. Your empathic strength is helping. So if you can rejoin us, we can certainly use you."

"This is what you warned me about." Now she just felt foolish. "You could have given me a little more detail."

"She's not always good at detail." A smile flitted across Opah's face before she asked, "Will you join us again? Please?"

As if she could refuse a request like that. "I'm sorry. I was just startled." Her hands touched their necks, and there it was again, that astonishing explosion of awareness. "Goddess above! I don't think I'll ever get used to that."

"Neither can we," Opah said. "It stuns us a little, every time."

Vellmar sank happily into the warmth of their welcome, surrounded by a depth of emotions that already seemed familiar. "Where do we go from here?"

"South," said Lancer Tal.

They took off, moving beyond the populated areas of Blacksun Basin and flying high over a landscape dotted here and there by a sprinkling of Alseans. Then there were no Alseans at all, and they were moving up and over the first range of mountains. Vellmar let her filter slip for a moment, hoping she might find a treecat, and was instead amazed to realize that she could actually sense the trees themselves.

"I never knew," she whispered.

They flew rapidly across the mountains, passing over sparsely populated lands, then slowed as they moved over the first larger town. Finding nothing there, they swung west for some distance, then turned south and east, the first leg of another search pattern. Steadily, they pushed on, and Vellmar began to wonder if they would go all the way to the ocean. But the Shared vision dimmed too soon, and she opened her eyes to see the glow fading from the women's hands. They sat up straight, breaking their connection, and Vellmar brought her own hands back into her lap.

Never in her life had she experienced anything so extraordinary—and that on top of an inconceivable intimacy, given the rank of her companions. She stared at her hands, feeling awkward and out of place. Her own limited emotions were a poor fit after the depth and glory of their Sharing.

"Damn, damn, damn!"

She looked up in surprise as Opah slumped back against the chair.

"It was a long shot, tyrina," Lancer Tal said gently. "But we didn't fail by any means. This works—we were almost to the sea. And we've ruled out a significant part of southern Argolis."

"Yes, so now we just need to rule out the north, east, and west parts, and then we'll find Herot's body on Pallea!" Opah's fear and frustration were palpable; she hadn't brought up her front.

Vellmar uncurled her legs and stood, knowing that she no longer belonged here. "I'm sorry I couldn't be of more help," she began, but the Lancer put a hand on her leg.

"Sit down, Vellmar."

She sat.

"Are you tired?" When she hesitated, Lancer Tal gave her a knowing look. "The truth."

"Yes," she admitted. "But not overly so."

"Can you Share with us again?"

"Of course."

The Lancer turned to Opah. "Then we'll rest for a few ticks, and after that we'll do it again, and again, until we can't anymore. And then we'll take a break while I round up every member of my Guard with a high empathic rating. I'd like to avoid that if I can, because it means making this far more public," —she gestured between the two of them— "but if that's the only way, then so be it."

"Thank you. I'm sorry; I'm just feeling so damned helpless."

"I know. But you're taking action, Salomen. That's not being helpless."

Vellmar watched them and belatedly remembered that Lancer Tal had called her bondmate *tyrina*. "Great Mother to us all. You're tyrees. That explains a lot."

Lancer Tal looked at her sharply. "It should also explain why Salomen's safety is as important as my own, so I know you won't be jeopardizing it by speaking where you should not."

"Of course not." She was insulted and didn't bother to front it. "I'm sworn to your service, even if we haven't had the ceremony yet. I'll swear myself to Raiz Opah as well if you'd like."

Lancer Tal's expression did not change. "That should be Salomen's choice, not mine."

Vellmar turned to Opah, whose eyebrows were at her hairline.

"Can you serve two people at the same time?" Opah asked. "I don't know the whole warrior code yet. I'm just accepting the oaths of my own Guards tomorrow morning, at the same time you're making yours to Andira."

Fahla, the woman was a newborn winden when it came to her position. Vellmar's regard for her took on a protective edge.

"Yes, I can," she said. "My primary duty would be to Lancer Tal, but I would have a secondary duty to you. And before you choose, you should probably know that I already decided I was serving you, before we Shared. I just wasn't going to do it officially."

Out of the corner of her eye she saw a smile flicker across the Lancer's face, though Opah was taken aback.

"Why?" she asked.

"Partially because you're my Lancer's bondmate. Serving you is a means of serving her. But also because...well, you're the Bondlancer, or you will be, but you've treated me like a regular guest. You act like we're equals."

"Aren't we?"

Vellmar would have laughed, but Opah was serious. She really thought that way. "Ah...no. You're the Bondlancer. Nobody is your equal except Lancer Tal."

"So you want to unofficially serve me because of a title I don't yet hold."

She felt the dismissal coming and leaped to stop it. "No, that's just why I was surprised. I would expect the first producer Bondlancer in generations to be very careful about the image she presents—about being seen as strong. And maybe you're too worried about your brother to be concerned with your image, but I've just Shared with you and I don't think that's it. You don't care about your image. I respect that."

Opah shook her head in bemusement, but the Lancer laughed softly. "She figured you out within a tentick of meeting you, Salomen. For what it's worth, I'd recommend you accept her service."

Vellmar found herself the object of an intense scrutiny.

"Tell me something about yourself, then. I know the histories of my own Guards, but nothing about you."

"My mothers are both warriors. I chose my birthmother's name because I couldn't imagine it any other way. She taught me everything I know about handling blades."

"Which is quite a bit," Lancer Tal interrupted. "Go on."

"I graduated from the Whitemoon Sensoral Institute, trained under Colonel Debrett at Whitesun, moved through four different assignments in five cycles, and ended up at Koneza a little over a cycle ago, where I headed a unit of nine Guards. And then I got the promotion of my dreams and came here."

Opah looked amused. "I see you also have the warrior characteristic of leaving a great deal out."

Vellmar blinked. What else did she want to know? "Ah…I'm not very good with a disruptor, but I make up for it with my blade handling. I'm not afraid of hard work, and I expect the warriors in my unit to perform to their full potential." She frowned; the amused look was still there. "My mothers taught me to trust my instincts and not accept things at face value, which is why I knew you were more than you appeared. Most people stepping into a position of power would feel a need to reinforce and defend it, but you don't. You show yourself as you are, and that takes a level of strength that I can honor."

She must have said something right. The amusement had been replaced by respect.

"And I can honor a warrior who sees beyond the surface. I accept your service, Lead Guard Vellmar." Raiz Opah looked at her bondmate. "Does that mean she'll swear her oath tomorrow, with the rest?"

"No, she's not free to offer you a public oath. That's reserved for one oath holder only. This is a private oath."

"Now is as good a time as any," said Vellmar. "Might as well do it before we tire ourselves out any more."

Raiz Opah watched her for a moment before nodding. "All right." She uncoiled from the chair, moved to an open section of floor, and stood waiting.

Vellmar slipped out of her own chair and stood before her, then realized that she was missing a major component of the ceremony.

"Wait a tick, Vellmar." Lancer Tal walked over to the bookcases beneath the windows, opened a wooden case, and turned with a sword grip in her hand. "You'll need this."

She tossed the grip to Vellmar, who caught it with ease and held her breath as she examined it. The Lancer's sword! She was going to swear an oath of service to the future Bondlancer with the Lancer's sword! Her mothers would burst with pride when she told them.

It was plainer than one might have expected. No gems, not even in the pommel where the main counterbalance weight was set, and no special engravings other than Lancer Tal's family crest, one on each side. Even those were small and discreet, serving mostly for orientation. By holding the grip so that one of the crests faced upwards, the user's hand would be in the correct position once the blade and crossguard extended.

At first glance, it seemed to be a simple sword of little worth, but Vellmar knew better. Two things gave it away: the stylized Y on the pommel and the teffalar wrap. Teffalar trees did not reach maturity until they were a hundred cycles old, after which the bark could be harvested only once per tencycle. When processed into thin, pliable sheets, it absorbed vibrations and sweat, never slipped, and took a lifetime to wear out. It was a rare, highly regulated product, and most warriors able to afford a teffalar wrap wanted the world to know about it. These grips were usually dyed and decorated to advertise their provenance, but Lancer Tal's was the original bark color, a rich brown with black and orange speckles scattered across its surface.

Back in her quarters, still sitting in a crate she hadn't yet unpacked, was a holobook of Yulsintoh swords. The image on the cover, and the first hologram to pop up when the book was activated, was of this exact sword. Vellmar would not have been surprised to wake up and find that she was dreaming.

Holding her arm straight out to the side and the grip parallel to the floor, she thumbed the control and smiled at the familiar sound as the blade extended. Faster than her eye could see, the blade sections shot out of the grip, assembling and sealing themselves into a seamless whole while the crossguard flipped up and out, protecting her hand. Less than one piptick after pressing the control, she held a fully formed and flawless sword. Though she understood the mechanics, it never lessened her awe for the sheer beauty of the result—and this sword was exquisite. Had she not already known it was a Yulsintoh, she would have guessed it by the perfect balance.

With a crisp motion she snapped her arm in, the sword now pointing straight up, and brought her other hand onto the grip. "Raiz Salomen Opah," she said, "I stand before you with a clear heart and an honorable name. Though I am primarily sworn to Andira Shaldone Tal, Lancer of Alsea"—this wasn't exactly true yet, but it would be—"my heart is free to serve another of my choosing. I wish to serve you, in any capacity I am able. I place my strength between you and harm, my sword between you and your enemies, and my last breath between you and death. This I swear in Fahla's name. I am Fianna Londin Vellmar, Lead Guard of the Lancer, and I ask this gift of you: Will you accept my service?"

She released one hand from the grip, let the sword fall to a horizontal position, and caught the flat of the blade on her palm. Dropping to one knee, she offered the sword to Raiz Opah. A moment later it was plucked from her grasp, and she heard the *sshunk* of the blade being retracted.

"Please stand, Fianna Londin Vellmar."

She stood and looked into the face of her new oath holder.

Opah handed the grip back to her and said, "You offer me a sword extended, and I return it to you sheathed. I accept the gift of your service with a glad heart, and trust that you will stand between me and harm. Should your last breath be expended in my defense, I swear to you that your name will be honored to the utmost of my ability, and the flames from your pyre will reach the stars themselves." A sudden smile appeared. "But I really hope that won't be necessary."

Vellmar smiled back at the unorthodox addition to the words of acceptance. "Thank you," she said. Holding the grip in one hand, she brought her other fist to her chest and bowed her head in the salute given all oath holders save one. Tomorrow she would give a different salute.

"I think this requires a drink, don't you?" Opah said. "That was my very first acceptance. I need to celebrate the fact that I remembered all the words." She turned toward the kitchen.

Vellmar stared at the sword grip with hungry eyes, loathe to give it up, but Lancer Tal appeared in front of her and held out her hand.

"That was a loan, Vellmar, not a gift."

"I know." She handed it over. "It's gorgeous. Thank you for allowing me to use it."

"You're welcome." The Lancer looked over the grip fondly. "I've had it since I was barely out of training. Cost me two moons' wages at a time when I could least afford it."

"It would cost more than that now. I tried to buy one from Yulsintoh last cycle—thought my promotion into the Koneza unit might be enough for me to afford it." Vellmar shook her head. "I'm willing to give up a lot for a good sword, but not that much."

"Really? What is he charging now?"

"Twelve thousand cinteks for a sword without gemstones."

"*Twelve* thousand? It's good to know he's making a fine living, but at those rates, only collectors can afford his swords!"

"Because you carry this one. Ironic, isn't it?"

Lancer Tal scowled. "Not in a good way. I may have to give him a call."

They were interrupted by the arrival of their spirits. "Give who a call?" Opah asked.

"The crafter who made my sword. He's upped his prices to the level of gouging. A warrior would need family money to afford him now, and that rubs me the wrong way."

"What can you do about it? That's the way the market works."

Vellmar watched in fascination as an almost feral smile settled on the Lancer's lips. "I can inform him that unless he makes his swords available to those who need them most, I'll be carrying another maker's sword at my bonding ceremony." She lifted her glass in a salute. "The market works both ways."

"Take note, Lead Guard Vellmar," said Opah. "Do not cross her."

"It never occurred to me," said Vellmar truthfully.

CHAPTER 26
Oath of service

TAL WATCHED PROUDLY AS SALOMEN accepted the oath of her last Guard on the floor of the Council chamber. Though she had uttered the words of acceptance nine times already, she made this one sound as fresh and sincere as the first. When the Guard saluted her and returned to the ranks, Tal found it impossible to keep the smile off her face. There was her tyree, standing in front of ten warriors and looking every bit the Bondlancer, despite having been so nervous this morning that she felt sick to her stomach. But she had performed the ceremony perfectly.

Because her status had not yet been announced, these oaths were not being made publicly. The only witnesses in the tiers were Tal's own Guards—now including Vellmar, who had sworn her oath before Salomen's ceremony. They were going about things rather backward, but there hadn't been time to do it the normal way. As it was, Tal was surprised they had managed to get Salomen's Guards fully trained before word about her true status had leaked out. Miltorin would make the formal announcement tomorrow, and Salomen would officially be the future Bondlancer of Alsea.

Which might be another reason for her bout of nervous stomach this morning, Tal realized.

Of course, a third and very likely reason was their failure to locate Herot the previous night. They had managed to search most of southern Argolis, but by night-three, all of them were swaying from exhaustion. Tal and Vellmar had wanted to continue, but Salomen refused, saying that she knew she had to be the one to do it. They sent Vellmar back to her quarters and tumbled into bed for barely three hanticks of sleep. Getting up for this oath ceremony was torture; she was definitely past the age when one or two hanticks of sleep were enough.

But seeing Salomen in front of her Guards made it all worth it. It was hard to believe that it had been only one nineday since the assassination attempt. Nine days ago, Salomen had still been afraid of their Sharing. Now she looked as if she were born to the title.

"More than that, I am honored to accept your oaths." Salomen was wrapping up her speech. "Every one of you has an impeccable record and an honorable name. Each of you was handpicked by Colonel Micah and the Lancer herself." Her stern expression gave way to a smile. "And believe me, they have very exacting standards. You represent the best of your caste, and I have no hesitation in trusting my safety to your skills. I am proud to have such a unit serving me."

She looked over at Tal, who took her cue. Joining Salomen in front of the unit, she said, "Tomorrow the State House will formally announce Raiz Opah's status as my promised bondmate. The bonding ceremony is planned for the twenty-third of Rosslin, but between now and then, she will still be a private citizen. Unfortunately, there will be those who do not see it that way, particularly in the media. Unless Raiz Opah informs you otherwise, you are charged with protecting her privacy along with her person." She paused, surveying the unit. They looked sharp and professional in their dress uniforms.

They had better be, she thought, and began their most important instruction.

"Recent events have demonstrated that the danger associated with my title cannot be overstated. That same danger can sometimes apply to the title of Bondlancer. I knew and accepted the risk to myself as a price to be paid for the honor of serving Alsea. But Raiz Opah never pursued her title. She never wanted the loss of anonymity or the risk that came with it. I am grateful beyond expression for the love she bears me, because it is the only thing that could have induced her to accept the role she must now play."

She and Micah had agreed that Salomen's Guards did not need to know their oath holder was tyree. Not yet, anyway. Though they were sworn to her service, they were also an entirely new unit. The potential for betrayal was there despite all efforts to choose the best. Tal would revisit the decision when the unit was more seasoned—or when the news got out on its own, she thought ruefully. In the meantime, she needed to impress upon them the importance of their charge without telling them exactly why.

"As you are now sworn to the service of Raiz Opah, I will share with you a truth that very few know," she continued. "Nine days ago, she nearly lost her life in the assassination attempt on me. The assassin was too far away to identify his target and took a wide shot instead. Though he did not know it, he was targeting Raiz Opah."

The Guards glanced at each other, their surprise obvious.

"She stands here as my future bondmate despite having already experienced the danger associated with my title. I believe that is all anyone needs to know about her courage. And now I charge you with a single, overriding duty. You all swore it in your oath, but the oath of service is ancient and has lost much of its original meaning. Not for you. You swore to stand between her and harm. You swore to give your last breath in her defense. You are warriors!" She raised her voice on the last word, and every Guard in the unit stood a little straighter. "You are defending the most courageous woman I have ever known. You are guarding the most valuable life on Alsea. There is no duty more important than the one you bear. *Do you understand?*" she shouted.

"Yes!" they shouted back.

"Who do you serve?"

"Salomen Opah!"

"What do you serve?"

"Alsea!"

"To whom do you swear?"

"Fahla!" they roared. *"For Fahla and Alsea! For Salomen Opah!"*

Their voices rang in the empty chamber, and Tal let the echoes settle before saying, "Then do your duty, and earn your honor." She looked at a dazed Salomen. "Raiz Opah? Do you require your Guards for anything else this morning?"

To her credit, Salomen showed no outward sign of her emotion as she faced her unit. "You do me great honor," she said clearly. "Thank you. Except for those now on active duty, you are dismissed for a well-earned morning off. Those on duty today will have a free morning tomorrow."

As one they saluted her, turned, and walked out of the chamber, talking excitedly among themselves. After such a high-intensity training, a free morning was a welcome reward indeed.

Of those on duty, one would join the Lancer's Guards in front of the hallway to their personal quarters. Once Salomen had her own office, that would be guarded as well. She could move freely as long as she was in the State House or on Blacksun Base, but the moment she stepped outside this building or off the base boundary, she would be accompanied by at least one of her Guards. Salomen would never be alone in public again, and Tal knew better than anyone on the planet just what that meant. It was a high price to pay for love.

As her own Guards climbed down from the tiers, she leaned toward Salomen. "Thank you."

"For what?"

"Accepting this." She gestured toward her Guards. "I remember a morning in your field when you told me they frightened you."

Salomen watched them approach. "I remember that, too. I told you I wanted someone who understood responsibility, stability, and tradition." She shifted her gaze to Tal. "I found her."

Tal would have given much for the chance to kiss her then, but with the Guards waiting for acknowledgment she had to settle for a brief brush of their fingers. "Ready to find Herot?"

"Are you going to tell them about what happens to our hands, or are you going to let them have the fright of their lives like Vellmar?"

Tal pretended to think. "I was leaning toward the 'fright of their lives' idea."

"I thought as much." Beneath Salomen's light words, her anxiety was all too apparent. "All right. Let's find my brother."

CHAPTER 27
Group Sharing

IN ALL HIS LIFE, MICAH never imagined himself standing guard over a group Sharing. Even if he had, he would never have imagined that Sharing to include Tal, her tyree, and almost the entire Lancer's Guard. When Tal proposed it right after the oath ceremony, he wondered if someone had slipped something into her food. But Vellmar spoke up, explaining what she had experienced the night before, and after that no Guard wanted to be left out.

They moved to the training room on the ground floor of the State House, where there was sufficient open space and privacy. Micah called in First Pilot Thornlan to help him stand guard, since every other member of Tal's Guard was either asleep in off-duty rotation or in the room with Tal and Salomen. He and Thornlan stood on opposite sides of the entrance, at the back of the observation deck overlooking the training floor. It gave them a perfect view.

The first two attempts failed. The traditional formation of a group Sharing—two lines of people forming behind the primary connectors—did not provide a sufficiently cohesive experience. Not only that, but the combined power of the Guards overwhelmed Salomen's ability to focus. At Tal's suggestion, they reformed into a huddle, with Tal and Salomen at the center and the Guards circling them in ever-widening rings. Vellmar theorized that the key might be having each individual touching the necks of two others, so they shifted around until they worked out the right geometry.

"Now remember," Tal called. "Focus on me, not Salomen. I'll channel it to her. And don't try to search actively. Salomen knows Herot's emotional pattern; our job is to support her and increase her range."

"Do her Guards know she's a stronger empath than they are?" Varsi asked. All of the Guards had been understandably astonished to learn of Salomen's talent.

"No," Salomen answered, "and I'd like to keep it that way for now. A Bondlancer has to have *some* secrets, you know."

Laughter rippled through the group. "We'll never tell," said Gehrain. "But we want to be there when they find out."

"Deal," Salomen said. "Are we ready?"

After the general affirmative, Tal and Salomen made their connection—and this time it succeeded. Micah couldn't sense what they were feeling, but he heard a gasp from every single Guard in the huddle.

"Fahla!"

"Great shekking…"

"Goddess above…"

The whispers filled the room, and Micah was envious. He knew he was serving Tal better by guarding all of them than he could inside that huddle, but damn, he wished he could see what was causing all of these experienced warriors to show such open astonishment.

Then his own jaw dropped. Tal had warned them about it, but for the love of Fahla, she just said their hands would glow!

"Mother of us all," murmured Thornlan, and Micah nodded in speechless agreement.

Tal and Salomen were enveloped in a shifting aura of gold, so bright that he found himself squinting. He couldn't even look at their hands; it was like looking directly at the sun. They were radiating a frightening power, but inside that brilliant glow they stood serenely, eyes closed and faces relaxed.

Surely they must feel that, he thought. With that much energy pouring through their bodies, how could they not? But they seemed not to notice the light crackling between them.

A hantick later, he was musing on the fact that a person could get used to just about anything. Nothing more had happened; Tal and Salomen were still standing calmly in a curtain of fire. But they had been standing there long enough that Micah had already come to see it as merely extraordinary rather than shocking. He'd enjoyed watching the other Guards make their own discoveries, though. It was easy to tell when they opened their eyes because of the sudden involuntary jerk of their bodies. But to their credit, not a single one of them broke the connection.

His wristcom vibrated, and a voice spoke into his ear.

"Colonel Micah, this is Colonel Razine. Lancer Tal's com code is locked out on a privacy setting. Do you know where she is?"

He tapped his earcuff and spoke quietly. "In the State House. I'm with her."

"I need to speak with her immediately. I'm outside her office now."

"Is this critical?"

"Yes."

The very lack of detail said it all. "Understood. She'll be there in three ticks." He tapped out of the call and punched a breakthrough code into his wristcom. A moment later Tal lifted her head, looking at Salomen for a moment before slowly bringing her hands away. The brilliant glow vanished, and Micah breathed a sigh of relief.

"Lancer Tal, you're needed in your office right away," he called.

Tal nodded. "Take a break, everyone. You deserve it after that. And thank you—we've now eliminated all of Argolis and the northern coast of Pallea. I wasn't sure we'd make it across the ocean, but at this point I think we may be able to reach all the way to Last Port."

A murmur of agreement followed her as she made her way through the huddle and trotted up the stairs to Micah. "What is it?"

"Colonel Razine is waiting outside your office. She says it's critical."

"Let's hope that for once, 'critical' means 'important in a good way.'" Tal went out the door.

CHAPTER 28
Traitor

Colonel Razine waited until they were inside Tal's office, with the door shut and the security lock engaged, before she shared her news.

"It worked," she said.

For a moment Tal thought they had found Herot. Then she realized. "Salir called our traitor?"

"Almost immediately. We've spent the time since then tracking financial records for verification. I don't think we have them all yet—they're very well hidden—but we have enough."

"Well? Who is it?"

"Parser."

"Parser?" Tal repeated. "We were looking for a warrior!"

"We made an assumption. We thought that if someone could interfere with an investigation, it had to be a warrior. But the abuse of power has never been limited to our caste."

Her words kindled the deep anger that had been simmering in Tal ever since her meeting with Donvall at the Pit. "So the man who created the task force is the one profiting from it. Our respected Prime Merchant, the one who spoke so eloquently about the integrity of his caste after the Redmoon fusion disaster. The one *I* chose to help fight corruption. That miserable pile of dokshin! Tell me you have him in custody."

"He's in holding at Blacksun Base."

"Hung upside down by his ankles, I hope. That anyone would betray the purpose of the task force has already been churning my stomach. That it's Parser, of all Alseans—I'd like to throw him on the Council chamber floor and tell the warrior caste to do as they see fit."

"And the merchant caste," Razine added. "They have every reason to feel just as betrayed."

"Yes, they do. When this goes public, Parser will have more enemies than he can count. If he ever gets out of prison, I wouldn't give good odds on him lasting more than a day." Tal stopped and took a calming breath. "Tell me everything."

"Salir called Parser less than three hanticks after you met with Ehron. She probably made the call as soon as Ehron passed on your order to meet with you; she was in a panic and wanted Parser to tell her what to do. Parser was angry that she'd called—I'm guessing she was never supposed to contact him via vidcom or anything that could be tracked. He told her never to call him again, especially not for something so trivial as answering a few questions about the task force. Then he killed the call."

"He knew it was being tracked. Everything he said gives him deniability."

Razine nodded. "But he can't deny his financial records. His accounts show an enormous increase over the last cycle, and that's just the ones we've found so far. There is no possible way Parser could be that wealthy from his Councilor's salary or his legal enterprises. By this morning we had enough evidence to detain him and search his house and office. Guess what we found when we combed through his reader card?"

"Fifteen hidden accounts where he's stashing his real wealth."

"Those, too. But that's not what will interest you most. We found a number of message accounts under false names, sitting in cities all over Alsea, and all collecting information from various sources. You know one of those sources. Or perhaps I should say, Raiz Opah knows him."

A chill went down Tal's spine. "The Granelle merchant."

"Spinner is Parser. He's been spying on you and making plans for several moons now, though to what end I'm not certain. He's not giving me anything useful, and I can't get any more information without a warrant for empathic force. But I did just complete his empathic scan, and there is no doubt of his guilt. Parser is our traitor."

"Damn that little worm!" Tal exploded. "How are we to repair this damage? The task force was corrupt from birth! And the damage to the Council is even worse. Any Councilor would have been bad, but the Prime Merchant? This will rock the public faith in the Council, as if we had that much to begin with."

She wanted to break something and thought darkly that Parser's face would be an excellent place to start. At the very least, she planned to be there when they executed that warrant for empathic force. She would take great pleasure in watching Razine split his mind wide open and pick every ill-gotten bit of information out of it.

"I'm not a politician, Lancer Tal, so I won't presume to advise you on Council issues. But it seems to me that if the merchant caste responds promptly, they might be able to resolve the issue of public trust by stripping Parser of his caste."

Tal raised her eyebrows, impressed by Razine's ruthlessness. "That hasn't been done in a very long time."

"Perhaps there hasn't been quite such an egregious abuse of power in a long time."

"Yes, there has. But this one was caught, and that makes all the difference." Tal was already weighing the pros and cons of approaching the Chief Merchant, Parser's second-in-command, and proposing such a drastic action. Then she wondered bitterly if the Chief Merchant was in as deeply as the Prime Merchant. Where did the corruption end?

"He asked to speak with you," said Razine.

Startled out of her line of thought, Tal snapped, "I do not wish to hear one word from that pathetic excuse for an Alsean."

"I don't blame you. I had to listen to him all morning. But he made what I believe is a credible threat."

Her first thought was to dismiss any threat made by a disgraced politician in detainment, but Razine was an experienced investigator who did not jump to conclusions, nor worry without cause.

"What was it?"

"He said that your lover has already lost one member of her family, and it would be too bad if she lost another. Particularly since you would be to blame."

Tal's anger contracted into a dense, icy core. *Anything to do with the Opahs*, Pendar had said, and she suddenly knew why Parser had been paying a spy in Granelle.

"You're right, it's a credible threat," she said. "Those were Parser's warriors in the transit station. He has Herot."

CHAPTER 29
Game of tiles

Tal rarely came to this part of Blacksun Base. The prisoners here were nearly always in judicial limbo: charged with a crime but waiting for their hearing. Somewhere in here, she knew, Cullom Bilsner was awaiting his hearing for attempted assassination. She also knew that it would be a very short hearing with a foregone conclusion. When a prisoner's guilt was already established by a corroborated empathic scan, there was little left to accomplish at the hearing itself other than an assessment of the severity of the crime, an accounting of any previous offenses, and the sentencing. Bilsner's crime had a preset severity of a level-five state offense; the sentence would be life imprisonment. Tal felt no pity for his self-destruction. He had come very close to taking away the most precious thing in her life, and that she would never forgive.

For high empaths, the procedure was different. Because an Alsean with sufficient strength and training could defeat an empathic scan, these individuals entered their hearings presumed innocent and the burden of proof fell to the state. Such hearings took much longer, and sometimes the quality of the final judgment was questionable, but there was no better alternative.

"He's in here." Colonel Razine stopped in front of a door halfway down the corridor. "I'll be outside."

Through the large window in the door, Tal saw Prime Merchant Parser sitting on the bunk, his expression one of martyred forbearance. He looked up at the sound of the door opening and smiled as she and Micah stepped into the room.

"Lancer Tal, what a pleasure. I would offer my hospitality, but I'm very short on spirits at the moment. Or a chair."

Tal stood in the middle of the tiny room, her arms crossed. "Or honor. Stooping to blackmail now, are you?"

Parser waved a hand in dismissal. "Blackmail would imply you have something to hide. We all know you have far too much *honor* for that. What I propose is more along the lines of an insurance agreement." His gaze moved past her. "Perhaps your Guard would wish to wait outside?"

"Colonel Micah wishes to break your neck, actually, but I've managed to restrain him for now. He stays."

"I see. Well then, since I have no hospitality to offer, and you don't seem to be in a hospitable mood, we should probably begin our negotiations."

Tal said nothing, hoping to unnerve him, but the man was insufferably confident. Parser was a mid empath, and she had no difficulty skimming him. She did not like what she saw.

"Let me be the first to congratulate you on an admirably quick investigation," he continued, unaffected by her silence. "I didn't guess you would find me so soon after your meeting with Donvall. But I'm quite pleased you did, since the cost of maintaining Herot Opah in proper security isn't cheap. I was hoping I wouldn't have to lay out that expense for too long."

"Wages are lower in southern Pallea," Tal said, taking a shot in the dark. She skimmed him, looking for his reaction to her guess, but found nothing. The worm was *smiling* at her.

"Ah ah." He waved a finger. "I don't know where he is, so probing me won't help you. That would be foolish of me, wouldn't it?"

"Get on with it, Parser. Or should I call you Spinner?"

His smile grew. "Oh, very good. I wasn't expecting you to hunt that one down. But I'm not surprised you did. Here's the difference between you and me: I never underestimate an opponent. That's why I win, because I respect the abilities of those I'm working against. But you don't even pretend to have respect for me. That has always been a failing of your caste. Warriors simply assume they're better than any other caste, despite ample evidence to the contrary. But it wasn't warriors who found your missing assassin, was it? It was the merchants. A man on the run can go a long way without ever being seen by a warrior, but he has to deal with merchants if he wants food or a roof over his head. My web is spread all over this planet, Lancer Tal. You may have the title, but I have the power."

"And you wield it with all the usual integrity of your caste. For a man who defended the merchants so eloquently, you're certainly proving the warrior caste's point. Shantu was right."

"Shantu is a fool. He helped me form the task force and never saw what I didn't want him to see. And if you're trying to anger me, you're failing miserably. What you call integrity, I call simple-mindedness. You hobble yourself with your beliefs. That's why you lost this game before you even started playing. The tiles are already laid on the board, and you stepped into the trap the moment you had me brought here."

"Not a very elegant trap," Tal said. "Holding a hostage and threatening murder seems a rather blunt instrument for a game player like you."

"What matters is the end result. Now, I did mention negotiations, but in truth I have only one offer. Don't fool yourself into thinking you have options. You will release me, and you will give me the vid that you are undoubtedly making as we speak." He waved at the featureless walls, where a tiny hidden cam was indeed documenting their meeting. "You will then record a special announcement for tonight's news broadcasts. In it, you will state that you had me brought in for questioning regarding corruption in the task force, but I've been absolved of any suspicion and you formally apologize for any mark on my reputation. You will then announce that the true culprits have been caught: a merchant named Falton Mor and a warrior named Alanor Salir. Detain them, give me your recording by eve-three, and I'll make sure it gets to the appropriate individuals in the media. Then you'll get your assassin back."

Tal had to admit the man was clever. By personally announcing his detention and then clearing his name, she would be mixing just enough truth into the lies to make it nearly impossible to bring him down later. Any attempt would no doubt be met with a media blitz that would be extremely damaging to her own reputation. Admitting she had made the original announcement to save the brother of her bondmate would only make her look worse, particularly to the warrior caste. She would expose herself as weak and easily controlled, and a vote of no confidence would be almost guaranteed.

"There's one problem with your plan," she said. "You're counting on the fact that I have a vested interest in Herot Opah's safety. I don't. If you kill him, you'll save me the effort."

"Oh, I don't doubt you have a personal issue with him. I'm also certain you wouldn't mind at all if he turned up dead. But it's not whether he dies. It's *how* he dies. If you don't agree to my very reasonable offer, Herot Opah will be killed by the Lancer's own warriors. I think that will be enough to put you right out of office, don't you? I can't imagine your lover will appreciate it, either."

His face grew hard. "You're still thinking you're better than me, when the truth is that I've outmaneuvered you at every turn. The moment your AIF warriors came to detain me, a vid made its way to every major media branch on Alsea. As you stand here, wasting time trying to find a way out, all of Alsea is watching Herot Opah being escorted out of the Napoline transit station by two Lancer's Guards. Imagine their surprise to learn that, instead of being detained, he was taken out and murdered. Two of your real Guards will also be found dead—the killers, of course. They'll go to an early Return from the shame of their actions, but fortunately, they'll leave a final communication explaining that you ordered the revenge killing. It's hard to see how such evidence might be questioned when the whole world already knows that your Guards found Opah and took him from Napoline. Bypassing justice…" He shook his head. "Not a good trait in a Lancer. Neither is murder. And violating the sanctity of family, as well—you ordered the death of your own lover's brother. Even if you subject yourself to an empathic scan, it can't be used in your hearing because you're a high empath. And adjudicators can be bought."

He made a show of brushing invisible lint off his trousers. "It's really not such a difficult decision. Agree to my terms and keep everything as it was. You even get to give your lover the gift of her brother's life." Looking up with vicious triumph, he added, "Or you can say no and be responsible for three deaths and the loss of your lover, your title, and your freedom. I don't imagine you'll last very long in prison, not without your precious Guards to keep the other prisoners from killing you."

It took every bit of Tal's empathic strength to front her rage. Her hands itched to beat that smirk off his face. And the worst of it was that she could not see a solution. She felt battered by the scheme Parser had laid out so matter-of-factly, every sentence another door closing on an avenue she hadn't yet had time to think of. He had even taken away her most desperate option of sacrificing Herot to the pursuit of justice. She would be forced to use the vid of their meeting to prove her innocence—but it would also prove her culpability in letting Herot die. Salomen would never forgive her.

There was only one weakness she could see in his plan, and she prayed he might be just a little overconfident.

"Very good," she said. "You've covered every possibility but one."

"And what is that?" He leaned back on his hands.

"You may have a broad web, but you're out of communication with it now. You can't order Herot's death from in here. I'm afraid we'll have to detain you a little longer—in the high empath block." Which would mean automated food delivery and zero contact with other Alseans, including warders.

His laughter filled the tiny room. "Go right ahead. I never intended to order his death." He stood, exuding nonchalance, and walked into her personal space. "I've been ordering his *life*. His guards have standing instructions to kill him in the absence of our daily communication. He lives from one day to the next because I say so. And the next scheduled contact is in, oh…" He craned his head to look at her wristcom. "About one hantick from now. You'd better hurry, Lancer Tal."

Her thumbs were pressed into his windpipe before she registered the thought. "Then you'll make that call from here," she snarled.

"Can't," he rasped.

For a moment she seriously considered crushing his throat. With an enormous effort of will she shoved him away, disgusted with herself that he had been able to break her control.

He stood at a safe distance, rubbing his throat but still giving her that damnable smile. "My warriors won't accept any communication unless it's from my vidcom unit at home, accompanied by a code. And just in case you're thinking of breaking the law yourself and empathically forcing me, don't bother. Their instructions also include a warning to kill Opah if I appear to be giving them any instructions that don't make sense or fail to coordinate with earlier communications. Give up, Lancer Tal. I told you the trap was sprung the moment you detained me. You're standing in it now. The only way you'll get out is if I open the door."

They stood in silence while she thought furiously. It didn't help. Parser had won, and Herot was the key to it all. If she could find him and pull him out before eve-two tonight, she could avert the whole disaster and take great pleasure in burying Parser. Failing that, her only other option was to give him what he wanted and work on a way to take him down later. It would mean a whole mudfield of cover-ups and lies, and she would have to play a very careful game. But she couldn't worry about that now.

"You've gone to a great deal of trouble," she said. "Everything neatly in place to strip me of my title and put me away. How do I know you won't do it once I give you what you want?"

"Because this isn't personal. It's business. I don't want a new Lancer in your place—then I'd have to watch and wait and set up a whole new trap to make sure your successor is under my control. I want a Lancer I can work with. You can keep your title; I know exactly how little it's worth." He straightened the sleeves of his jacket. "Time for a decision. Will you keep me here and lose everything? Or will you taint yourself with just a little whiff of corruption?"

As she stared him down, she knew he was lying. It *was* personal. Whatever secondary goals Parser was accomplishing, the primary one was to stain her reputation with the very thing she had publicly ordered him to regulate in his own caste. This was revenge.

She turned and looked through the window at Colonel Razine, who nodded and opened the door. Tal stepped into the corridor and snapped, "Free him."

"What?" Razine was so stunned that it took her a piptick to get her front back in place.

"You heard the Lancer." Parser emerged behind her, followed by a murderous-looking Micah. "It appears that my detention was an unfortunate mistake." He looked at Tal. "The vid?"

Gritting her teeth, Tal said, "Get him the vid of our meeting."

Razine looked between them, her eyes narrowing. "Yes, my Lancer."

"I'll accompany you," Parser said, stepping to her side.

Razine stalked away without acknowledging him, and the two of them vanished through one of the many doors in the corridor. Tal heard raised voices, then a sharp order, and a moment later they reappeared. Parser was insufferably smug, and Tal would have given almost anything for the chance to kill him. Herot had no idea what he was costing her.

"Process him and get him out of here," she told Razine. The colonel clearly wanted answers, but she pressed her lips together and silently walked away.

"Have the announcement at my house by eve-three," Parser reminded her. "If it's not there by then, I'll assume you're breaking our agreement." He gave her a mock bow. "Good day, Lancer. It's been a pleasure doing business with you. Oh, and one more thing: be glad it was Herot. My original target was Jaros, but Herot made himself far more useful."

He turned and caught up with Razine, leaving Tal faint with fury as she watched them disappear around the corner.

"What are you going to do?" Micah asked quietly.

Tal was still staring down the empty corridor. "Make two announcements," she said. "And pray that we can find Herot in time to air the right one."

PART THREE:

PLAYING TO WIN

CHAPTER 30
It's still magic

ON THE RETURN FLIGHT, TAL ordered Micah to redirect Salomen's entire Guard unit to Hol-Opah, retaining only her Lead Guard. While he was doing that, she made a vidcom call to Shikal explaining why.

"Well, at least Jaros will enjoy this," she said bitterly after ending the call. "He gets his own personal Guard at last. Shikal and Nikin aren't quite as happy about theirs."

Micah couldn't think of a single appropriate reply. Instead, he busied himself with his own order to Tal's Guards, instructing them to return to the training room in half a hantick. Tal would produce the announcements by that time and rejoin them for their next attempt at finding Herot. At this point, every tick counted.

When Tal tapped her earcuff, Micah knew who this call was going to and why she wasn't using the vidcom. In the four-seater transport, he had little room to give her privacy, so he looked out the side window and tried not to listen to Tal's strained voice.

But it was impossible not to hear. Salomen wasn't taking it well, and when Tal finally tapped out the call, she simmered in a tense silence that lasted the rest of their flight. Micah felt guiltily grateful when she vanished the moment they landed. He had seen her this tightly wound only once before, and felt just as helpless now as he had then.

When she was late for the next Sharing, Micah used the opportunity to fill in the Guards on what he could. As he expected, they immediately channeled their anger into a cold determination. What he hadn't anticipated was that Salomen would do the same thing. His respect for her rose another notch; the woman really did have a warrior's heart.

Tal arrived ten ticks later. Her expression was thunderous, and she swept into the training room as if she planned to walk right through the wall on the other side. The hum of conversation ceased instantly as every Guard stood alert.

"Has everyone rested enough to try it again?" she asked without preamble.

The general affirmation didn't change her expression.

"Good, because we need to finish this. Right now. Salomen, are you ready?"

"We're *all* ready," Salomen answered.

"Then get in position, everyone. We'll go straight to Whitemoon and start from there." She turned to Salomen and whispered something to her as the Guards formed their huddle. They made a curious picture as they stood there, a motionless island in the center of the shifting Guards. A few pipticks later the shifting ceased; by now the Guards had this down to a routine.

Micah watched carefully while Tal and Salomen made their connection, and this time he saw it from the start. It began with their hands, which first glowed red, then orange, then the yellow-white color of molten trialloy. The streaks of light shot outward, swiftly merging with others and weaving themselves into the rippling curtain of fire he had seen during the previous Sharing.

He had asked Salomen about it while they waited, learning to his surprise that she had never seen it before, either. The glow was a visible form of the energy being channeled by their Sharing, she said. It was tremendously boosted by all the Guards focusing their own powers and manifested itself in this extraordinary, all-enveloping flame.

A perfectly sound explanation, he thought. But it was still magic.

Tal's face showed no signs of her prior anger; she had slipped back into whatever mental state allowed her to guide the combined energies of twenty-three people. In the silence, Micah settled himself against the wall, preparing for a wait. He prayed to Fahla that it wouldn't be too long.

CHAPTER 31
The payoff

Parser tightened the belt on his robe as he walked into his study. He had taken a shower immediately after arriving home, needing to wash off the stench of the holding cell. It had been a necessary part of the game, but that place was more unpleasant than he had anticipated. A single bunk, no chair, a toilet in full view of anyone watching from the corridor—how could a person be expected to live in such conditions?

He popped the top off a bottle of Tollisan and poured himself a glass. It was still early in the day, but he deserved this. After ten moons of patient waiting, his plan had come to fruition. By the time he went to bed tonight, he would be the most powerful man on Alsea.

And that was just the beginning of what he planned to accomplish. Even after he spelled it out for her, Lancer Tal still didn't know what she was dealing with.

But she had a clue now, didn't she?

He sipped his Tollisan, appreciating the fine flavor, and smiled to himself. If he lived to be a hundred and twelve, he would never forget the look on Lancer Tal's face when she realized the trap had closed on her. That alone had been worth every bit of his planning and investment. That she had lost control to the point of trying to kill him...

He rubbed his throat and laughed.

"And the best part," he said aloud, "is that I have it all on vid." Sipping his drink, he crossed the room to his desk, where the vid chip sat in the exact center. It was another insurance policy: proof of the Lancer's corruption. She had let him walk out of prison despite his confirmed guilt. Of course, it was proof of his corruption as well, but in certain circles, that wouldn't matter. What did matter was the evidence of his ability to control her.

He picked up the chip and held it to the light. An insurance policy and a source of endless entertainment, all in one. In fact, he was going to watch it now and relive one of the finest moments of his life.

Right after he gave the order to let Herot Opah live for one more day.

CHAPTER 32
Plan of action

Tal lost all track of time. The effort of focusing so much power from such diverse sources took every bit of her concentration; she had none left to be aware of anything outside their link. For that matter, she had none left even to help Salomen search. If Salomen had any doubts about the strength of her own gift, this would surely lay them to rest. She was single-handedly leading all of them, taking the energy Tal poured into her and flying all of their minds high over Pallea, methodically eliminating one sector after another. It was painstaking work, with none of the pleasure they normally found in a Sharing. But it was also covering more ground in a single morning than an entire army of investigators could cover in a moon's time. They were already at the midpoint of Pallea, and since this part of the continent was sparsely populated, they should be able to cover it quickly. Tal just hoped she had the strength to keep going. The first Sharing today hadn't been nearly as taxing as this one, so she guessed they had been in the link quite a bit longer.

The directed pattern of their flight suddenly shifted. Salomen was doubling back, taking a closer look at something. She had done this several times already, and Tal wearily waited for her to satisfy herself and move on. But now Salomen was circling, homing in, and the hope that blossomed in her mind touched every person in their link.

"Is it…?" Tal whispered.

"I don't know. I think, maybe… Oh, thank Fahla! It's him! It's him, oh, Herot…" Salomen's emotions overwhelmed her, shattering the concentration that had enabled her to guide their Shared search.

With the sudden disappearance of a focused receptacle, all of the power Tal was channeling ricocheted back and crashed into the power still coming in from the Guards. The opposing streams detonated in a white-hot storm of energy that roared through her, immobilizing her limbs and burning out her empathic senses in an agonizing flare. Her body flew backward, slamming into Gehrain and the Guards behind him and sending three of them down in a pile with a stunned Tal on top. Still paralyzed, she could not even put out her hands to stop her fall. She rolled to the floor, landing at an awkward angle and fighting her sluggish lungs as she tried to breathe.

"Andira!" Salomen was next to her, an arm around her back, her panicked voice loud in Tal's ears. "I'm so sorry! Are you all right? Please, please be all right!"

Much as she wanted to, Tal couldn't answer.

"Everyone step back. Give her some air," Micah said from somewhere above her.

Thank you, Micah, she thought. And perhaps it was simply the knowledge that she wasn't so hemmed in, but as the press of bodies moved away, her rasping breaths eased. Now if only her head would shrink back to its normal size so she could lift it.

"Talk to me, anything, please! I can't tell if you're—" Salomen stopped with a small gasp, and the sheer terror in her voice gave Tal the strength she needed.

"I'm all right," she said thickly, and tried to push herself up. Unseen helpers pulled her into a sitting position, but her head was still too heavy and she cradled it in her hands. "Damn, that hurt. Let's not do that again."

Salomen moved closer, reaching out with shaking hands. "No, never, I didn't mean to," she said in a rush. "I didn't even think—" She stopped again, and even through the throbbing in her skull, Tal knew this wasn't just about her.

"It's all right. I'm fine. Really."

"Are you sure? I can't feel you."

"I'm sure." With an enormous effort, she lifted her head. "But I have to tell you, that was the biggest shekking flash of all time."

Salomen's laugh was too harsh and higher than normal. "Fahla, you scared ten cycles off the end of my life!" She laughed again, then sucked in a breath as Tal leaned over to rest her pounding head on her shoulder. Holding Tal's head with one hand, she kissed her hair and whispered, "I'm sorry, tyrina."

"Don't be," Tal mumbled into her shoulder. "You found him. That's the important thing."

"I can't believe it. Honestly, I didn't think we would."

"But you did."

"We did." The emotional overload was easing; Tal could hear it in her voice. "But I lost it. Andira, he was hurt and frightened. They're hurting him."

"That's about to end." Tal took a deep, grateful breath of air and straightened. The throbbing was beginning to fade. "Do you remember where we were?"

"In general, yes, but we lost the link before I could really focus on it."

"Micah?"

"I'm right here." He knelt beside her.

"We need a topographic map of central Pallea," she told him. "Detail to one hundred paces."

"I'll have one here in two ticks. Anything else?"

"How about a new head?"

He smiled. "Sorry, my friend. You'll have to make do with that one. But I can bring in some food and water if that would help."

Come to think of it, she was starved. "What time is it?"

"Mid-one and twenty."

"We've been in the link for two hanticks?" Great Goddess, no wonder she was tired. She looked up, seeing for the first time the ring of concerned faces around her. "You must be ready to eat the practice mats in here."

"Well, the black one was starting to look pretty good," Gehrain said, causing a ripple of nervous laughter among the other Guards.

"Micah, while you're getting the map, contact the kitchen and get a midmeal sent down." At his nod, she looked back at her Guards. "We're taking a break. It's past time to eat, but we'll have to make it fast. Hopefully, by the time we've gotten some food inside of us, I'll have a normal-sized head again and we can go back for another look. Now that we know where Herot is, we need to examine his location more closely. I want to know how many Alseans are there, what they're feeling, and where they are in relation to Herot. I want all of you to pick up as much detail as you can, because we're going on a mission. Herot will not be spending one more night as a hostage."

CHAPTER 33
Fear and failure

Their assessment of Herot Opah's location revealed three warriors in close proximity: one in a holding area with him and the other two posted just outside. They hovered as long as they dared, waiting to see what the nearest warrior was doing, but to everyone's dismay, he did nothing at all. Vellmar watched in sympathy as Lancer Tal explained to her bondmate that there were only two reasons to put a warrior inside the holding area with a prisoner. One was to question or intimidate him, but this warrior had done neither.

The other was to ensure the prisoner's instant death in the event of a rescue attempt.

Given the situation, Raiz Opah took this news surprisingly well.

They found five other warriors in the near vicinity, most likely the second shift, and a careful examination of the surrounding area revealed two additional guards posted at a perimeter. Both external guards were posted at high points in the topography, giving them good views of a large area. Parser was taking no chances with his valuable hostage. Lancer Tal said she was not surprised; her interview with the man had made it clear that he believed in covering all possible options. While he had never expected Herot to be found, he had taken precautions just in case.

Their best option was immediately ruled out. They had the numbers and weaponry to simply overrun the building where Herot was being kept, but the threat to him made that impossible. Instead, they would need to land their transport at a distance, hike in unseen and unheard, take out the two perimeter guards, and then send in two teams. One would silently disable the guards near Herot and extract him, while the other would neutralize the five guards off shift.

Since the off-duty guards were spread throughout the building, it would be difficult to coordinate the two mission objectives. Until Herot was secured, the team in charge of neutralization would not be able to act for fear of raising an alarm. Nor would any use of disruptors be possible until then. That left knives, and as the best blade handlers in the group, Lancer Tal and Vellmar were natural choices for the primary mission.

There could not be a more perfect vindication against all the warriors who had ever looked down on her for having subpar accuracy with a disruptor.

After her practice session with the Lancer, Vellmar had mere ticks to pack for the mission. She hurried to her quarters and gathered her gear with glee. Perhaps it was inappropriate to be so excited when the Bondlancer's brother was in danger, but she couldn't help it. A covert mission her first day on the job? And as the Lancer's chosen second? Life did not get better than this.

When Lead Guard Ronlin caught her on her way out, she remembered that not everyone was so fortunate. Opah's new Guards had just sworn their oaths and then promptly been left behind. Not that keeping the Bondlancer's family safe was a bad assignment, but…it certainly wasn't a rescue mission.

"Where are you going with that?" Ronlin crossed his arms over his broad chest.

Vellmar shifted her bag over one shoulder. "You know I can't tell you."

"That's dokshin. You think I don't see what's happening here? You're going with *my* oath holder! I'm her Lead Guard, not you! She's my responsibility."

In his indignation, he pushed himself into her personal space, making their height difference clear as she looked down at him. But he was built like a cargo transport. With his arms bulging and his face nearly as red as his hair, he looked as menacing as the Bondlancer's Lead Guard should.

She would have been just as angry in his place. Lowering her voice, she said, "It's a covert mission. Only those trained for it are going. It's no reflection on you, just that you're too new on the scene."

"And you're not? I was here before you. Don't try to feed me that fanten food."

"Lancer Tal chose me for my blade-handling skills. She needed a specialist."

There was little he could say to that, though she thought she could hear him grinding his teeth. When he uncrossed his muscular arms and poked her in the chest, it was like being hit with the end of a staff.

"Then you're Lead Guard for both of them right now, which means I am holding you personally responsible for Raiz Opah's safety."

"I'm sworn to Lancer Tal first. But I promise you that I will look after them both."

His scowl lessened slightly. "On your honor?"

"On my honor."

"See to it, then." Without another word, he stalked away.

When she rejoined the others in the staging room, she found another disappointed Guard. Standing next to Lancer Tal and looking startlingly like her was Varsi, now with blonde hair and blue eyes. The colorizers had done a good job, and in one of the Lancer's fine suits, she could easily pass for her at a distance. Her part of the mission was to be seen around the corridors and grounds of the State House in case Parser's spies were watching.

Chief Counselor Aldirk arrived, looked Varsi up and down, and said, "She makes a better Lancer Tal than you do."

The Lancer smiled. "At least we know that if I don't return, there will be no interruption in government."

Vellmar laughed along with the other Guards, but when she caught sight of Raiz Opah, her amusement ended. Opah was fronting it perfectly, but the fear was visible in her eyes.

She forgot about it during the excitement of leaving. The Lancer's long-distance transport was a luxury ride, its enormous main cabin effortlessly swallowing all of its passengers and their gear. Vellmar chose a seat near the back, wanting a quiet location to complete her mental preparations.

To her surprise, Lancer Tal and Raiz Opah walked past her to sit in the very last row. She would have expected them to fly in their private cabin, but after a moment's reflection, she realized that Lancer Tal did not want to remove herself from her team before the mission. She was not the Lancer now; she was the team leader.

For two hanticks, Vellmar watched the scenery pass beneath them, letting her mind go quiet and calm. When the coastline of Argolis floated past, leaving nothing to see but ocean and a few clouds, she emerged from her mental state and became aware of a hushed conversation going on behind her.

Remembering Opah's look of fear, she guessed what this might be about. When their voices suddenly rose in volume, her guess became a certainty.

"What more can I say to convince you? This is part of what I do!"

"You are the leader of our world! How can you risk yourself like this? It's folly!"

Vellmar blinked at the anger in Raiz Opah's voice.

"Because I'm also the leader of my caste, and I don't lead by staying safely behind a desk while others take the risk! Trust me, that's not the way to earn the respect of the warriors." Lancer Tal paused, then continued in a calmer tone. "Tyrina, I've trained all my life for missions like this, and I've successfully completed quite a few before now. Please give me some credit for being good at my job."

"'Good' is not good enough. You expect too much from me. How am I supposed to sit here while not one but two members of my family are in danger?" Raiz Opah lowered her voice slightly. "You had better damn well be perfect."

"I promise you that I will be."

"You cannot make that promise."

"Then what do you want me to do?" The Lancer's voice rose again. "You're asking for assurances you won't believe!"

"I want you to stay here! You have twenty Guards on this shekking transport, and only six of them are going in with you. Surely you can find someone among the other fourteen who can throw a knife."

Vellmar winced. She was embarrassed to be hearing such a private argument, but if she got up and moved now, it would look too obvious. She slid lower in her seat and stared fixedly out the window.

"Thank you very much for your staggering estimation of my skills."

"I'm sure your skills are just fine. I'm also sure that this transport is full of equally skilled Guards who have less to risk."

"Equally—! Goddess above, Salomen! Do you have so little understanding of who I am? Whatever happened to the greatest warrior of her generation? Did you think I spent the Battle of Alsea hiding in a transport, letting others do the work?"

"You cannot compare the two! Our entire world was at risk then. This is not the same thing."

"No, now it's my title, my government, and your brother's life at risk!" Lancer Tal let out a frustrated growl. "I should have known this was coming. You never asked because you didn't want to know. And you really *don't* know."

A harsh clink indicated a harness buckle being thrown aside with some vigor.

"Where are you going?"

"To my cabin! Maybe I can get the mental space I need to *not get myself killed* there! Please do me the courtesy of giving me a little privacy. I cannot do this now, Salomen. I just can't."

Lancer Tal brushed past, her anger showing in the stiffness of her bearing as she strode up the aisle.

Vellmar watched out of the corner of her eye, trying not to appear as if she had noticed anything. She sympathized; an argument like this was extremely detrimental to a warrior's readiness. Raiz Opah was tough and strong, but she clearly did not understand her bondmate.

Several ticks passed as Raiz Opah shifted repeatedly in her seat. Vellmar wondered if she should go back and say something. Perhaps she could help. But it wasn't her place, and she had no right to presume that level of intimacy. Then again, no one on this transport had that level of intimacy. Perhaps she should brave it after all.

She went back and forth in her mental argument at least three times before the issue was taken out of her hands when Colonel Micah walked past her. The creak of a seat indicated his greater weight settling down.

"Are you all right?" he asked quietly.

"Not really." Raiz Opah's voice was strained. "Colonel Micah, can you not talk sense into her? She doesn't need to do this! I don't understand why she's insisting on it. It's dangerous and unnecessary, and it scares me halfway to my Return. And it's not as if she can claim she doesn't know what it's doing to me. I'm sitting here terrified, and she's angry with me!"

"Ah. You argued over her choice to lead the primary mission?"

"Why is she doing it? Why? It's…it's just foolhardy!"

There was a long pause.

"Salomen, I must ask you—did you say that to Tal?"

"No. Well, not like that."

"What did you say?"

"I just pointed out the fact that there are other people on this transport who could be going instead of her."

Vellmar could almost hear the colonel stifling his groan. His front was weak.

"What?" Raiz Opah asked. "What was so wrong about that? It's true."

"No, it's not. And you offered her grave disrespect by saying it."

"For Fahla's sake, I did not disrespect her. I just—"

"Implied that she is no more accomplished or qualified to lead than any of the Guards who serve her. But worse than that, you told her that she's not likely to succeed."

"That is *not* what I meant."

"But it's what you told her. And it's what she's feeling from you, isn't it? She feels your fear."

"How am I supposed to not be afraid? I can't hide that from her."

"No, but you can tell her that despite your fear, you know she's the best person for the mission and that she's coming back to you. That's what she needs to hear. No, please, listen to me. This is important, and your understanding may affect whether Tal walks out unscathed or not."

After an electric silence, Raiz Opah said, "I'm listening."

"Thank you. You're a courageous woman, and I know that has been taxed to the limit recently. You have every right to be fearful. But you're Tal's bondmate, and that means you have a power no one has ever had until now. You can give her strength, or you can take it away. And right now that power is more important than anything you personally feel. If you let your fear for her overwhelm you, she'll be handicapped at a time when she needs every advantage. She'll be distracted by worry and the echoes of your fear, and that can easily mean her death."

Though Raiz Opah's front never wavered, Vellmar knew the colonel's words were hitting her hard.

"If you're trying to frighten me even more, you've certainly succeeded."

"In a way, I am. I need you to understand the power and responsibility you hold. And you need to understand who Tal is. You are not bonded to a scholar; you're bonded to a warrior. And not just any warrior, but the leader of our caste. She did not reach that position by standing in the back of her unit while others earned the honor. She got there by being out in front, every time. Sometimes her role as leader of Alsea is secondary to her role as leader of our caste, and this is one of those times."

"With all due respect, that's dokshin. She is the *Lancer*. That should never be less important than her caste role. She has a responsibility to the people of Alsea."

"Yes, she does. A responsibility that she cannot carry out without the support and respect of her caste. We're not a perfect caste by any means, and Fahla knows we have our quirks. We'll overlook bad judgment and poor decisions—up to a point—but we will not overlook cowardice or dishonor. Tal understands that, and she knows the obligations of her role. She knows she has to do this or lose face in the eyes of her caste at a time when their support is critical. More than that, she *wants* to do this. We all do. There are quite a few Guards back in Blacksun who were unhappy to be left behind, including all ten of yours. You must accept that this is part of Tal's identity, the same way she accepts that your bond with Hol-Opah is part of yours. The question is not whether she should go. You need to set that aside. The only real question is whether you will help or hinder her, and right now, you're hindering her."

Vellmar was impressed, not just with Colonel Micah's argument but also with the fact that he was speaking with such brutal honesty to the Bondlancer. Apparently, there *was* someone on this transport who could presume a high level of intimacy with her.

"All right, fine. I don't like it, but I can see that I have no choice."

"No, you don't. I'm sorry for that, and I could wish that you'd had much more time to learn and understand our code. You've been on a ride you never asked for, and I have nothing but the deepest admiration and respect for how you've handled it so far. Truly, I could not have chosen a better bondmate for Tal."

"Thank you. Though I don't feel like a good bondmate at the moment. She's up there in her cabin, seething because of me. At least I understand a little better why she's so upset. But I don't know how to fix it. I cannot change my emotions, and I can't front them from her."

"But you can choose which emotions you give the most weight to. We're two hanticks away from a dangerous mission, and each of us prepares for that in our own way. I know how Tal prepares because I taught it to her. It's one of the fundamentals of our code—visualize your success and achieve it; focus on your failure and sink. Tal is imagining the mission, from every angle she can think of, with every possible variation. And every one of them ends in success. If one of her imaginings leads to failure, then she goes back and rethinks it until she figures out a way to make it end successfully. But I suspect she's finding it difficult to concentrate because she thinks you don't believe in her. And if she can't visualize her success, then there's a very good chance it won't happen. So you need to tell her that you *are* sure she'll succeed, and that she *is* the right person to lead the primary mission. She understands your fear. But she needs to be able to set it aside, and she cannot do that if she believes that your fear comes from a certainty of her failure."

"Shek. You ask as much from me as she does."

His voice was gentle. "I ask only what the Bondlancer should give."

After a pause, Raiz Opah spoke so softly that Vellmar could barely hear her. "I'm just so tired of being afraid."

Their voices dropped even further, and Vellmar became aware that she was putting far too much effort into listening. It was one thing to be unable to avoid hearing and another to actively intrude on someone's privacy. Ashamed, she yanked her gear bag open and noisily rustled around in it before taking out a well-worn book. Opening it to her marker, she did her best to lose herself in the text. But she had barely read two pages before Raiz Opah walked past, her head high as she made her way to the other end of the main cabin. Vellmar lowered her book and looked after her. It had never occurred to her how difficult it might be for members of other castes to understand her own.

A heavy hand on her shoulder nearly jolted her out of her seat. Colonel Micah looked down at her with a knowing expression. "And how are you doing?"

"I'm counting the ticks," she said, trying to ignore her embarrassment. "And looking forward to bringing Raiz Opah's brother back."

He squeezed her shoulder. "You and me both, Vellmar. Let's make sure it happens."

"Oh, it will," she said confidently. "Lancer Tal is leading us."

He smiled broadly, squeezed once more, and moved back to his seat.

CHAPTER 34
Extraction

Leaving Salomen in the transport was even more unsettling than Tal had expected. First Pilot Thornlan and two heavily armed Guards remained with her, while four more kept a perimeter around the landing site, scanning for any approach. Thornlan was under strict instructions to evacuate if the perimeter was breached.

She made sure Salomen was nowhere in hearing range when she gave that order.

It had been a difficult decision to bring her at all. Tal had wanted to leave her in the safety of the State House, preferably surrounded by at least thirty warriors, but Salomen objected vociferously. She pointed out that she could hardly be safer than in a transport filled with Tal's most trusted warriors, which Tal acknowledged was true—until most of those warriors left the transport to carry out the mission. Then Salomen reminded her that magnifying their range required both of them, and if Tal wanted any more information on Herot or his captors once the transport left Blacksun, she had two choices: bring her tyree, or walk up to that building, knock on the door, and make polite inquiries.

There were times when Tal wondered if she would ever win an argument again.

But Salomen was right. The presence of those outlying guards necessitated a landing two valleys away from Herot's location, and only by Sharing after their landing was Tal able to determine that they were still undetected.

Her final preparation entailed pulling Salomen into a long, fervent warmron. Just before she stepped out, Salomen stopped her with a touch and said, "Come back to me."

One hantick of hard hiking later, Tal was still reeling from the words and their staggering import. This mission had the single objective of rescuing Herot, but Salomen had made her own priority very clear. She had not said, "Bring Herot back."

Tal would do everything she could to prevent her from living with such a choice.

It had been several moons since she last hiked terrain this steep. Central Pallea was nothing but high ridges and narrow valleys, blanketed by dense forest that shut out the light but not the stifling heat. The forest floor was soft with the remains of leaves from many winters past, making their footing difficult. They could not see the true contours of the land, and at one time or another, all of them found the seemingly solid ground giving way beneath them. It was impossible to hike quickly when every step had to be taken with such care.

Vellmar stepped into a hole so deep that she toppled over, forced to twist and fall to save her leg. Tal halted in alarm, dreading the thought of losing their best blade handler, but Vellmar pulled herself up again, took a few steps, and gave Tal a nod.

They moved even more carefully after that.

Though they were all in excellent physical condition, every one of them breathed a sigh of relief once they made the top of the second ridge. When they settled onto the spongy ground for a well-earned break, Tal popped the mouthpiece of her water flask between her teeth and gratefully sucked down what seemed like half her supply. She was certain she weighed less now than when she had left the transport, and her damp uniform was palpable proof.

They were all wearing covert mission uniforms, which used nanotechnology built into the fabric to detect localized light wavelengths and match them. Here in the deep forest, their uniforms blended perfectly with the various shades of green. The fabric was also effective at conducting moisture across a one-way differential, so the fact that she could feel any dampness at all meant she had been sweating a great deal.

She gave everyone five ticks to rest and hydrate before motioning to her two optics teams to start the search. Somewhere on this ridge, far to the left, one of Parser's warriors was keeping watch. The other was on the ridge across from them. While the optics teams scanned for the outlying warriors, the rest of them studied the large, dilapidated domed building sitting in a clearing below.

"I see Parser spared no expense for housing," Tal whispered to Micah. "That thing looks like it could fall on their heads at any moment."

Micah nodded, still watching the building through his own scanning glasses. "Not good," he whispered back. "Old construction like that is going to make noise when we move through it."

"Think we should keep the secondary team outside until Herot is secured?"

"Too dangerous. The moment you start taking out guards, you elevate the risk of discovery. You don't need five other warriors descending on you while you're trying to get Herot out."

The air shifted next to Tal, and Vellmar noiselessly crouched beside her. "Heat signatures show no change in their numbers," she whispered. "And there are no unusual animals inside."

Tal nodded. Since heat scanners were in the toolboxes of most well-equipped warriors, a means of defeating them was a necessary defensive capability. The technology to completely conceal body heat had not yet been invented, but it could be redirected via a small powered unit worn on a belt. Different models produced different heat signatures. If by any chance the enemy guard on the next ridge focused a heat scanner on them, they would appear as a herd of boren, grazing animals common to this terrain.

The fact that the enemy numbers hadn't changed meant their original count, based on the empathic search, was accurate. There were no warriors in there maintaining a perfect front. Tal and every one of her Guards, on the other hand, would be doing just that the moment they moved off this ridge. Only Micah lacked the ability, but Gehrain was strong enough to wrap his own front around Micah's mind. Their empathic stealth would enable both teams to move through the building while maintaining an invaluable advantage: they knew where their enemies were, yet were invisible themselves. Only a visual sighting would set off an alarm.

"Targeted," came the whisper from her left. Tal watched a Guard press the stabilizer on her optic scanner and then back away. The scanner hovered in place while her partner moved in behind it, peering through toward the opposite ridge. He nodded, deactivated the scanner, and handed it back. Both of them looked at Tal, who pointed toward her eyes and then made a fist.

Get a target lock. Go.

The two Guards vanished without a sound. Theirs was the most difficult job of all: they had to get over to the opposite ridge as quickly and quietly as possible, working through an area under constant observation. The primary and secondary extraction teams could not move until both outlying guards had been neutralized.

The guard on this ridge was more difficult to locate due to their near-parallel positions, but a slight curve of the topography gave them the angle they needed. As soon as the second optics team found their quarry, Tal sent them on their way. She and the remaining ten Guards settled in for a wait.

Twenty ticks later, a message on Tal's wristcom notified her that the second team was in place. The team crossing the valley took another thirty ticks, no more than expected given the terrain. As soon as she received their notification, Tal tapped her earcuff and whispered, "Neutralize. Now."

Both confirmations arrived mere pipticks later. Her warriors were swift and deadly, but they had still burned up half a hantick just to remove the two easiest guards. Tal looked up at the sun, already low in the sky, and shook her head. They were on schedule, and she had planned the operation for just after dusk, but she couldn't shake the sense of a looming deadline.

She rose, drawing the eye of every Guard, and made an "O" shape with her fingers and thumb.

We're clear to proceed.

In less than half a tick, all eleven of them were over the ridge and moving silently downslope. They would be joined at the bottom by the other four Guards, who had been instructed to regroup just outside the clearing around the house. Their new job would be to guard the house and clearing, watching for any possible reinforcements or escapees once the real assault began. A second set of four Guards would also remain outside the clearing, ready to storm the house the moment the extraction team was clear. To make that easier, they would wire the front door for a quick entry.

They arrived at the rendezvous point and paused to check their gear one more time. The sun was below the ridge now, drawing a lengthening shadow across the valley, but it wasn't yet dark enough for Tal's tastes. She was not about to lead six warriors across that clearing until she was sure they wouldn't be instantly visible to anyone looking out a window.

She centered herself and extended her senses, verifying the locations of Herot and his keepers now that she had the building in front of her. The situation near Herot was unchanged: he still had one warrior with him and two just outside. Of the other five guards, two were relaxing—and probably drinking—in a room upstairs, two were together on the opposite side of the building from Herot, and one was walking away from Herot's location. He was fronting, but not well, and she could sense irritation and relief. She frowned. He had most likely just been relieved of duty, which meant that one of the guards with Herot was fresh and alert. Probably all three of them; the guards upstairs weren't relaxed enough to have been drinking long.

Her wristcom vibrated, and she looked down to see a message from one of the Guards on the perimeter.

Opah's window is boarded. No entry.

Well, she hadn't expected it to be as easy as killing Herot's in-room guard with one quick shot through the window. That was why she and Vellmar had spent most of a hantick practicing their throwing. Not that Vellmar had needed it; that woman was deadly accurate from the very first throw. But Tal hadn't done much blade handling in the last moon except for a hantick here and there, when she found time to unwind with Micah. Still, it didn't take long before her muscle memory kicked in. Once she was warmed up, they worked on coordinating their throws, which Tal enjoyed despite the situation. Accurate throwing required a perfect bonding of brain with body, and there was something almost poetic about the feeling it brought.

The shadows were deepening. It was time.

Tal chose a first-floor window on Herot's side and broadsensed once more to be sure that none of the guards were looking outside. Their emotions showed no sign of nervousness or alarm. Satisfied, she held up her forefinger and thumb in an L shape and looked at each member of the two teams in turn. Every one of them responded with a short nod, and she closed her hand into a fist.

Let's go.

Vellmar and Senshalon were right behind her as she ran to the window. Senshalon was the largest of her Guards, and she had chosen him specifically for his physical strength. The three of them flattened themselves against the wall, watching, sensing, and waiting. Then Tal held up her fist, and Micah led his team across the clearing to join them.

So far, so good.

Vellmar pulled out a power-sensing unit, scanned the window, and held up her hand palm outward. The window was wired for an alarm. She took four thumb-sized power routers from her pack and attached one outside each corner of the window, routing the alarm's power up and over the window before it continued on its normal path. After a second scan, she nodded.

Senshalon reached into Vellmar's pack and extracted a large suction cup. Pressing it to the window, he used a plasma pen to melt the glass in a thin line, drawing a person-sized square around the suction cup. The bottom cut was flush with the window frame, allowing for the easiest entry. With a soft exhale, he lifted out the glass and walked away, carefully leaning it against the wall several paces from the others.

Tal put her hands on the frame and silently hauled herself up.

She was facing a dark bedroom, sparsely furnished with a bed and desk. The bed was directly below the window, and she prayed that it wouldn't creak when she stepped on it. Turning herself in the opening, she lowered her legs onto the bed and only gradually allowed her weight to settle, holding her breath. It made no sound, even when she stepped off it.

Vellmar and Senshalon followed her in, and when the bed stayed quiet even under Senshalon's weight, she knew it would be fine for the rest. As he was stepping off, Tal moved to the door. Micah would monitor his own team; this was where they split up.

The house was old, its doors opening on hinges rather than power slides. Tal had anticipated that possibility and quickly sprayed the hinges and latch with lubricant. The door opened without a sound, revealing a curving hallway.

Herot was being held down the hall to her right, toward the back side of the dome. She extended her senses, relieved to read Herot's guards in the same place as before and no others within a dangerous range. Holding up her fist, she opened the door all the way and moved out, keeping to the wall.

They were halfway to Herot's room when Senshalon's weight caused a floorboard to creak. To Tal's sensitive ears, it sounded like a falling rock hitting a boulder.

All three of them froze in place.

Tal had been constantly monitoring the guards outside Herot's room and knew they heard the creak. One dismissed it. The other was curious, but not enough to leave his post to investigate.

She pointed at Senshalon and motioned for him to go in front. As he passed, she unsheathed one of her throwing blades, hearing a soft snick behind her as Vellmar pulled hers as well.

They made it ten more paces before Senshalon set off another floorboard. Once again they froze, and this time the guard's curiosity turned into suspicion. Voices indicated a short, irritable argument between him and his partner at the door; it sounded as if the suspicious guard was being accused of manufacturing a reason to leave his post. These two were bored with their duties.

With a final sharp statement to the remaining guard, the suspicious one began moving toward them. Tal waited, expanding her senses to all of the guards in the house. None seemed concerned, least of all the woman still at Herot's door. Her strongest emotion was annoyance.

Senshalon dropped into a crouch three paces ahead, poised for a sprint, while Tal and Vellmar drew their arms back. The footsteps approached, the emotional presence grew stronger, and then the guard came around the curve of the hall.

Tal made an instant adjustment for his height and let her blade fly, seeing Vellmar's arm flash down at the same moment.

The guard saw them, widened his eyes, and died with one blade embedded in an eye socket and another in his heart. He did not utter a sound as he crumpled, nor could his last thoughts betray them. Tal had wrapped her own front around him, shutting off his surprise from detection by the others.

Senshalon was already running toward him even as the knives had been released, and just managed to catch him before he hit the floor. He lowered the dead man the rest of the way, pulled out the knives, and wiped them clean as Tal and Vellmar joined him.

Once the three of them had repositioned for the next strike, Tal readied her knife and centered herself. Focusing on the other guard at Herot's door, she projected emotions and doubts.

Curiosity. Where did he go?

The guard was reluctant to leave her post. She had her orders, and due to Tal's forceful prevention of suspicion, she saw no reason to override them.

Curiosity. Annoyance. No harm in leaving for a moment. Probably just a stupid joke. Idiot. Tal injected an expectant annoyance.

No harm. No harm. Just for a moment. Curiosity...annoyance...joke.

She felt the guard's purpose tilt over the edge and nudged Vellmar.

They waited as she continued to project onto the guard, whose footsteps were now sounding down the hall. Before the woman came fully into view, Vellmar's blade was in the air, followed almost instantly by Tal's. They struck in precisely the same locations as before. Senshalon was in a better position for this kill and caught the dead guard while she was still upright.

From there it was just a few steps to Herot's unguarded door.

Tal reached into her thigh pocket and pulled out a small device, remembering vividly the last time something like this had been used on her. She motioned Senshalon to one side of the door and Vellmar to the other while she stood directly in front, her thumb hovering over the activation button. Focusing once again, she projected emotions onto the guard inside.

What the shek...? Idiots. What are they doing out there? Irritation.

This one was more resistant than the woman; he was better trained and more highly skilled. But he was no match for Tal. In fact, all three of these warriors were less skilled than she had expected. They felt more like mercenaries than sworn warriors.

Sharpening her senses, she pressed harder.

Irritation. Am I the only one who does my duty? Irritation…irritation…anger!

At last he responded, and she wrapped her front around him as he moved. A heavy footfall landed just inside the door as it was yanked open. "What the—?"

He froze under the assault of her immobilizer, his mouth still open in the middle of the last sentence he would ever utter.

It was not the way she would have preferred to deal with him, but his proximity to Herot meant they could not risk an attempt to kill him with a knife. The only way to be sure he couldn't get off a shot was to prevent him from moving at all.

He thudded to the floor, his tongue partway out and his eyes bulging. This time Senshalon could not stop the noise of his fall. The effects of an immobilizer passed easily through touch, and this was a lethal model.

Tal pushed the door open as far as she could with the guard's body blocking it and found Herot sitting on a rumpled bed, his eyes wide with fear. Had Vellmar not wrapped her front around him before they even opened the door, his terror would have given them away.

"Lancer Tal!" he said much too loudly.

She shook her head and put a finger to her lips, then focused on the dying guard.

He was by far the worst one. The other two had died instantly, but death by immobilizer was slower and much more terrifying. He stared up at her, unable even to blink, desperate and panicked in a way that came not from the higher emotional center of the brain, but from the more primal core of instinct. Buffeted by the sheer power of this deeper fear response, Tal struggled to maintain her extended front. This felt like the foulest kind of violation, denying him the chance to be empathically heard even in his final, dying burst of terror. It was one of the worst deaths imaginable, and the only way she could even slightly redeem it was to look into his eyes, giving him a connection with another Alsean as he felt his life draining away. At the last piptick, his terror faded and was replaced by another deeply instinctive response: the acknowledgment and acceptance of death.

Then he was gone.

Tal closed her eyes and took a deep breath as she reached out for her tyree. It was impossible to absorb a death like that and not feel emotionally soiled. She needed to touch something more innocent, something far removed from the reality of what she had just done. Salomen was there, and Tal knew she had some idea of what had just happened. But her support was unwavering and exactly what

Tal needed. Opening her eyes again, she met Herot's gaze. For just a moment, she saw his sister's eyes looking out from his face, and smiled without thinking.

Though the eye color was the same, the fear in them was not. Tal snapped back to reality, pocketed the immobilizer, and pushed through the narrow opening. Vellmar scooted in after her, and the two of them dragged the guard farther into the room. Senshalon entered behind them and closed the door.

Tal crossed to Herot and whispered, "Can you walk?"

He looked with horror from the dead guard to her. At last he said, "No. I tried to escape two days ago, and they broke my ankle. I can't put any weight on it."

She wasn't surprised. When Salomen had first sensed his pain, she suspected it might be from beatings that could result in a lack of mobility. It was another reason for choosing Senshalon.

"Anything else hurt?"

"No."

He was lying. His face was bruised and scraped, and the stiff way he held himself indicated more bruising under his clothes. But nothing seemed in need of immediate medical attention, and Tal respected his pride.

"He'll carry you," she whispered, pointing at Senshalon. "Do not make a *single* sound, do you understand? No matter what you see or hear."

"I understand. But I can't leave."

She followed his pointing finger downward. He was shackled to the bed with cuffs and heavy cables.

"I see you managed to irritate these guards too." She motioned Senshalon forward and pointed to the cuffs.

He pulled the plasma pen from a thigh pocket and quickly severed the cables. Turning his back, he crouched down and whispered, "Climb on."

Herot put his arms over Senshalon's shoulders and scooted up against him. Without so much as a grunt of effort, Senshalon straightened with his arms under Herot's thighs, hoisting him on his back. "Ready," he whispered.

Tal expanded her senses and was relieved to feel no alarm from the other guards. She tapped her earcuff and said, "Target acquired." The secondary team was now free to use disruptors if necessary. It was going to get noisy very soon.

Leaving the com channel open, she led the way out. This time they didn't worry about creaking floorboards, moving as quickly as they could back the way they had come. Tal stayed out in front and Vellmar covered their rear, both of them constantly scanning for any approach. To Herot's credit, he did not utter a sound as they passed the two dead guards in the corridor.

A shout shattered the silence, followed quickly by the sound of disruptor fire. None of it was near them, and they reached their destination without being seen. As they flattened themselves against the wall, well out of the way of the front door, Tal barked, "Blow the door!"

With a deafening roar the door exploded inward, setting off a screeching alarm. Two Guards leaped through the opening, disruptors at the ready. Two others began raining disruptor fire on every window in the front of the house, preventing any chance of an enemy warrior getting off a shot as Tal's team sped through the gaping hole and across the clearing. As soon as Herot was in the cover of the woods, Tal called out, "Target is safe! Wrap them up!"

It was all over in a few ticks. Though the alarm still shrieked, the shouts and disruptor fire had gone quiet. The whole operation had been flawless, and Tal allowed herself a sigh of relief. Time to get out of here.

"Lancer Tal to all teams. Check in."

"Team green, two enemy dead upstairs. All clear."

"Team red, two enemy captured, three dead downstairs. All clear."

Tal waited, then frowned at the delay. "Team blue, check in."

No response.

"Team blue, respond." She waited another five pipticks, but there was still no answer.

"Shut off that shekking alarm!" she shouted to no one in particular, and two Guards scrambled to obey. "Teams green and red, stay put and wait for further instructions." Pulling a frequency locator from her pocket, she snapped, "Who has the heat scanner?"

"Right here, Lancer." Vellmar appeared in front of her.

Tal scanned for the frequency signatures of every wristcom in the area and frowned. "I've got Gehrain's, but not Micah's."

"And the heat scanner shows eleven bodies in the house," Vellmar said. "We're missing three."

They stared at each other.

"Basement," they said simultaneously.

"Shek! Damn that Parser!" Tal tapped her earcuff again. "Lancer Tal to teams; we're missing one enemy warrior and possibly more that didn't show up on heat or empathic scans due to underground locations. Team blue may be in pursuit. Start looking for an access to a basement."

She tapped out and thought furiously. Gehrain's wristcom was transmitting a strong signal, so there was no reason for him to be silent unless he was in pursuit of the last guard—or unable to respond. And where the shek had Micah gone?

"Vellmar, see if there are any suspicious large animals around here."

"You think there's another entrance to the basement?" Vellmar asked, watching her scanner as she slowly turned in a circle. Her voice was loud in the sudden silence; the alarm had stopped at last.

"I'm certain there is. The question is whether anyone has popped out of it."

Vellmar completed her circle. "And the answer is…no."

"So far." Tal looked up at the Guards waiting nearby. "Assume that we still have active enemies in the area and take no chances. Senshalon, you're with me.

Vellmar, you're in charge out here. Stay on Opah with two others, put four on perimeter, and watch that heat scanner like a winden with a newborn."

Vellmar immediately began organizing assignments while Tal called Thornlan.

"*Yes, Lancer,*" came the instant reply.

"Get ready to transfer to my wristcom location. There's room to land. Don't come until I give the word; we're still securing the area. But you can tell Raiz Opah that her brother is safe. Call Aldirk right now and tell him to activate the safe vid. And tell Colonel Razine that she is now free to act."

"*Confirmed.*"

Tal made a sharp motion to Senshalon and jogged back across the clearing. She swore quietly as they crossed the shattered threshold. Having to reenter the site of a covert mission was a sign of bad planning.

"Why didn't we think of a basement?" she muttered.

"We were in a rush," Senshalon said. "And basements aren't common in Blacksun Basin."

It was an understandable lapse. But Fahla, that fantenshekken Parser thought of *everything*. Which made her wonder why he hadn't kept Herot underground as well. If he had, they would never have found him.

She could think of no answer to that one. A tick later, she forgot the question.

CHAPTER 35
Team blue

By the time Micah's team had gathered in the dark bedroom, Tal's team was already out the door. Gehrain confirmed that none of the guards in the house were alarmed. Everything was going according to plan.

If this house was like most, the staircase would be near the front door. They had entered to the right of it, as close to Herot's location as they could safely get. Micah led his team out of the bedroom and turned left. When they arrived at the staircase, he held up two fingers and pointed. Dewar and Nilsinian peeled off and began ascending the stairs, while Micah waited just long enough to be sure that no creaking steps would give them away. Sure enough, the old stairs protested their weight, but if any of Herot's guards heard, they assumed it was from one of their own. Gehrain kept his hand in a fist, indicating that they were still undetected.

Nilsinian gained the second floor and waved behind him.

Micah left his Guards to their work. He knew them well, and as far as he was concerned, the upstairs was already secured.

Their own targets were still separated. Two guards were together in one room, and a third was unmoving some distance away. Micah crept cautiously to the arch on the other side of the stairs, freed a tiny cambot from his belt pouch, and sent it just around the corner. The vid feed on his wristcom showed a living area furnished with old chairs and a rug that looked ready to crumble. The room had an abandoned air; this wasn't where the guards spent their time.

A flick of his finger sent the cambot across the empty room to the archway on the opposite side, where it revealed another curving corridor that most likely went around to the back side of the dome. Two doors were visible before the curvature of the hall hid the rest.

He motioned to Gehrain, and they quickly crossed the living area to crouch against the wall beside their hovering cambot. Micah sent it into the corridor to peek through the first doorway, seeing an office crowded with dusty bookshelves and a large, dented wood desk. A man and a woman sat in overstuffed chairs in front of the desk, which housed a pile of papers, an open bottle of spirits, and two mostly empty glasses. They were speaking animatedly, and Micah quickly tapped his wristcom to activate the audio feed and send it to his earcuff.

"—*getting tired of it. I think they might walk.*"

"*Yeah? I'm getting tired of their complaining. They try walking and they'll see the wrong end of my disruptor. Does no one understand the significance of an oath anymore?*"

"Shek, Oren, none of us swore a damned oath. Except Periso, and that woman is insane. The pay isn't enough for the kind of duty we're pulling. For Fahla's sake, we're in the middle of shekking nowhere! Why are we killing ourselves guarding that little dokker? He's not worth anything alive. I hear the Lancer wants him dead."

"She doesn't want him dead, you grainbird, don't you ever check your caste account? She put out a directive ordering him to be kept safe."

"Well, I have no idea why. If I were her, I'd want him dead. Come to think of it, I want him dead anyway."

The man laughed. "Still upset about the nose, eh?"

"Shut the shek up."

With another laugh, Oren picked up the bottle and refilled their glasses. Micah wished he could hear more, but they had no time. He pulled the bot out of the doorway and left it hovering just outside as he held up two fingers for Gehrain, then pointed at the arch and held up one.

Two guards. First door.

Gehrain nodded, and Micah sent the bot to the next door. Finding it closed, he dropped the bot all the way to the floor and extended a tiny tube into the space beneath the door. Though the image it sent back was difficult to make out, it was enough to eliminate the room, which appeared to be an empty closet.

The doorway after that revealed their third guard, relaxing on the bed with a reader card. Micah showed Gehrain the footage, then pointed at the arch and held up three fingers.

Reconnaissance completed, he recalled the cambot, plucked it from the air, and returned it to its pouch. From a second pouch he produced a thin, transparent cable and snapped one end of it into an adhesive peg.

Gehrain held out his hand for the cable and second peg. As he snapped in his end, Micah attached the first peg to the side of the archway, less than two handspans above the ground. Gehrain secured his peg on the other side, wound the cable tight, and locked it down while Micah set an immobilizer to wide dispersal. Once it was connected to the trip line, they put their backs against the wall on either side of the archway and drew their goodnights.

Micah had a special fondness for these weapons, so rudimentary yet effective. They were nothing more than a grip and a spring-loaded shaft with a flat, weighted end, designed to disable without permanent damage. One swing and an opponent would be instantly unconscious. Sometimes, he thought, the simplest things still worked the best.

The house was silent, save for the murmur of voices and an occasional laugh from the office. Micah didn't need Gehrain's senses to know that Tal's team was operating undetected. These two had no idea that they were losing their hostage and their salaries even while they drank.

He was jerked out of his musings by the silent vibration of his wristcom. Lifting it, he read the message from Tal.

Target acquired.

He smiled. She had Herot.

Still they waited. Unless it became absolutely necessary, no one on his team would make a move before Tal's team was out.

A shout sounded upstairs, followed instantly by disruptor fire. Nilsinian and Dewar had been seen.

"What the shek?" Oren bellowed from the office.

Chairs scraped as Oren and the female guard scrambled out. They barreled through the archway, flying over the trip line and sprawling paralyzed on the floor. Keeping clear of the immobilizer's dispersal angle, Micah and Gehrain swung their goodnights and put both guards out of commission. Gehrain deactivated the immobilizer and jumped through the arch in pursuit of the last one, while Micah pulled out tielocks and swiftly locked the wrists of the unconscious guards. He had just snapped the second one shut when the front door blew in and disruptor fire began tearing up the outside of the house. Tal had gotten Herot out quickly.

Micah pulled his own disruptor and ran after Gehrain.

"Colonel! Down here!"

Following Gehrain's shout and the sound of weapons fire, he found a closet door standing open in the now-empty third room. But when he reached it, he realized it wasn't a closet—it was a wooden staircase leading down.

"Damn," he muttered. They hadn't considered a basement. There could be anything or anyone down here. He tapped his earcuff and opened his mouth to alert the unit, but a tremendous crash distracted him, followed a piptick later by a disruptor shot impacting the doorway over his head. Debris rained down and knocked him off his feet. He fell several steps down the stairs before stopping, then had to throw himself the rest of the way down as disruptor fire tore chunks of dirt and rock from the wall where he had just been. At the bottom he dove under the staircase, taking the nearest cover available.

"Micah to unit," he said breathlessly. "There's a basement access in the third room from the living area. We're in pursuit—"

The steps just over his head blew apart, and he flattened himself to the dirt floor. Deciding that his unit knew enough for now, he concentrated on saving his skin and finding this damned guard. He pulled out his cambot and sent it airborne, looking to his wristcom for the vid feed and sucking in a breath when he saw the damage to his arm. Between his uncontrolled descent of the stairs and the rock shrapnel flying around, he had managed to scrape a good portion of the skin off his arm, resulting in a bloody mess. That wasn't the problem, however. The shattered and blackened screen of his wristcom worried him a good deal more. He was cut off from his unit.

"Gehrain!" he shouted. There was no answer but the sound of someone running away from him, deeper into the dimly lit basement. Carefully, he poked his head out.

A shape flitted away, too short to be Gehrain and with the wrong stride. He sent several shots after it, his aim hampered by the stairs, then scrambled out and went in pursuit.

The guard stopped and fired, and Micah dove to the side. Rolling to a crouch, he returned fire, cursing the lack of cover. What little there had been was back by the stairs.

His quarry resumed her dash, running in an irregular zigzag for the opposite wall of the basement, where a metal power panel reflected what little light there was.

Micah noted the shiny newness of the panel compared to everything else in this house and made a snap decision. If it was important enough for this woman to ignore disruptor fire, then it was important enough to be destroyed. Adjusting his aim, he sent a series of shots at the panel, blowing it out in a shower of sparks and metal shrapnel.

With a shout of rage, the guard turned on the spot and fired.

Micah pushed off, rolling away, but there was nowhere to hide and the disruptor fire followed him faster than he could move. A searing heat ripped through his side, shoving him backward and slamming his head into the dirt floor. Disoriented, he clenched his hand around his disruptor and tried to lift it, but the weapon seemed to weigh far more than normal.

It didn't matter, he thought calmly. He couldn't see anything anyway.

He heard running footsteps, the deep slam of a heavy door, and then nothing.

CHAPTER 36
Path of the Return

"Lancer Tal! Over here!"

Following Nilsinian's voice, Tal and Senshalon ran into the living area and paused at the sight of two unconscious guards lying facedown with their wrists bound behind them.

"We found the entrance." Nilsinian led them across the room and down the curving corridor. "Colonel Micah and Head Guardian Gehrain got those two, so we started looking here. We didn't have to go very far."

He jogged past an office scattered with papers and turned into a bedroom that showed signs of recent use. Rubble littered the floor near an inside door, and Tal stopped at the opening. Crashing sounds emanated from below.

"Are the others already down there?" she asked.

"Yes. It's clear; no heat signatures except our own. Colonel Micah and Head Guardian Gehrain are injured. We don't know how badly; the others just went down. I was just about to call you."

Tal was halfway down the stairs before Nilsinian finished speaking.

"Look out for the last few steps!" he called after her.

She barely registered the destroyed steps with their sharp and blackened splinters, vaulting onto the floor from the last intact step above them. Now she could see the source of the crashing sounds: a Guard was pulling crates off a pile and throwing them to one side. As she ran over, a body came into view beneath them.

"Lancer Tal." The Guard grunted, pulling off another crate. Now that she was close enough, she could see it was Corlander, one of the assault team members who had gone in after blowing the door. "Head Guardian Gehrain isn't badly injured so far as we can tell. But you need to see Colonel Micah." He threw the crate away and pointed into the dimness, where two light beams flashed and shifted.

"Senshalon, help Corlander." She trotted as fast as she dared across the uneven dirt floor.

The lights were from headbands worn by Dewar and Windenal, Corlander's partner. They were bent over a huddled mass on the ground.

Tal sprinted the last distance, skidded to a halt, and dropped to her knees. "Oh, no," she breathed. "What happened?"

"We don't know." Dewar sealed the oxygenator over Micah's nose and mouth. "But whoever did this is gone. And they didn't come up the stairs."

Belatedly remembering her own headband, Tal pulled it from her pocket and slipped it on. Her eyes watered as she looked more closely at the wreck of Micah's body.

A disruptor hit to his right side had done horrific damage, tearing open his lower torso, hip, and thigh. The dirt beneath him was wet with blood, and only after seeing it did Tal realize that the knees of her uniform pants were soaked. The blood loss was severe, and they were in the middle of nowhere.

She couldn't accept this. Micah bore as many scars as the rest of them, but he had never been badly hurt before. She hadn't thought it was possible. Not Micah.

Something soft thumped to the ground beside her.

"Lancer Tal, I need to wrap him," Dewar said gently.

Tal nodded and stood back, watching in helpless grief as her medic unrolled the pressure sack. Dewar called Nilsinian over and fired off rapid instructions to both of her assistants. It would take all three of them to gently maneuver Micah's body into the pressure sack, which would prevent additional blood loss and give them more time to get him into surgery.

Tal was now a bystander, her main task that of staying out of the way. She should have been offended at the way Dewar had simply elbowed her aside, but she couldn't summon the emotional energy. Instead she felt sluggish and foggy, staring at Micah's white face until she had to close her eyes against the sudden sting.

He would not Return. It was not his time! They would get him to a healing center, and the healers would take care of him, and he would be back to normal. He had to be. She refused to consider any other option.

Healing center. Yes. She needed the transport. Tal felt the fog thinning, and with an enormous effort she pulled herself out of her stupor. Taking a few steps away, she called Thornlan and quietly told her to retrieve her perimeter Guards and make haste to the new landing coordinates. "We have a medical evacuation," she finished. "Notify Redmoon. They're the closest."

"We'll be there in five ticks."

Her next call was to Vellmar, informing her of their medical situation and the transport arrival. "Get everyone onboard the moment that ramp hits the ground," she said, watching the activity around Micah. "We need to be in the air as soon as possible."

"Yes, Lancer."

Wrenching her gaze away from the sight of Micah's limp body being lifted and handled, Tal looked around. Why had he let himself get caught so far from cover?

Her eye was drawn to the blown-out power panel on the opposite wall, and she walked over to inspect the ruined contents. She didn't think it was an accident that this panel had been hit. Beyond the melted and scorched area, it shone with the brightness of new metal, an aberration for the dusty old house.

"What were you doing, Micah?" she murmured.

A metal tube led from the panel to the ceiling, where it branched and ran in both directions along the edge. Wires sprouted from it at regular intervals, perpendicular to the main trunks, carrying power somewhere. Her light showed a wiring grid overhead and a regular series of holes drilled into the ceiling. She took a few steps away from the wall, shining her light over the ceiling. The grid reached as far as she could see. Turning in place, she looked at the panel once more, then played her light along the wall. Hidden in the dimness just a few paces away from the panel was something else that didn't belong.

She stepped to the new metal door, reaching out with her senses and finding herself quickly blocked. At least she knew there was no one directly behind it. This had to be the other exit from the basement, and given her limited empathic reach, she guessed it led to a curving tunnel.

Carefully, she pulled it open a crack and shone her light through. In contrast to the thick, heavy door, the tunnel behind it was narrow, rough-hewn, and barely large enough for her own head to clear. Anyone taller would have to walk bent over. She was examining the oddly thick door when Senshalon walked up.

"Lancer Tal, Gehrain's awake. He was just knocked out by the crates collapsing on top of him." He looked down the tunnel. "Well, now we know where the last guard went."

"Yes," she said bitterly. "And we don't have time to give chase."

Senshalon stepped through and investigated the entrance from the other side. Ducking back into the basement, he said, "There's old framing around the other side. The door is new, but the original frame isn't. And that tunnel smells old, too."

It did. She hadn't consciously noticed, but the tunnel smelled just as stale and musty as the basement. "So this house was built by someone paranoid, and repurposed into...what? Why such a heavy door?"

"Well, it would stop disruptor fire."

"It would stop just about anything." She didn't have time to think about it anymore. "Go help Dewar with Micah."

As he walked toward the frantically active group around Micah, she recrossed the basement to where Corlander was crouched by Gehrain's prone figure.

When she reached Gehrain, he was rubbing his eyes. "Lancer Tal," he said as she came into his view. "I'm sorry; I couldn't stop her. She was down the stairs before I even got through the door, and I never could catch up."

"You did your best," she said. "None of us thought about a basement."

"Senshalon wouldn't tell me about Colonel Micah. Is it bad?"

"May I see him?" Corlander asked.

"Go. Dewar can probably use all the light she can get." She knelt beside Gehrain. "It's not good. Dewar is putting him in a pressure sack, and we're getting him to Redmoon as fast as Thornlan can fly. I'm just glad you weren't seriously hurt. How do you feel?"

He rubbed his eyes again. "Fine, except for the lights. I must have hit my head pretty hard."

"Your vision is affected?"

"I think so. I'm seeing pinpoints of light—wait a tick." His gaze sharpened as he looked at her. "I'm not seeing them on you." Looking straight up again, he said, "I'm seeing them up there."

Tal followed his gaze and found a small red light blinking at her, directly over Gehrain. Another blinked a few paces away, and now she could see several others in the ceiling around them, forming an incomplete grid.

"Spawn of a fantenshekken. That's where the power was going. It was another shekking trap!"

"What? I'm sorry, my brain isn't in full working order yet."

"Micah's was," she said, glancing back at what she could see of him between the others. "He saved a lot of lives today. Can you stand up?"

"I think so." He sat up carefully, then took her hand and allowed himself to be helped upright. "I'm fit," he said as he took a limping step.

Tal thought that might be an overstatement, but she wasn't about to argue. "Everyone not needed for evacuating Micah, get out of this building *now*," she shouted. On the other side of the basement, five light beams sliced toward her. She pointed upward and added, "The whole building is wired to blow. Micah managed to cut the power to most of the charges, but there are still a few operating." And she didn't think an attempt to cut the remaining power was something they wanted to chance, not with the panel already partially destroyed. "We have a missing enemy guard, and if she has a backup transmitter, we could be in trouble. Move it!"

"Goddess above," Gehrain said, staring upward.

Tal heard a burst of voices at the other side of the basement, recognizing Dewar's in the end. Two shapes left the huddle around Micah and began racing toward them.

She wrapped her arm around Gehrain's waist and pulled his arm over her shoulders. "Come on. Let's get you out of here."

Corlander and Windenal joined them as she led him to the stairs, wondering if she was making the right decision. The tunnel was undoubtedly the safer exit in terms of a potential explosion. But she had no idea what else—or who else— might lie in wait there. Or how long it was, or where it ended. No, better to count on the building staying intact for just a little longer.

She released Gehrain into Corlander and Windenal's care, watching as they helped him past the damaged steps. When they were clear, she hauled herself up and crouched on the first intact stair. "Dewar, how close are you?" she called.

"Right behind you." Dewar, Nilsinian, and Senshalon emerged from the dimness, carrying Micah in a clasped-arm sling formation. "I would have preferred waiting for a stretcher from the transport, but…"

"I know. We can't afford to wait." Tal reached out and took the weight of Micah's upper body, backing up two steps until Dewar and Nilsinian climbed past the damaged section and retook their positions. As soon as Senshalon was on the stairs, she turned and hurried to the top. Kicking the rubble out of the way, she led her last Guards out of the bedroom and down the corridor, the back of her neck tingling with every step. Knowing what was right under her feet was disquieting, to say the least, and she breathed a sigh of relief when she emerged through the blown-out front door and saw blessed stars overhead.

The transport crouched in the empty clearing. The only Alseans in sight were two Guards standing watch just beyond the ramp and Vellmar racing toward them with a stretcher.

"Put him on!" Vellmar called over the roar of the engines. "We're ready to go as soon as we get him in."

"Have you counted bodies? Do we have everyone?" Tal was taking no chances.

"You're the last," Vellmar answered, watching as the others gently lowered Micah onto the stretcher. "Our missing warrior never did appear."

"She must still be in the tunnel. What I wouldn't give to drop a shock charge down it," Tal said darkly.

"Words for Fahla," Senshalon said. The others murmured their agreement.

Several hands made short work of the security straps. Vellmar and Senshalon picked up the stretcher and dashed toward the transport at a near run, with the rest in hot pursuit. Tal brought up the rear, and the last two Guards swung in behind her when she hit the ramp. They crowded into the main cabin, the engine noise fading as the door slid shut.

The moment Micah's stretcher was locked into the equipment rack by the door, Tal called Thornlan. "We're all in. Get us to Redmoon."

They were rising even as Thornlan responded. *"They're waiting for us. Estimated flight time is twenty-three ticks."*

Dewar was crouching by the stretcher, holding a medical scanner against Micah's wrist. "His blood pressure is low but stable. The pressure sack is working. But…" She looked up. "His pulse is erratic. Lancer Tal, I don't know if he has twenty-three ticks."

Tal had not taken her eyes off Micah from the moment she had come through the door. Under the bright lights of the transport, his condition was starkly clear, and she could feel the final wisps of denial evaporating. He was going to his Return even now.

"Then we'll have to convince him that he does," she said. In two steps she crossed the distance and settled on her knees next to Dewar. "He knows me, and he knows I won't take no for an answer."

She reached for his energy points. It wasn't a perfect match; the oxygenator made it impossible to get her hand in quite the right position on his cheek and jaw, and she was at the wrong angle for the ideal integration of their forehead ridges. But it was close enough.

She leaned over and rested her forehead against his.

A warm, liquid darkness enveloped her. She was Sharing with a mind that was traversing the shadows between life and death. The first time she had done this, back when she was a Lead Guard, the sensation had sent her into a panic. It felt like dying, and she had broken the connection almost immediately, breathing hard and shivering at the idea of going back in. Intellectually, she knew that her body was whole and functional, but as soon as she had connected with her injured Guard, her mind had been convinced that it was losing the body that sustained it. Sharing a second time took every bit of her courage.

She had learned a few things since then. As the darkness pressed in, she forced herself to relax and began floating upward. Where there was life, there was always a surface above which the darkness did not extend.

But Micah's darkness was deep, deeper than she had ever been before. It seemed as if she had been rising forever, and she felt a moment of panic. What if he had completed his Return already? What if she was too late?

She struggled, a primal fear holding her back. If there was no light at all—

Then she saw it: a slight shading of the darkness to dim gray. Reassured, she let herself relax, and her journey upward increased in speed. The surroundings grew progressively lighter until finally, with an instinctive gasp, she broke through the surface.

Micah.

He was there, a tiny little piece of him that had not yet left. With a shuddering relief she embraced him. He was tired, so tired, but she had strength to spare.

Stay, she thought, projecting it with all her might. *Don't go.*

He responded, his exhaustion easing slightly as he accepted the strength she offered. Though she felt herself growing weaker the moment he touched her, she would not let him go.

I'm all right. Just stay with me.

Vaguely, she heard a murmur of voices, but it had nothing to do with her. That was elsewhere, in the conscious world. She could not be there right now. Micah was doubtful; he sensed her draining strength. It was taking everything she had to convince him to stay.

Another presence appeared at the edge of her awareness, sending an empathic plea. Her mind translated the projection into words.

Hold on.

For one wild moment, Tal thought she was hearing Fahla herself. Then she realized that someone else was coming up through the darkness.

Hold on.

It was more powerful this time, and a wonderfully familiar strength burst into the light.

I'm here. Hold on to me.

Tal reached out, her own weariness easing instantly at their touch, and Micah relaxed in their embrace.

CHAPTER 37
Counting heartbeats

Vellmar had seen and done a great deal in her career, including taking part in the heaviest fighting of the Battle of Alsea. She prided herself on being cool in any situation. But her jaw nearly came unhinged when Lancer Tal dropped to her knees and lined up the energy points on Colonel Micah.

The colonel was dying. Vellmar knew it, and Lancer Tal definitely knew it. She couldn't possibly be considering—

Oh, shekking Mother, she was. Vellmar felt a chill as Lancer Tal lowered her head to complete the Sharing.

Her oath holder was insane.

She bent down to Dewar and whispered, "Is that safe?"

Dewar was already pulling a second medical scanner from her pack. "Was anything about this mission safe?" She held the scanner to the Lancer's exposed wrist and swiveled her head back and forth, checking first one patient and then the other.

Vellmar was about to request a more specific answer when Raiz Opah joined them.

"Dear Goddess, I didn't know it was this bad. I was hoping she was reacting that way because it was Colonel Micah."

"It's not good." Dewar didn't take her eyes off the scanners. "I don't know if she can hold him. She may not have enough time."

"I didn't even know this was possible. How can she Share if he's not conscious?"

Something had caught Dewar's attention on Micah's scanner. Frowning at it, she said, "Until the Return, everyone has some part of consciousness, even if we can't see it on this side. She's looking for it now."

"When will we know she's found it?" Vellmar asked.

"When her heart rate and blood pressure start dropping."

A dead silence fell over everyone within hearing range.

"Guard Dewar," said Opah in a clear and too-precise voice, "Exactly what did you mean when you said she might not have enough time?"

Dewar had a flawless front, but when she looked up, the nervousness showed on her face. "No one knows precisely how this procedure works. Somehow, the connection of the minds translates to a connection of the bodies. Lancer Tal is using her own strength and health to bolster Colonel Micah's. Theoretically, if she stays too long, she could drain herself past the point of recovery. But I've never heard of that happening. And the Lancer knows her limits."

"Do you mean she's done this before?" Lancer Tal's caste record, or at least the parts of it that Vellmar was allowed to access, hadn't been nearly detailed enough for this.

Dewar checked the readouts again. "Yes. Once that I've personally witnessed, and—"

A gasp from the Lancer startled all of them, and her body stiffened before slumping.

"She found him," Dewar said. "His pulse is steady again." She waited, watching his numbers. "And it's slowly climbing." She turned to the Lancer's scanner.

"Well?" Opah's voice was unnaturally calm. "Is she sliding?"

Dewar nodded.

"Can you extrapolate the rate and predict whether she has enough time?"

"I think so. But I'll need to watch the rate for another two ticks."

Opah settled onto the floor just behind the Lancer, closed her eyes, and visibly relaxed.

Recognizing the technique, Vellmar stepped around her and crouched down. "Do you know what you're doing?" she whispered.

"No. But I know I can't sit here and do nothing. I've already done plenty of that this evening."

Apparently, both of them were insane. But Vellmar had to admire her courage. She glanced at Dewar, still reading the scanners, and tried to wait patiently.

"She'll have to back out before we arrive," said Dewar at last. "He's drawing too much strength from her. But it might be enough. He may be able to hold on after that."

"If there's one thing I've learned about Andira, it's that mights and maybes are unacceptable. Especially when it comes to someone she cares for. Do you have a third scanner?"

"No. Raiz Opah, I really cannot advise—"

"Then don't. Tell me what to expect."

When Dewar looked to her for help, Vellmar could only shrug. "She's the Bondlancer. In reality, if not yet in name."

"Thank you," Opah said without glancing at her. "Guard Dewar?"

Outranked and outflanked, Dewar gave up. "I only know what I've read. It will feel like you're Returning. Your mind will fight it, but the more you fight, the longer it takes. You have to make yourself relax, and then it will happen naturally. You'll float to the surface." She gestured with her chin toward Lancer Tal and Colonel Micah. "Somewhere in there, you'll find a light above the darkness. That's where they are. He may not want to stay. But so far he's staying with the Lancer, and that's a good sign."

"Salomen."

They looked up at the unexpected voice. Herot had hobbled over with the aid of a crutch and stood looking down at them, fear etched in his face. "Please," he said. "I just got you back. Please don't go."

Brother and sister stared at each other, and the occupants of the main cabin collectively held their breath.

"You're here because all of these people risked their lives for you, Herot." Opah's voice was sharp enough to cut glass. "I will not stand by and let one of them die if I can do something about it. And let me tell you this: if Colonel Micah goes to his Return, then you will have finally created a mess that nobody can clean up. Andira will never forgive you, and I cannot forgive anything that would hurt her so badly. So you had better pray."

She turned away, ignoring the pulse of anguish that burst out of him, and gently brushed the Lancer's bound hair aside. Laying one hand on the back of her neck, she reached out to slide the other under the colonel's. Her eyes closed.

"I can't do it all," Dewar said urgently. "Check her pulse. Tell me if it goes below thirty-five beats per tick."

Vellmar hesitated, then traced her fingers against Opah's throat, searching for the pulse point. Right about…here. She pressed harder and felt a strong beat against her fingers. Holding up her wristcom, she began counting to establish the base rate. Fifty-five beats per tick; healthy and normal. She relaxed the pressure, watching Opah for signs of contact with the others.

Herot hovered over them, and though she tried to ignore him, she found his presence distracting and annoying. She had disliked him from the moment she first touched his emotions and felt his terror at seeing Lancer Tal. Herot and his sister must have come from two different planets; it was the only explanation.

"I don't think you've been officially informed yet," she said, making no effort to hide her irritation. "Herot Arrin Opah, you are in the custody of the Lancer's Guards on the charge of direct enabling of an attempted assassination. You will be remanded to the Alsean Investigative Force upon our return to Blacksun. In the meantime, I suggest you sit down and get the shek out of our way."

He nodded slowly and turned away, only to twist back as his sister gasped and stiffened. Vellmar immediately began a new count.

Already fifty-three beats per tick. This was going to be a long trip.

CHAPTER 38
Redmoon

Tal was more tired than she could ever recall. Holding on to Micah and Salomen had become instinct rather than active intent. Though time did not exist here, she knew enough from her state of exhaustion to understand that out there, in the conscious world, she was approaching the point of departure. She would either have to leave this place or leave her body.

But if Salomen was here with her, why would she want to go back?

It was a seductive thought. Back there lay responsibility and stress and fear for Micah. Here it was…peaceful.

She had been in this link long enough to view her pre-Sharing self as someone else entirely. That other Andira Tal was juggling too many things, dealing with too many betrayals, and scrambling to keep up with the latest threats to her title, her governance, and her loved ones. She was living a ridiculously stressful life compared to this quiet, comforting place. The greatest draw of that life were two very special people, and they were linked with her now, so what was left? It was so simple here.

Voices murmured in the distance, and someone jostled the body she had left outside. She drew away, willing those who would disturb her to leave her alone. A small alarm sounded in her mind, telling her she had gone too deep, but it was easy to ignore.

She floated in the link, her exhaustion giving way to a feeling of contentment. No, there was nothing left. It was too late anyway, wasn't it?

The voices grew louder and the jostling more violent. At first Salomen responded with the same irritation Tal had, but it changed to relief. Tal wondered about the odd emotion, her thoughts moving slowly as she drifted.

Salomen let go.

Shocked into a moment of clarity, Tal reached out. *No! Salomen!*

But her tyree was already sinking, and Micah was trying to pull away. Everything had gone wrong.

Come back.

She felt the call as clearly as if Salomen had spoken aloud. The voices broke in, their words taking shape.

"Lancer Tal, you *must* come back. We cannot move him until you do. Lancer Tal, please!"

Slowly, the realization dawned. They were in Redmoon. She was only here to hold Micah as long as necessary. This wasn't her place—and Salomen had gone back.

When she let go, Micah retreated at an alarming speed. With one last empathic plea for him to stay, she turned and followed Salomen into the darkness. It closed around her, enveloping her in its soft weight, pushing her downward. Faster and faster she sank, too tired to slow herself down.

She slammed into her body, her physical senses reeling with a sudden flood of input. So much light and noise, and Fahla, she was weak as a newborn! As she slumped to the side, someone caught her, gently lifting and pulling her backward until she was resting in something soft. Her eyes fluttered open in time to see Vellmar and Senshalon pick up Micah's stretcher and vanish out the door.

Dewar stayed, holding a medical scanner over her wrist. "You're going to need a long nap after that," she said. "I suggest you both stay here for a few ticks before running after the colonel. Especially you, Lancer Tal. You went right up to the line."

No, she had gone over the line. But Dewar didn't need to know that, and Salomen really didn't.

Tal lifted a heavy arm to rub her forehead ridges, which ached where they had been pressed against Micah's in that awkward angle. "I've never had to go that far before. He's ready to Return. He only stayed because we asked him to, and he pulled away just before I came out. I don't know how long they have before he forgets about us."

"He's in the hands of the best trauma healers on Pallea. If there's any chance at all, they'll bring him back." Dewar pressed a skinspray against her wrist. "That will help with the fatigue and the rubbery muscles." She turned to Salomen, who sat slumped in the next seat, and sprayed her as well. "But the best thing for you is a little sleep. Don't fight it."

"I promise that if a nap knocks on my door, I won't argue," Tal said.

Salomen was silent, her head resting on the seat back and her eyes closed. Judging by her diminished presence in their link, she was even more exhausted than Tal.

"Are you all right?" Tal asked.

"I think so," Salomen said without opening her eyes. "As long as you don't ask me to move. I feel completely drained."

"You are," Dewar said. "It's a good thing we weren't any farther away than this. But the two of you kept Colonel Micah stable. Given the situation, we couldn't have asked for better."

Tal rolled her head from side to side, stretching the kinks from her neck, and stopped when she saw who sat on the other side of the aisle. One seat away, with a crutch leaned up against the hull, was the man who had caused all of this. A surge of anger energized her as their eyes met. Without breaking their gaze, she pushed herself up and slowly walked to stand in front of him.

"Have you been informed of the charge?" she asked.

Herot nodded. "Lan—"

"Save it. You and I are going to have a long talk later. Until then, I don't want to hear a shekking word out of you. Dewar, Nilsinian, escort the prisoner to the healers to get that ankle treated. I suspect he's got a few other scrapes and bruises that may need looking at. Do *not* let him out of your sight. And Gehrain, go with them." She saw the look on Gehrain's face and raised an eyebrow at him. "That was not a suggestion. You need to get your head checked."

"We've been saying that for a long time," Nilsinian muttered, and the other Guards chuckled.

Tal recognized the humor for what it was. "I know we're all worried. And we might as well worry in the healing center, so let's go in there and frighten the natives." A unit of Lancer's Guards in full mission gear was guaranteed to do just that, but none of them had planned on a side excursion. They were fresh out of regular uniforms. "I want two Guards on our other guests and four on the transport perimeter. The rest of you can go. And Dewar, I want to know everything about Micah just as soon as you know it."

"Of course," Dewar said. She and Nilsinian helped Herot from his seat and flanked him as he hobbled past. He turned his head, watching his sister, but Salomen's eyes remained closed.

As the remaining Guards discussed among themselves who would stay on watch, Tal glanced toward the back of the transport. Parser's warriors were still unconscious, which meant someone had sedated them. They were going to be considerably surprised to wake up and find themselves secured to seats in her transport.

She walked up the fore corridor to poke her head in the pilot's cabin. "Thornlan?"

Thornlan turned around. "Twenty-one ticks. I think I need to go out and apologize to my engines. Will he be all right?"

"We won't know for a while. Do you want a break? I'm staying here." Regulations required at least one qualified pilot to remain in the transport whenever it was off base.

"I could use the chance to stretch my legs."

"Then go. And thank you for getting us here so quickly."

"Colonel Micah gave me this post." Thornlan smiled at her. "Over someone's objections, I heard. I owed him."

"Sooner or later, everyone does. And I have no idea whose objections you're talking about. I've always thought you were the best pilot for the post." Tal waved her out and followed her into the main cabin, now empty of all Guards except Corlander and Windenal, who were sitting near the prisoners. As Thornlan went down the ramp, Tal stopped in front of Salomen and spoke to the Guards.

"I want to know the moment they come out of it. Even if I'm asleep. If you knock on my cabin door and don't hear an answer, come in anyway."

They exchanged glances. "Yes, Lancer," said Windenal.

"Don't worry, we're too tired to be caught in any compromising positions." It was only partially a joke; she could feel Salomen on the verge of more than just exhaustion. "Wouldn't you prefer to rest in my cabin?" she asked quietly.

Salomen held out a hand, allowing Tal to help her up and lead her into the private cabin.

With the door shut behind them, Tal wasted no time pulling her into a warmron. "Finally," she murmured.

Still Salomen said nothing, simply holding on tight. Tal pushed down her own emotions; one of them hovering near a breakdown was enough. She projected what little calm she could, prepared to stand there for as long as it took.

At last Salomen loosed her hold and pulled back. "I'm all right. Don't worry."

"Of course I'm going to worry. You're never this quiet."

"Little do you know. I've been quiet for the last several hanticks." The weariness and grief showed in her eyes. "And terrified for you. Turns out I was afraid for the wrong person. I'm so sorry about Colonel Micah."

Tal couldn't talk about that. "I need to change and make two quick calls. And when I'm done, you and I are going to sit here and just be alone for a while. Is that all right?"

"Do what you need to." Salomen pulled out the nearest chair at the conference table and sat heavily.

Tal leaned down to kiss her temple. "Thank you for what you did."

"I just hope it was enough." She looked more alert, and Tal sensed her control sliding back into place. Once again she was reminded just how strong her tyree really was.

She pulled a clean uniform from the clothing cupboard, set it on the counter, and peeled off her mission clothes. The pants were the worst. Micah's blood had dried, making the knees stiff and crusty. She felt sick as she threw them in the storage cupboard, and even worse when she saw that her hands were stained red. She scrubbed them ferociously in the small sink, then took a quick sponge bath before sliding on the clean clothes. It was remarkable how something as simple as a fresh uniform could make her feel like a new woman.

Salomen watched as she tucked in her shirt. "Now you look more like the Lancer I know," she said. "You were a little intimidating in that mission uniform."

"That wasn't the design intent, but I'll take any advantage I can get." Tal ran a light hand across the back of Salomen's neck as she stepped past her.

It was the work of moments to unlatch the fold-down desk and pull the chair from its recessed cubby. She slid it into place, locking it out of habit even though the transport was on the ground, and a few pipticks later had Colonel Razine on the large vidcom above the desk.

"Lancer Tal! I'm glad to hear from you. I presume from your message that you recovered Herot Opah."

"Yes, we did. Do you have Parser back in custody?"

"Oh, yes," Razine said, a rare smile lighting her face. "That was the most enjoyable thing I've been able to do all cycle. He was not a happy man. He said the game wasn't over, but I think that was just hot air."

Tal frowned. "Did you scan him?"

"There was no need."

"Do it anyway, and ask him what he means about the game. I have a nasty feeling you'll find too much confidence. We were almost caught in a trap—Colonel Micah stopped it from killing him and five other Guards. I'm on edge enough to think Parser might have other traps set as well."

Razine swore softly. "We underestimated him."

"Not anymore. I want you to go to the High Tribunal and get a warrant for empathic force. I'm done playing that zalren's games. He's going to tell us everything."

"I was already planning to be there first thing in the morning. Is your team all right?"

"No. We're at Redmoon right now. Colonel Micah suffered a severe disruptor injury."

"Oh, shek. I'm sorry, Lancer Tal."

"So am I," Tal said grimly. "This is one case I'm going to speak for. If my recommendation has anything to do with it, Parser will have to dig up to find the fifth level of the Pit."

"Good." Razine's eyes were flinty. "I'll give him a dull spade. Do you need anything in Redmoon?"

"Actually, yes. I don't know how long we'll be here, and I have three prisoners to offload: Herot Opah and two of Parser's employees. He called them warriors, but I don't think they were sworn. They felt more like mercenaries to me. And as long as you're flying a transport out here, all of my Guards need their regular uniforms. They're not dressed for a healing center at the moment."

Razine made a note and nodded.

"We didn't get them all. The one who shot Micah got away, and with Micah's injuries, we couldn't run her down. So I want Parser's hired thugs scanned and questioned, and if they don't give the right answers, I want warrants for empathic force on them, too."

"I'll take care of it. The transport can be there in five hanticks."

"Good. Contact Redmoon Base and have them send out an explosives team to the coordinates I'm sending you." She quickly accessed the transport's logs and tied in the record. "There are explosives wired directly into the basement ceiling of the house where Herot was being held. The entry to the basement is in the third room from the living area, left of the stairs. Tell them to be extremely careful—some of the lead lines are already carrying a ramp-up current. My guess is they all were before Micah destroyed the control box."

Razine sucked in a breath. "That was the trap? How much of the basement is wired?"

"All of it. And it extends beneath the entire house."

"Great Goddess."

"I think the warrior who got away was trying to blow the house. There's a blast door built into the basement wall right by the panel controlling the charges. She probably planned to set off the charges and be safely behind the door when the floor blew and the house dropped into the basement." Tal paused as a memory flickered. "Parser said Herot would be found dead and it would be blamed on my Guards. He said two of my Guards would be found dead as well. Now I'm wondering if this was his backup plan. If the warrior in charge of destroying the house had realized we were inside just a few ticks earlier, she could have blown it with Herot and six of my Guards inside—and me."

She felt the spike of horror from Salomen and shot her an apologetic glance.

"And most of Parser's crew as well," Razine said. "Then he could flip the whole thing over and say his warriors died trying to rescue Herot from us."

"Exactly. And I would have just made a worldwide announcement of his innocence in the corruption investigation, so his word would have carried more weight than it should. Not to mention the fact that everyone on Alsea already saw what looked like my Guards taking Herot out of the Napoline transport station on the afternoon news. Though I don't think his plan included catching me as well. It was a lot of work to go to on the remote chance we might find Herot, but Parser really did think of everything. He had backup plans for his backup plans, which is why I'm worried about him saying the game isn't over."

Razine whistled softly. "Then we shouldn't wait for the High Tribunal to convene at its normal time. I'll send a message to the adjudicators to meet me at hantick seven; that way I should have a warrant in hand and be inside Parser's brain before eight."

"Good." Tal hoped she tore him apart.

"I must confess, this is a conversation I'm looking forward to. That merchant has much to answer for. I'm beginning to think you were lucky to have only one injury."

She winced at the growing anger coming from Salomen. "I'm thinking the same. I need to make another call, Colonel. Oh, one more thing. Tell the Redmoon team they'll be collecting five bodies in the house and two more up on the ridges. I'll have Vellmar send the coordinates of the outpost guards. And find out who that house belongs to."

"Consider it done."

Tal signed off and held up a finger. "I know. Just one more." Hurriedly, she punched in Aldirk's code.

Her Chief Counselor informed her that the correct vid would be aired on the news broadcasts. "Even though I somehow did not receive notification until it was very nearly too late," he said.

Tal had to smile. No matter what else was going on in the world, Aldirk would always be Aldirk. "I sent word the moment I could. We hadn't even wrapped up the mission."

He nodded, mollified. "Then I presume our delightful Herot Opah has rejoined your company. I'm glad for Raiz Opah."

Tal raised an eyebrow. "Do I detect a favorable opinion of my bondmate?"

"Why would this surprise you?"

"Because she's neither warrior nor scholar."

Aldirk sniffed. "Not all of us can choose our caste. For a producer, she seems quite accomplished."

A snort came from behind her. "Indeed she is. Aldirk, I need you to clear my calendar tomorrow. I'm going to be in Redmoon."

He looked briefly horrified before schooling his features into his usual calm expression. "That's not possible. I've already—"

"Do it," she said. "Colonel Micah is seriously injured. I'm staying here."

To her surprise, Aldirk seemed saddened by the news, asking no more questions and promising a new schedule by mornmeal. Two ticks later, Tal turned off the vidcom and tensed for the next encounter.

"Salomen, I know you're angry, but—"

"I'm not angry at you." Salomen stepped over and laid a hand on her shoulder. "Parser, Herot, the woman who hurt Colonel Micah, yes. But not you."

"Thank the Goddess." The relief loosened her spine, and she rested her head against Salomen's waist.

"Come on, tyrina. We're supposed to be napping, and it won't happen here." Salomen pulled her up and led her across the cabin, where they settled on the wide reclining seats.

Now that she had taken care of the most urgent tasks, the drive that had kept Tal going sputtered to a halt. Still holding Salomen's hand, she turned in the seat to face her and thought that might be the last physical effort she could manage today.

"If Micah lives, it will be because of you," she said. "I know for a fact I couldn't have held him long enough."

"I was just glad I could finally do something to help."

"What you did took immense courage. The first time I did that, it scared me halfway to my own Return. And I had much more time to get used to the idea."

"It wasn't courage," Salomen said. "It was fear. Of you losing Colonel Micah, and me knowing I hadn't done anything to stop it. Besides, I knew you were there. That got me through the dark part."

Tal shivered as she remembered just how deep that darkness had been. "I've never chased someone so far down the path of their Return. For a moment before I broke out, I thought he was already gone."

"Andira…" Salomen looked down at their clasped hands, then met her eyes. "Why do you think he's so ready to Return?"

Tal's throat closed, preventing an answer. She took a shuddering breath, forcing it back open, and said, "Because this is what he wanted most. This is redemption. Not the kind I wanted or even imagined, but it's redemption for him. He'll have died on duty, with a disruptor in his hand, in the act of protecting me and my interests. There is no better death."

"But wouldn't he want to live now that he's proved himself? You said he saved himself and five other Guards. Isn't that a better redemption than Returning?"

"I don't know. He may not realize exactly what he did. We don't know what happened down there." A tear slipped down her cheek, and she angrily swiped it away. She had no time for this. "I'm sorry. I just—"

"Shh." Salomen's knuckle brushed her face, catching a second tear. "Every one of these is an honor to him."

"Then he's about to drown in honor," Tal managed before dropping her face in her hands. She could have controlled herself in front of anyone else, but Salomen's gentle understanding undid her. Her breath came in short gasps, her throat burned, and her head felt two sizes too large.

"He cannot Return, Salomen! It's not right; I can't lose him. What am I supposed to do? He's all I have left." She realized what she had just said and raised her head, trying to ignore the tears streaming down her face. "I'm sorry. I didn't mean—"

"I know." Salomen was soothing her with both touch and emotion, and Tal closed her eyes in gratitude. "Stop apologizing, tyrina. You're right, there is no one else in your life like Colonel Micah. If he Returns, you will have lost family."

"Thank you for understanding," Tal whispered. "And for being here."

With a soft exhale, Salomen wrapped her in a warmron. "This is a dokshin trade, isn't it? You gave me back my brother, and now it's Colonel Micah in danger. I'm the one who's sorry, believe me."

Tal thought that if she could choose, there would be no trade at all. Micah was worth twenty Herots.

"I had planned to be here for your reunion," she said, wanting to change the subject.

"Such as it was. I told him that if he weren't already so bruised, I would have slapped him right across the face."

"You really said that?"

"I would have done it. I've spent all day watching you and Colonel Micah and twenty others giving everything they had to pull his backside out of the fire. He has no idea, *no* idea what has been done for him. And there are five Alseans lying dead in that house because of him. I felt you kill one of them, and I know what that did to you. And then I saw Colonel Micah. I'm so angry with Herot that I can't even look at him."

Tal couldn't help the snort of laughter, then a second one at Salomen's confusion. "I know, you think my boat is sinking. It's just that I spent the whole hike into that house imagining how happy you would be when I brought him back. And you wanted to slap him? I couldn't have gotten it more wrong if I'd tried." She laughed again, a great, gulping sort of laughter that turned into tears as she shook her head, embarrassed to be so out of control. She knew it was just her body releasing tension; right now laughter and tears served the same purpose. That didn't make it any easier.

"I wish I could feel that happy," Salomen said. "Before, all I wanted was to get him back safely. And now that he's back I seem to have skipped right past the relieved stage and straight into anger. I'm furious with him."

Salomen's emotion helped Tal get control of hers. Wiping her wet cheeks, she said, "Not that I ever want to defend him, because I'd like to knock him out the transport door myself. But Parser said Jaros was his original target. It would have happened anyway. This much of it is not Herot's fault." Even as she spoke, she realized the truth of it. Herot carried a great deal of blame, but he could not be blamed for Micah.

"But Parser couldn't have used Jaros for anything other than a hostage. He couldn't have threatened you with political annihilation the way he did with Herot. And that *is* Herot's fault." Salomen sighed. "I don't know what to think anymore. And Herot is a changed man. I've never felt him so…subdued. He doesn't have that edge of arrogance and entitlement that drove me so insane."

"Herot had no idea what was in the world beyond the borders of Hol-Opah and Granelle. He got hit with a large dose of reality and found out how small he really is. That usually does change a person. And…" Tal hesitated.

"And what?"

"You should probably know this anyway. That warrior you felt me kill? Herot saw it. All of it. And he saw two other dead bodies on the way out. So I think he's learned more about the world than even I could have wished. He looked terrified when I killed the guard in his room."

"Good. Then maybe he'll think twice before talking big in a tavern about how easy it would be to kill you."

Tal stared.

"What? You thought I'd be horrified that my innocent brother saw death? A nineday ago, I would have. But everything has changed since then. Herot lost the right to innocence the moment he told Cullom Bilsner which window to shoot at." Her voice caught as she added, "But he did not have the right to take away my innocence at the same time."

With an aching heart, Tal enfolded her in a warmron. "No, he didn't."

Salomen tucked her head under Tal's chin. "I've learned more about the world than I wanted to as well."

Tal wished she could blame all of it on Herot, but she could still hear Salomen in that field, furiously informing her that she had dreamed of a producer tyree, not a warrior. And today had been one long lesson in the difficulties of being Tal's bondmate. What had she given up for this bond? An emotional privacy she no longer cared about? Salomen was the one making all the sacrifices.

"Stop feeling guilty, for Fahla's sake." Salomen lifted her head. "What I lost to Herot, he took. What I've lost to you, I gave. There is an ocean of difference between the two."

A tiny smile tugged at Tal's lips. "We need to get you assessed. You might be the first Alsean telepath."

"It doesn't take a telepath to know what you're thinking. You take on too much, Andira. Leave some responsibility for the rest of us."

"A fitting speech from the woman who would rather have been reported than give up responsibility for her family and holding."

"Not the same thing."

"You walked the path of the Return with me, too."

"Because it—"

"…had to be done," Tal finished with her. "Exactly. And that's why you'll be such a good Bondlancer."

Salomen made a noncommittal hum. "I do wish you had given me the manual earlier." After a pause, she added, "I was just remembering how afraid I was when I first understood what was happening between us. But the truth is, you're the one who should have been afraid. My family has caused you so much pain. And now there's Colonel Micah."

Tal had only just boxed that up; she was not about to reopen it. "Your family didn't cause this. And you had every reason for your fear."

"It doesn't really go away, does it? It just changes to a different form."

"As long as we have something to lose, we'll always have fear." For the first time, she wondered if the common interpretation of the Truth and the Path—of warriors not giving their hearts—was meant to make them impervious to fear. If that was the case, whoever came up with that was a dangerous fool.

"I have so much more to lose now," Salomen murmured, her eyes closing as she rested her head against the seat.

Her weariness seemed to exacerbate Tal's own, and she could barely lift her heavy arm far enough to press the seat controls. As the chairs reclined to a horizontal position, she said, "So do I. But I would fight to my last breath to keep from losing you."

Salomen snuggled in sleepily. "I know. That's why I feel so safe with you."

Tal nuzzled the top of her head, reveling in the clean scent of her hair. A faint spiciness still clung, not any lingering perfume but the unique scent of Salomen herself.

A warrior with a whole heart is a better servant to Alsea, Micah had said.

She smiled into Salomen's hair, letting the wave of drowsiness wash over her. The last thing she thought was that Micah was right. As usual.

CHAPTER 39
Prisoner waking

VELLMAR LOOKED AT HER WRISTCOM one more time and gave up. She had been in the notification area for almost a hantick now, and the assistant healer kept telling them the same thing over and over: "We cannot know anything until the surgery is complete." Which was a lie; of course they could know by now whether Colonel Micah was likely to survive or not. Healers were alike the world over—they all seemed to feel that false hope was better than none.

"I'm going back to the transport," she told Senshalon. "At least the seats there are more comfortable."

"True words," he said. "These were made for pre-Rite children."

She hid a smile as she rose. The chairs weren't that small, but Senshalon was a big man. "Join me if you want."

"Thank you, but I'd rather be here."

She understood. Every Guard not on watch was crowded into the notification area, waiting for the first whisper of news. They were being given a wide berth by the locals, who continually cast sidelong glances as if they were watching some sort of exotic species. Vellmar thought they should have charged a viewing fee.

Turning away from the "Main Arch" sign, which pointed toward the public entrance, she walked down the curving corridor toward the back of the huge dome. A "Landing Arch" sign marked a smaller side corridor, which opened onto the healing center's brightly lit landing pad. Their transport took up almost all of it. She expected they would be asked to move it by sunrise.

Before the Guards at the bottom of the ramp could ask, she shook her head. "No news," she said, moving between them.

"That's probably good," one of them said behind her.

The transport felt like home after the crowded, pungent confines of the notification area. Healing centers always smelled like narnell root, the plant extract used for sterilization. She had hated that smell since childhood.

"Vellmar! Any news?" Corlander asked from the back.

"No, they won't tell us anything. We did learn that Gehrain has a mild concussion, which was no surprise. He's under observation now and complaining to anyone who will listen. And Herot is getting his ankle properly wrapped. His torso looks like someone held a village dance on top of him." She took a bag of shannel from the storage unit and squeezed it to activate the heating reaction. When the indicator strip turned from yellow to red, she pulled off the top and sucked on the mouthpiece. "Aggh," she spluttered. "I forgot how much I hate bagged shannel."

"It's probably still better than that recycled piss in the healing center," said Windenal.

"I didn't try it, but if it's the same here as it is in Whitesun, then yes. They must import it straight from the fanten farms." She walked to the back of the transport and leaned against the nearest seat. Still sucking on her shannel—which at least was hot and energizing—she eyed the prisoners. "They've been out a while."

"This one twitched just before you walked in." Corlander reached across the aisle and poked the male prisoner. "I think he may be coming around."

"Did you tell the Lancer?"

They exchanged uncomfortable looks.

"What?" she asked.

"Well…" Corlander began.

"She's in her cabin with Raiz Opah," said Windenal.

"So? Did she ask not to be disturbed?"

"No…she told us to come in even if she didn't answer a knock."

The man groaned and shifted his head.

Vellmar looked from him to her Guards. "And the reason you're sitting on your hands instead of obeying her order is…?"

They looked like pre-Rite children caught with their pants down, and she rolled her eyes. "Are you afraid of seeing something that might burn your retinas?"

"Yes," they said in unison.

"Fahla on a funstick, what a pair of grainbirds. I thought you were sworn warriors." They all looked at the prisoner, who moaned again. "I'll tell her," she said. "But the next time you piss around instead of obeying her order, or mine, I will roll over you like a boulder. Clear?"

They were still a little too relieved, but she had gotten her point across. Half a tick later she rapped sharply on the private cabin door. "Lancer Tal?"

No response. She tried again, counted to five, and touched the palm pad. The door slid open silently, revealing a spacious room with large windows. In front of her stood an empty conference table surrounded by six chairs that locked into place, and the forward bulkhead was dominated by a large vidcom unit above a rather ingenious pull-down desk and another locking chair.

She stepped in and turned, taking in the waist-high preparation cabinet right by the door, with its plates and glasses in polished wooden racks. Next to it was a sink and a food storage unit, and the aft bulkhead was solid drawers and cupboards. Four wide, very comfortable-looking seats sat in two facing rows by the windows. Two of those seats were reclined into a horizontal position, forming a bed.

Lancer Tal, now in her regular uniform, was lying on her back. Raiz Opah was wrapped around her, an arm and leg draped over her bondmate's body in a casually possessive position while her head rested on her shoulder. It was more intimate than anything those two grainbirds outside had been afraid of, and Vellmar was suddenly glad that she was the one standing here.

She crossed the cabin and knelt next to the Lancer, whose breathing indicated a deep level of sleep. "Lancer Tal," she said in a low voice.

The breathing didn't change. She put a hand on her shoulder and jumped as her wrist was caught and held in a tight grip.

Alert blue eyes bored into hers. "What is it?"

"One of the prisoners is waking."

Lancer Tal nodded as she released Vellmar's wrist and rubbed her eyes. "No news about Micah?"

"No. I'm sorry."

"How long has it been?"

"About eighty ticks."

"Too early anyway." She stroked Opah's hair away from her face. "Salomen. I need to get up."

"Hmm?" Opah tightened her grip and snuggled in deeper.

Vellmar felt her face grow warm.

"Salomen." Lancer Tal kissed her forehead. "You can stay here, but I have to go."

With a sudden intake of breath, Opah raised her head. "Colonel Micah?"

"No. One of the prisoners is waking up."

"Oh. Damn." She rolled over onto her back, rubbing her eyes as Lancer Tal sat up and swung her legs over the edge. "I'll come with you."

"There's no need, tyrina. Just sleep."

"Not without you." She opened her eyes and saw Vellmar for the first time. Her lips curved in a knowing smile. "You look a little red, Lead Guard. We weren't doing anything compromising, were we?"

Vellmar flushed even more. "I'll be in the main cabin," she said, and fled.

CHAPTER 40
Scope of betrayal

"Stay here," Tal said, gently resting a hand on Salomen's chest as she tried to rise.

"Why?" Salomen settled back on her elbows.

"Because I'm about to question two prisoners who have no motivation to tell me anything."

"I don't—"

"So I'll have to give them motivation."

Salomen's eyes widened. "Oh."

"You said you'd learned more about the world than you wanted to. I don't want you to learn this. Please stay here, and don't open the door until I come back."

Salomen watched her in silence, then nodded. "All right."

"Thank you." Tal pushed off the bed but was halted by a hand around her wrist.

"Andira…I know you will do what you have to and no more."

She heard the unspoken request. "I promise."

By the time she entered the main cabin, Vellmar had recovered sufficiently to have a normal skin tone again. Tal nodded as she passed her, then dropped into the seat directly opposite the conscious prisoner. He sat straight, his eyes wide and his fear soaking her senses, though he was trying to front it. Beside him, the woman was groaning and rolling her head from side to side. Tal eyed the bandage across her nose before returning her attention to the man in front of her.

"Welcome to my transport," she said. "I would have offered a ride to your friends as well, but unfortunately, we killed the rest."

He swallowed hard. "Are you…?"

She watched him until he finally answered his own question.

"You're Lancer Tal."

"Yes, I am. And you're a man whose life depends on what he says in the next few ticks."

"I don't know anything."

"That was the wrong answer. I can feel exactly how much you know. And you're going to share it with me. You can either do it now, voluntarily, or you can do it later, under a warrant of empathic force. Now would be better for you."

The woman opened her eyes, looked up blearily, and snapped awake at the sight of Tal. "Shekking—" She tried to lunge from the chair, then stared at the ties binding her to the armrests. Disbelief and dread leaked through her weak front.

"I was just telling your friend that you're the only survivors of your little club," Tal said. "And suggesting to him that it would be better to tell me everything now, rather than having it forcibly pulled out of him later. Wouldn't you agree?"

The woman glanced at her partner, who shook his head slightly. She settled a practiced scowl on her face and stared straight ahead.

Tal smiled to herself. She knew how to play this game and who the target would be.

"Who was the guard in the room with Herot Opah?" She waited several pipticks, then added, "He's already dead. I hardly think you can betray him by telling me his name. I just thought it would be easier to refer to him by a name when I tell you how he died."

They might have been a matched set of statues, but they could not mask their fear. Tal breathed it in and let it settle in her stomach, a salve to her own worry about Micah. In this, at least, she had control.

"I killed him with an immobilizer," she said conversationally. "A nasty way to go. The two guards at the door got a much quicker death, but we couldn't take any chances with your friend in the room. I watched him die. He was in agony."

She leaned forward and spoke in a lower tone. "My intent is to turn you over to the Alsean Investigative Force in Blacksun, but I have an entire unit of Guards traveling with me. None of them are very happy about my decision to keep you alive. I'll be spending the trip to Blacksun in my private cabin, which means I won't be here to watch you. It's soundproofed, so I won't be able to hear you, either. If any of my Guards develops an itchy finger on an immobilizer, I'm afraid you'll find out just how agonizing a death that is."

The man broke first, unable to remain quiet in the face of her not very subtle threat. "You won't do that. You have to obey the law."

"Who told you that?"

He looked away.

"You're correct, actually. I do have to obey the law. Which is why I'll be somewhere else when you tragically die in transit. My Guards won't see a thing, and my report to the AIF will be very short. Clean and legal. Would you like a preview?"

Their eyes rounded, and she smiled at the spurt of terror. "No, not like that. That would be *illegal*. I'm just offering you the chance to honor your fallen comrade, by feeling what he felt."

When they still refused to speak, she gestured for Corlander to stand behind the man. "Hold his head back."

"Wait! What are you going to do?" The man craned his head around, trying to watch Corlander, but the Guard wrapped two strong hands around his head and forced it back against the seat. "You can't do this!"

"You don't even know what I'm going to do. How can you object?"

He tried to struggle, an effort rendered useless by the bindings on his forearms and shins. "No..."

"Are you going to answer my questions?"

"No!"

She lunged from her seat, slapped her hands on his energy points, and pressed her forehead to his. Her skin was crawling, but she needed answers. She called up her memories of the guard she had killed: his abject terror, his despair at dying alone, his agony at being caught without a breath in his lungs—knowing that because he exhaled just before being immobilized, he had lost that many more pipticks of life. All of the horror she had absorbed from him, she threw toward the man under her hands. He struggled, screaming, his own terror blending with the memories she was sending until she wasn't sure which was which. Revolted, she pushed herself away and sat back, watching him sob.

"Fahla, no, I don't want to die!"

"Get me a wet cloth," she ordered.

The woman had lost all pretense of stoicism and was straining at her bonds, instinct driving a flight response despite knowing she could not get free. "What did you do to him?" she demanded, her voice cracking.

"Exactly what I said I would. Remember that. I do not lie, and I do not bluff. Corlander, you can release him. For now."

The man had stopped sobbing, but his breathing was harsh and panicked.

His friend gave up her ineffective struggles and leaned over as far as she could. "Are you all right? Oren? Oren! Talk to me!"

He shook his head, still gasping.

"Oren," said Tal. "Finally, an answer. You know I couldn't have done that if I hadn't experienced those feelings myself. What you just felt is precisely what your friend felt. The difference is that you're still alive, but he felt that way until he died. As I said, it's a nasty way to go."

Vellmar held a wet cloth in front of her. She took it without looking up and gratefully wiped her forehead and hands. It helped, but she wouldn't feel clean again until she had showered.

"Would you like to answer a few simple questions, Oren?" she asked.

"You said you had to obey the law." His voice shook with fear and hatred. "That was not legal!"

"Of course it was. I offered you the opportunity to honor your friend. You agreed."

"I did not! I said no!"

"You said no, you would not answer my questions. Not no, you did not wish to honor your friend's death. Now, let me ask you again. Will you answer my questions?" She felt the answer, but before he could say it, she turned to the woman. "Or would *you* like to honor your friend?"

"You can't do that to her!" Oren shouted.

Tal held her gaze. "Is keeping someone else's secret worth it?"

She licked her lips, glancing nervously at Oren and back to her. "No," she said.

"Dalset!"

"Seal his mouth." Tal did not look away from the frightened woman staring at her. "Your name is Dalset?"

She hesitated, then nodded, and Tal knew she had her.

"Don't you tell her—" Oren's shout was cut off midsentence as his mouth was taped shut.

"What was the name of the guard in Herot Opah's room?"

Dalset glanced at Oren, then back at Tal. "Swifan," she said.

"Thank you. I appreciate your willingness to cooperate. You know I wasn't lying when I said Swifan died a terrible death. What I didn't tell you was how much I regretted that death. We killed the guards on the ridge tops and the ones outside Herot's room quickly and with a minimum of pain, but we knew that Swifan was assigned to kill Herot if anything went wrong." She noted Dalset's surprise. "Yes, we were watching you. That's how we were able to plan such a clean mission, except for Swifan's death. I wish it hadn't been necessary. But you made it necessary."

"It wasn't me! I didn't have anything to do with how this was set up."

"Who did?"

"Periso. She was in charge of everything. I just did what I was told."

"First name?"

"Hedron."

"And Hedron Periso was with you in the house?"

"Yes. She was the one who hired me. She said it was just a guarding job. I didn't know it would involve anything illegal until I got there."

"Of course you knew it was illegal. You don't have a very strong front; don't even attempt to lie to me. The more truth you share, the better it will be for you in Blacksun."

Dalset looked down.

"Periso must have paid well. That was a dokshin job in the middle of nowhere. You must have been bored out of your mind."

"I was," she said. "We all were. Some of us were talking about leaving."

"A pity you didn't. Did Periso pay Oren and everyone else, too?"

"Yes. I told you, she was in charge."

"So she's the one who kidnapped Herot from the Napoline transport station?"

"Her and..." She paused, trying too hard not to look at Oren.

"And Oren," Tal finished for her, sensing the truth of it. "Was Oren the second-in-command?"

"In a way. Periso didn't trust any of us, really. She was a paranoid shekker."

"Which room was hers?"

Dalset looked at her oddly. "The one by the office, why? Is that important?"

Tal had known it before she said it, but it was nice to have the confirmation. "In a way. Did you know there was a basement under that house?" No, she clearly didn't. "The access was in Periso's room. There was only one other exit, a blast door leading to an escape tunnel. Here's something else that might surprise you: the entire basement ceiling was wired with explosives. You were living on top of a bomb. Periso was killed right by the escape tunnel as she was trying to set them off, with you—and Oren, and everyone else—still in the house."

"What?" Dalset gaped at her, then narrowed her eyes and tried to present an unconcerned front. "You're lying."

Tal reached across and touched her hand. "Ask me if the house was wired to blow."

Dalset stared at their hands, startled by the physical touch. Shakily, she asked, "Was the house wired to blow? With all of us in it?"

"Yes."

Her jaw slackened as she sensed Tal's sincerity through their physical connection. Even Oren was shocked into belief.

"That spawn of a fantenshekken!" Dalset spat. "She was *using* us!"

Tal drew her hand back. "Yes, she was. You were just tools in a high-stakes political game."

"I'm glad she's dead!" Dalset was burning with the fury of betrayal. "And I hope you kill Shantu as well. Damn them to Fahla's worst nightmares!"

Tal went still. "Shantu? Do you mean…Prime Warrior Shantu?"

"He's the one who wanted Opah kept alive. Periso was sworn to him. The rest of us were just hired tools. That's why we were expendable, I guess. Shekking dokkers!"

Tal looked at the stunned faces of her Guards, then back at Dalset.

"Thank you," she said in a voice that didn't seem to be hers. "I have no other questions for now." She rose and walked back through the main cabin, her shock gradually melting into anger. By the time she reached her cabin, she was incandescent.

Salomen looked up when she entered. "What hap—"

"Damn them!" Tal shouted, startling her into silence. "Fahla damn them all, those shekking excuses for Alseans! How far does this go? Is there *anyone* left on the High Council who isn't betraying me?" She wanted to break something, but everything in the room was bolted down.

"Andira—"

"Not now, Salomen!" She threw herself into the desk chair and began to punch in Razine's code, but Salomen's bewildered pain stopped her. "Sorry," she said curtly. She was too furious to mean it and knew that Salomen was even more hurt by her insincerity. Shaking her head, she entered the rest of the code and hit the call key so hard that it was a wonder her finger didn't break the transparent cover.

Razine came on almost immediately. "Lancer Tal! Do you have new—?"

"I'm not calling about Micah. I just finished questioning the prisoners. They're not Parser's."

"What?"

"They were hired by Shantu."

Razine's intake of breath was audible. "Great Goddess above."

"My sentiments exactly. Though I'm a little more homicidal than you."

"Are you certain?"

"Yes, I'm certain!" Tal snapped. "The Prime Warrior is colluding with the Prime Merchant, and there's only one possible reason. Those two hate each other. They must have a common goal."

"A caste coup."

"Good guess, Colonel. I want him brought into custody one hantick ago."

"Lancer Tal." Razine's tone was overly calm. "I cannot bring the Prime Warrior into custody without cause. Your word, however trustworthy, is not sufficient."

Tal closed her eyes and took a deep breath. Now she wanted to kill Razine, but the part of her that was still logical knew the colonel was right.

Think, she told herself. What do you have for cause?

Her eyes popped open. "Check the caste records for a warrior named Hedron Periso. She's sworn to Shantu. She was the one in charge of the operation with Herot; the others were just hired mercenaries. She's also the one who shot Micah and got away. Periso and a mercenary named Oren—one of my prisoners—are the ones who kidnapped Herot out of the Napoline transport station. I can get Herot to confirm that. And I have two mercenaries here who will finger Shantu under questioning. One of them will probably need empathic force, but the other will talk without a warrant."

"That will work once we get them here and can conduct a properly witnessed empathic scan. In the meantime, I'll work on the caste records. But until we have corroboration of Periso's connection with Herot, the fact of her being sworn to Shantu will not be enough."

"You have the connection already." Salomen's voice came from right behind her. "The news vid. If Periso and Oren are the ones who kidnapped Herot, then you have them on a vid. One the whole world has already seen."

Razine looked from Salomen to Tal. "She's right."

"Of course she is. Is that sufficient cause?"

"Yes. If the vid shows their faces, that is. I imagine it was recorded from an angle to avoid that, but all we need is one frame with an identifiable profile. Send me images of your prisoners, in case I can't find them in the caste records. They may not be using their real names. We won't be able to hold Shantu for long without the corroboration of witnessed testimony, but we'll have enough to bring him in."

"Then do it. Put those two zalrens in the same holding cell. Maybe Fahla will smile on us and they'll kill each other."

"I'll let you know the moment we have him."

"Thank you." Tal ended the call and turned in her seat. "And thank you, too. I—" She stopped at the thunderous expression on Salomen's face.

"Don't you ever do that to me again."

Tal's anger had been so overwhelming that it had actually blocked Salomen's, but she certainly felt it now. Worse, she knew it was justified. "I'm sorry," she said, shrinking under the icy glare. This time she meant it.

"You should be. I'm on your side. I know you've had a dokshin day and it just got worse, but even that does not give you the right to treat me like some annoying underling clamoring for your attention. I deserve better."

A cloud of remorse settled on Tal's shoulders, where it clashed with the anger that still held her in its grip. She couldn't meet Salomen's eyes, and she couldn't speak, either. At this point, she had no idea what would come out of her mouth. Instead she closed her eyes and nodded.

She was so tired of this whole mess. She just wanted to wake up and find it had all been a bad dream. Then she wouldn't be facing a caste coup, with no idea whom she could trust. And Micah would be fine. The gaping hole in his side would never have happened, and she would never have scrubbed his blood off her hands, or felt him drifting away from her, so far down the path to his Return…

She was gathered into a warmron, her head held against a soft stomach, and only then noticed that Salomen's anger had been displaced by a tangled ball of guilt and concern.

"I'm a dokker's backside. You didn't need that. Andira, I'm sorry."

Tal shook her head, still unable to speak.

"I'd rather have you mad at me than this."

That brought her voice back. "I wasn't mad at you."

"Would you like to be? I'm sure I could say something inflammatory."

Tal's snort broke the paralysis. Wrapping her arms around Salomen's waist, she said, "Let's save that for another time."

"All right. You had me worried for a tick."

With a final squeeze, Tal pulled away and looked up. "I'm fine. Just tired and overwhelmed."

Salomen nodded, her dark eyes troubled. "How bad is this? I mean, with Shantu?"

"It's bad. I don't know who to trust anymore. Shantu wouldn't plan a caste coup without support, which means there are other warriors on the Council standing ready to betray me as well. And I don't know who any of them are. I never saw this coming; that's what frightens me. I thought I had the support of my caste. I don't understand how something like this could have gotten so far without me getting even a hint of it." Another thought occurred to her. "Oh, no—Aldirk!"

Salomen crouched down, resting her hands on Tal's knees. "What about Aldirk?"

"I asked him to track Parser after that last emergency Council session. I thought he was up to something then, when he switched sides and supported Shantu in a call to halt the implementation of the matter printers. But Aldirk never reported back on anything unusual. He couldn't possibly have missed this. There is no way Parser could be colluding with Shantu and a majority of the high-powered warriors on the Council without Aldirk picking up on something."

She looked at Salomen in growing horror. "Aldirk knows *everything*. Absolutely everything. If he's in on this, I…I can't even calculate the damage." She put her face in her hands, the weariness overtaking her. Everything was caving in, and why did it all have to happen now?

Salomen wisely said nothing, simply communicating her support through her touch.

"I am *so* tired of playing catch-up." Tal raised her head. "Parser was right. I didn't even know the game had started before it was already half over. I've been behind every step of the way. I'm not even sure I want to fight back a caste coup. Is it worth it?"

"It's worth it," Salomen said.

Her conviction got Tal's attention. "Then tell me why, because right now I'm not seeing it."

"Because we need you. If you really want to retire, then I'll gladly take you onto Hol-Opah and turn you into the best warrior-producer on Alsea. But I don't think you're the retiring type, and I know for a fact that Alsea is far better served with you in the State Chair than with a man who would kill innocent citizens to gain power. And it's better served with Parser in prison where he can't hurt anyone else. If Shantu wins, so does Parser. Do you want to leave Alsea in their hands?"

"No."

Salomen nodded. "You care too much. And you've worked too hard to give up on us now. So start counting the people you know you can trust without question. I'll top the list, though I'm not much use in an internal caste battle. But you have Colonel Micah, Colonel Razine…all of your personal Guards…Councilor Ehron, too. And those are just the ones I've met so far."

Tal's laugh held no humor. "Yes, at least Ehron is on my side. That's one warrior out of thirty on the Council."

But she couldn't let Shantu win. Though she had always believed him to be far more principled, she had never been in doubt as to his lust for power. That lust had apparently overwhelmed his caste ethics, which made him unfit to lead. With sufficient evidence, she could put him in prison and cut the head off the coup, but that didn't necessarily mean the coup would die. It all depended on who else was involved.

She needed information, she needed it now, and she would start with Aldirk.

A smile crossed her face as she realized where her thoughts were going. She was already planning her next move. No, she was not the retiring type.

She looked back at Salomen. "You'll top the list?"

"You know I will."

Tal squeezed her hands. "That's all I need. If they want my title, they'll have to fight for it."

CHAPTER 41
Isolation

WHILE WAITING FOR NEWS ON Micah and Shantu, Tal took care of a few more immediate needs. First came a call to Aldirk, who was startled to learn that he was needed in Redmoon immediately. He sputtered and protested, but she told him nothing other than to pack for two days and be on the next transport out of Blacksun. It was too bad she hadn't learned about his possible involvement earlier; he could have caught the transport Razine had sent. Aldirk had naturally pointed out that fact, but if he had hoped for additional information, he was sorely disappointed. As far as Tal was concerned, her Chief Counselor was guilty until proven innocent. She could not afford to act otherwise.

After a call to the commander of Redmoon Base, she recalled all of her Guards—including Gehrain, who was delighted to be released from observation—and had the transport moved to the base. Her Guards were housed in guest quarters and given spare uniforms to wear until their own supplies arrived. Shantu's men were still being held on the transport, since Tal trusted no warriors but her own. After considerable discussion with Salomen, she decided to hold Herot on the transport as well, but gave him the aft cabin to keep him separate from his captors.

Gehrain and Vellmar set up a duty rotation schedule, with two Guards keeping watch over the prisoners, two stationed outside the transport, and four guarding Tal and Salomen in their temporary quarters. Not surprisingly, every one of the off-duty warriors opted to take local transports back to the healing center, where they kept vigil into the night. It was Dewar who called Tal from there at night-one and seventy. Micah was out of surgery.

Tal borrowed a short-range transport from the base and flew it to the healing center, creating a stir as she exited with Salomen and four Guards. The local journalists, having learned of her presence in town, had gathered on the landing pad in hopes of seeing something exciting. The Lancer entering a healing center with her lover in the middle of the night certainly qualified, and they clamored for news. When Tal walked through them without answering, they turned their attention to Salomen. Tal felt her dismay at the chaos, which was a far cry from their carefully planned announcement of her new status. Putting her arm around Salomen in a clear display of intimacy, she informed the journalists that they would learn everything they needed to know about Raiz Opah from tomorrow's State House announcement. Then she swept past them and into the healing center, where the peaceful environment was rigorously enforced by the staff. In the past, she had run afoul of the stubborn mentality of healers and their support staff, but on this occasion she welcomed it as they repelled the eager journalists and closed the doors in their faces.

"I suppose that was my first taste of the future," Salomen said as they followed an assistant healer toward Micah's room. "No wonder you assigned me my own Guards. I'll need them just to push through the crowd."

"It's not always like that."

"Sometimes it's worse?"

Tal squeezed her hand in reply; she knew Salomen was trying to lighten her mood. "Look on the bright side. If there's a successful coup, you won't have to worry about the crowds."

"Every flood brings new growth," Salomen said cheerfully.

The assistant led them to a closed door and stood to one side. "Healer Elwyn is waiting."

"Thank you." Tal entered the small room as her Guards took up positions outside the door. She was so focused on the figure in the bed that she didn't notice the slender man sitting in the corner until he stood up to introduce himself, and even then she hardly heard a word.

Micah appeared so much better that she felt real hope for the first time that night. The oxygenator was gone and his color had returned, and for a moment she expected him to open his eyes and give her a knowing smile. *Did I make my point?* he would say. *There's still some usefulness in this old warrior.*

"—a strong man," the healer was saying. "He sustained significant bone and soft tissue damage. He now has a synthetic hip joint and several spans of new intestine, both large and small, and we had to reconstruct all of the major muscles in the affected area. Your team did a commendable job of minimizing the blood loss and getting him here quickly."

"That sounds positive," Tal said. "Do you expect a full recovery?"

"We only finished surgery forty ticks ago. It's still early in the healing process. I really cannot answer that question just now."

"But you can make an educated guess."

"Healing is not about guessing, Lancer Tal. It's about observation and response."

"And what have you observed that prevents you from giving me any kind of answer at all?"

He pressed his lips together, glancing at Micah.

"Did someone on your surgery team Share with him?" Salomen asked.

"You're familiar with this procedure?"

"Not until tonight. Lancer Tal and I both Shared with him on the flight here."

"You never heard of that until tonight and you performed the procedure? You're either extremely courageous or blissfully ignorant of the usual myths. Most people believe that Sharing with a dying person is a one-way trip to a Return."

"Put me down for ignorance, then. And I notice you sidestepped my question."

Tal almost smiled at the expression on Elwyn's face. "I'm also curious about your response."

After a pause, he said, "Yes, we did. When he arrived, it was obvious that he would not survive surgery without extreme measures. I called in a colleague who is known for her skill in retrieval. She held him, but afterward she told me that he was not willing. It was a forced hold."

"But he's stable now, correct?" Tal asked. "Does a forced hold matter once the physical danger is past?"

"Now you're moving into an area that has eluded our science since the First Healer. Sometimes, for reasons we still don't understand, Alseans simply do not wish to be healed. Their bodies recover, yet they never regain consciousness. Sometimes they Return for no physical reason we can find. Other times they lie dormant for days or ninedays or even moons, and wake up as if nothing had ever kept them away. I know of cases where Alseans awoke as much as five cycles after their original injury. In all of these cases, the patient underwent a forced hold."

He held up his hand in a placating gesture. "It is far too early to determine whether Colonel Micah will fall into this category. Please don't take this as any sort of diagnosis on my part; I'm merely sharing information. It's just as possible that his forced hold was necessary because he believed his injury was fatal. Once his body understands that it was not and transfers that information to his consciousness, he may awaken almost immediately. His body will heal, though it will take time. As to the rest, I simply cannot say."

Tal looked back at Micah. His square jaw and short, bristling hair belied the frailty of the body beneath the cover, but she knew that his true frailty was not physical. Healer Elwyn could not touch the real injury.

"Is there any issue regarding my Sharing with him now?"

"No, not at all. In fact, it might help."

"Would you like me to join you?" Salomen asked.

Tal shook her head. "What I'd like is for you to Share with him after me. I think Micah is content with his Return. We need to let him know that the rest of us aren't nearly so happy about it."

With the healer's assistance, she tilted his head slightly to enable a better match of their forehead ridges. Slipping her hands into place, she lowered her head and soon found herself in a familiar darkness, but this time she quickly broke through. Micah could be awake right now; he was just on the other side of the barrier. He was tired, but the utter exhaustion that had marked their prior Sharing was gone.

Come back. Please.

She felt his sorrow; a sense of longing for something. Whether it was for his final release or something else, she wasn't sure.

I need you. She projected her fear, her grief, her love, her own longing for his safe awakening. But she never felt a direct response. It was as if she could not quite make the connection, and with a sinking heart she understood why. Micah was no longer allowing her to touch him. He had been held back against his will and was now keeping his distance.

She tried again and again, each time getting the same result, and finally withdrew in defeat. The first thing she became aware of was Salomen's hand on top of hers where it touched Micah's jaw. She straightened, pulling both of their hands back.

"He's not listening. I can't make the connection. I don't even know if he's aware of me."

"Do you think it will make any difference if I try?"

"It can't hurt. Perhaps we should just take turns until we annoy him so much he'll have to listen."

Salomen gave her a sad smile before stepping into place.

Tal watched her eyes close as she rested her forehead against his. "Good luck," she whispered.

But Salomen had no better results, and they were forced to leave Micah in his self-imposed isolation. After thanking Healer Elwyn, Tal led Salomen to the notification area to break the news to the Guards.

They crowded around as soon as she appeared.

"How is he?"

"Will he recover?"

"They won't tell us anything, the dokkers."

Half of them were talking at once, and Tal raised her hands. When they had quieted down, she said, "Colonel Micah came through his surgery just fine. The healer said that we did a commendable job of stopping the blood loss and getting him here. Though he didn't say it in so many words, I know the colonel would not have made it without Guard Dewar's quick thinking and efficient treatment."

Dewar looked embarrassed as her fellow Guards clapped her on the back. "But how is he now?"

"Physically on the mend. I just Shared with him, and he's right on the other side." Tal paused, wondering how much to say.

"There's a very large caveat coming," Gehrain said. The others nodded, looking at her expectantly.

"You might as well tell them," Salomen whispered. "They already know."

She was right, but Tal needed a moment to find the best way to say it.

"The colonel is not responsive on the emotional plane," she said at last. "He's there, but he won't allow a connection. Healer Elwyn gave us some possible explanations, the most common being that Colonel Micah doesn't yet realize his injury was not fatal. Once he understands that, he may wake up immediately." Their expressions were still expectant, and she shook her head. "I don't think that's the case. I think he has decided that his time has arrived. He suffered an injury in the line of duty that sent him a long distance down the path of his Return, and the fact that we prevented his Return may be irrelevant to him. Salomen and I both attempted to persuade him to come back, but he's not listening."

They looked at each other, a few of them murmuring quietly. Gehrain caught Tal's eye and said, "Colonel Micah can be a little stubborn." Amid a few chuckles, he added, "I'd like to Share with him as well, if the healer doesn't think that would cause any problems. Perhaps he needs to hear that we don't accept his resignation."

Tal smiled at his choice of words. "It won't cause any problems. Healer Elwyn suggested that a Sharing couldn't hurt and might help. Thank you, Gehrain."

"Then I want to Share with him, too," Dewar said.

"Me too," said Senshalon. "I've been serving under Colonel Micah for nearly four cycles, and in my opinion we've just now got him broken in. Starting all over again with someone else is not an option."

That set off a chorus of voices as nearly every other Guard in the room pressed forward, eager to take part.

"All right, all right!" Tal called, and they settled down again. She looked them over with considerable pride. Her Guards were just as stubborn as Micah; they weren't about to stand quietly and do nothing.

"You just hate waiting around, don't you?" she asked, causing another chorus of agreement. Looking at the one Guard who had held herself apart from the requests, she said, "Vellmar, you'll be the liaison with Healer Elwyn. Find out what he advises regarding the number and duration of Sharings, and set up a schedule. In the meantime, there's no need for all of us to be cluttering up the notification area. I suggest that once you've established your Sharing times, you head back to Redmoon Base and get some sleep."

The vibration of her wristcom distracted her, and she checked the screen to find a cryptic message from Razine, carefully worded against interception.

Vid yielded enough frames for identification. We have a match for both. Guards found an empty house and no sign of the occupant. Request immediate consult.

Shantu must have known about Herot's rescue, then. Periso had probably told him. And now he had gone underground.

The head of the coup was free to organize his followers.

Leaving Vellmar surrounded by Guards trying to establish their place in the lineup, Tal tapped Gehrain's shoulder and led him over to a window.

"We need to talk," she said.

PART FOUR:

ENDGAME

CHAPTER 42
Loyalty test

Aldirk spent the entire flight to Redmoon staring out the window and calculating possibilities. His political success depended on staying one step ahead of Lancer Tal, ready to provide or maneuver before she herself knew what she was going to do. For her to yank him out of Blacksun on the very night that Parser had been neutralized, and put him on a public transport where he had no access to his usual sources, spoke of an urgency that might not be explained by Colonel Micah's injury. If that urgency had to do with Parser's plan, then Aldirk had just been taken out of the game. He did not like to consider what that might mean.

His agitation was exacerbated by the indignity of his current mode of travel. How did anyone fly this way? The seats were narrow, the food was disgusting, and someone nearby had not bathed in far too long. Lancer Tal was going to get an earful when he arrived. "Offense before defense" was not just a warrior creed.

He was somewhat mollified, upon exiting that foul-smelling mobile crate, to find that the Lancer had at least sent her highest-ranked Guard to meet him. Head Guardian Gehrain was waiting at the bottom of the transport ramp, his uniform causing nearly every passenger to look at him while trying to appear nonchalant.

Aldirk marched up and deposited his gear bag in Gehrain's hands. "Please tell me you have a military transport for the rest of this trip. I have no desire to cross Redmoon on some public magtran that stinks of old fanten."

"Yes, Chief Counselor. Please follow me." Gehrain turned smartly and led him around the nose of the large transport, revealing the much smaller craft behind it. They walked up the ramp and into the familiar confines of a military short-range craft, with its wide seats, large windows, and—best of all—complete lack of people.

Settling into the first seat, Aldirk let out a grateful sigh. "Thank Fahla, breathable air."

Gehrain closed the door and stored the gear bag. "We'll be at Redmoon Base in ten ticks," he said. "The Lancer is waiting for you."

"Yes, I'd rather imagine she is, since she put me on that damnable flight in the middle of the night. Does the woman never sleep?"

Gehrain paused, then turned toward the pilot's cabin. "Make yourself comfortable, Chief Counselor." The pilot's door shut behind him. Barely a tick later, the craft rose and the enormous transport station fell away beneath them.

Redmoon was an attractive city, Aldirk had to admit. Particularly now, with all of the domes flushed a light pink in the sunrise. The Telano River looked like a lava flow as it wound through the center of the city, and boats of all sizes were carving its waters, their wakes sparkling. The fisher craft were easy to spot with their gear and brilliant colors, each painted with the unique crest of its family. Ponderous cargo carriers shoved through the current to the docks, and tiny sporting boats dashed in all directions, full of people out for their morning exercise.

He had little time to observe this before the city was behind them, which was the main reason he could never live here. Redmoon was too small for his tastes and much too far from the center of power.

They followed the river downstream, leaving all of the sporting boats and most of the cargo carriers behind. Then Gehrain banked the transport, and Aldirk caught a glimpse of the vast bay as they began their descent toward the landing pad at Redmoon Base. Looking down, he had no trouble picking out the Lancer's long-distance transport from the rest. Beside it was another transport with Blacksun markings—the one he had missed by a bare hantick, thus consigning him to the horror of a public flight.

They settled to the ground, and with excellent efficiency Gehrain was out of the pilot's cabin, picking up Aldirk's bag and escorting him down the ramp. To Aldirk's surprise, he was led directly to the Lancer's transport rather than the guest officer quarters on the base.

It was cool, dim, and empty inside. This was not among the scenarios Aldirk had envisioned, but before he could ask, Gehrain led him down the short corridor to the Lancer's private cabin, rapped on the door twice, and opened it.

"Lancer Tal, Chief Counselor Aldirk is here."

"Good. Bring him in."

Aldirk stepped past Gehrain and found the Lancer sitting at her conference table, facing the door. "I've come as ordered, though I must protest the manner of transport I was forced to take. You would not believe—"

"Sit down, Aldirk."

He closed his mouth and sat across from her. Her front was perfect as usual, but her expression was disturbing. Not for what it showed, but for the careful lack of showing anything at all. She simply watched him, and in the uncomfortable silence he heard Gehrain moving into the room behind him. With a quiet whisper, the door slid shut.

"I have an unusual request to ask of you," she said at last. "I would like you to submit to an empathic scan."

He gaped at her. Criminals submitted to empathic scans, not law-abiding citizens. He had been scanned only twice in his life: once when he became a member of the Council and was being given his clearances, and again when Lancer Tal had named him her Chief Counselor, requiring new clearances. The only reason she could possibly have to ask him for another submission was if she suspected him of criminal activity.

"I don't understand," he said. "I've done nothing." Suddenly, the silent, empty transport felt threatening. He was locked in here with two people who could make him disappear.

"I wish I could take you at your word. I cannot tell you why I'm asking, Aldirk. I can only ask. Will you submit?"

"What am I accused of? I have a right to know."

"Will. You. Submit."

It was no longer a polite question, and for the first time in his association with her, he saw a ruthless warrior under the Lancer's uniform. The chilling blue of her eyes sent a shiver down his spine.

"I will submit," he said. "But only because it appears that I won't be leaving this transport unless I do."

She made no response other than to narrow her eyes slightly, and he felt the intrusion. Not just her probe, but the Head Guardian's as well. Instinctively he blocked them, causing an instant headache as they pushed against his defenses.

"Aldirk." Her voice was nearly a growl.

"I'm trying!" He took a calming breath, let it out, and forced himself to drop his blocks.

Their probes punched through with too much force, the sudden lack of resistance surprising both Lancer Tal and Gehrain. Aldirk clutched his head, panting through the pain, and was grateful to feel them pulling back to a safer level. They didn't trust him, but at least they hadn't actually meant to hurt him.

Yet.

"Where do your loyalties lie?" Lancer Tal asked.

He dropped his hands and straightened, frowning at the last question he had expected. "With you, of course. Why would you doubt it?"

"Are you working for or providing information to anyone else?"

"No! I have never betrayed you. What is—"

"Did you mention anything, to anyone other than Colonel Razine, regarding our mission yesterday?"

"Yes, I spoke of it with Guard Varsi. She was very distressed to have been left behind."

"What do you know about the relationship between Parser and Shantu?"

He blinked at her. "You mean besides working together on the Anti-Corruption Task Force? They have no relationship beyond that. At least not that I know of."

She watched him for several pipticks, then sat back with a sigh and rubbed her temples. "Let him go, Gehrain."

They retreated, Gehrain swiftly and Lancer Tal with more care. Only then did Aldirk realize that the majority of the pressure in his head was from the

Lancer's probe. Had she pulled out as abruptly as she had pushed in, he would have been reeling from the pain.

The moment they were out, he slammed his blocks back into place and sagged with relief. Then he stiffened, anger bolstering his courage. "Do you mind telling me what that was about? Did I pass your loyalty test?"

Her face, which had been so cold moments before, now looked weary. "Yes, you did. Please accept my apologies. I never thought I would be in the position of questioning your loyalty, but it's been a difficult day and a worse night. Gehrain, have a seat."

Gehrain came around to the Lancer's side of the table and sat beside her. "I apologize as well, Chief Counselor. It was necessary."

A retort was on the tip of Aldirk's tongue, but another look at Lancer Tal's obvious weariness stopped him. "You haven't slept, have you?"

"Not more than a couple of hanticks." She gave him a tiny smile. "You have no idea how glad I am that you're on my side."

"I didn't realize there were sides." A sudden suspicion blossomed. "Parser and Shantu?"

"Shantu is planning a caste coup. He's the one who was holding Herot Opah, not Parser, though they're working together. And he was fully prepared to kill Herot and frame me for the murder, in order to expose me as a leader bent on personal revenge. We've upset his plans by extracting Herot, but he's gone underground now and I don't know what his next step will be. I assume it will be to contact his supporters and initiate action. Since there's a warrant out on him, he can no longer afford to wait. He needs to get me out of my position so the criminal charges can be conveniently dropped."

Aldirk shook his head, trying to come to terms with the impossibility of it. "Are you certain of all this? Because if he's truly planning a caste coup, it's the quietest one I ever heard of."

Her gaze sharpened. "You haven't heard anything?"

"Absolutely nothing. If Parser and Shantu are working together, they're showing no sign of it at the State House or at social functions in Blacksun. The only time they're together is when they're working on the task force. And if Shantu has been rounding up support on the Council and among Blacksun warriors, then he's found a way to do it without raising even a breath of gossip. I find that especially difficult to believe. When the warrior caste was preparing to unseat Tordax, I knew about it nearly three ninedays prior to the event. And I was only a Councilor then; I have more sources now as Chief Counselor. Nothing is happening. I would stake my good name on it."

She looked from him to Gehrain. "Maybe I've overestimated his timeline. Maybe he *hasn't* gotten support yet."

"He doesn't have the political capital for it now," Aldirk said. "If you hadn't turned around public opinion on the matter printers, he would have. But you recovered from that. He needs you to make a public stumble that he can pounce on, and you haven't stumbled."

"Great Goddess," she said, a light dawning on her face. "Is something going to go right at last? I may faint from the shock of it."

"Herot was your public stumble," said Gehrain. "We pulled out his most valuable source of political capital."

"I would advise an emergency Council session." Aldirk was already strategizing. "We can eliminate what political capital he has by laying everything out in front of the Council. The Councilors will wake up this morning and find that the Prime Warrior is now pursued by the AIF and the Prime Merchant is already in custody; that will be the biggest news since the Voloth invasion. If we follow that up with the details of Shantu's plan regarding Herot Opah—perhaps even have Herot testify before the Council—we can make it impossible for Shantu to find support. No one wants to associate with a known criminal. An unknown one, perhaps, but not a known one."

"Hm." Lancer Tal rested her head on the back of her chair and gazed at the ceiling. "There's one piece missing, and I don't like it." Raising her head again, she looked from Aldirk to Gehrain. "Parser's plan. Given the way he covered all possibilities, I cannot believe he wouldn't have planned for the possibility of losing Herot."

"He may have," Gehrain said, "but he probably didn't plan for the possibility of losing Shantu as well. Even the Chief Counselor didn't know of their association outside the task force. The only reason we know is because we collected two prisoners along with Herot, and how could Parser possibly have planned for that? As you said, that was Shantu's show. Parser didn't even know where Herot was being held."

"It's not likely," she conceded. "But I'm still not comfortable. I don't want to make a move until Razine has her warrant and takes Parser apart."

Aldirk felt ill. "Empathic force?"

She nodded. "I need to know what he knows. We should have the information before midmeal today."

Aldirk had no great love for Parser, but he wouldn't wish empathic force on anyone other than the Voloth. Even in the hands of highly trained interrogators, things could go wrong. He had heard stories of Alseans who never fully recovered from it. "That's a nasty procedure," he said.

"Yes, it is." Her eyes chilled again. "And I've learned that Parser is a rather nasty person. He brought this on himself. It's not as if he made a single bad decision. He planned all of this, far in advance. Herot Opah nearly died, simply because he was a tile for Parser to play. And if it hadn't been Herot, it would have been Jaros."

"What!"

They looked at Gehrain, who was embarrassed by his outburst. "You didn't mention that in my briefing," he said.

"Put it down to a lack of sleep. Yes, Parser made sure to tell me, when he thought he'd won the first time, that his original target was Jaros. It was a message."

"A very pointed message," Aldirk said. "None of the Opahs would be safe unless you turned a blind eye to him."

Gehrain's face darkened. "Now I'm sorry I can't be there to personally assist in his questioning."

"Perhaps you can personally escort him to the Pit." Lancer Tal looked at Aldirk thoughtfully. "I like the idea of Herot testifying before the Council. Putting a face and a personal story to the situation will make matters even worse for both Parser and Shantu."

"Are you sure you want to do that?" Gehrain asked. "Can we be certain Herot won't damage you as much as they have?"

Aldirk had to concede his point. "This *is* the man who nearly got you killed. Perhaps my idea was ill considered."

"I think Herot can be motivated to do the right thing." She drummed her fingers on the table. "I need to speak with him anyway. And the prisoner transport is ready to leave, so I suppose now is the time. Aldirk, when the hantick is more reasonable, see if you can find out anything about Shantu without letting anyone know why you're asking. And depending on what Colonel Razine gets from Parser, I may be asking you to assemble that emergency Council session. I'll let you know as soon as I can. In the meantime, we have accommodations ready for you on base." She smiled briefly. "The guest officer quarters, not the detention block. I was hoping for this outcome for more than just my own peace of mind. Gehrain, please escort the Chief Counselor to his quarters. I'll be on the other transport."

Gehrain stood immediately. "Whenever you're ready, Chief Counselor."

Aldirk pushed his chair back and looked around for his bag.

"Aldirk."

Somehow Lancer Tal was standing next to him. He hadn't even heard her chair move.

She held up her hand. "I truly am sorry for the necessity of scanning you. And even more so for the discomfort we caused."

He touched their palms together, feeling for himself the sincerity of her apology. "As Head Guardian Gehrain said, it was necessary. I cannot say I enjoyed the experience, but I understand why you had to do it."

"Do you?" she asked. "Do you realize that of all the people in the State House, you're the one Shantu should have recruited? He overlooked the best resource in Blacksun."

He smiled. "Shantu is not a fool. Had he tried to recruit me, his caste coup would have been over before it began."

There was appreciation and respect in her touch as she returned his smile. She stooped to pick up his bag and handed it to Gehrain. "Get a few hanticks of sleep while you can."

"You should take your own advice."

He walked out the door ahead of Gehrain and thought that the transport seemed rather peaceful in the early morning light.

CHAPTER 43
Herot's education

Tal nodded at Nilsinian and Dewar as she entered the military transport. While Razine's warriors were taking a break, her own Guards were continuing their watch over the prisoners. They would rotate out when the others returned, but Tal was not about to leave Herot alone with anyone but her own people. She had chosen the two best-rested of her team to accompany the transport back to Blacksun, with orders not to let Herot out of their sight until they were relieved by fresh Guards from the State House.

"Any trouble over here?" she asked.

"No, Lancer. It's been very quiet." Dewar yawned and turned red. "My apologies."

Tal shook her head. "People who draw the dawn rotation shouldn't be holding all-night vigils at healing centers. And yes, I know that's the knife calling the sword a blade."

"You should get some rest, Lancer," Nilsinian said.

"I keep hearing that. Don't worry, I'm going back to my quarters as soon as I have a talk with Herot." She noted that the Guards had wisely separated Herot from his captors by the length of the cabin. Oren and Dalset were bound to the front-row seats, where they studiously avoided looking at her. Herot was asleep in the farthest rear-facing row, his seat reclined as far as it would go. "Nice to see that someone is getting some sleep," she said as she headed down the aisle.

He didn't move when she slipped into the last row to take the seat facing him, and she used the opportunity to study him more closely. According to his medical report, his injuries showed evidence of two separate beatings, one considerably harsher than the other. Tal guessed that the second, nastier beating had been after his escape attempt. Other than the broken ankle, the injuries were limited to bruising and scrapes, though some of the bruises were quite deep. Dermal treatment had healed all but the deepest, and his ankle was now in a hard case. She suspected that he was enjoying his first pain-free sleep in six days, and felt almost guilty about waking him.

"Herot," she said in a low voice. "Wake up."

The muddled emotions of sleep jumped to the higher plane of awareness, but he didn't move, feigning unconsciousness.

"Herot. We need to talk."

His eyes flew open. "Oh, it's you. I thought I was back there."

As he yawned and stretched, she wondered if he was aware that it had been her order to leave him unbound. Prisoners were not normally left to run around free, but he wasn't going anywhere.

Pulling his cased ankle into a more comfortable position, he looked up at her in resignation. "Is this the long talk you threatened me with last night?"

"Probably not. But we need to get a few things out of the way."

He twisted in his seat, looking toward the front of the cabin, then settled back with a sigh. "She didn't come, did she?"

"She's asleep."

He bit his lip. "Is she ever going to talk to me again?"

"Knowing Salomen, yes, eventually. But not this morning. She's having some…mixed emotions about you."

Salomen was right; that irritating edge of arrogance and entitlement was gone. In some ways, his emotions felt younger. There was a bewilderment mixed in with his guilt and fear, and the longing of a child for comfort. Salomen was the closest thing Herot had to a mother figure, and she had made her anger abundantly clear. For the first time, Tal felt a tiny stirring of sympathy for him.

"I'm sorry," he said. "I've been wanting to tell you that for days. I tried last night, but you wouldn't let me. I tried to tell Salomen, too, but she hardly even looked at me."

Her sympathy vanished. "Perhaps you might have noticed that we were a little busy trying to save Colonel Micah's life."

"I know, but Salomen wouldn't look at me afterward, either. Even when we flew the transport to the base. I thought maybe she'd come talk to me when I was moved to this transport, but she hasn't."

"Great Goddess, Herot!" Tal saw her Guards look toward her, then quickly away again. She lowered her voice. "In all those days you were a prisoner, didn't you spend any time thinking about what you've done?"

"Of course I did! What else did I have to think about? I even prayed to Fahla for the chance to see my family one last time, just so I could tell them how sorry I was. I never really believed that she answered prayers, but here I am, she gave me the chance, and Salomen won't even see me!"

Tal took a deep breath and tried to rein in her impatience. After all, Herot had missed a few details in his absence.

"Salomen prayed, too. She was worried sick about you."

"She was?" The hope that bloomed through his emotions startled her with its intensity. "I didn't know. She was so angry last night."

"It's possible to be angry and worried at the same time. You've put her through Fahla's own nightmares. You have no idea how much damage you caused."

He looked down. "Yes, I do. Believe me, I do."

"No," she said firmly. "You don't. Because you think the worst thing you did was act like a fantenshekken when you were drunk and say some stupid things that had unfortunate consequences. You think a simple apology will fix it, but it won't. Not until you understand."

"What else can I do besides apologize? I can't change what happened."

"But you can change your understanding of what happened. You didn't just talk like a drunken dokker. You betrayed a trust. You betrayed the hospitality of your home. In some ways that's even worse than betraying me personally, but you did that, too. I watched your message, Herot. You said you were glad I only sustained a minor injury. Do you realize what you were saying, even while you were trying to apologize? You were saying, 'I'm glad she was only hurt a little.' Not, 'I'm so sorry she was hurt; thank Fahla it wasn't worse.' There's an enormous difference."

"I didn't think of it like that. It's not what I meant."

"Isn't it?" She held his gaze, willing him to face it. "Can you tell me that you were truly sorry I was hurt at all? Or were you sorry about the destruction to your home and the fact that you had just turned yourself into a criminal and hurt your entire family?"

There was a long silence. "I was sorry about everything," he said at last. "But...I was more sorry about the rest than about you. But you *weren't* hurt badly."

She wanted to shake him. "Will you listen to yourself? Whether or not I was badly hurt is not the point!"

Frowning, he looked away, and she forced herself to calm down and regroup.

"Let me ask you this," she said in a quieter tone. "When you were telling Cullom which window to shoot at, did you ever stop to think that I wouldn't be the only one in the room? You told him I was there at a certain time every night, but the reason I was there at those times was because I was meeting with your sister. You *knew* that. But you were being such a selfish ass that you didn't think beyond your immediate desire of hurting me. What if you'd hurt Salomen instead?"

He stared in dawning horror. "She was there?"

"She was the one in the window seat. Not me. She almost died, Herot. That plasma shot was aimed at her, and you're the one who told Cullom where to aim it."

"Wh—" He clutched his stomach with a pained groan. "Oh, no. No, no, I didn't know...Salomen..."

"You didn't know because you didn't *think*. You turned selfishness and self-pity into an art form, and it nearly killed your sister. Do you suppose a simple apology will fix it now?"

His eyes were brimming with tears. "I don't know," he whispered. "I don't know how to apologize for that. There's nothing I can say. Fahla forgive me, I never thought..."

"No, you didn't. And then you ran like a coward instead of facing your family. They were cleaning up the destruction, Salomen was at the healing center with me and Micah, and on top of everything else, they had to worry about you. For six days you let them wonder whether you actually meant to cause that much damage, or whether you'd just done it because you were thoughtless and dangerously stupid."

The tears overflowed. "I know I was a coward. I'm sorry, Fahla, I'm so sorry! I'll do anything to make it right."

"You can start by telling your sister the truth. Not the dokshin you just tried to feed me. Don't tell her you never meant for anyone to get hurt, because she knows better. That's why she's so angry. She spent five nights in the healing center with me, knowing that her own brother helped put me there. It wasn't a minor injury, Herot. That's just what the media was told. You succeeded in hurting me; I was severely burned over half my body. But you hurt Salomen more. My injuries were just physical, but hers go far deeper. She lives every day with the knowledge that you almost got her killed through sheer spite and small-mindedness. Her own burns were nothing compared to that. And you didn't even stay around to see how badly she was hurt."

A great, gulping sob escaped, and he clutched his stomach again, bending over as he cried. She watched him with very little pity, but as he continued to weep, she finally felt her own anger giving way to a quieter sorrow over the whole situation.

"There's something you need to know," she said more gently.

"Wh...what?" He took a deep breath, trying to get himself under control.

"In three hanticks, my communications advisor will hold a media conference to make a special announcement. Salomen and I have set a bonding date for the twenty-third of Rosslin."

His weeping stopped with his breathing as he stared at her. "A bonding date?" he managed. "You and Salomen?"

She smiled for the first time. "My intentions were always more honorable than you gave me credit for. Your sister will be the Bondlancer of Alsea."

Though his shock faded, he seemed incapable of speech.

"I petitioned your father for inclusion, and he accepted me. Your family is my family now, so you'll have to get used to the idea. I'm not going away. Ever. That's another reason Salomen is so angry. She would have been furious if you'd hurt anyone under her roof, but you happened to hurt her chosen bondmate."

"Shek," he whispered. "Bondlancer?"

She nodded, and he sagged back against his seat. When nothing else was forthcoming, she dropped the topic.

"I have to send you back to Blacksun soon. Before you go, I'd like to know what happened after you were taken from the Napoline transit station. How did those two warriors convince you to go with them?"

He looked as if he had eaten something sour. "They told me you sent them, and that you'd worked out a deal with the High Tribunal so I wouldn't face charges. I thought the whole world had magically righted itself." He gave a derisive snort. "I was an idiot. I believed them. So I went with them, and as soon as we got into the transport, I knew it was a mistake, because it was filthy. Your Guards don't even let their boots get dirty; they'd never allow their transport to look like that one did. So I tried to get out, but Oren punched me in the face. I fought back, but he was too big and too fast. And when we got to that house, he put me in the room and told me that I needed to learn a lesson about touching them."

"A memorable lesson, I take it." Tal gestured toward the fading bruises on his face, and he nodded.

"Part of me felt like I deserved it. I didn't think I could get any lower. But every tick from that point on, there was a guard in the room with me, holding a disruptor. One of them told me that he had no idea why they wanted me alive, since their orders were to kill me if anyone other than them tried to get to me. I kept looking at that disruptor and thinking I didn't want to die. After two days of it, I snapped. Dalset was the one holding the disruptor then. I waited until she was distracted and jumped her. I thought if I could get her disruptor, maybe I could escape. But I wasn't good enough."

"You jumped Dalset?" A light dawned. "Are you the reason her nose is bandaged?"

"I broke it. She paid me back by breaking my ankle. I thought she broke my ribs, too, but the healer said they were just severely bruised. I gave up hope then. It was just a matter of time before I died. And then yesterday, you came."

"And you thought I was there to kill you."

He looked away, embarrassed. "I hate that you can feel everything."

"Actually, I couldn't feel you then," she said. "Lead Guard Vellmar wrapped her front around you to keep your emotions from warning any of your other captors. But it was written all over your face."

"You killed Swifan," he whispered. "You killed him and your expression didn't even change. It was nothing to you. You even shushed me while you were doing it—and then you *smiled* afterward. I thought I was next."

"Sorry to disappoint. At least you're consistent in always expecting the worst of me."

"Does Salomen know what you do?"

"Does she know I'm a cold-blooded killer, is that what you mean?" Her anger was rising again. "No. She knows that I'm a warrior and that I do precisely what I have to. And you should thank our Goddess for that, because if I and fourteen other warriors hadn't been prepared to kill in order to save you, you would have died yesterday and we wouldn't be having this conversation about my killing instincts. Unlike you, Salomen knows who I really am. She also knows exactly what I did yesterday and what it cost me. If you want to learn any more about that, you'll have to ask her."

"What do you mean, what it cost you?"

She looked at him for several pipticks as he grew progressively more uncomfortable.

"Just think about it," she said. "Put yourself in someone else's place for once in your whole damned life and try to imagine it. I never saw that man before, but I had to watch him die. I had to *feel* him die. To save you." She shook her head. "We're drifting off the navigation beacon. I came here to ask if you would be willing to testify to the Council about your experience."

"Ah...do you need me to?"

"It would be helpful, yes. If you want to make things right with Salomen, you can start with this. The man responsible for your kidnapping was Prime Warrior Shantu. He's one of the most powerful Alseans on the Council. Since I've put out a criminal warrant on him, the other Council members will be questioning why. Your testimony will make it very clear."

He furrowed his brow. "Why would the Prime Warrior want to kidnap me?"

"For the same reason you told Cullom Bilsner where to aim. He wants to hurt me. Though he's after a political wound, while you were after a physical one. It's ironic, don't you think? You became a weapon, and the reason you were chosen is because of what you did."

"I don't understand."

"Shantu was going to kill you and frame me for your murder. Then he could lead a caste coup against me. You were his ticket to the title of Lancer."

"But I'm—oh." A sharp edge punctured his comprehension. "That's why you rescued me. To save your title."

"I was already looking for you before you were kidnapped, Herot. Before I had any idea about Shantu and his scheme. But if you were hoping that I rescued you because you're an innocent man who was treated badly, then I'll have to remind you of something you seem to have overlooked. You're not an innocent man."

His gaze dropped as a wave of shame washed through him.

"Will you testify?" she asked again.

"Yes," he said, still not meeting her eyes. "I owe it to you."

Tal started to correct him but changed her mind. "Thank you. I'll tell Salomen you asked after her." She rose and was halfway down the aisle when his voice stopped her.

"Lancer Tal!"

She paused, her back to him.

"Please. I need to know something."

With a sigh, she turned around. "What is it?" she asked when she reached him.

"You said Salomen was in the window seat. But you were the one who was hurt. What happened?"

He reminded her of Salomen as he looked up at her, and she finally realized why. For the first time in their acquaintance, he was showing concern for someone other than himself.

"I felt Cullom on the property," she said. "His emotions gave him away. I pulled Salomen out of the window seat just in time, but I couldn't get us far enough back to avoid the molten glass from the window. One of us was going to be burned…and I couldn't let it be her."

"But you said she *was* burned."

"She was. But only on the parts of her legs that I couldn't cover. I couldn't save her from everything, though Fahla knows I tried."

He stared at her for a long moment before looking out the window. "I never took Cullom seriously. He was so angry about everything, all the time. I think that's why we became friends, because I was angry, too. We fueled each other. At the end, he was furious about what he thought you were doing to our caste—and about his father losing face after he'd taken such a public stand against you and saying you had to be stopped. It made all of them look stupid."

When he turned back, there was a new sharpness in his gaze. "But I think he always hated Salomen, too. Because she refused Gordense's bond offer, and everyone in Granelle knew it. Everyone knew Iversina was the second choice. And then word got out about Salomen being your lover, and Gordense tried to throw that in her face at the caste house meeting, and she reminded him in front of Iversina and every landholder in the district that she'd turned him down. Gordense lost a lot of respect. Cullom said the whole town was laughing at them. And I wonder…I just wonder if he didn't care who he hurt, you or Salomen."

"If that's the case, then I have even less pity for him now than before. And I had none before."

"I want to tear out his throat," Herot said flatly. "You'd better make certain we never meet, or my sentence will be a lot longer. I think that's Fahla's joke on me—someone I thought was my friend almost killed my sister, and someone I thought was my enemy saved her. I will never be able to thank you enough for that."

Great Mother, Herot Opah thanking her? The world had come to an end.

"You don't have to," she said. "I did it for her. And for myself. It would have destroyed me if anything had happened to her."

"It kills me just thinking about it. I don't blame her for not wanting to talk to me after that. I wouldn't either."

A few days ago, Herot would have been angry at Salomen for being angry at him. His acceptance of her reaction showed more maturity than Tal would have thought possible. It was also the one thing that could have induced her to offer comfort.

"She'll talk to you eventually," she said. "Probably sooner rather than later. You hurt her and you disappointed her, but you have one very important thing in your favor. You're her brother, and Salomen does not let go of her family. She's one of the most loyal people I have ever known."

"I know. I took a lot for granted." He gave her an intent look, a sudden shyness coloring his emotions. "Can I ask you something?"

She nodded, wondering if she was ready for it.

"Do you…" He paused before finishing in a rush, "You really love her, don't you?"

She smiled; that was an easy one. "How could I not? When someone like Salomen loves you, it's impossible not to love her back."

"True words. I guess this is the part where I'm supposed to warn you against ever hurting her, but…" He shrugged, embarrassed. "I know you'll take care of her."

"I'm doing my best." Tal hesitated, then held up her palm. "Good-bye, Herot."

His touch was firm. "Good-bye."

This time she only got a third of the way down the aisle.

"Lancer Tal!"

She turned in place.

He was struggling to his feet, using the seat back as a crutch. "I know this doesn't mean much, coming from me. But I'm glad to have you in our family."

Surprised, she gave him a brief smile. "It means something."

The sun was well over the horizon as she stepped off the ramp, but she could feel that Salomen was still asleep. Her stride lengthened as she walked toward their temporary quarters, already imagining herself curling around Salomen's warm body. She wouldn't have long, but she meant to make the most of it.

And Herot was glad to have her in the Opah family.

Maybe Micah would wake up today. They had already had one miracle; why not two?

CHAPTER 44
Morning in Redmoon

"Andira."

Tal reached out, her hand settling on a sleeve. "Why are you dressed?" she mumbled. Salomen needed to be in bed. The sooner she got undressed and climbed in, the sooner Tal could snuggle up to her and sleep again.

"I'm dressed because we have to get up." Tal's hair was pushed away from her face, and a gentle kiss touched her forehead. "I let you sleep as long as I could. But it's our turn with Colonel Micah."

Tal groaned as she sat up, the vestiges of sleep still gumming up her brain. Her head dropped in exhaustion. "Didn't I just get in bed?"

"You've been sleeping for over two hanticks." Salomen kissed the back of her neck.

"Really?" She couldn't believe it and checked her wristcom just to be sure. "Damn. I would have sworn I laid down five ticks ago."

"You've been dead asleep. I wanted to let you stay that way, but you told me to wake you up at hantick nine."

"I know. But did you have to listen?" Tal threw the coverlet back and slid her legs over the side, the movement helping to clear her head. "No, you're right. We need to check on Micah, and Colonel Razine should be getting some results soon." She stood up and took a single step, right into Salomen's arms. "That's far enough for now," she said into her shoulder.

Salomen squeezed her gently. "I've never seen you so tired."

"I think I'm better off just staying up all night than getting a hantick of sleep here and a hantick there." With a sigh, she pushed herself away and padded through the bathroom doorway.

Salomen followed her in. "Would you like a cup of shannel?"

"I'd sell my title for one." Tal activated the water shelf and stood under it gratefully. "Ahhh. That's helping." She rinsed her hair, slicked it back with her hands, and opened her eyes to find that Salomen hadn't budged.

"I know you're not in the mood, and we wouldn't have time to do anything about it even if you were. But watching you do that is killing me. You're truly beautiful." Salomen's gaze made a slow trip down and up again. "And very sexy when you're wet." She pushed off the doorway and turned. "I'll get your shannel."

Tal watched her go, her skin tingling. "All right," she said to the empty room. "I'm awake now."

The Blacksun military transport was conspicuous by its absence. Salomen said nothing, but Tal saw her looking out the window as they strapped into their seats. They were in the pilot's cabin, while the four Guards sat in the back. Tal wasn't about to be chauffeured around Redmoon when flying her own transport was an option. She did a quick check of the flight controls, engaged the engines, and said casually, "He asked after you."

"Did he?" Salomen was trying for casual as well, but it didn't go below the surface.

"He wanted to know if you would ever talk to him again." Tal lifted off the landing pad and moved into the base's transit airspace.

"Did you tell him I haven't decided yet?"

"I told him you were having mixed emotions."

They crossed the base border and began following the river. Several silent ticks passed before Salomen said, "What an understated term for it. Makes me sound as if I can't quite decide which shirt to wear." She intercepted the hand Tal held out, clasping it tightly. "I just couldn't talk to him. I'm not ready."

"I know. You're not under any obligation."

"Of course I'm under an obligation. He's my brother. And I know it probably hurt him terribly that I let him go back to Blacksun in a prison transport without even saying good-bye. But I'm afraid that if I see him before I get a handle on my anger, I'm going to say something that can never be taken back."

"Good thing I didn't have to worry about that. I said quite a few things that can't be taken back."

"Do I want to hear this?"

Tal glanced at her. "I told him you almost died. That he'd hurt you and didn't even have the courage to stay around and see how badly. I think it was the first time he truly understood what he did."

"What did he say?"

"He broke down completely. Fahla knows I haven't much use for Herot, but I'll give him credit for one thing: he loves you very much."

"Sometimes I've wondered," Salomen said darkly. "Did he tell you that?"

"I don't think that's a message he would want to convey through me. It's not hard to sense, though. And I suspect it will be the second thing he tells you when you talk to him. Right after 'I'm sorry.'"

"Yes, but is he sorry for the right thing?" Salomen stared straight ahead as the domes of Redmoon approached. "I never doubted that he regretted hurting his family and throwing his life down the fanten feeding chute. And I'm sure he's sorry about what nearly happened to me. But is he sorry for what he did to you? Is he sorry that the whole world now associates the Opah name with betrayal and attempted murder? Is he sorry for turning his back on everything of value our parents tried to teach him?"

Tal banked around to skirt the city, skimming over the outlying homes toward the shining dome of the healing center. "I don't know. But I think he's on the road toward some self-examination. Something has clearly changed—he actually thanked me."

"He did? So he *can* see beyond his own nose. That's encouraging. Did you tell him that he also owes a debt of gratitude to twenty other people?"

"He didn't thank me for saving him. He thanked me for saving you."

"Oh."

Salomen offered nothing more, but a tiny blossom of happiness whisked across Tal's senses. She glanced over in time to catch a small smile on her face.

"And you forgot one thing," she added. "Exactly half a hantick from now, the whole world will associate the Opah name with you, not Herot."

"Shek," Salomen groaned. "I'm not certain that's an improvement."

CHAPTER 45
Family

The quiet of the room was stifling.

Vellmar had never been fond of healing centers; they gave her the spine crawls. She had seen more than one fellow Guard go through the front archway and never come back out again, and even though she knew nothing could have been done to prevent their Return, she still associated healing centers with death. It didn't appear that this time was going to be any different. Colonel Micah hadn't died yet, but he certainly wasn't living.

Carefully, she walked to the colonel's bedside, then realized she had fallen into the same automatic response everyone else did. People instinctively tiptoed in these places, even though a patient like the colonel wouldn't wake up if the Redmoon Symphony played an entire windhorn suite in his room. If it were that easy, Lancer Tal would have had the symphony playing at night-two.

Every Guard had now taken a turn, and the rotation was starting over in a quarter hantick with Lancer Tal and Raiz Opah. Vellmar had never seen anything like it. Warriors owed loyalty to their superiors, but this was more than just something owed. This was a loyalty earned. Colonel Micah's warriors seemed to see him as partially a unit leader and partially family.

She looked around to make sure no one was in the doorway before placing her hands on his energy points. It felt odd and wrong for several reasons, but she had made her decision and she was sticking with it. Taking a deep breath, she bent over and rested her forehead against his.

Darkness. Heavy, liquid darkness, pushing and constricting. It was so different from Sharing with a conscious person, and she instinctively wanted out. For a few moments she thrashed around uselessly, until Dewar's description came back to her.

Right. She needed to relax.

That was far easier said than done. She managed it only by taking herself to her place of serenity, which finally calmed her enough so that she began floating upward, just as Dewar had said. Moments later she popped out into a light, airy space above the darkness.

Colonel Micah was here, though her sense of him was faint. She didn't know how to connect with him. He certainly didn't know her well enough to respond to just her presence. But Sharing with a nonresponsive person should be similar to an intense projection, and she had experience with that. Of course, the last time she had used projection was against the Voloth in the Battle of Alsea. She needed to find a middle space between that kind of force and the light projection she would use with a conscious person—all while accessing emotions that were not her own.

Feeling like a trespasser, she focused on what she had seen the night before, using her memories to guide the emotions.

Colonel Micah, I know you can't hear me, but you really need to come back.

You have twenty worried Guards out here. Lancer Tal and Raiz Opah are beyond worried; I think the Lancer is already grieving for you.

She's worried and afraid.

Don't do this. We all need you.

Come back, please.

A simple set of thoughts, repeated over and over. With each round she recalled the emotions she had absorbed from her oath holders as well as the Guards and reflected them outward. If the colonel was paying any attention at all, he couldn't miss them.

Most of all, she focused on the grief she saw in the Lancer. If anything could get Colonel Micah's attention, surely that would. Again and again she called up her memory of the look in Lancer Tal's eyes as she had stood just inside the transport door, staring at him while Dewar checked his readings. Grief and fear and determination…

Vellmar felt the strain of projecting someone else's emotions, but she pushed on. She recalled the way Lancer Tal had unhesitatingly dropped to her knees and Shared with Colonel Micah to hold him during their flight; the way Raiz Opah had joined her despite having no prior experience; and the way they had both needed to be helped to a seat afterward, having given so much of their strength to him.

When she had thoroughly tired herself out, she focused on her own feelings.

You have people here who would give their all for you. I've never seen anything like it. This is not just honor. This is family. And I just joined the family, so please don't leave before I've even had a chance to know you.

At last she backed away, sinking willingly into the darkness. She was more than ready. She wanted to see through her own eyes again, to feel the vivid senses of her own body. And she wanted a nap.

The darkness rushed in on her, pushing her deeper and deeper until she hit the bottom and came back to herself with a start. The muffled sounds from the corridor, the feel of the colonel's skin beneath her hands, the slight current of air from the open door, the irritating smell of narnell root: all were welcome signs of her own consciousness.

She raised her head, squinting against the too-bright light—and froze in place as a pair of ice-blue eyes looked back at her.

"Are you all right? I was just about to come after you."

Vellmar relaxed at the concerned expression on the Lancer's face. "I'm fine, thank you." She turned her head to find Raiz Opah on her other side, watching her with a similar expression. "I, ah…I hope this was acceptable."

"Why wouldn't it be?" Opah asked. "Every voice helps."

Lancer Tal took Vellmar's arm and steered her toward the chairs in the corner. "Sit down. You look a little wobbly."

She sat gratefully. "I feel a little wobbly. What time is it?"

"Nine and sixty," Lancer Tal said, taking the seat next to her. "We've been watching you for a tentick."

She had been Sharing for thirty-five ticks? Vellmar groaned to herself. They had come at their scheduled time and—shek. "I apologize for making you wait."

Lancer Tal shook her head. "There's no need; I was glad to see you here. Why would you think otherwise?"

"I didn't feel it was my place. This kind of Sharing…" She gestured at Colonel Micah. "It's only done with family. This unit is more family than anything else, but I'm new here."

"And you don't feel like family yet." Raiz Opah walked over to stand beside the Lancer's chair. "Well, you did just arrive two days ago. I can understand your feeling."

"Was it only two days ago?" Lancer Tal said. "I'd swear it was a nineday at least."

"I can tell you that this post is a good deal more exciting than my last one. You people pack a lot into two days."

Lancer Tal snorted a short, unamused laugh. "Believe me, this is not normal. And I pray to Fahla we never have two days like it again." She gave Vellmar a keen look. "What changed your mind?"

"My entire unit has Shared with the colonel. I'm their Lead Guard. That means I don't sit in the back while they get things done. I'm supposed to be in front of them, not behind."

Lancer Tal nodded. "And the other reason?" she asked shrewdly.

This was more difficult. Vellmar looked down briefly before meeting her gaze. "He's not just your Chief Guardian. I saw it in your face last night. I hope that's not too personal, but it's clear that you're worried about him. More than you would be for someone who was merely a good warrior."

There was an uncomfortable silence in the room.

The Lancer was letting nothing slip past her front, but her expression showed that she was taken aback. Finally, she quirked an eyebrow and said, "Welcome to the family, Vellmar. I know it's difficult to come into an established unit like this one. You feel like everyone has a history that doesn't include you. But history is made at different rates of time, and as you said, we've packed a lot into two days. You're a part of this unit now. Everyone who came on this mission shares a common bond with him, and that includes you. You were one of his stretcher-bearers. Your Guards won't soon forget that. Neither will I."

"Nor I." Vellmar glanced at the colonel. "I told him that he needs to come back so I can get to know him. I think he has a lot to teach me."

A slow smile crossed the Lancer's face. "Yes, he does."

CHAPTER 46
Bondlancer

Tal waited until she was sure Salomen had connected before walking over to Vellmar, who had stayed through her Sharing with Micah. She was more and more impressed with her new Lead Guard. Vellmar was a confident, accomplished warrior, yet for all her experience, she still showed an endearing desire for approval. Tal suspected that she cared less about advancement and more about doing the best job she could for her oath holders—which guaranteed her swift rise in the ranks.

Vellmar was watching Salomen with a slightly puzzled look as Tal sat beside her.

"You might as well ask," Tal said.

"Ask what?"

"Whatever it is you're trying to figure out about her."

"That obvious, eh?"

Tal raised her eyebrows, earning a slightly sheepish smile.

"I was just wondering how a producer could have the kind of empathic strength she does. Why isn't she scholar caste?"

"Why not warrior caste?" Tal countered, just to see what she would say.

"There's not a doubt in my mind that Raiz Opah could hold her own in our caste. She's fierce, and she's a protector. But…" Vellmar trailed off, and Tal took pity on her.

"But she's not a killer," she said.

"No."

"The warriors who haven't killed far outnumber those who have."

"Yes, but the caste responsibility requires a readiness to commit that act. I can't see Raiz Opah accepting that responsibility, no matter how remote the chances of an actual obligation."

"No," Tal admitted. "It's not in her character. You're right. Had she changed castes, she would have been a scholar."

"Then why isn't she?"

"Because she beat the testers and never told a soul until just last moon."

"You're joking!" Vellmar burst out. Seeing Tal's smile at her reaction, she lowered her voice and added, "Children don't have that kind of power. If she beat the testers, then she must be—"

"In a class of her own," Tal finished. "I don't know exactly how powerful she is. She's never been assessed. But I wouldn't be surprised if her strength is off the scale, and I suspect she may have some abilities we haven't yet tapped."

Vellmar shook her head. "Fahla hides her seeds in the most unlikely of places. How did she acquire her skill if she never told anyone?"

"I've been working with her for the last moon. She won't leave her holding to attend any of the institutes, so we worked out a compromise."

"She has an impressive front for someone with only one moon of training. You must be a good instructor."

From anyone else, Tal might have interpreted that as flattery, but she really didn't think Vellmar was the type. "It has more to do with the student than the instructor. Salomen learned quickly because she worked hard at it. I would love to see what she can really do, but for now she's content with fronting, blocking, and a little focused sensing."

"But you don't think she'll stay content with it."

Tal shrugged. "It's not for me to say. When and if she's ready to move to a different level, she'll tell me."

"Beating the testers—I've never even heard of that. I can think of several instructors who would be tripping over their own feet to work with her."

"So can I. But she doesn't want them." Tal glanced at Salomen, standing immobile over Micah, and wondered how she was doing with him. After several days of a full tyree bond, it was…uncomfortable to be cut off from her while she was traversing the planes of the unconscious.

"May I ask a different question?" Vellmar said.

"Will I regret saying yes?"

Vellmar hesitated, then forged ahead. "What you said to Oren and Dalset—what you told them we would do—how much of that was a bluff?"

Tal gave her credit for having the horns to ask. "You didn't swear your oath to a lawbreaker." She watched Vellmar exhale and added, "Advanced behavioral management wasn't in your file."

"No. I only took enough to qualify for officer training. And even that much didn't come naturally to me."

"That's not a bad thing, Vellmar. Don't undervalue the trust you can gain simply by being yourself."

"But you made Dalset trust you. Even though she was terrified of you. How did you do that?"

"By breaking the stronger of the two. She's a follower. When I broke Oren, she lost her leader. I stepped into that void, and nearly everything I said to her after that was the truth."

Vellmar looked down for a moment, the clicking gears almost visible in her head, and then snapped her fingers. "When you touched her hand. You pulled back before she could ask anything else. So she could only feel truth."

"Good eyes." And good memory, Tal thought.

"Hm. Maybe I should have taken those courses."

"Not if it didn't come naturally. Manipulation only works when it's seamless. You should either be wholly yourself, or wholly the role you need to play. Anything in between and you'll show cracks that even a low empath can see through."

Vellmar nodded, out of questions for now. In the comfortable silence that fell, Tal mentally catalogued the things she needed to get done as soon as they left the healing center. Find out what Aldirk and Razine had learned, start making lists of who supported her and who was backing Shantu, deal with the public acknowledgment of Salomen's new status…

"Shek," she muttered. Vellmar looked over in surprise, and Tal waved her hand in a not-you gesture. "I just remembered the media conference is happening right now. I hope we can get out of here before it starts raining journalists."

"I'm sorry," Vellmar said immediately. "If you hadn't had to wait for me, you wouldn't be running so close to the conference time."

Tal gave her a level stare. "Are you apologizing again, after I already told you there was no need?"

"Ah…" She was clearly trying to decide which way to jump. "No?"

For all her stress and worry, Tal couldn't help laughing. "Right answer. I hate repeating myself." Sobering, she added, "I'm truly glad you Shared with him. As Salomen said, every voice counts. I'm not reaching him, but maybe a new voice will."

"Do you sense any response at all?"

"No. In a way, he's less there now than he was on the transport. He doesn't drain me like he did then, but…he's more distant."

After a pause, Vellmar asked, "Has Healer Elwyn mentioned anything to you regarding his opinion?"

"You mean since the surgery? No. Why, has he spoken to you?"

"Not to me. To his assistant. I overheard him saying that there was no physical reason why Colonel Micah is still unconscious."

Tal wasn't surprised at the news or the fact that Elwyn had not told her. The healer would probably wait another two or three days before admitting his own lack of hope. "I could wish for better. But my instincts tell me Elwyn is right."

"I don't understand it. He's at the top of our caste, he's your Chief Guardian, he holds your trust and friendship…" Vellmar held out her hands, palms up. "He lives a life the rest of us can only hope to achieve. Why would he not be fighting to come back to it?"

"That's a question only Micah can answer." Tal reasoned that it wasn't quite a lie. Though she was fairly certain she knew why, it was still a guess. Her next words died in her throat as her wristcom vibrated, showing an incoming message from Colonel Razine.

Interrogation completed.

She certainly wins the prize for brevity, Tal thought as she cleared the message. "As soon as Salomen is done, I want you to accompany us back to the transport. We may need you to help clear the way."

"You mean if it's raining journalists?"

"Exactly." Tal got up and poked her head out the door, unsurprised to find a few healing center personnel lingering at the end of the corridor. They were in a tight huddle, speaking softly, but as soon as one of them glimpsed her, the whole group went quiet and looked at her with wide eyes. Elwyn's assistant was among them. Tal crooked her finger at him, hiding a smile as his coworkers subtly moved away. The assistant came down the hall and carefully skirted around the four Guards outside the door.

"Lancer Tal, what may I do for you?" he asked.

"You can bring Healer Elwyn. I need to speak with him."

He bobbed his head and whisked down the hall, leaving a waft of relief behind.

Tal rejoined Vellmar. "Sometimes I wonder what sort of reputation I have. The support staff here act as if I'm about to eat one of them."

"It's not every day the Lancer brings her top Guard to a healing center. Especially one so far from Blacksun. Besides, do they know for sure that you *won't* eat any of them?"

"No. Do you?"

Vellmar gave her a quick smile. "I'm new to the unit. I haven't learned your dining habits yet."

"It doesn't include healer staff. Though I've been known to chew up a warrior now and then."

"So have I."

They sat quietly for several ticks until a rustle outside the door heralded the arrival of Healer Elwyn. "Lancer Tal," he said in greeting. "My assistant said you asked for me?"

"I did." Tal rose from her chair and stood beside Salomen. "In your opinion, do you think it would be safe to move Colonel Micah tomorrow morning?"

"That depends. Move him to where?"

"Blacksun."

His eyebrows rose. "That's quite a distance."

"Yes, it is. But I cannot run the government from here, and I would rather not return without him. Is he stable enough to be moved?"

Elwyn walked to the other side of the bed and checked Micah's readouts. "I believe he is. I'm not enthusiastic about the idea of moving him, but we've done all that can be done. The staff at Blacksun can handle his current needs." Seemingly unaware that he had just denigrated an entire city's worth of talented healers, he added, "I'll send one of my healers with him to monitor the transport and brief the Blacksun staff on his condition. What time do you wish to leave?"

"I'll inform you when I know it myself. There are—" She stopped as her empathic senses flooded with Salomen's renewed presence.

"Damn him," Salomen muttered, raising her head and massaging her forehead. "If anything, he's farther away than he was last night. Is that what you sensed, or is it just me he's running from?"

"That's what I sensed," Tal said. "I didn't want to tell you in case you had a different reaction."

Salomen radiated dismay and sorrow as she reached for her hand.

With her throat suddenly tight, Tal turned toward Elwyn. "Are we fighting a losing battle?"

He pursed his lips, looking from Micah to her. "Where there's a beating heart, there's hope. I've seen much worse cases than this pull out of the darkness, so I would not assume that the battle is lost."

Typically vague healer-speak, but at least it was not a yes. "Is there anything we should know about his transport?"

Five ticks later, Elwyn had exhausted his supply of advice and bade them farewell, leaving a quiet room behind him. The silence stretched out as Tal stared at Micah, until Salomen finally squeezed her hand and said, "Shall we go?"

Tal looked up to see identical expressions on their faces. "Don't look like that. You heard the healer. Micah's heart still beats."

"Yes, it does," Salomen said. "And until it stops, we'll be in his mind, annoying the shek out of him until he wakes up just to make us leave him alone."

"If annoying him will do the trick, perhaps we should bring Aldirk in here for a turn."

"Perhaps we should." Salomen smiled at her, and Tal felt just a little bit better.

The four Guards fell into step as they left the room, two ahead and two behind. Vellmar walked just behind the front Guards, far enough from Tal and Salomen to be unobtrusive, but close enough for instant action.

"Be prepared for a possible media storm," Tal said as they walked down the corridor. "The announcement was made while you were with Micah. It's still early enough that most of the journalists in the city probably haven't arrived, but…"

"I know," Salomen said. "I'm ready."

"Just don't hurt any of them. You need to establish a good image first. *Then* you can start abusing them."

"Right. First the false advertising, then reality."

They went out the arch to find that the number of journalists had doubled. "Damn," Salomen groaned. "How did they get here so quickly?"

"They knew we were in town," Tal said. "They were probably in their transports before Miltorin got past his first three sentences."

As the journalists caught sight of them, a swarm of vidcams rose into the air.

"Lancer Tal! Will your bonding ceremony be public or private?"

"Raiz Opah! How does it feel to be the future Bondlancer of Alsea?"

"When did you first know how you felt about the Lancer?"

"Have you heard from your brother?"

"Lancer Tal, are you concerned about the warrior caste's reaction to your choice?"

Tal hid her displeasure at that last one, continuing toward the transport as her Guards kept the journalists at a distance. Only when they were two paces up the entry ramp did she turn to face them, all five Guards lined up below like a breathing wall.

"We can give you five ticks," she said, and pointed toward a man she recognized from the night before.

"Thank you, Lancer Tal. Raiz Opah, as the first producer Bondlancer in sixteen generations, do you see your position as striking a blow for caste equality?"

"I wasn't aware that my caste was unequal to the others," Salomen said. "Do you know something I don't?"

"Ah…" He fumbled for a moment, and Tal put an arm around Salomen's waist in appreciation. "Of course the castes are equal in name and theory, but the reality doesn't always match, does it?"

"Perhaps your reality does not. Mine does. I'm an Alsean first and a producer second, and I'm proud of my caste. If someone gave me the opportunity to change castes, I would say thank you, but no."

If the journalists ever dug up the truth in that statement, Tal thought, Alsea would be talking of nothing else for a nineday. She watched as Salomen took the initiative and pointed at a woman toward the back.

"Raiz Opah, your brother is the object of an investigation regarding the assassination attempt—"

"I will not comment on a continuing investigation," Salomen interrupted. "Is there something else you wish to ask?"

Instantly switching gears, the woman said, "You met the Lancer when you became a delegate for the matter printer planning meetings. Did you form a bond then? Is that why the Lancer spent a moon working on your holding?"

"Lancer Tal spent a moon on my holding because she's almost as brick-headed as I am."

There were a few muffled chuckles.

"If we formed a bond during the delegate meetings," Salomen continued, "we were both unaware of it. We didn't understand our attraction until the Lancer's challenge moon was more than half over. The nice thing about her bond offer is that for once I know, beyond a shadow of a doubt, that I am wanted for myself rather than my land."

"You've had bond offers before, then?"

"Five," she said, to the audible surprise of the crowd. "As you can see, I was waiting for the right person." She pointed toward a man to the left.

Having learned from his predecessor's mistake, he said, "The title of Bondlancer is far removed from the experience of most of us, regardless of caste. How are you preparing for this new responsibility?"

"Lancer Tal has already assigned Colonel Micah as my Chief Counselor, to help me learn what I need to know. He's..." Salomen's voice caught, and she covered it by clearing her throat. "He's the reason we're here in Redmoon."

Her panic slithered through Tal's senses. She had just gotten herself onto a topic she didn't know how to handle.

"Colonel Micah was injured on a mission," Tal said. "The full details of that mission will be available later, when we've had a chance to bring it to its final conclusion. Are there any other questions for Raiz Opah?"

She squeezed Salomen's waist, silently telling her to take over again. Salomen got the message and pointed toward the woman directly in front of them.

"Is it true that one of your rejected bond offers came from Gordense Bilsner, the father of Cullom Bilsner?" asked the woman with a deceptively pleasant expression.

"Yes, that's true."

"Is it possible that family honor might have been a motivating factor in the assassination attempt?"

"That's a question for Cullom Bilsner, not me. I cannot even begin to put myself into the mind of an assassin."

Tal silently cheered as Salomen pointed to a man at the far edge, effectively ending the topic.

"Raiz Opah, since no one else has said it, please allow me to be the first to congratulate you on your upcoming bonding."

Salomen smiled for the first time. "Thank you. I was wondering how long it might take before someone offered congratulations. But then, I'm new to media conferences. I thought perhaps journalists simply didn't operate under the same codes of courtesy that the rest of us do."

Tal fought back the grin that threatened to break over her face as the journalists shifted on their feet, a palpable sense of discomfort arising from most of them.

The man in the back smiled broadly. "Some of us tend to forget the courtesies in our enthusiasm for the story. I think we won't soon forget again around you. Will your ceremony be public, I hope?"

"The ceremony itself will involve only our friends and family. We're somewhat limited by the capacity of Whitemoon Temple. However, it will be recorded and aired in real time, so that anyone who wishes can share in it."

"Whitemoon Temple is beautiful," he said, "but rather far from Blacksun and Granelle. Why not Blacksun Temple?"

"Because Whitemoon holds special meaning for both of us. For me, it will be fulfilling a dream of my mother's. She always wanted to see it but was never able to before her Return."

"And for you, Lancer Tal?"

Tal was not above using the moment to her advantage. "Whitemoon is where Fahla herself chose to communicate with me."

Several audible gasps could be heard. "Can you tell us about that?" the man asked.

"I went there after my speech last moon, to show my gratitude for the gift she had given me." Tal kissed Salomen on the cheek, making it clear exactly which gift she was referring to. "I prayed to her for the wisdom to make Salomen happy, so I could give her the kind of life she deserves. Fahla gave me a very clear sign that she was listening." She raised her hand to stop the questions. "No, I'm not going to share the precise nature of that sign. It's personal. But I can tell you that I've seen it several times since then, always in connection with Salomen, and there is not a doubt in my mind that she and I are both on the path that was chosen for us."

A chorus of voices rose, but Tal called out, "That's all we have time for. Good day." She slipped her arm from around Salomen's waist, caught her hand, and held their clasped hands up in a farewell gesture that caused the entire swarm of vidcams to swoop in. Leaving the Guards to hold back the journalists, they made their way up the ramp and into the transport, where Salomen waited only until the door closed behind the last Guard before turning to Tal and resting her head on her shoulder.

"You did beautifully, tyrina," Tal said as her Guards discreetly found other places to look.

Salomen took a deep breath in, let it out slowly, and raised her head. "Thank you. I felt like a fanten on slaughter day."

"But you looked like a Bondlancer in full control." Tal gave her an encouraging smile. "I particularly enjoyed watching you slap them down for their lack of courtesy. I think you've already established your reputation."

"Might as well start now," Salomen said.

Tal tugged her into the pilot's cabin, shut the door, and pulled her into her arms. "You're magnificent," she said, holding her tightly and stroking the back of her head. "And you make me so damned proud. Those journalists thought they'd be dealing with a meek little dokker, but they learned a quick lesson about the Bondlancer."

"Will they always think of me as the producer Bondlancer?" Salomen pushed herself back far enough to look into Tal's eyes. "Am I going to be fighting caste prejudice for the rest of my life?"

"Perhaps in the beginning. But I think you'll give your caste a brand-new face and reputation. When Micah had his first dealings with you, he was instantly impressed. He told me that you would make an excellent unit trainer. And I told him that if you trained units, we'd have an entire Alsean Defense Force cowering at the sight of a producer."

Salomen laughed, her mood lifting. "You said that? Before you even arrived at Hol-Opah?"

"Oh, yes. And Micah said that he was certain you would consider it a positive development."

"He was wrong about that. Now that I know your Guards, I can't imagine seeing any of them cowering at anything. And I really cannot imagine you cowering." She paused, a decidedly evil expression taking over her face. "Well, except for—"

Tal kissed her then, partly to stop her and partly because she had wanted to since watching her take control of the journalists. Salomen's response was gentle at first, but her passion soon flamed up, igniting Tal's as well. For a moment Tal entertained a wild fantasy of joining with her right here in the cabin. She pushed Salomen against the door as they kissed, the desire heating her blood and making her forget for a few blessed pipticks just how much she had hanging over her head. But reality intruded and she broke off reluctantly, resting their foreheads together. "I probably sound like a lovestruck fool, but I miss you already. We haven't had a peaceful night together in too long."

"It's only been two nights. But given the fact that we only had three nights to begin with, I know what you mean. Why did you stop?"

"I have to call Colonel Razine, and then I have to—"

Further speech became impossible as Salomen surged forward to kiss her again. Her hands slipped between them to cup Tal's breasts, softly squeezing as she kissed along a cheekbone ridge and then tugged on an earlobe. "You will always have things to do," she whispered as Tal squirmed. "If you wait until nothing is pressing, I'll never feel your touch again. And I want to feel that touch."

"Now?" Tal gasped.

"Now."

It was all the invitation she needed. With a growl, she knocked Salomen's hands away and reached up to hold her head in place, nipping at her throat where the ridges were already beginning to emerge.

"You felt it." She bit a ridge more aggressively, a thrill shooting through her at Salomen's sharp intake of breath. She backed off just enough to push Salomen's jacket off her shoulders and a moment later had her shirt off as well. "I'll have to be more careful about my little fantasies around you."

"Don't ever be careful." Salomen leaned against the door, naked from the waist up and looking dangerously beautiful. "I love knowing when you want me."

"I always want you. I just can't always do anything about it." Tal took two steps to the control boards and activated the privacy screen, frustrating the vidcams that were already hovering outside. The sun glaring off the front window kept them from focusing on the cabin doorway, so they were positioned at the sides, watching the pilot's and copilot's seats instead. But Tal had plans for that copilot's seat.

"Sorry to disappoint," she said with satisfaction as the vidcams sank down. In a heartbeat she was standing in front of Salomen again, looking her over with a tingle of anticipation. "Now, where was I?"

"You hadn't gotten started yet. I think I'm being very patient."

"Good for you. Patient is not something I'm feeling at the moment." Tal's mood had shifted into something far more aggressive, and she knew Salomen was receptive. With other lovers she might have tempered her desires, but Salomen was watching her in defiant invitation, all but daring her to show what she could do.

With a swift movement, she captured Salomen's wrists and pinned them against the door, pressing their bodies together and taking her mouth in a demanding kiss. Salomen didn't struggle, but her kisses were just as demanding, letting Tal know that she was not a quiescent partner. Their emotions abruptly merged, and Tal's aggression roared into a flame she could barely control.

"Goddess," she panted, pulling back. Her gaze drifted to the half-emerged neck ridges, then to Salomen's bare shoulders, the slope of her breasts, and her hard nipples. "I don't want you. I need you."

"Then why are you standing there looking at me?"

Tal took one step back, pulling Salomen with her, then shifted her captured wrists to the small of her back. With the improved leverage she crushed Salomen to her, bent her head to a breast, and sucked hard on the nipple.

"Yes..." Salomen arched back, offering an even better angle.

Tal used it to her advantage, holding her in that position long past the point of comfort while she switched from one breast to the other. Salomen's arousal climbed steadily, fed by the aggressive treatment and the restraint of her arms, until Tal had reached her limit. With no gentleness whatsoever she spun them both around and pushed Salomen into the copilot's chair, hearing the *whuf* as she landed.

"Take the rest off. Now."

Salomen complied quickly, tossing her clothes to the side, and the sight of her naked in the chair was fuel to Tal's fantasies. She dropped to her knees between Salomen's legs and pulled her to the edge of the chair. "You knew I didn't have time to spare, but you wanted it anyway. So I'm not going to apologize for this." With that she slid two fingers into Salomen's center, the ease of her entry goading her on.

Salomen gripped the armrests. "Who asked for an apology? Get on with it."

Tal twisted her fingers, wringing out a groan. Twisting back to line up her fingers with the inner ridges, she took Salomen hard and fast, watching with intense fascination. Nothing compared with the feeling of sinking herself inside another, and with Salomen the sensation was even more overwhelming. For this proud, strong woman to allow and even invite such entry was arousing all by itself. Watching it took her breath away.

She lifted her gaze and looked into a pair of smoldering brown eyes. Their expression would have told her exactly what Salomen was feeling even if their emotions hadn't been merged. Changing the tempo, she pulled nearly all the way out and slowly pushed back in, and the next time she looked up, she saw what she had been waiting for. Salomen's throat ridges had popped out into sharp relief.

Rising to her feet, she braced herself with one hand on the armrest and sank her teeth into the nearest throat ridge.

Salomen's body jerked, her groan of pleasure sending a shiver down Tal's spine.

"The Guards certainly heard that," she said, and bit down again. This time Salomen made no sound, holding it in with a difficulty that Tal could easily feel. It was an instant challenge, and her third bite was harder. The fourth was enough to leave a mark, and the fifth broke Salomen's resolve.

"Fahla! You're killing me!"

"No, just giving you precisely what you wanted. Hold on to those armrests; you're going to need them." Tal sank her teeth in one last time, keeping them closed on the ridge as she pulled her fingers out. For several long pipticks she simply let Salomen sit there, her chest heaving as she caught her breath, but unable to move with Tal's teeth holding her in place. Then Tal reached up to grasp one nipple in each hand, squeezing them as she gradually increased the pressure of both fingers and teeth. It was a slow, intense assault on the senses, and before long Salomen was writhing, her fingers digging into the armrests.

"Goddess!" she gasped. "I can't take it!"

Tal knew that was not true; she hadn't felt any glimmer of pain yet. Silently, she increased the pressure further still, watching Salomen's back arch to an impossible degree, and only when she felt her tyree reaching the threshold did she finally release her.

Salomen slumped against the seat, her breathing a harsh rasp as she rubbed her throat ridge. "Shekking Mother," she whispered, a profanity Tal had never heard from her. "No one's ever done that before. I thought I was going to die."

"No one has ever pushed you to your limit before." Tal held up three fingers, watching Salomen's eyes widen, and then reached down. Salomen bit her bottom lip as they went in, her eyes shut tight against the pressure. Alsean internal anatomy was quite variable, and Salomen's was really made for two fingers. Three did not quite fit her ridges, resulting in a feeling of fullness and overstimulation that would have been uncomfortable for her had she not been so aroused. As it was, Tal reveled in the sensations she absorbed through their link, knowing that Salomen was on the knife edge between pleasure and pain. She began a slow thrusting but soon picked up speed, watching as Salomen's hips met her every stroke.

Her distraction left her open, however, and the sudden weight around her neck was her only warning before Salomen forced her head over. A sharp bite to one of her own throat ridges nearly buckled her knees. She hadn't even felt them emerge.

"You look incredible like this." The voice in her ear was ragged. "I wish you could see yourself." Salomen bit her again, and this time it was only Tal's hand on the armrest that kept her upright. She wanted more; an assertive Salomen sent her straight to the stars. But she also wanted to finish what she had begun.

"I'm happy with what I'm seeing right now." She jerked her head away, and since her knees were already weak, she swung her leg back over and let herself sink to the floor.

In front of her was the most arousing view she could imagine, and the scent was driving her wild. Salomen's scent reminded her of sallgreen trees, when she crushed the thin, needlelike leaves in her hand—bracing and fresh, a fragrance that burned a path from her nose straight to the back of her head. She inhaled deeply, then leaned forward to run her tongue along the sweet curve of the molwine.

Salomen jumped at the first touch, then went limp. "Oh, yes," she murmured. "Please keep doing that if it makes you happy."

Tal smiled and repeated her gentle caress. "Believe me, it does. And I will." She glanced up to see Salomen's head resting on the back of the seat, her throat ridges sharply defined. The right one glowed with marks that Tal's teeth had left, and not for the first time, she wished she could be everywhere at once. It was hard to see those throat ridges and not be able to do anything about them.

But there was a ridge right under her mouth that needed her attention, and she began a gentle nibbling as she resumed her hand motion, this time slow and deep. With every thrust she softly closed her teeth on the molwine, careful not to use too much pressure. The molwine was far more delicate than the throat ridges, easily overstimulated, and she was approaching the limit already. As she pulled her fingers nearly all the way out, she released the bite and licked that spot instead. Then she pushed back in and gently bit a different place.

Salomen's fingers sank into the armrest as she tensed. The shift to this deliberate pace left her trembling and moaning with each deep movement, but Tal kept the tempo precisely the same, even when Salomen's body began to shake. Every thrust, every bite, and every lick was now an agony of pleasure, the sensations pulsing through both of them. Tal's own arousal was not far behind, and she groaned from the overwhelming heat of it.

The sound seemed to be all Salomen needed. Her hips rose into the air, straining and shaking as the release roared through her body and Tal's mind. The force of it wrung a strangled cry from both of them, though Tal managed to keep going, prolonging it for as long as she could. At last Salomen slumped down, gasping for air, and pushed her away.

"Enough! Goddess!" Her arms fell limply to the side.

Tal slowly withdrew her fingers, which glittered with the lubricating powder. The scent was stronger now, the powder combining with her own skin oils to create the unique fragrance of a joined couple. It was intoxicating, like an entire forest of sallgreens on a rainy night, when the trees released their scent into the cool air. She sucked her fingers clean, humming happily as the fresh flavor expanded into her nose and down her throat.

The lazy, sated warmth emanating from Salomen vanished under a jolt of shocked arousal. Tal looked up and smiled. "Ready for another one, then?"

Salomen laughed weakly. "Not if you want me to walk out of here. But great Mother, you look sexy doing that."

Tal wrapped her arms around Salomen's waist and rested her head against her stomach. "You're the sexy one. And so beautiful," she whispered as an aftershock vibrated the body beneath her.

Salomen made an incoherent sound, her hands landing heavily on Tal's back, and they stayed in that position until long after her breathing had returned to normal. At last her grip tightened, and she ran her hands up to caress Tal's hair.

"I'll probably think twice before I push you like that again," she said with a smile that Tal could actually hear. "I got a little more than I expected."

Tal tried not to feel too smug, but it was impossible.

"Don't bother. I know you're proud of yourself."

"Maybe just a little." Tal lifted her head. "But this whole thing started because I was so proud of you. There's something about watching you take care of yourself that makes me…"

"Hot as a black rock on a summer day?"

"Well—yes."

Salomen laughed. "So you get aroused by me being pushy and taking no grief. Good to know. I think that's a first."

"What can I say? I'm in love with you. When I first met you, that attitude drove me insane. But even then I respected it."

Salomen's mood grew more serious. "That's something I will never take for granted. Your respect. It means everything to me."

"Great Goddess, Salomen, no one who meets you can keep from respecting you. They may not like you, but they have to respect you."

"I'm not so certain about that. I don't think respect is what motivates Gordense Bilsner."

"It may not motivate him, but I'd be surprised if he doesn't feel it." Tal muffled a groan as she climbed to her feet. "Damn. This floor is hard on knees." She collected the scattered clothing and handed over the pieces one by one as Salomen dressed. Before the shirt went on, however, Tal dropped a soft kiss on each breast, followed by one to the reddened area of her throat. "I'm afraid I left a mark," she said, brushing her finger over it.

"So did I." Salomen flashed a rather evil smile, then pulled her shirt over her head and tucked it in. "Though I'm guessing mine is quite a bit larger. I still can't believe what you did. That was incredible."

"Yes, it was," Tal said, remembering the way Salomen's body had moved while she had held her trapped.

Salomen brought her back with a soft slap to her stomach. "Just remember," she warned. "I learn by observation and imitation."

"I know. I look forward to it."

Tal wasn't quite ready to face her Guards, so she took the coward's way out and notified them via com that they were now departing.

Salomen looked over as they lifted off. "Do you really think the Guards heard me?"

"More than once, I'm afraid."

She faced forward again. "Poor Vellmar. She may never recover."

CHAPTER 47
Strategy session

FOR THE SECOND TIME THAT morning, Aldirk strode across the Redmoon Base landing pad with Head Guardian Gehrain at his side. Their destination was the only thing that remained the same. At dawn he had been alarmed by his abrupt summons and irritated by the uncomfortable flight; now he was a member of an elite team charged with a task of planetary importance.

He was still reeling over the idea of a caste coup being planned right under his nose, but his discreet inquiries had uncovered more of an association between Parser and Shantu than anyone would have suspected. Different people had heard or seen different things, which meant little by themselves but acquired significance when added together. When he informed the Lancer of his findings, the look in her eyes made him very glad he was not Shantu. She was on her way in from the healing center and asked them to meet her as soon as she arrived.

They walked up the ramp and through the empty transport to the Lancer's private cabin. This time the door stood open, and Lancer Tal and Raiz Opah were waiting on the far side of the conference table. Gehrain closed the door behind them and took the seat next to Aldirk.

"Are we ready?" Lancer Tal asked.

"Yes," Aldirk said, "but before we start, may I congratulate Raiz Opah? I saw your media conference on one of the local stations. Very well done, I must say. You gave the world something to talk about. Our new Bondlancer is clearly not going to be a meek and quiet armband for the Lancer."

"'Armband' is not the first thing anyone would imagine when they think of Salomen," said Lancer Tal. "Not if they've ever interacted with her."

"Neither is meek…and especially not quiet." Raiz Opah turned her head to smile at her bondmate, and Aldirk's eyes widened when he saw the marks on her neck. A closer look at the Lancer revealed a similar mark. He was certain it hadn't been there this morning. Goddess above, when had they found the time? The woman really didn't sleep. And judging by the size of Opah's marks, Lancer Tal was an aggressive lover.

That was not something he wanted to know.

Lancer Tal's answering smile made Aldirk feel as if he shouldn't even be in the same room, but when Raiz Opah turned to him, her expression was serious. "Thank you, Chief Counselor. I admit to being a bit nervous. But it's really no different than addressing a caste house meeting. In fact, they were less combative than a roomful of producers."

Since he couldn't imagine a roomful of producers, he would take her word for it. "Then it appears that your caste house meetings were excellent practice. I'll enjoy watching your first Blacksun conference. The journalists there will no doubt have learned from watching your performance here."

"I look forward to it as well," said Lancer Tal. "But we have a little matter of a caste coup to deal with at the moment. Shall we?" She pressed a recessed control, activating the vidcom unit, and everyone turned to face the screen.

Colonel Razine appeared almost immediately. She took in the group at a glance and said, "Ah, you've already established Chief Counselor Aldirk's loyalty. If you hadn't, I was looking forward to giving you at least that bit of good news."

"That doesn't bode well for the rest of it," Lancer Tal said.

"That depends on what you hoped to gain from the extraction session."

Aldirk concealed a shudder at her casual use of the phrase.

"I hoped to gain enough information to cut Shantu's legs out from under him."

Razine shook her head. "Then I won't be able to give you good news. Parser doesn't know what Shantu's plans are. He was assured that if they lost their leverage with Herot Opah and could not pursue Parser's alternative, Shantu would have an effective back-up plan. Beyond that, he knows no details because he instructed Shantu to tell him nothing. It appears he anticipated that you might call in his tiles, Lancer Tal. He carefully divided his resources so that if he were pulled off the game board, Shantu would still be a player."

"That sounds like something he would say." Lancer Tal sighed. "Well, what *do* we know?"

"We know how far he was willing to go to ensure your compliance. And how he learned your greatest weakness." Razine glanced at Raiz Opah. "I'm sorry, but this will probably be difficult for you to hear."

"I already know it's about Herot. Go on."

Looking back at the Lancer, Razine said, "Parser wanted to know why you weren't taking advantage of the publicity opportunities at Hol-Opah, so he sent an employee to Granelle to nose around. The employee learned that Herot could be found almost every night at the Harvester."

"The most disreputable tavern in Granelle, yes," Raiz Opah said resignedly. "Is that where he found Withernet?"

"No, he found Withernet by checking the finances of Granelle merchants and learning who was in trouble. Withernet was happy to accept a substantial fee in exchange for switching his normal tavern choice to the Harvester. All he had to do was sit, drink, and listen, and he collected a great deal of information. Your brother was not quiet while complaining about the Lancer's presence on his holding."

"Hol-Opah is *not* Herot's holding. It's mine."

Aldirk glanced over, startled by Opah's tone.

"I understand that," Razine said. "My apologies. I was quoting Parser."

"No, I'm sorry. I'm a little on edge about Herot. Please continue."

Razine nodded. "It was through Herot's conversations with his friends, mostly Cullom Bilsner, that Parser learned about Lancer Tal's affection for Jaros. He knew that she pulled Herot off Jaros in a fight one morning and gave him a lesson in courtesy. Of course, Herot's version of that was probably somewhat skewed. He also knew that Jaros walked to and from school every day at the same time, unaccompanied, and he knew all about Lancer Tal defending Jaros against the three boys who bullied him. The fact that she went so far as to take those boys to the Pit for a lesson of their own is what cemented Parser's initial choice. He planned to have Jaros kidnapped while he was walking home from school." She paused. "The kidnapping was scheduled for the day after the assassination attempt."

Raiz Opah gave a perceptible shudder and crossed her arms over her chest, gripping her upper arms tightly. Behind her, the Lancer reached over and rested a hand on her shoulder.

"I never thought I'd be glad Bilsner took that shot," she said. "But that was what put Herot in Parser's targeting lens instead of Jaros."

"Parser saw at a glance that Herot could be your political downfall. He had his network looking for him from the moment the assassination attempt hit the news. I think it's something of a testament to Herot that he managed to avoid Parser's net as long as he did." Razine cleared her throat. "But until he realized you had survived, Parser was furious about that attempt. Withernet exceeded his orders. Parser thought he had wasted moons of effort and planning."

"Because he didn't want a new Lancer. He told me he had the trap set and didn't want to have to do it all over again with someone else."

"That was half of the truth," Razine said. "He preferred to have you under his control and be done with it, and he was reasonably sure that his initial trap would work. He was more certain that even if it didn't, if you were actually willing to fight it out with him in the public arena, a subsequent warning delivered via Jaros would be sufficient. That warning would not have been a mere ransoming but a contract killing, made to look like an accident."

Startled by a searing blast of rage, Aldirk turned to look before he could stop himself.

Lancer Tal leaned toward her bondmate. "Salomen," she whispered, and a moment later the emotion was cut off.

"Please tell me that extraction process hurts," Raiz Opah said in a voice Aldirk would not have recognized. "I want to know."

"That depends on how much empathic force is required for the desired results," said Razine. "Parser was very determined to resist. He is now recovering in the healing unit on base."

A shiver ran down Aldirk's spine, but all Raiz Opah said was, "Good."

"What was the other half of the truth, Colonel?" Lancer Tal asked.

"One moment, please." Razine took a quick sip from a glass of water, her hand shaking slightly.

Aldirk stared in horrified fascination. That tremor came from the extreme energy output required for prolonged empathic force, which meant Razine herself had done the extraction. Looking from her shaking hand to her calm, stern face, he marveled at the kind of mentality a warrior must have to perpetrate so much harm on another being and then go about her business with such a matter-of-fact attitude.

He was very glad to be on the right side of these people.

Razine put her glass down. "Parser knew there was a chance that you could not be controlled, so he was simultaneously working toward putting Shantu in power. Shantu had no idea of Parser's true corruption, but he was certainly amenable to the idea of taking the title and putting an end to your implementation plan for the matter printers. He's also never forgiven you for the Voloth asylum vote. Apparently, he didn't stop to consider that his direct involvement in the kidnapping and murder of a civilian was the very thing that would give Parser an unbreakable hold on him. He simply saw it as a necessary means to the noble end of saving Alsea from your misguided policies, and Parser played on that."

Lancer Tal shook her head. "So he made Shantu his insurance policy by virtue of his involvement. I hate to admit it, but it was an elegant plan."

"I don't find it elegant at all," Raiz Opah said. "That man is a heartless monster."

"For him it's just business. If I hadn't cooperated, Herot would have turned up dead, my Guards and I would have been implicated, and Shantu could have risen up as the righteous warrior who would sweep the corruption out of the State House. I'd have been fighting both him *and* Parser, and the warrior caste would have swung behind Shantu when my reputation was destroyed."

"Precisely," Razine said. "Parser had every possible path covered. He would get his desired outcome whether you cooperated or not: a Lancer who was under his control. And then he would have what he really wanted—what this whole thing was all about. Through his various companies, which would quietly be given all the contracts by secret order of the Lancer, he would end up owning all of the commerce in the space elevator station and eventually, the space dock. He already had secret agreements with former Ambassador Frank regarding the import and export markets."

"Great Mother." Aldirk couldn't believe all of this had happened without even a hint reaching him. "He really was planning ahead. That would have made him the richest man on Alsea."

"What a master manipulator," Lancer Tal said. "No wonder he was so furious about the assassination attempt. Had I died, Shantu could have stepped into the title and Parser would have had no hold on him. All that planning for naught."

"Wait." Raiz Opah was shaking her head. "Are you telling me that all of this…this *horror*, it was just about wealth?"

"It was about more wealth than most of us can even imagine," Aldirk said. "And an influence forevermore not just in Alsean politics, but in Protectorate politics as well. Parser wasn't just setting himself up for life. He was planning a dynasty."

The room was silent.

"And it all came crashing down because of the one thing he couldn't predict," Lancer Tal said at last. "Salomen's empathic strength."

"*Our* empathic strength," Raiz Opah corrected. "And Colonel Micah's quick thinking."

Razine picked up her glass again. "That reminds me. The explosives were Parser's idea as well. He had great respect for your ingenuity, Lancer Tal. While he could barely credit the thought that you might actually find Herot, he planned a way to turn it to his advantage just in case."

"And if the alarm had been raised just two ticks earlier, that plan would have worked. Did you find out who owned the house?"

"Parser used one of his illegal enterprises to funnel cinteks to a representative who purchased the home for Shantu. No financial trail to either of them, and Parser never knew its location."

"Well, we can only hope that Shantu isn't as good as Parser. Do you have any idea at all what he might be planning?"

"None. I'm sorry, but I pressed particularly hard on that one. Parser simply doesn't know. He didn't want to."

Lancer Tal turned to face Aldirk and Gehrain. "Any ideas you might have would be welcome. The only thing I can think is that it must have something to do with the Voloth asylum and breaking Fahla's covenant. Those are my only political vulnerabilities, now that we have Herot. The matter printers would have been a vulnerability last moon, but public opinion has swung back to my side."

"Not all of it," Aldirk said. "You have the majority of the public on your side, yes. But the economist coalition's report had a powerful impact. There were dissenters before it came out, and there were more after. They may be a minority, but they're a frightened and less-educated minority. Those are the very people who are most easily swayed by simple rhetoric, which is what Shantu will offer. If he can add that bloc to the war criminal bloc, he'll have a decent-sized base."

"But he's in no place to be offering any rhetoric. I don't think being a wanted criminal figured into his plan. So how will he reach those people?"

"By privately reaching the Councilors who agree with them."

She nodded. "You're right. That's the only route he has left."

"Parser gave him that bloc," Razine said. "He's the one who arranged that report."

"What?" Lancer Tal's tone was sharp. "Darzen Fosta wrote that report. Was she in Parser's employ?"

"Yes, but she didn't know it. He used an intermediary and a dummy philanthropic organization to offer her research funding. It was enough for her to take a leave of absence from her position and spend six moons working on the report and organizing the signatories."

"He certainly had his web spread all over Alsea." Aldirk couldn't help feeling a grudging respect. "How did he know that this obscure economist in Whitesun would be able and willing to devote six moons to that?"

"I didn't ask," Razine said. "That didn't seem important. The fact remains that Parser arranged for the report which undermined Lancer Tal's support and which may give Shantu the base he needs. He did know two of the Councilors currently backing Shantu for a coup: Zalringer and Denson."

"Not surprising," Aldirk said. "Those are his closest cronies on the Council. They would agree with him if he proposed changing the warrior caste color to purple."

"I would have guessed those names as well," said Lancer Tal. "They don't really help us. What we need to know is, which of the other Councilors might be in agreement? Are there enough for him to make a stand?"

The three of them began discussing names, political histories, and voting records. Aldirk kept track on his reader card, and sixty ticks later they had as clear a picture as they were likely to get with their current information. To go any deeper, he would have to put his information network in high gear.

But it was good enough for now. They had seven Councilors likely to join Shantu, thirteen considered loyal to Lancer Tal, and nine whose loyalties might be swayed.

"It seems to me that the one thing Shantu needs more than any other is time," Lancer Tal said. "It takes time to line up loyalties, and he couldn't start that process earlier without word getting to me. He had to wait for Parser's plan to play itself out. If we hold an emergency Council session and share everything we know, including Herot's testimony, we'll almost certainly bring several of these nine to our side. And we only need three of them to break Shantu's chance at a majority vote. Without that, he'll have a very hard time convincing the warrior caste, particularly given the charges against him."

"Tomorrow is too soon," Aldirk said. "Some of the Councilors need time to travel to Blacksun. The day after tomorrow will be the soonest we could do it."

The room was quiet as the Lancer considered.

"Tell your office to make the calls," she said. "We're flying back to Blacksun as soon as Healer Elwyn will let us move Colonel Micah. And give me a list of calls to make to start rounding up our support. You and I can divide that between us."

The meeting broke up soon after. Lancer Tal and Raiz Opah stayed to speak further with Razine—probably about Herot, Aldirk guessed—and Gehrain followed him down the corridor.

"Chief Counselor, a moment?"

Aldirk turned at the transport door. "Yes?"

The Head Guardian looked uncomfortable. "If Colonel Micah were here, would he have contributed to that discussion? Does he know the politics and history of the Councilors the way you and Colonel Razine and Lancer Tal do?"

Not nearly the way I do, was Aldirk's first thought, but then he reminded himself where the colonel was at the moment. It was one thing to denigrate him while he was healthy and capable of fighting back; it was something else when he was injured and unconscious.

"He knows quite a bit, yes. Why do you ask?"

"Because all the time I was sitting in there with nothing to offer, I was thinking about how much I'd have to learn to fill the Colonel's position." Gehrain looked at him with clear hazel eyes. "I pray it doesn't come to that, but I may be knocking on your door someday for a few lessons."

Aldirk stared at him. Until that moment, he hadn't consciously considered the possibility of Colonel Micah actually Returning. Certainly, he knew the details of his injuries and the ongoing effort to bring him back, but Shantu's treachery had occupied all of his attention since his arrival. Now he looked at the man who might become Chief Guardian and knew that for all his determination and effort, Gehrain would still need several cycles to come up to the colonel's level.

"If it does come to that, you're welcome to knock on my door," he said.

"Thank you." Gehrain nodded courteously and started down the ramp.

Aldirk watched with a vague sense of disappointment, feeling as if something were missing. He had half-expected the Head Guardian to make a snarky comment before leaving. Colonel Micah would have, and Aldirk had come to expect it after all these cycles. But Gehrain was so earnest—and so damned young. For a moment, Aldirk found himself wishing for a little of Colonel Micah's sarcasm and gamesmanship.

Just for a moment.

As soon as the door closed behind Aldirk and Gehrain, Tal looked back at Razine. "Thank you for diverting Aldirk away from Darzen. I trust his discretion, but there are some things he doesn't need to know."

"You're welcome."

"Does that mean Parser was spying on her even back then?" Salomen asked.

"No," Razine answered, and Tal breathed a sigh of relief. "But once he did begin collecting information, he sent an agent to that village to see what he could learn. When he discovered you had courted someone there, he made it his business to learn everything he could about Darzen. And then he used her."

Tal rested her forehead on her hand. "Great Mother. I think I need a shower."

"You might be interested to learn that Darzen changed her mind."

Her head snapped up. "She did?"

"She sent a letter to that dummy philanthropic organization, saying that after your speaking tour, she had redone her calculations and come to a different conclusion. She wanted to retract the report, or at least take her name off it. Parser made sure she was informed that any attempt to discredit the report she'd been paid to produce would result in the end of her career."

"She changed her mind," Tal repeated in amazement. "I wonder if that was why she came to my speech in Whitemoon. I thought she was there to make her case in a more public forum, but…maybe it was just the opposite." But then that little girl had offered such a perfect opportunity, and Tal had mercilessly gutted Darzen's credibility in front of a worldwide audience. Her stomach twisted at the thought.

"She could have called you," Salomen reminded her. "She's had every opportunity to tell you she supports your policies now."

"But Parser frightened her off. Goddess above, how many victims does he have? And the only reason he was able to use her was because of her association with me." After all this time, Tal finally had the answer regarding Darzen's motivation, but it didn't make her feel better.

She watched Razine take another sip of water, her hands still slightly shaky. It had clearly been a long and arduous session.

"Colonel, I know you could use a rest, so I won't keep you much longer," she said. "There's just one more thing I wanted to know."

"I can guess what you're going to ask, and the answer is yes. It was personal."

Salomen looked back at Tal with a furrowed brow. "What was personal?"

"Parser's plan. When the colonel said he would have gotten his desired outcome whether I cooperated or not, she wasn't telling all of it. I asked her to keep that part private."

"It's true that his main objective was a Lancer under his thumb," Razine said. "But he certainly had a preference as to which Lancer it would be. He wanted Lancer Tal in his power."

"But why her in particular?"

"Was it really because of the Redmoon disaster?" Tal asked.

"That's where it began. Ironically, it was because Parser assumed you knew more than you did. When you singled him out in front of the entire Council and ordered him to control the corruption in his caste, he thought you were sending him a message. He already had half a dozen enterprises going by then, though none of them had anything to do with providing materials for the fusion facility. So he assumed that you were warning him of his ruin unless he acted against his own caste."

"He thought it was political blackmail?" Great Mother, had all of this started because she'd been angry during a Council session?

"Well, it was," Razine pointed out. "You threatened him with legislation against the merchant caste if they didn't come up with a plan on their own. But he thought it was *personal* blackmail."

"He weighed your grain by his own half bin," Salomen said.

Both Tal and Razine looked at her. "I haven't heard that one," said Tal.

"You're not a producer. It refers to someone who puts a false bottom and a weight in a bin, then sells it as a full bin of grain. Anyone who cheats that way will assume others are cheating, too. Parser doesn't deal fairly, so he assumed you weren't either."

"Then he realized that you didn't know about his activities," Razine said. "And for reasons I still don't fully understand, that made him dislike you even more. He hated your ethics and the fact that you would judge his lack of them so harshly."

"So instead of cleaning up his own code of honor, he decided to bring mine down to his level."

"And provide long-term security to his network at the same time. Which of course had grown tremendously due to the very task force you ordered him to help create."

"Fahla, what a mess. And I was oblivious. The only reason I found any of this out was because Parser finally made an enemy who was willing to talk."

"Because he lost his entire business to him. It was Parser's idea to infiltrate Donvall's smuggling ring with a man of his own and plant the idea of recruiting high empaths. He knew that would bring you running."

"And he was right. I took out the entire ring, *except* for his man, and left him free to take over the business!" Tal slapped the table. "I feel like a shekking tile. Parser played me wherever he wanted."

"I'm afraid he played you even more than you know. He wanted you to find out. He made sure Donvall heard about his business being taken over, knowing he'd be angry enough to tip someone off. Parser knew that if you learned that the Anti-Corruption Task Force was in fact corrupt, you'd take it personally and hunt it down to the source. That whole scene in the Blacksun Base detention unit—he planned all of that out. His strategy was to get himself detained, then freed with a public apology from you. After that, he'd have you where he wanted you. Remember the security vid of your interview with him? He's already shown that to former Ambassador Frank, to prove that he controlled you."

Tal remembered the horrible feeling of watching every possible door slam shut while she'd spoken with Parser in his cell. It felt a bit like that even now.

"And yet Parser is the one who warned us about Ambassador Frank," she said. "He told the High Council that it took a merchant to know a merchant, and that Frank didn't give a dokker's ass about Alsean interests because he was here to control the import and export markets."

"Which was perfectly true," Razine said. "Parser just didn't mention the part where he'd already made agreements with Frank. Then he made sure the ambassador was kicked off the planet before he could make agreements with any other Alseans."

"So even Ambassador Frank ended up shekked by Parser." Was there anyone on or off this planet who hadn't been outsmarted by that little fantenshekken?

Salomen slid her hand over Tal's. "Parser is in prison now. His plan failed. And Shantu will fail as well. It's over, Andira."

"I wish I had your confidence. It's not over until Shantu shares Parser's cell and I have the assured loyalty of my caste. Right now I'm too jumpy to assume anything. And I still have a nagging feeling that Shantu has more in his pocket than I can see."

"Perhaps you'll see it better when you're not so tired."

Tal sighed. "Perhaps." She looked up at Razine, whose exhaustion was all too evident. "Perhaps we all need to take a break and look at this again when we're fresh. Colonel, I know you were up late last night and early this morning. Take the rest of the day off."

"Lancer Tal, this is hardly the time—"

"This is precisely the time when I need you at your best," Tal interrupted. "Leave it to the politicians now, and get some rest. That's an order."

Razine gave her a tiny smile. "I suppose I could use a nap."

"You and me both. Thank you, Colonel. You've been invaluable these last few days."

"It's my duty and my honor." Razine signed off, leaving the room in silence.

"Will the Lancer obey her own order?" Salomen asked.

"I'm not sure I can. I'm too wound and too worried."

"Then come to our quarters and let me try to relax you."

"Tyrina, I don't think—"

"That's not what I meant. There are other ways to relax, you know. Or is that something I need to teach you?"

Tal pretended to consider it. "I'm willing to learn."

"Good." Salomen rose, tugging Tal up with her. "Because I'm an excellent instructor."

Tal followed her out, thinking about instructors, which made her think about Micah, which wasn't the best of ideas at the moment. Her worry for him, always active in the background, quickly came to the front and expanded until it overwhelmed everything else. It was horribly unfair that he should be gone just when she needed him so much.

"By the way, we still need to send Aldirk in to Share with Colonel Micah," said Salomen.

The very thought of it lifted some of the clouds in Tal's head. "It might be worth suggesting, just to see the look on his face," she said as they stepped off the ramp.

"Whose face, Aldirk's or Colonel Micah's?"

Tal reached for her hand and held it tightly. "Thank you."

Salomen glanced over and smiled, her understanding clear to Tal's senses. Hand in hand, they walked across the landing pad, while behind them the two Guards at the base of the ramp fastened their coats against the late morning breeze.

CHAPTER 48
Stuck in the web

Parser woke with a gasp and instinctively slammed his eyes shut again. He was afraid of…of what? Something. Something had terrified him, but he couldn't quite remember.

Was it here, in this room?

His breathing was too rapid, too loud. If something was in this room, it knew he was awake. He would fool it by pretending to be asleep.

But slowing his breath just made him desperate for more air, and he ended up gasping loudly, filling his lungs in relief, terrified at the same time that he had given himself away.

His eyes flew open.

He was on a bed, in a small room full of equipment. It was brightly lit—no dark corners for something to hide in. Whatever was after him, it wasn't here.

Relieved, he tried to sit up but found himself immobile. What? No! If he couldn't move, he couldn't get away! They had left him here to die!

He jerked his arms, kicked out with his legs, thrashed as hard as he could. Nothing worked. His wrists and ankles were locked in straps, held against the rails at the sides of the bed, and a broad strap across his chest pressed him down.

He screamed, then coughed. His throat hurt, as if he had already screamed too many times. What had they done to him? Who were they? Why couldn't he remember?

The door opened, and he went stiff in terror.

"For Fahla's sake, shut up!" A big man moved into his line of sight and checked the straps around his wrists. "I had to listen to you scream all morning. Don't start again now."

Parser licked dry lips. "You…you have to let me go. I can pay. I'll make it worth your while."

The man laughed. "You couldn't pay a dokker to kick right now."

"But if you let me go—"

"After what I heard this morning, there aren't enough cinteks on Alsea to make me let you go." The man leaned over, shoving his face much too close. "You were going to kill a *little boy*. You called him a tile. A game piece to be played. Where I come from, we have names for people like you." He smiled suddenly. "And where you're going, they have other names."

Where was he going? He couldn't remember that, either.

Wait. There was something about being underground…

The Pit! They were going to put him in the Pit!

"No," he whispered. He couldn't go there. That wasn't part of the plan.

The man turned to check his ankle straps. "Sometimes I think five levels aren't enough." With a snort of disgust, he walked out and slammed the door behind him.

Parser's heart hammered in his ears. Not the Pit. He would die there. He wasn't meant to live in a place like that. He was meant for bigger things, greater things. Shantu would…

Would what?

He combed through his brain, trying to remember. Slowly, it came back to him. Shantu had said he had a foolproof plan. Parser hadn't wanted to know about it then, but he did now. His life depended on Shantu's plan.

Would he murder Lancer Tal?

It seemed like the sort of unimaginative, blunt-weapon idea Shantu would go with. Just remove the competition and dodge the shrapnel afterward.

But he didn't see how that could work. Shantu might have gotten away with assassination before, but he was a fugitive now. He would be the first one suspected. It had to be something else.

Think, he told himself. If you were Shantu, what would you do?

CHAPTER 49
Dream job

VELLMAR THOUGHT THE SCENE LOOKED eerily familiar as Colonel Micah's stretcher was brought into the transport. But this time there was no blood, no oxygenator, and no pressure sack, and Lancer Tal appeared rested and in control as she spoke to the healer.

The Guards had spent the remainder of yesterday continuing the Sharing rotation, and Vellmar had taken part twice more before giving up and returning to base early in the evening. She had slept for eight straight hanticks, making up for the night before, and by the looks of her warriors, they had all done the same.

This time she was sitting in the front row, having no need for a quiet space to prepare for a mission. She was also feeling a great deal more confident about her role and less inclined to remove herself from the group. Over the past three days, these warriors had become *her* Guards, her unit, and she knew she had already earned their respect. It was a tricky thing to come into an established unit and replace a well-liked commanding officer, but their mission had given her the opportunity to pack three moons' worth of proving herself into a single day. Thank the Goddess she hadn't blown it.

She hoped she had earned the Lancer's respect as well. Most of the time she felt positive about it, but Lancer Tal had a front like a stone wall, and her face didn't give much away either. Except when she looked at Colonel Micah or Raiz Opah. Especially Raiz Opah—anyone with eyes could see how the Lancer felt about her.

A large body loomed in her peripheral vision, and Senshalon sat next to her.

"Every time I see him, I expect him to open his eyes," he said, looking for the straps to his harness.

"I know. Me too." Vellmar watched him struggling and finally knocked his hands away. "How do you function without normal-sized people to help you with things like this?" She located his strap ends and handed them to him.

"That's why Fahla made small people like you." He flashed her a smile as he attached the harness.

"I am *not* small." Vellmar towered above every other Guard except Gehrain and Senshalon, and her height was something she had always been a tiny bit vain about.

"You are compared to me."

There wasn't much she could say to that, so she contented herself with popping open one of his harness buckles.

"Why, you—"

"You're not about to say anything you might regret, I hope."

He glared at her, but the expression soon gave way to an open grin. "No, Lead Guard."

"Good." She smiled and looked past him at the healer, who was taking his own seat as near to the colonel as he could get. The Lancer vanished into the fore corridor, no doubt to spend the flight in her private cabin with Raiz Opah. The engines spun up to full strength, and she felt the slight jar of the transport lifting off.

"It's good to see her back to normal," Senshalon said in an undertone. "The colonel's injury hit her hard."

"I think it hit everyone hard."

"Oh, it did. But you didn't see her in that basement. Dewar said she looked absolutely lost. And when I saw her a few ticks later, she still seemed like someone had kicked all the fight out of her. I've never seen her like that before, and I never want to again."

"You really respect her, don't you?" she asked curiously.

"Of course! Don't you?"

"Are you joking? I would have given up my salary for the opportunity to work with her. For that matter, I'd have paid to do it. It's just that…" She paused, trying to think of a way to put it. "I've never been in a unit before where the directing officer was so…familiar with her warriors. She doesn't keep the kind of distance I would have expected."

"Maybe not with you. She treats us like professionals, but she's usually pretty reserved. I think that's how she is with most people, though, not just us. But she's been different lately. We think it's Raiz Opah."

"Different how?"

"A little more open. And she laughs more…and she even took the time to help Varsi over her newbie nerves."

As a newbie herself, Vellmar pricked up her ears at that. "What did she do with Varsi?"

"Took her aside and told her that she valued her opinions. Varsi was walking a body length off the ground."

Vellmar tried to remember any superior officer telling her that her opinions were valued and came up blank. Then she remembered her first night in Blacksun, when Lancer Tal asked her how she would find something that couldn't be found, and realized that the message was precisely the same. The Lancer wouldn't have asked if she didn't value the answer.

"You don't keep much distance yourself," Senshalon said.

"I'm too new in the role. I haven't had time to acquire my lofty superior-officer airs yet."

"Well, in case you value my opinion, I advise you to watch Colonel Micah and see just how lofty he is. There's a reason we're all breaking our backsides trying to wake him up, and it's not because of his professional distance."

"Senshalon, there's nothing I'd like more than to watch the colonel and learn from him. I just pray I have the chance to do it."

He nodded soberly. "Me, too."

There wasn't much to say after that, and they passed most of the flight in a comfortable silence, reading or watching the scenery out the window. Twice Vellmar saw the healer check on Colonel Micah, and once Chief Counselor Aldirk wandered up the aisle from his aft cabin and vanished into the fore corridor, no doubt to consult with the Lancer on something. He returned half a hantick later, staring straight ahead and meeting no one's eyes. Vellmar knew nothing about the man, but it seemed clear that he was a scholar caste snob.

By the time they reached the southern coast of Argolis, she was tired of her book and took a moment to make fun of Senshalon's, which was a well-known historical romance set during the fall of Blacksun. Senshalon protested that he was reading it for the depictions of the battle, and Vellmar suggested he try nonfiction if he wanted accurate battle descriptions. After a few enjoyable ticks of banter, Vellmar was returning to her view when Senshalon said, "Wait. I wanted to ask you something."

His tone got her attention, and she looked back to see a serious expression on his face. "Go ahead."

"Is it true that you carry blades because you're not accurate with a disruptor?"

"I carry blades because I'm *more* accurate with them than with a disruptor, and a good warrior always uses her best tools," she snapped. "Anything else you want to know?"

"Whoa." He held up his hands. "I didn't mean that the way it sounded. I, ah…shek, this isn't working." He took a deep breath and asked in a rush, "Will you teach me your technique?"

"Why?"

"Because I'm not a perfect shot with a disruptor either. My best skill is hand-to-hand combat; I leave the long-distance accuracy to our snipers. And watching you and Lancer Tal in that house made me think that a better knowledge of blade handling could be a real asset for me in close-range fighting."

She eyed him, trying to determine his agenda. He seemed earnest, but she had been burned before. "It takes a lot of practice to get that kind of accuracy."

"I know, and I'm not striving for that. At least, not right now. It's just that I saw an opportunity to expand my skills, and I was hoping you'd teach me."

"Are you talking about knife fighting?"

"Yes. To start with, anyway. Eventually I'd like to learn to throw, too. What you did back there—it was spectacular."

Her instinctive wariness finally retreated. "I can teach you. As long as you don't mind getting a few holes at first."

An enormous grin lit his face. "Speedy! Thank you!"

"You sound like you're eighteen," she said with a laugh.

"It's not every day that a warrior gets the daughter of the world champion to train him. I'll be learning from the best. When can we start?"

"Today, if you want."

"I do," he said instantly. "That would be great."

"All right. Bring heavy gloves."

His brow furrowed. "How am I supposed to handle blades with gloves?"

"Very carefully," she said. "That's the point."

He looked at her suspiciously while she held a straight face for as long as she could. Then it cracked, and she laughed at his expression of disgust. "Sorry. I couldn't resist."

"Wonderful, our new Lead Guard thinks she's funny." But he was smiling as well. "Were you serious about the gloves?"

"Very. I found arm pads in the training room, but no gloves. You'll need them until you learn some basic techniques. Remember your early sword training?"

"Oh," he said. "That's what you meant by a few holes."

"Unavoidable. Better to get them in training than elsewhere."

He nodded. "Have you ever considered entering the Global Games?"

"And go up against my birthmother?"

"Hm. That *is* a problem."

"Actually, I've thought about asking her not to enter one of the competitions for that very reason. But it seems a little selfish, asking her to forego a prize just so I can enter."

"I think you should do it," he said. "I can't imagine your birthmother not being proud to see you accepting a prize, even if means she has to give one up. She's the one who taught you, isn't she?"

"Yes, but—"

"Then she'll be proud."

"Is that your opinion?" She lifted an eyebrow.

"It is. If you value it."

She caught the meaning and looked at him with new eyes. Though she was only a few cycles older, she had the rank and experience he was still dreaming about. And she was the one who could provide for him what Lancer Tal had provided for Varsi…and for her.

"I value it," she said. "Thank you. Perhaps this winter I'll get further than just thinking about entering."

He grinned. "Good! We'll all be there cheering you on. You'll be the first in our unit to be in the Games. Nilsinian almost got into the sniper competition two cycles ago, but he was knocked out of the final elimination round by half a point."

"Ouch."

"Yes, he sulked for days."

"Why didn't he try again last cycle?"

He shrugged. "You'll have to ask him that. We tried, but he just growled at us."

They got into a discussion of last cycle's Games and who should have won, until Vellmar had a shannel craving and left to get a bag from the storage unit. By the time she returned, Senshalon was reading again.

She settled into her seat, her own book forgotten as she watched the first outlying mountain pass beneath them. They were almost home.

"Vellmar?"

"Yes?" she said, still looking at the view.

"Thank you again. I appreciate your taking the time for me." She turned to face him as he added, "And don't be surprised if some of the others want to join up once they see what's happening."

"You're welcome. I'll be happy to train anyone who wants it."

He nodded and buried his nose back in his book. Vellmar watched as they approached the highest peaks, a tingle of happiness buzzing through her. For once in her life, it looked as if she would not have to battle the prejudice of warriors who saw her lack of disruptor skills as a handicap. Senshalon had called her the best; he wanted her to teach him.

A smile crossed her face. Her first impression about this unit was right—this *was* her dream job.

CHAPTER 50
Siblings

They landed at the Blacksun Healing Center first. Tal accompanied Micah's stretcher and watched as the staff transferred him to his new bed. Part of her had secretly hoped that being in Blacksun might have some sort of magical effect; after all, this was home. But of course it didn't. This room looked the same as the one in Redmoon, just with a different view out the window.

As soon as they were left alone, Tal went to his bedside and held his hand.

"We're home, Micah," she said softly. "And the dokshin is falling from the sky, and I really need you. Please, *please* come back."

His eyes moved briefly under his eyelids, but she had seen that before and no longer took it as a sign of impending consciousness. She stood with him for another tick or two, then reluctantly laid his hand on the cover. "I can't stay. But I'll be back. So will the Guards, including everyone who stayed behind, so don't start thinking you'll get to relax. We're not done annoying you. And I'm bringing the entire Opah family here tonight, so you'll be seeing some old friends. Well, except for Herot."

It was hard to leave. Every single time was hard to leave, because she never knew if he would still be there when she came back. All she could do was hope, and that was getting more difficult every time she saw him.

Their next stop was the State House, where Aldirk, Gehrain, and Vellmar disembarked. As ranking officers, Gehrain and Vellmar had dual housing in the State House and on base, sleeping where Tal did while on duty. Since their leave took effect the moment they arrived in Blacksun, neither of them had any obligation to be at the State House, but they both said they planned to use the time to settle into their new quarters. Vellmar hadn't even seen her base quarters yet, but she had decided to save that for later.

When they arrived at Blacksun Base, the remaining Guards piled out and scattered to their quarters. Tal, Salomen, and Thornlan were soon the only ones left on board, and Thornlan was only there to finish her post-flight review. Tal poked her head in to thank her and wish her a good day off, then went back to her private cabin.

"Delaying won't make it any easier," she said, leaning in the doorway.

Salomen looked up from where she was repacking several items in her bag. "I just wanted to get these put away."

"And the four-hantick flight wasn't enough time?"

When Salomen looked down without answering, Tal pushed off the door and walked over to crouch beside her. "I know you don't want to do this. But you'll feel better afterward."

"Is that a theory or a guarantee?" Salomen asked sharply, focusing on her packing. Tal was quiet, and Salomen's hands finally stilled. Staring into her bag, she said, "I'm sorry. I'm nervous and upset and taking it out on you. You're right, I need to get this done."

Tal put a hand over hers. "I'll be right beside you."

Salomen let out an inelegant snort. "It's a sad statement when you have to support me while I speak to my own brother."

"It won't just be me."

"What do you mean?"

"You have company waiting for you outside. Shall I bring him in?"

Salomen frowned at her, then stood abruptly and left the cabin. Tal followed her to the transport door, where one of Salomen's Guards was just arriving with Shikal.

"Father!"

He smiled at her as he stepped inside. "Hello, Salomen. Welcome back."

She touched his palms and rested her forehead against his. "I'm *so* glad you're here."

Tal breathed a sigh of relief and motioned for the Guard to make a discreet exit. As he tiptoed down the ramp, she turned and went back to her cabin, where she pulled her reader card from its pouch and settled into a chair at the conference table.

The Salomen who reappeared at her door was a different creature than the woman who had left it twenty ticks earlier. She walked straight over, threw her arms around Tal's neck, and kissed her.

"Thank you," she said. "This was exactly what I needed."

Tal smiled up at her, happy that she had guessed right. Any answer she might have given was forestalled by Shikal's low whistle as he came in.

"Lovely," he said. "Now this is the way to travel."

Tal reluctantly disentangled herself from Salomen and stepped over to offer Shikal her palms. "It surely takes the sting out of getting from one place to another. Well met, Shikal. It's good to see you again."

"Well met." He curled his fingers around hers. "I don't know how to thank you for bringing my son back. And I'm even more at a loss to express my sorrow about Colonel Micah. I know we're scheduled for a Sharing tonight, but do you think I'll be able to see him earlier?"

"Of course. He'd appreciate that. As for Herot, has Salomen told you that the only reason we were able to bring him back is because she found him?"

"*We* found him," Salomen corrected. "And yes, he knows all about it. I called him from Redmoon yesterday, while you were sleeping."

"Difficult times." Shikal squeezed Tal's hands once more before letting go. "There has been too much anger in our family, and too much betrayal for all of us. I can't do anything about your political situation, but at least I can start the healing process for our family."

Salomen went to her bag, tossed in the remaining items without a care for where they landed, and stood up with the barely closed bag over her shoulder. "I'm ready. Let's get this over with."

He shook his head at her. "We're getting nothing 'over with.' That sounds as if we will see Herot once and be done with it. He's still a member of our family, and he needs healing just as much as the rest of us."

"You'll forgive me if I don't agree. His wounds were self-inflicted. Ours were not."

"But they cause the same pain," he said. "And don't forget that the wound which began all of this is one we all share."

"I think the time has long passed when Herot could claim Mother's Return as an excuse. He has no excuses, and I don't want to hear any. I just want to hear that he understands what he's done."

"And if you hear that, will you forgive him?"

"I don't know." She motioned toward the door. "Shall we go?"

Tal looked at Shikal, who nodded. She picked up her own bag and led the way out.

It was a somber walk into the detention quarters, dampened even further by the light rain that began to fall. They left their bags at the front desk and were escorted through several corridors and locking barriers, finally halting by a door near the end of a long hallway. A warder unlocked the palm pad and stepped to the side.

When Salomen and Shikal stood still, Tal gently pushed in front of them, opened the door, and walked into the cell.

Herot was lying on his bunk, his back to the door. Though he did not stir at the sound of her entry, she knew he was awake.

"Herot," she said.

He started in surprise and rolled over. "It's you! Did you—?" His voice died when Shikal and Salomen stepped in.

"Hello, my son. I would say well met, but..." Shikal looked around the small cell, letting the implication finish his sentence.

Herot's eyes were enormous as an extraordinary range of emotions flitted across his face. He started to rise, thought better of it, and slumped onto his bunk with a defeated air. "I hoped you'd come. And I wished you wouldn't."

"Why would you wish that?"

Herot mutely gestured at his cell, his face taking on the stony stillness of someone who was trying desperately to hold himself together. Tal had to block her senses against the strength of his and Shikal's emotions, but she couldn't block Salomen, who had not moved since her entry. Herot seemed afraid to look at her, alternating between staring at his father and the floor, and Tal knew he could sense her anger. Salomen was barely controlling it as she stood there, arms crossed tightly over her chest.

"You are family regardless of your location." Shikal was speaking for Salomen's benefit as well. "Will you not give me a proper greeting, or have you forgotten how?"

Herot stood instantly, limped to his father, and held up both palms. "I didn't know if you would want it."

"Of course I do." Shikal clasped their hands. "I've been angry, yes. And hurt and grief-stricken and bewildered…but I've also worried about you, and I'm very, very glad you're safe."

Herot took in a shuddering breath of air. "I'm so sorry," he said in a small voice.

"I know. But tell me, exactly what are you sorry for?"

"Everything." A tear slipped from his eye, but he was still holding on. "Every single thing. The way I treated all of you, the things I said, the way I saw only what I'd lost and never what I still had…and especially that night. I can never make up for that night."

"No, you cannot."

The words were cold and clipped, and Herot visibly shrank as he met the rage in his sister's eyes. Letting go of his father, he took a careful step toward her. "I know I can't," he said. "I know, believe me."

"What the shek do you know, hm? Do you know that we lost Mother's portrait? And all of her books? Do you know that we had to throw the quilt in the trash, along with everything else? The quilt she made when she was Jaros's age and her mothers taught her how to sew?" She closed the small space between them, standing nearly chest to chest with him. "Do you know that I burned just as much as Andira when I tried to help her with the pain? Do you know that I watched her pass out from it? *What do you know?*" she shouted, and as he flinched, she shoved him, sending him flying back onto his bunk.

He landed awkwardly, pulling himself back into a sitting position as the tears streamed down his face. "I'm sorry—"

"That's not *good enough!*" she shouted again.

Shikal put a calming hand on her shoulder. "Salomen…"

"No!" She brushed his hand away, her eyes never leaving Herot's as she advanced to his bunk. "Sorry isn't good enough. Sorry doesn't *begin* to make up for what you put us through. And I know you've suffered as well, and I've hurt for you, and that made me even angrier. I don't want to hurt for you. How can I still have any feelings like that when you've hurt me and Andira so badly?"

He looked up, a tiny blossom of hope on his face. "Because we're family," he whispered.

"We're family," she repeated. "So you *do* know that. Then tell me, please, how you could have done what you did to your own family? Because I really don't understand. Family is something you love and protect. But you didn't love and protect us. You sneered at us, and denigrated us in public, and told an outsider how to hurt us. And then when he did hurt us, you ran away. You *saw* the flames and you ran away. You left Andira and me lying on a burning floor, in the wreckage of that room, and you *ran away!*"

His face crumpled as he cried, but even in his distress he couldn't take his eyes off his sister's. She held him with the power of her fury, hammering him with every word.

"I know you were jealous of Andira. And maybe I was too distracted by what I was feeling for her to pay quite enough attention to you. But most people deal with jealousy a little differently, Herot. Most people don't consider murder an acceptable solution. And if you thought that hurting Andira would change things between you and me, well, you were damned right about that. It has. I can never feel the same way about you, do you understand that? Never. You betrayed me, you betrayed your family, and the price is still being paid. Other people are paying the price, not just you, and you had no right to force them into that!"

He covered his face, sobbing uncontrollably, but Salomen was unaffected. She bristled with rage as she stared down at him, and Tal was shocked at the lack of mercy in a woman she thought she knew so well. Even Shikal was afraid to intervene. He looked at Tal helplessly and shook his head. His children would have to work this out themselves.

Herot cried for long ticks while no one in the room moved, and the silence finally seemed to get through to him. He uncovered his face, finding Salomen still staring at him, and wiped his cheeks.

"You're right," he said in a voice tight from weeping. "About everything. I did all those things, and even though I never meant for all that to happen, I'm still the one who made it possible." The tears continued to stream down his face, but he was calmer now, merely wiping them away with every few words. "Lancer Tal said I had to tell you the truth, and I've been thinking about that ever since. The truth is…I wanted to hurt her."

"Oh, Herot." Shikal's shoulders slumped.

Herot looked over at Tal. "I didn't want to admit that even when you talked to me, because it means admitting that I did wish for at least some of those consequences. But not like that, never like that. Never in my wildest dreams did I envision Cullom acting on our stupid boasts. If I'd had an inkling that he was actually capable of it, I never would have told him anything. I thought he was my friend. I thought I could speak openly to him; that's what you do with friends. You can be an idiot and it doesn't matter. But it did matter this time, and it's my fault, and I can't blame Cullom without blaming myself." He took a deep breath. "I…saw you as a rival."

"I know. But do you understand that there was never a question of Salomen loving one or the other of us? Her heart is too big; she didn't have to choose."

He gulped, fresh tears washing down his cheeks. "I know that was true then. I'm not sure of anything now." He looked up at his sister, but she gave him no encouragement.

"As soon as she came to our holding, you changed," he told her. "I'd never seen you so fascinated by anyone. You turned down five bond offers without a second thought, but the moment she set foot in our home, you were different. At first I didn't think much about it, because…well, I was fascinated too. But she never gave me a second glance; it was always you she wanted. That wouldn't have been a problem except I could see you wanted her, too. And that made her a threat."

"A threat to what?" Salomen asked, breaking her silence at last. "Did you think I would leave our home? Our family? Did you think I would forget everything else in my life?"

"I thought she would enjoy you for as long as you were convenient," he said. "And then she would drop you."

Salomen's head went back. "Are you—" She stopped, visibly gathering herself. "Are you telling me that all this was some twisted way of *protecting* me?"

"That was part of it, and I wish I could say it was all of it. But I was even more afraid that she might actually be serious." He met Tal's eyes. "When you punched me on the porch—that's when I saw it. You were defending Salomen's honor. You were doing what I was supposed to be doing. I admired you for it, and I hated you at the same time."

Tal nodded. "So part of the time you were trying to earn my respect, and the rest of the time you just wished I would leave."

"Something like that."

"Do you know what the real irony was? I had planned to cut my usual run short on my last day and invite you to come with me. I was keeping track of your progress; you went farther every day. I wanted to show my respect for your determination. But I never had the chance."

He closed his eyes, then looked up at his sister. "If you're hoping I can explain everything I did, I'm sorry, but I can't. I've been going over it and over it, and it all seems so far away now. I look back at it, and sometimes even I don't know what I was doing or why. But…I think I was afraid. Afraid of losing you and afraid of being so much less than Lancer Tal."

Salomen ran her hands through her hair in bewilderment. "If you were afraid of being less than her, why didn't you try to be more?"

"I did."

"When? You were unconscionably rude to her and to your family. You went out drinking almost every night, with people you knew were not our friends. You aired your complaints and anger loud enough for everyone in Granelle to hear, and you told Cullom Bilsner exactly how to kill Andira. You acted as if our family was a burden to you, rather than the other way around."

He winced at that. "Because I was still angry about everything."

"Just what do you mean by 'everything,' Herot? Don't give me that vague dokshin."

He looked from her to Shikal, nervously rubbing his hands on his pants. "I, ah…I don't feel that way anymore. I know now that I just didn't understand that you all showed your feelings differently, and you fronted different things. But…" He sensed Salomen's ill-concealed impatience and finished in a rush, "I thought the rest of you didn't love Mother the way I did. Because you all got over her Return so quickly."

"Oh, *that* is the last straw!" Salomen growled. "How dare you, you *shekking*—"

"Salomen!" Shikal stepped up and laid a hand on her shoulder. "That's enough."

To Tal's surprise she went silent, but she was nearly vibrating with renewed fury.

Shikal looked down at his son and said, "And this is how you would honor Nashta's memory? With anger and self-pity, disrespect for everyone who cares for you, and a betrayal that tore your family and your home apart?"

In just a few words he reduced Herot to tears once more. "I'm sorry," he choked, and this time the tears flowed faster than he could wipe them away.

"Let me explain something to you, Herot. I loved Nashta more than I thought it was possible to love. I had a long and wonderful life with her, and when she went to her Return, I thought it was a crime against Fahla that I should even be breathing. It hurt to be alive when she was not. The first time something made me laugh, it felt like a betrayal of her memory, because how could I possibly be happy without her?"

Herot mutely shook his head, pulling up his shirt to wipe his eyes.

Tal cautiously opened her senses and was instantly battered by the strength of his grief. Shikal might as well have been describing Herot's emotions.

He had never mourned her.

Salomen looked over, her eyes wide with the same understanding.

"But life cannot be lived that way," Shikal continued. "I had three sons and a daughter who missed her just as much and needed me more than ever. I had to move past it; to go on with my life because there was no other way. I miss her every tick of every day. I talk to her at night, when I get into the bed that I shared with her for longer than you've been alive. Do you know that I still sleep on my side of the bed? A lifetime of habit cannot be broken so easily, and there's still a part of me that would feel guilty for taking up her side. She's with me when I go into the fields, and she's with me when I come into the dining room and see our children at the table. She took a piece of my heart with her when she Returned, but she also left a piece of her heart in mine. As long as I breathe, that piece of her breathes with me."

He reached down and touched Herot's shoulder. "There's a piece of her heart in you as well. And in Salomen, and Nikin, and Jaros. She loved all of us, and she would never leave us for good. Your mistake was in thinking she left you alone. She did not. She left you with her family. With the people she loved, and the people who love you."

Herot leaned forward, burying his face in his father's stomach as his shoulders shook. Tal had to block her senses again; she was too raw to handle this. These emotions were much too familiar to her, and she knew that if Micah died, she would be in precisely the same condition as Herot.

Salomen looked at her with tears in her own eyes before sitting on the other side of her brother. "You stupid grainbird," she said. "How could you ever think we didn't love her as much as you did?"

He pulled away and sat up straight, wiping his face with his shirt. "Because I was an idiot."

"Yes, you were."

"I was angriest of all with you," he said. "Because you seemed to get over it before anyone else. You just buried yourself in the holding and took Mother's place as if you'd been waiting for it."

She shook her head. "I buried myself in the holding because it was the only thing I could do. And I took Mother's place because she told me it was my responsibility. She asked me for three things: to take her role as head of the family, to watch over Jaros, and to remember how to be happy someday. I fulfilled her first two wishes right away. It wasn't until last moon that I finally fulfilled the third."

She smiled at Tal, who was startled by this revelation. Her feet moved of their own volition, carrying her to Salomen's side where she reached for her hand. "Once again I'm wishing I could have met her," she said. "The pieces of her heart that you all carry tell me what a special person she was."

"I think she would have liked you," Herot said, surprising her for the second time in as many ticks.

"She would have," said Shikal. "I've told her all about you. And I get a warm feeling whenever I do, so I know."

"Salomen..." Herot hesitated. "You said sorry wasn't good enough. I understand that. When Lancer Tal told me what really happened, I wanted to die. No," he amended, "I wanted to kill Cullom first, and *then* I wanted to die. There's nothing I can do to make up for it. I swear in Fahla's name that if I could undo that night, I would. But I can't. All I can do is ask your forgiveness." He took a steadying breath. "Please, Salomen. Forgive me for my blindness, and my stupidity, and most of all for betraying the people I love."

The room held a charged silence as everyone waited for her answer.

"I cannot," she said finally. "Because I'm not the first person you should ask. You betrayed me by accident, but you betrayed Andira intentionally."

Tal took a surprised breath, finding herself unaccountably nervous about what she knew was coming.

Herot turned to her, and they looked at each other for a moment that stretched to an uncomfortable length. At last he mumbled, "I guess this is the rest of Fahla's joke on me."

For all the tension in the room, Tal couldn't stop her smile. "I guess it is."

He gathered himself and looked her straight in the eye. "I've done a lot of stupid things, I know. But the worst by far was what I did to you. Because I wanted to hurt you, even while I convinced myself that it wasn't my fault. Can you forgive me, Lancer Tal?"

There was no quick response, she realized, because he was really asking for two different things. But everyone was watching her, Herot was waiting anxiously, and Salomen had put the whole thing in her hands. She had to say something.

Slowly, she answered, "I can forgive the physical harm you caused me, because I know it was more than your intention. And I can even forgive your intention, because I've done much worse myself. But I do not have it in me to grant absolution for the anguish you caused Salomen. You hurt the woman I love, and that I will never forgive."

To his credit, he did not speak a word in his defense, simply nodding in acceptance.

"My answer is the same," Salomen said. "I can forgive what you did to me, but I still feel Andira's pain in my dreams. She was hurt because of my own family, in my own home, and I will never be able to forgive you for that. So I guess you'll have to settle for two halves of a forgiveness, because it's the best we can do."

"It's the best I can expect," he said. "Thank you."

An awkward silence ensued as everyone looked at everyone else, none of them having any idea what to say. Finally Shikal cleared his throat and asked, "What can we expect regarding Herot's sentence?"

"The range for his crime is two to ten cycles," Tal said. "And I'm sorry to say that because of my title, the adjudicator will almost certainly declare the maximum sentence."

"So much," Shikal said in dismay. "I thought it might be less because of his lack of intent. I mean, his lack of intent to kill."

"It would be, had I been anyone else. But justice is not the same for everyone. I wish it were different, but that's a fact of our system that cannot easily be changed. However, the title that will make Herot's sentence longer is the same title that will give weight to my statement."

Herot gaped at her. "You'll petition the adjudicator?"

"Yes, I will. And I'll ask for the minimum sentence, on the basis of your apology, your understanding of your crime, and your request for forgiveness. I think the adjudicator will listen."

"I don't know what to say."

"Try 'thank you,'" Salomen suggested.

"Thank you, Lancer Tal." He was completely sincere. "That's more than I had a right to hope for."

"Yes, thank you," said Shikal.

"Well, he *is* family." Tal raised an eyebrow at Herot, whose expression gave him away. "Not comfortable with that idea yet, are you?"

Before he could answer, Salomen said, "He'll miss the bonding ceremony, won't he?"

"Not necessarily. Leaves can be granted in the cases of bonding ceremonies or funeral pyres, so we should be able to count him among our guests…if he wants to come."

"Of course I want to come! I wouldn't miss Salomen's bonding for the whole world." He looked at his sister. "You really did keep this close. I knew you were fascinated by her, but I never had any idea you felt…well, like that."

"You mean that I love her?" Salomen said pointedly. "Yes. I do."

"It just occurred to me that Herot missed the most startling news about our family," Shikal said.

"What? What else could possibly have happened?"

Shikal smiled at him. "There's something you need to know about your sister," he began.

CHAPTER 51
A breed apart

After leaving Herot—who had taken the news of his sister's empathic gift surprisingly well—Tal sent Shikal's Guard back to the State House in his transport so she could fly Salomen and Shikal privately. Both Opahs were subdued after their meeting with Herot. Other than Shikal's appreciative comments over her luxury personal transport, the flight back to Blacksun was quiet. It wasn't until they were over the outermost homes of the city that Salomen finally said, "You were right, Andira. I do feel better. But I also feel worse, in a whole different way."

"Why is that?" Shikal asked from his seat behind her.

"Because as long as I was angry, I wasn't so upset about him being in prison."

"Ah. And now the reality is coming home."

"It came home already. I just put it out of my mind when I was so furious with him." She sighed. "I've wished so many times that none of this had ever happened. It still feels like a bad dream. I want to go home and look at Mother's portrait or pick up one of her books, and then I remember that I can't. Not anymore. And now Herot is in prison, and Colonel Micah nearly died in the rescue mission, and the consequences keep rolling on."

"Don't forget what those consequences would have been had Herot not betrayed us," Tal reminded her. "Rescuing Jaros would have been much harder and far more scarring to him." She didn't even want to think about having to kill someone in front of Jaros.

"I'm missing something," Shikal said. "What's this about Jaros?"

Salomen explained what they had learned from Parser, and his normally calm manner vanished. "This man will be in prison for a very long time, correct?" he demanded.

"Yes," said Tal. "Not just in prison. In the Pit. Fifth level."

"Good," he said, and his simmering anger suppressed any conversation for the remainder of the flight. When they landed, Salomen invited him to see their quarters, but Shikal said he needed a little time to himself.

"I believe I'll walk to the healing center and visit my friend Corozen," he said, pulling his rain cloak a little closer. "I miss his company, and perhaps it will help to have a chat with him. I do want very much to see your quarters and the parts of the State House that aren't on the normal tour. Perhaps this evening would be better; then you can show it to Nikin and Jaros as well."

"Of course," Salomen said.

They made their farewells and watched him walk toward the main gate as his Guard unobtrusively joined him.

"Perhaps I shouldn't have mentioned Jaros," said Tal.

"No. No more secrets. Not about my family. Not even if the truth is something we would rather not hear."

Tal put her arm around Salomen's waist and turned them toward the side entrance. "Come on, tyrina. I hear a soft chair and a good book calling my name. I still haven't finished the one you gave me."

"I swear I have never seen anyone read as slowly as you."

"I don't read slowly. I just don't read often."

They shook the drops off after entering the quiet, warm corridor. "I think I prefer the weather in Redmoon," Salomen said as they walked toward the lift. "It was so nice to be dry."

"Didn't you say you loved the rain?"

"I do. In moderation."

They were passing the training room when Tal heard something unexpected: Vellmar's voice, loudly ordering someone to get their elbow up. Curious, she opened the door and looked in to find Vellmar attacking Senshalon, who was in full protective gear. Vellmar stopped short when Tal appeared, only to have her wrist nearly snapped by Senshalon's blow as he disarmed her.

"Shek!" Vellmar held her wrist against her body, grimacing.

"Fahla, I'm sorry!" Senshalon sheathed his knife and reached for her, but she twisted away.

"I'm fine. Don't worry." She looked up at Tal. "Lancer Tal, you surprised me." Awkwardly, she brought her fists together and saluted.

Senshalon turned around, seeing Tal for the first time, and saluted as well. "Lancer. We were just doing a little sparring."

"I can see that." Tal trotted down the steps and reached for Vellmar's wrist, raising her eyebrows when the Guard hesitated before letting her take it. "I do apologize," she said, gently checking the joint. "Had I realized, I wouldn't have just barged in."

"Maybe we need a sign for the door when someone's training. That's what we had at Koneza."

"Senshalon, did you forget something?" Tal asked.

He looked down at his feet. "We do have a sign. A light over the door. I forgot to turn it on."

Vellmar shot him a look of utter disgust. "Thanks for the helpful tip."

"It's still in one piece." Tal released her grip. "He has a punch like a dokker's kick, doesn't he?"

"You've experienced it, eh?" Vellmar rubbed her wrist, clearly feeling better.

"Oh yes, more than once. Senshalon is our best at hand-to-hand. So he's talked you into teaching him knife fighting?"

Senshalon raised his head and grinned. "I did. She's already taught me two new moves I've never seen before."

"Don't you people ever take time off?" Salomen asked from the edge of the observation deck. "I should think after these last few days you two would be… oh, I don't know…perhaps lounging around your quarters, enjoying a well-earned day of leave?"

"This *is* time off," Vellmar said.

Tal laughed at both of them. "Salomen isn't used to the warrior concept of leisure time. She's a producer. She'd never dream of going back into the fields as a means of relaxing on her day off."

"Not in this lifetime," Salomen said.

"Actually, now that I think of it, I haven't had a good sparring session myself in too long. How are you at sword fighting, Vellmar?"

"Not bad," Vellmar said too casually.

"I'm going to take that as code for 'I could enter a competition and win.' Would that be about right?"

She smiled. "About, yes."

"Good." Tal enjoyed the familiar thrill of excitement. "Because I need to get a few things out of my system. Perhaps later this afternoon?"

"It would be my pleasure, Lancer."

"Then I'll leave you to it. Senshalon, remember that we just got her. I really don't want her incapacitated her first nineday."

"A little credit, please," Vellmar said. "Now I'm going to have to take him apart just to prove myself."

"You can try," said Senshalon.

Tal and Salomen left them circling each other on the mats, and this time Tal made sure to activate the training light before shutting the door.

"You warriors really are a breed apart," Salomen said as they made their way to the lift. "One tick you're talking about relaxing on a soft chair with a good book, and the next you're making an appointment to pick up a sword."

"It's been half a moon since I last sparred. My normal partner is in the healing center, and tomorrow is going to be tense. I need to blow some of the spinner's webs out of my mind."

Salomen shot her a sharp look, then wrapped an arm around her waist. "Come on, my warrior tyree. I'd like a chance to blow some things out of your mind."

CHAPTER 52
Sparring

As it turned out, Tal wasn't allowed to relax. Blacksun had been electrified by the news of Parser's and Shantu's sudden fall from grace, the new Bondlancer, and tomorrow's emergency Council session. Not counting the Voloth invasion, the capital hadn't seen this kind of excitement in fifty cycles, and Tal's vidcom never seemed to go dark. Given the political demands of her situation, she took every call and made the best of every opportunity to lay the groundwork she needed. But each time she had to explain she became a little more angry, until finally she called Aldirk and told him that unless there was a significant natural disaster somewhere, she did not want to be disturbed for the next two hanticks. Twenty ticks later, she left Salomen reading under the windows and stalked downstairs in a frame of mind that did not bode well for Vellmar.

The Lead Guard was waiting for her in the training room, a well-worn sword grip in her hand. "Lancer," she said, saluting.

"I should probably warn you that I'm looking at this session as a means of sublimation," Tal said.

"I can handle it."

"Good." Tal held out her hand. "May I?"

Vellmar extended her sword before handing it over.

"Double-edged; I'm not surprised." Tal cast an appreciative eye along the shining blade, which was longer and heavier than her own, though very well balanced. The grip was longer as well, and too wide for her hand. But Vellmar had the reach and strength for a weapon like this.

"My birthmother taught me the classical style," Vellmar said. "I got my height from her. My bondmother is shorter; she prefers the modern sintalon style and a single-edged blade."

Tal nodded as she admired the engraving on the crossguard, a subtle depiction of a mountain range with the sun rising over one end and both moons setting over the other. "All of my early instructors thought I should use a single-edged blade, too. But I never got used to it."

"I know."

Tal looked up. "How do you know that?"

"Yulsintoh devoted an entire chapter to your sword in his book. He said you wouldn't allow yourself to be limited to one style because you thought there were advantages and disadvantages to both. You wanted a blade that did everything, and that meant two edges. He thought your early instructors were blinded by tradition and expectations, so he took special pleasure in creating a sword that defied them."

"I can see I'll have to buy that book. I had no idea he remembered everything a young warrior told him all those cycles ago."

"I don't think Yulsintoh has ever forgotten a detail about any sword he designed. He said the biggest challenge in making yours was finding the proper balance—making it heavy enough for the power you wanted but light enough for your speed and style."

"And height."

"I wasn't going to say it."

"Everyone else does." Tal held out the sword. "You have excellent taste. It's very well made."

"Not as well made as yours. But someday I'll get there."

"I have no doubt. Have you already warmed up?"

Vellmar nodded. "I'm loose and ready to go."

"Then show me what you have."

They started slow in deference to Tal's half-moon hiatus. She focused fiercely, cursing herself for every move that wasn't perfect, but Vellmar matched her rhythm and parried each attack with a control that made Tal's moves seem better than they were. Gradually, Tal relaxed into her own body, letting her muscle memory take over from her brain, and as things smoothed out, they picked up the pace.

"'Not bad,' she says." Tal exhaled as their blades clashed and held at chest level. "I knew that was a pile of dokshin."

Vellmar looked over their crossed blades with a full, natural smile, the first Tal had ever seen on her. "My bondmother taught me not to advertise. It's better for an enemy to learn about my skills the hard way."

Tal pushed her back and tried a low, sweeping cut, finding it effortlessly blocked despite Vellmar's height. "I'm not your enemy."

"You are right now." Vellmar whipped her sword around in a blur, and Tal deflected it by pure instinct, feeling rather than seeing where it would end up.

In that moment, she realized that Vellmar was an opponent she could fight, truly fight, without worrying about the delicate dance of balance she always played with Micah. It was precisely what she needed, and she gleefully threw her normal caution to the wind.

The clanging of their swords came faster and faster, and Tal threw in a kick just to see what Vellmar would do with an unplanned blending of fighting styles. Her Lead Guard was surprised by it, but she avoided the worst of the impact by twisting away and still had her sword over her head in time to catch Tal's downward cut. Tal grinned at her, and from that moment their sparring match became an outright battle. Vellmar gave as good as she got, all respect for her Lancer forgotten in the heat of the fight. She landed a glancing blow with her fist and followed it up with another that snapped Tal's head back. Tal ducked under a third and struck out with the hilt of her sword, feeling the shock travel up her arm as it found its mark. Vellmar's mouth opened as the blow landed, but she made no sound even though it had clearly hurt. Her eyes narrowed and she came back low, pushing Tal's abilities in a rapid series of feints and thrusts she had never seen before. Tal parried all but one, a sudden change of direction that caught her by surprise and slipped past her desperate block. The sharp, thin pain shocked her, and they both stopped, staring at the blood trickling down Tal's arm.

This was not a blood match; they were not equipped for it and they had not agreed to it. Vellmar had crossed a line. As Tal looked from the blood to her Lead Guard, her shock morphed into pure anger. Without warning she fell on Vellmar, channeling every bit of the rage she had been suppressing and unleashing her aggression in a furious blur of attacks. Micah, Parser, Shantu…their faces and others drifted through her mind as she fought, holding nothing back. A lesser opponent would have shattered under the onslaught, but Vellmar took her on and even taunted her, driving her into a mental space she had never experienced in a sparring session. She forgot where she was and who she was fighting, conscious only of a murderous need to do damage. Every cut was accompanied by a cry of rage and a desperate desire to hurt, and when Vellmar made a sound of pain as a particularly violent lunge slipped past her, Tal was vicious in her glee. Her fury poured out, seemingly without end, and she drove Vellmar from one side of the room to the other. It wasn't until she began to tire that she finally came back to herself enough to realize what was happening. Horrified by her own behavior, she stepped back and held up her hand.

"Stop!"

Vellmar lowered her sword, breathing hard as she wiped the sweat from her eyes. "What's wrong?"

Tal retracted her sword, threw the grip onto the nearest mat, and turned around. "Great…shekking…Mother," she swore between gasps for air. What in the name of the Goddess did she think she was doing?

"Lancer Tal? Are you all right?"

Tal turned back to face her. "Are *you*?"

Vellmar looked confused. "Of course. It was a good match. You're an excellent sword fighter. Especially considering that you don't do this as often as you should."

Tal gaped at her. "I tried to kill you!"

"So? You warned me ahead of time. I told you I could handle it, and I did."

Her expression made it clear that she didn't see the problem, and Tal's laugh came out of nowhere. "Don't advertise, eh? I think I've met my match and then some. Thank you; I feel lighter than I have in days."

"Believe me, it was my pleasure. I don't often get the chance to spar with a left-hander. And no one at Koneza could really challenge me, so I'm delighted to have an opponent who makes me work."

"If my wanting to kill you just makes you work, I'd hate to see what it would take to make you break out in a real sweat."

"Oh, I'm sweating," Vellmar said with a grin. "Who do you normally spar with?"

"Colonel Micah."

The grin vanished. "I'm sorry."

"So am I." Tal reached down and scooped her grip off the mat. "About many things. But this felt good, really good. I've never been able to let go like that before. Sign me up for regular sessions. And show me that parry you used against my overhead cut—the bind that pulled my blade down and inside. You almost disarmed me with that one."

Vellmar's eyes lit up. "Right now?"

"Of course right now."

They spent half a hantick going over that move and two others, and when Tal finally returned to her quarters, she felt positively languid. She crossed the main room without stopping, only waving at Salomen as she passed through, and walked straight into the shower. The hot water felt divine, except when it hit the cut on her upper arm. She washed it carefully, then soaped the rest of her body and spent several ticks just standing there, letting the water loosen her muscles. Before the lassitude could completely take over, she stepped out, dried off, and hoped Salomen would not take it upon herself to check on her while she treated and skin-sealed the cut.

She didn't, and Tal was able to hide the newly sealed cut under a robe before emerging into the main room. With a blissful sigh, she poured herself onto the seat next to her tyree.

Salomen looked at her over the top of her book. "Well, that seems to have worked. I don't even want to know what you were doing. Just tell me that everyone is still alive."

"Oh yes," Tal said in tired contentment. "It worked, and Vellmar still lives. Micah really knew what he was doing when he picked her. I'll have to thank him."

"Will you be ready to thank him in a hantick? Or have you forgotten that we're meeting my family at the healing center?"

"I'll be ready." Tal shifted position, laying her head in Salomen's lap and closing her eyes as a gentle hand began brushing through her hair. "Just let me know when it's time to leave."

"I think I'd better let you know a little before that."

"Mm-hm." Tal wasn't even sure what she was agreeing to. She drifted in a comfortable haze, barely aware as Salomen picked up her book again, and a moment later was asleep.

CHAPTER 53
Bedside visit

THE OPAHS AND THEIR GUARDS were already in the healing center's notification area when Tal and Salomen arrived. Tal barely had time to get through the door before a small body barreled into her.

"Lancer Tal!" Jaros looked up, his arms wrapped securely around her waist. "I knew you'd bring him back! Those warriors didn't have a chance against you."

Tal didn't know if he was talking about Micah or Herot until Salomen crouched down for her own warmron. "No, they didn't," she said as Jaros threw himself into her arms. "Hello, Jaros. Herot is safe, but he won't come home for a while yet."

"I know. Father said he's being punished." Jaros looked over at Tal. "He said you would get his punishment reduced, but not even you can take it away altogether. Even though Herot never meant for anyone to be hurt."

Salomen's no-more-secrets policy did not apply to a boy of nine cycles.

"No," Tal said, "and I think he's learned something about how to choose his friends."

"Cullom Bilsner is a dokker's backside," Jaros announced, and Salomen had to turn her head away. With Jaros's attention on her, Tal had no such option and managed to keep a straight face only with the greatest of effort.

"I couldn't have put that better myself," she said with a nod.

"The Bilsners have no name in Granelle anymore," he said with the importance of someone holding great news. "Did you know that Gordense has put the holding up for sale?"

Salomen looked back at him, then up at her brother and father, who stood waiting for their own acknowledgment. "Really?"

Tal stepped over to Nikin, holding up her palms. "Well met," she said warmly. "It's good to see you."

"Well met, La—Andira," he said with a wry smile. "I haven't gotten used to that name yet."

"Take your time." She clasped their hands and squeezed; Nikin's calm presence was truly a pleasure.

He matched her grip as his smile grew. "We've missed you at the holding. But I hear you've been rather busy." The smile dropped as he added, "Our family is indebted to you. When I thanked you for helping my brother that day, I never dreamed it might take this form. And I'm so very sorry about Colonel Micah."

"Don't be sorry. Just help me bring him back."

"Father and I will do all we can. Have you seen the schedule for his Sharings? That poor man won't get a moment's peace."

"I know. That's the idea." She turned to greet Shikal. "I hope you had a good chat with him."

"I did. But I missed his input."

Salomen kissed both of them on the cheek as they touched palms. "Now what is this about Gordense selling the holding?"

They turned as a group, surrounded by seven Guards from two different units, and made their way down the corridor. Jaros maneuvered himself so that he was walking next to Tal, who put a hand on his small shoulder as she observed Ronlin. Salomen's Lead Guard had practically glued himself to her side, radiating watchfulness as his head swiveled in all directions. It was the first chance he'd had to guard her, and he was taking it very seriously indeed.

"Jaros said it best," Nikin said. "The Bilsners have no name in Granelle."

"They cannot hold up their heads," Shikal added. "Even if their public shame wasn't an issue, there's also the fact that most of the other producers refuse to have anything to do with them. Several of the merchants are refusing their business. It wouldn't have been such a problem if Cullom had been acting on his own, but Gordense made his beliefs loudly public. He said too many times that the Lancer had to be stopped. Those words have come back to haunt him."

"It doesn't matter how loudly he protests now," said Nikin. "The fact remains that Cullom acted on his father's beliefs, and no one in Granelle will ever forget that."

"I told Andira what he said at the caste house meeting." Salomen turned toward Tal. "Do you remember asking me about his intentions?"

"Very well. You were convinced he wasn't a threat."

"But he was, indirectly. And it never occurred to me to look past him to his son. I don't think I ever realized until now how damaging words can be."

"There is still an immense gulf between speaking and acting," Tal reminded her. "It's the same gulf that divides Herot from Cullom. Gordense deserves his shame, but he's not the one who fired the shot."

"At least the shame isn't limited to our caste," Nikin said. "Word is already out about Withernet spying for Parser." He caught Tal's surprised look and added, "It's Granelle. Nothing stays secret there. And of course the news is all over Alsea about Parser, so the merchant caste is carrying its own shame."

"And the warrior caste," said Jaros, eager to be a part of the conversation. "The Prime Warrior is a criminal, too. But Lancer Tal will catch him."

Tal squeezed his shoulder. "I'm your bondsister now, Jaros. You can call me Andira."

"I know," he said seriously. "But I prefer Lancer Tal."

Salomen winked at Tal and said, "It sounds better at school."

"If I called you Andira, nobody would know who I'm talking about," Jaros explained.

Tal wanted to laugh but contented herself with pulling Jaros close to her. "Doesn't the fact that you have your own Guard give your friends a clue?"

He grinned. "They are *so* envious about that!" Turning, he waved at one of the Guards behind them, who waved back with a smile. "That's Deladan," he confided, as if Tal wouldn't know the name of the warrior she had assigned to him. "She's really good at kickball."

This time Tal couldn't keep the smile off her face. "Is she?" she asked, catching the Guard's eye and seeing the instant flush. "Don't tell me she plays on your team."

"Oh, no. That wouldn't be fair. But she's been helping our coach. She knows a lot of tricks."

A few more steps brought them to Micah's room, and the Guards took up positions in the corridor. Tal hesitated, suddenly unsure about taking Jaros inside. She didn't know what was safe to say.

Salomen sensed it and took his other hand. "Before we go in, Jaros, do you remember what Father told you?"

He nodded. "We have to be careful about touching Colonel Micah because he's hurt. And something happened to keep him from waking up, but you're all going to Share with him to try to bring him back. Can I Share with him, too?"

"I'm sorry," she said gently, "but it's not a good idea. It's not like what you felt when you Shared with Andira and me."

As Jaros slumped in disappointment, Shikal said, "How interesting. That's precisely what I said when he asked me."

"Jaros!" Salomen's tone made even Tal cringe. "Why are you asking me if Father already said no?"

He looked from his sister to his father. "Ah...because...because..."

Tal took pity on him. "Because Colonel Micah is your friend too?"

"Yes!" He turned to her gratefully. "I want to help."

"I know you do." Salomen shot Tal a look that said *Don't encourage him*. "And you can help just by being here with him. But don't ever try that trick again. Your father and I will know if you try to play one of us against the other. Just because I'm not at Hol-Opah every day doesn't mean that you can take advantage of me."

His head dropped as he shuffled in place, mortified at being scolded in front of his idol.

Tal stayed quiet, mindful of her own near scolding, and Shikal defused the moment by opening the door to Micah's room. "Come on, Jaros. Let's go see the colonel."

Jaros gladly followed his father, and Tal gave Salomen an appeasing smile. "I did that when I was his age, too."

"So did Salomen," said Nikin.

She gave them a mock glare, which soon dissolved into a smile. "Yes, but I was never stupid enough to do it in front of both of my parents. I expect better of Jaros."

Nikin laughed. "You expect him to be just as devious as you were? Why would you wish that on us?"

"Nikin," said Tal in a confidential tone, "perhaps you'd like to have a drink with me sometime later? When your sister is busy? I think you have stories to tell."

"I do indeed," he said, matching her tone. "You'll be amazed at some of the things she got away with."

"You're both walking a dangerous line." Salomen turned and entered the room, her head held high.

"That's what makes life worth living," said Tal.

Nikin touched her shoulder with a smile. "Then your life with her should be extremely rewarding."

True words, Tal thought as they walked into the room.

Her momentary good humor vanished when she saw Shikal and Jaros standing by the bed. Jaros was already telling Micah about having a Guard at school, his small hand resting on Micah's arm. Salomen caught Tal's eye and held out her hand in invitation.

"Guess we'll have to wait our turn," she whispered as Tal came over.

"I don't mind. Every voice helps, even the ones on the outside. I've talked to him, too." Though Tal took Salomen's hand, she kept her gaze firmly fixed on Micah and Jaros. She couldn't bear to see in Salomen's eyes what was already too clear in her emotions.

How could she keep her own hope alive when Salomen was losing hers?

CHAPTER 54
Awake in the dark

THE OPAH FAMILY'S VISIT TO the State House was an enjoyable affair—or at least as enjoyable as it could be under the circumstances. Nikin worked hard to keep the mood light, and Jaros's awe at the size and luxury of their quarters was a delight to watch. But Tal's vidcom continued to demand her attention, and she could not afford to take any more time away from it than she already had. Too much was riding on tomorrow's Council session. So Salomen took over the duties of hostess, and Tal grew increasingly resentful of the whole situation. This was her family, and she deserved a few shekking hanticks free of political concerns. Her anger toward Shantu took on a new dimension as she discussed his actions with the various Councilors and powerful caste members who called her. The only consolation she had was that the groundwork she was laying tonight had already guaranteed tomorrow's outcome. She had the votes she needed; Shantu was finished. But she was still obligated to play the political game, gathering as much support as possible to be certain that no other warrior would be tempted to take advantage of the rift Shantu had created.

By the time their guests returned to Hol-Opah, Salomen was tired and Tal was both tired and short-tempered. They went to bed with a minimum of conversation, simply holding each other and taking quiet reassurance in their bond. Tal had so much whirling through her head that she found it nearly impossible to sleep. When she finally managed to drop off, her sleep was restless, punctuated by dreams that took her from one scene to another with dizzying speed. Nothing made sense, everything was disturbing, and at last she came wide awake, horrified at the single clear thought in her mind.

She knew exactly what Shantu had planned. And she had made it easier for him by scheduling tomorrow's emergency session.

She sat up, looking at Salomen by the light that filtered in through the windows. Fahla, she had so little time. She had wasted too much of it on a useless strategy, because she and everyone else were thinking like politicians. How many times had Salomen said it to her? *That is a politician's answer, and you are not a politician.*

"Oh, Salomen, I'm sorry," she whispered in the darkness. She leaned down to kiss her on the temple, holding her lips against the soft skin as long as she dared. Then she rose, threw on a robe, and went to the smaller vidcom built into her desk.

The call was answered quickly in spite of the time, and Tal looked into the face of the only person who could save her.

"I need your help," she said. "Right now."

CHAPTER 55
Looking for the Lancer

ALDIRK WAS TAKING A HURRIED mornmeal when the call came in from the Lancer's private com code. He wiped his mouth and hastened to his vidcom to accept the call.

"Lanc—" He stopped at the sight of the unexpected face on his screen. "My apologies, Raiz Opah. I expected the call to be from Lancer Tal. What can I do for you?"

"Have you seen her? Do you know where she is?"

"She's not with you?" he asked.

"No. She's not even in the State House or anywhere in Blacksun. I can feel her, so I know she's safe, but...she left me a note this morning saying she would see me at the Council session, and this isn't like her. I'm worried."

Aldirk was worried too, but she didn't need to know that. "Lancer Tal never does anything without reason. I'm sure she's simply making preparations for this morning's session."

"What kind of preparations involve leaving in the middle of the night?"

He shook his head. "I have no answer for that. Have you tried reaching Head Guardian Gehrain? Or Lead Guard Vellmar?"

"No. I thought it might look a bit odd if the future Bondlancer was calling around the State House searching for her bondmate."

He approved of her political astuteness. "Then let me make the calls for you. May I call you back in a tick?"

"Yes, of course. Thank you."

He reached Gehrain in his State House quarters, but the Head Guardian was still officially on leave until hantick seven and fifty; he had no idea where the Lancer was. Vellmar was on the same leave and could be found in neither one of her quarters. It was too early for the support staff to have arrived at the Lancer's office on Blacksun Base, so Aldirk tried the contact desk next, getting a stern-faced warrior who informed him that the base never gave out information on the Lancer's whereabouts.

"Check your com code, you idiot," Aldirk snapped. "I'm not some journalist. I'm calling from the State House."

The warrior raised an eyebrow in remonstrance as he leaned forward and pressed a key on his console. The other eyebrow rose to join the first, and he straightened into a more formal posture. "My apologies, Chief Counselor. The Lancer is here. But she left explicit instructions not to be disturbed for any reason."

Aldirk nodded. "Very well. Please inform her, if she accepts any messages later, that we in the State House are looking forward to seeing her in the Council chamber." He knew Lancer Tal would understand who the message was really from.

"It will be done," the warrior said.

Aldirk ended the call and a moment later had Raiz Opah on his screen.

"She's on the base," he said, and saw her visibly relax. "I don't know what she's doing, but whatever it is, she does not wish to be disturbed. I can only speculate that for some reason she needed to be alone and away from any possible interruptions before the Council session."

She looked briefly distressed before schooling her expression into one of calm acceptance. "I'm certain she knows what she's doing. Thank you for your assistance, Chief Counselor. I'll see you in the guest gallery."

He wished her a good morning and stared at the blank screen thoughtfully.

"What have you figured out?" he said aloud. "And why don't you want your bondmate to know?"

CHAPTER 56
The warrior's challenge

TAL WAITED UNTIL THE LAST possible moment before returning to the State House with Vellmar. It had been beyond difficult, feeling Salomen's worry and concern this morning, but she couldn't face her. Not last night and not now. There would be too many questions, too many arguments, and she didn't have time to deal with them. So they slipped into a service entrance, and Vellmar went up in the lift while Tal made her way down the back corridors to a little-used set of stairs. She ran up to the tenth-floor landing, where she waited until she could feel that most of the traffic in the hall above had thinned out. Salomen was already in the guest gallery, and while Tal stood there, she expanded her senses, identifying the people near her tyree. Lead Guard Ronlin sat on one side and Nikin on the other. Around them were Aldirk, Razine, Gehrain, Vellmar, Shikal—and Jaros. Great Goddess, why had they brought Jaros?

Because she hadn't told Salomen. They didn't know.

"Oh, shek," she whispered. But there was nothing she could do, and her time was up. If she waited any longer, she wouldn't get to her dais before the session was scheduled to open.

She took the stairs two at a time, popped out into the corridor, and strode through the remaining attendees with a stiff bearing and an attitude that warned off those who would have spoken with her. A few people still called greetings after her, but she made no response save to lift a hand over her head.

She unlocked her private entrance and ducked through, breathing a sigh of relief as the door sealed behind her. This was her sanctum, a small, soundproof room where she could gather herself before facing the Council. A pitcher of water and a bowl of fruit sat on the low table, and she was dismayed to see her hands shaking as she poured herself a drink.

It's just nerves, she told herself. They'll be steady enough when you need them.

She drank the water and held the cool glass against her forehead, taking a few moments to simply be still. Then she replaced the glass on the table, crossed the room, and opened the other door.

The roar of hundreds of conversations assaulted her ears when she stepped onto the dais, though the sound level declined when people saw her. The usual swarm of vidcams rose into place as she picked up the staff from its holder on the wall, walked to the bell, and gave it a sharp blow.

All remaining conversations ceased instantly. In the silence she looked up to the guest gallery, meeting Salomen's eyes with an almost physical impact. She sat in the front row, an insurmountable distance away. Tal had made certain of that distance, but now that she was looking at her, she wished she had done it differently. She could only hope that Salomen would understand.

Breaking their gaze, she looked from one side of the chamber to the other, taking in the packed galleries and the nearly full attendance of Councilors. Two seats were conspicuously empty.

"This Council session is now open," she said. "I have called this emergency session to put the rumors to rest, and to shine a bright light into the darkness that has deeply wounded us. Alsea has lost two of her leaders to their own worst instincts. Our former Prime Merchant has confessed to a corruption that will astound you with its breadth and reach; you will hear every detail before this session is over. And our former Prime Warrior is running from arrest, charged with kidnapping and conspiracy to murder. He was prepared to kill for political gain—a cold-blooded, premeditated murder for the worst of reasons. The victim of his crimes, Herot Opah, is here this morning to testify about his experience.

"We have a task of enormous importance before us today. When one-third of the Council leadership falls to corruption and murderous behavior, the belief of the Alsean people cannot be expected to stand. We must address this now, today, not tomorrow and not a moon from now. We are in crisis. Though it is not a crisis of our making, we are nevertheless bound to resolve it or risk losing the trust of the people we serve. And that is why I will be proposing a swift and unmistakable response." She paused, sweeping her gaze across the attentive faces of the Council. "When we have finished presenting the evidence to you, I will ask the warrior and merchant castes to consider the only realistic judgment they can make. I will ask them to strip former Prime Warrior Shantu and former Prime Merchant Parser of their caste."

Gasps of astonishment filled the air, but a number of merchant and warrior councilors sat with grim faces, nodding their agreement. Most of them had already promised either Tal or Aldirk their votes. Though a majority vote of the Council was not binding in internal caste matters, in this case its recommendation would almost certainly be followed. Parser and Shantu were about to lose everything that made life possible. They would be outcastes, Alseans of no identity and almost no rights. Even a sentence to the Pit paled in comparison.

Though they would get that, too.

When the whispers had died away, Tal said, "We will begin with the case of Parser, as we already have his confession and full details of his criminal activities. I will no longer call him by his former title, since his crimes have rendered him unfit to hold it. Though these crimes stretch back many cycles in time, for brevity's sake I will start his story with the fusion facility crisis of last cycle, when he cynically used the sorrow of our world to fill his own—"

She stopped as the great chamber doors were flung open, thudding back against the walls with a hollow boom. A solitary figure advanced onto the empty chamber floor, and shocked whispers mounted in volume as he was recognized. The doorway behind him filled with Guards, though none made an attempt to stop his progress. He walked to the center of the floor and stood still, letting the wave of whispers crest and recede before speaking in a voice long used to reaching every part of the Council.

"Fellow Councilors, you know me. For those in the galleries and those watching in their homes, I will identify myself. I am Prime Warrior Shantu, and I am here to defend my name and honor against the egregious accusations the Lancer has already leveled. But I have no faith in the justice of our tribunals or even this Council. It is all too clear that I have been judged and convicted before my voice was even heard."

He paused, standing tall in his dress uniform, his perfectly cut hair sweeping his shoulders and his appearance that of the hero of Whitesun, the man who had commanded the Pallean forces to fight back the Voloth. He looked noble and unworried, and Tal had to admire his theatrical poise.

"Nice entrance, Shantu," she muttered. She didn't care that the nearest vidcam had probably picked up her voice.

"If I am such a criminal, guilty of such crimes as to warrant a stripping of caste, then why do these warriors stand idle in the doorway?" he asked, pointing back at the Guards who were indeed motionless. "I'll tell you why. Because they know and accept my ancient right, the right I am invoking now. The only right I have left in a misguided Council, led by a Lancer with a personal vendetta, who would ruin my name and bury my honor under a stinking cloud of lies. The right of challenge."

The entire tier of warrior caste Councilors burst into shouts of outrage, shock, and in a very few cases, support, while most of the other Councilors sat in stunned silence. Councilor Ehron stood up and shouted to be heard above the rest.

"You have no right of challenge! You threw it away when you stole the rights of your victim!"

"I have every right!" Shantu shouted back. "Has anything been proven? Have I been convicted in a fair hearing? No! But I *am* unjustly accused; I *am* pursued by the legal forces of the warrior who rules us! The right of challenge was created for precisely this situation, when an honorable warrior stands helpless before the overwhelming might of a sitting Lancer. It was created so that a single warrior might still defend himself, even with the accusation of crimes over his head. It was created so that I might stand here, without fear of being shot in the back, and look this Lancer in the eye to say *I am innocent!*"

He had turned to Tal for his last words, and she met his gaze evenly as the Council chamber erupted into pandemonium. It wasn't easy with Salomen's horror pulsing through her. Perhaps it had been a mistake not to tell her; to give her what time she could to accept the idea and control her response. But she'd had so little time as it was.

The shouts flew back and forth as she and Shantu stared at each other.

"No one has invoked the right of challenge in four hundred cycles! It's defunct!"

"The law still stands; it was never revoked!"

"He has no right!"

"He has every right!"

"We will not allow it!"

"And who are you to stop it?"

"This is an embarrassment! How can we even be discussing this?"

Shantu's lips curved into a small smile of triumph. This was going precisely as he had hoped, and she would not let him bask in it.

She picked up her staff and struck the bell. The debate came to a sudden halt, leaving behind a silence underscored by the low hum of the bell's reverberation.

"Shantu is correct," she said. "He has the right of challenge, however cynically it is now being used. Chief Counselor Aldirk, do you concur?"

She would not look at the guest gallery; Aldirk was sitting too close to Salomen. Instead she held Shantu's gaze as the entire chamber waited in breathless silence to hear what the Chief Counselor would say.

"This is a most…unexpected request," Aldirk said. "And may I add, entirely unworthy of a civilized society. We left this barbarism hundreds of cycles in our past, and I think it safe to say that very few of us here ever expected to see its return." His voice grew stronger. "Shantu, your request shames this Council. Justice cannot be proven by might of arms, and no matter the outcome of this challenge, no Alsean alive today will ever forget that you have chosen to hold up a past that should have been left buried. Unfortunately…" He paused, and Shantu's smile returned. "The right of challenge predates the formation of the Council. Nor was it ever made unlawful by a vote of the Council. It was thought to be an artifact of a barbaric past. To my eternal regret, that assumption does give you the right to challenge Lancer Tal."

After a moment of utter silence, the whispers began. Tal silenced them with another strike of the bell.

"I also regret that such barbarism should have been returned to the seat of government. Shantu has ensured that this day will be forever remembered as one of deep shame for all Alseans. But if he insists on invoking an ancient excuse to shed blood on the Council floor, I will not deny him. I accept Shantu's challenge in the name of his victims, past and present, and in the name of those who would fall to his ambition should it be left unchecked. You are defending an honor that is already lost, Shantu. But I am defending Alsea. I think we both know who Fahla will favor."

"I knew you would understand the law and your own obligations to it," Shantu said. "Though you have led this Council and our world down some unfortunate paths, you have always known your legal limitations."

Tal ignored the double-edged words. "As the challenger, you have the right to choose the date and time of combat. What is your choice?"

"Right now," he said, as she had known he would. Salomen's shock slammed into her with an almost physical force, and she had to steel herself against it.

"I require enough time to have my sword brought, to change into appropriate clothing, and to speak with my future bondmate," she said. "I will not fight you before one hantick from now."

He gave her a short bow. "Agreed."

"Then at hantick ten and twenty-five, we will reconvene this Council to witness a ritual combat. By the ancient laws, this combat will end only with the death of either challenger or challenged. May Fahla forgive me for what I must do."

She turned and strode off the dais, closing the door behind her and sinking onto the nearest chair with a long exhale. "Goddess," she whispered, putting her face in her hands. "I hoped I was wrong."

No time for useless wishes. She pulled off her boots and set them neatly against the chair. Her jacket, dress shirt, and trousers followed, leaving her in a light bodysuit. The material was tougher than it looked and would not tear or puncture easily, but that didn't matter in the kind of combat she was now entering. She had just wanted clothing that would give her some modicum of protection without restricting her in any way. Its solid black color was originally a style choice, but this morning it had a strategic advantage: it would not show blood.

She had just finished folding her trousers when she sensed them arriving outside. After dropping the clothes on the chair, she went to the door and opened it, her heart skipping a beat as their eyes met.

"I don't suppose I can talk you out of this," Salomen said in a ghastly attempt at hiding her terror. Vellmar and Ronlin stood just behind her, their heads respectfully lowered.

Tal drew her into the room, enfolding her in a warmron without a word. Behind them, Vellmar walked in and closed the door.

"I'm sorry I couldn't tell you," Tal said.

"Why?" Salomen's voice was choked. "Why did you leave like that? So I could spend our last morning alone, worrying about you? Vellmar says he was a competition fighter!"

"I'm sorry, Lancer Tal. She asked how good he was, and I…don't lie very well."

"It's all right. Don't ever lie to Salomen." Tal pulled back enough to look into Salomen's face. "He's a very good sword fighter; it's true. But his competition days are long past, and he doesn't move as quickly as he used to. Besides, I have something he doesn't. I have right, and honor, and you."

"And is that enough? Is it enough against a man fighting for both his life and the biggest prize he could ever want?"

"It has to be."

Salomen looked at her incredulously. "It has to be? That's the best you can do?" Her fear rose on a wave of anger, and she struggled to hold it back. "How could you not tell me about this? You knew last night, didn't you?"

"Lancer Tal," said Vellmar, "your bag is on the chair. I'll be outside with Ronlin."

"Thank you, Vellmar. For everything."

"You're welcome." The door slid shut behind her.

Salomen's gaze had not wavered, her eyes brilliant with the emotions that were searing Tal's senses.

"Yes, I knew last night." Tal winced at the lash of betrayal and hurried to explain. "And I knew that the only chance I had was if I could get in enough practice to make what I do out there something that requires no thought. He's not going to give me a warm-up period; I have to be in top form from the moment this combat begins. I should have figured this out days ago. I should have been practicing day and night to bring myself up to the very best level I can be. Instead I wasted time strategizing and rounding up votes I didn't need. That's what Shantu was counting on—he planned to walk in here and catch me by surprise. By the time I figured it out last night, every tick counted. Don't you see, I couldn't wake you up! You would never have let me walk out the door without a long explanation and probably an argument, and I couldn't afford it. Not the time, and not the mental distraction."

"So you went to the base with Vellmar."

"Yes. We've spent every piptick practicing. She's good, very good, and in just a few hanticks she's taught me some moves that might be the difference between living and dying."

The word hung between them, and Tal cursed herself for her tactlessness.

"Three nights ago, you were almost ready to let a caste coup happen. You said you weren't sure it was worth fighting. You talked about retirement, for Fahla's sake. How can you stand here now and tell me that not only is this worth fighting for, it's worth dying for?"

"Because there's a difference between retiring with full honor and forfeiting everything that makes me who I am. If I walk away from this, it's not just my rank that I'll lose. I'll lose all of my honor with it, no matter how unfair this is and how much everyone out there knows it's a farce. It doesn't matter, Salomen. I cannot walk away. I cannot live that way, one step short of outcaste. It's not a life."

"Not even if it's a life with me?"

Tal closed her eyes. "Please don't do this to me."

Salomen stepped back, breaking her hold. "Don't do this to you?" she repeated. "Can you not feel what you're doing to me?"

Yes, she could, and she had made a colossal mistake. Their bond felt raw and wounded, clouding the mental clarity she needed. "I would give anything not to hurt you," she said, her voice ragged.

Salomen's laugh was painful to hear. "Not anything, apparently. Just anything except your Fahla-damned honor."

"I will not be the person you fell in love with if I walk away. It's not just my honor; it's me! It's everything I am, everything I've worked for, everything my parents taught me. How am I honoring their deaths if I destroy myself and let Shantu win?"

"How are you honoring their deaths if you *die?*" Salomen covered her mouth, her eyes brimming. When Tal moved toward her, she took a step back. "You have asked me for the impossible since the night of that first warmron," she said shakily. "And every time I find a way to give it to you, you ask for even more. You might have hit the limit this time."

A night of preparation was falling apart around her, and Tal stood helpless to stop it. If she went out there like this, death was a near certainty.

"Salomen, I—"

"You're in no condition to fight," Salomen interrupted. "I felt you before you rescued Herot, and I feel you now, and there is no comparison."

"Because I need you," Tal whispered in despair.

"Then why did you leave me?"

Because she had not learned a damned thing. Because she was a shekking idiot who might have just killed herself and left Salomen with a broken tyree bond. "It was a tactical decision."

"Didn't work out very well, did it?" The sarcasm could not cover Salomen's pain. Once again Tal tried to approach her, and once again she stepped back. "What if…what if you chose a champion?" she asked in sudden hope. "Isn't that your right?"

Tal shook her head. "Only scholar caste Lancers could choose a champion. That was never an option for a warrior, unless she was physically incapacitated. And I don't think anyone would believe me if I suddenly broke a leg."

"I could shekking well break it for you. No one but a warrior would blame me. That you could leave me like that, and let me learn about this in front of three hundred—" Salomen stopped with a shuddering breath as her anger crested and crashed, leaving behind an agony of fear. She lowered her head, the breath rasping in her throat, and held up a hand as she fought back the tears.

Tal could only watch in silent guilt, paralyzed by that upraised hand and the bitter magnitude of her mistake.

"I'm sorry," Salomen whispered at last. "I know this isn't what you need from me. I'm trying, Andira, I really am."

This time she didn't back away, and Tal wrapped her in a desperate warmron. "I'm the one who's sorry. I should have told you. I should have prepared both of us for this fight, not just me. And I'll spend the rest of my life making up for it, but right now you *have* to believe in me. Be furious with me, I deserve it, but I need your faith."

Salomen made a choked sound as her body jerked once, twice, and then went still. She was trying so hard to be the Bondlancer that the Lancer needed, despite what Tal had done to make a bad situation worse.

"Every time I think I cannot love you more, you prove me wrong," Tal murmured. "I don't even have the right to ask your forgiveness."

Salomen's voice was deceptively steady. "Do you need my forgiveness or my faith? Because right now I'm only capable of one."

"I—"

She was not allowed to finish her sentence. In a sudden surge of strength, Salomen pulled back, seized her head, and kissed her with a bruising need. Tal could barely keep up, gasping when Salomen broke off only to attack her jawline and throat with equal ferocity.

Salomen's hands were all over her, grasping roughly, pushing her back. The abrupt shift in emotions left her feeling as if she were in the grip of a sea storm, powerless to do anything but let her tyree take what she needed.

Her compliance fed Salomen's aggression. The heat surged through their bond, energizing them both and clearing Tal's head. When her back hit the wall, she realized that she was being marked and claimed. Salomen would not let her go until she understood exactly what the true stakes were. There was no way out—but there was a way back, and this to come back to.

The assault stopped as abruptly as it had begun. Salomen rested her forehead on Tal's shoulder, breathing hard, then pushed herself back. Her face was streaked with tears, but she met Tal's eyes with a startling calm. Somehow she had gathered all of her fear and pushed it into sheer determination.

"I have faith," she said. "Because you have me. Shantu will have to fight both of us."

Tal watched her in stunned admiration. "Then he will lose. I've never heard of anyone crossing you and winning."

"Not until you."

"I didn't beat you at anything. You were my nemesis from day one."

"Then I suppose I should tell you. You won the challenge. You said I had no idea what your life was like, and you were right, I didn't. I thought you were a politician with little understanding of how most Alseans worked for a living, but you work harder than anyone I've ever known. And you care more than I ever dreamed. So I concede."

Tal caressed her cheekbone ridge, savoring its feel beneath her fingers. "If we're making confessions, I have one as well. Not since my first moons of training have I ever been as sore as I was on your holding."

A tremulous smile broke through. "You tried so hard to hide it."

"At the time, I thought I'd sooner give up my title than show you any weakness."

"Oh, tyrina. Haven't you learned yet that it's your weaknesses I love the most?" Salomen kissed her again before gently putting Tal's arms away from her and stepping out of their embrace. "Help me move these."

They pushed two of the chairs off the thick rug occupying the center of the room, making enough space for them to lie down in as much comfort as their situation would allow. For most of a hantick they simply held each other, murmuring whatever thoughts came to mind, wrapping up loose ends, savoring every touch and look and word. At times one or the other of them would silently weep, but the tears never lasted long, and their hands never stopped moving.

Their bond hummed between them, strong once again despite the wound beneath the surface. Somehow Salomen had cauterized it, but healing would take longer. Tal shuddered to think how close she had come to crippling herself through the very strategy she had thought was her best chance. In that moment, she missed Micah with a grief that bordered on anger. He had taken his counsel away from her when she needed it most. And she had chosen the wrong path twice, using political tactics when a warrior was needed, and warrior tactics when a tyree was needed.

At least she knew what to do now.

When she could put it off no longer, she kissed Salomen one more time and moved away, plucking her bag off the chair and pulling out the low shoes Vellmar had brought for her. As she put one on, Salomen picked up the other. Then she tilted her head and looked more closely.

"What's this?"

"Armor." Tal pulled her straps tight and accepted the second shoe. Running her fingertip along the dark metal alloy ridge at its front, she added, "Not for my protection, though. This one gives me more destructive power in a forward kick." She turned the shoe and showed Salomen the second ridge, along the outside edge of the heel. "And this one is for side kicks. They weigh almost nothing, so they won't slow me down, and they're invisible unless someone gets as close as you just did. Not exactly regulation, but they're not specifically excluded by the laws."

"You mean you're cheating?"

"Let's just say I'm taking every advantage I can. Shantu will beat me in swordplay. There's no question about that. I don't have the skills I need. But I have other skills, and that's where I'm pinning my hopes." She adjusted the straps, rose to her feet, and held out a hand.

Salomen looked at it for several pipticks before taking it and allowing herself to be pulled up. "Don't break my heart," she whispered as they embraced one last time. "It's not just your life at risk."

"I know." Tal held her so tightly that she was afraid of hurting her. Letting go was nearly impossible, and it took several attempts before her muscles would obey. She stepped back, putting distance between them. "You have to go."

Salomen nodded, biting her lip as her composure cracked. They stared at each other, both trying to memorize every detail of a beloved face; both wishing the moment would never end. Tal felt the surge of determination just before Salomen turned and walked out, her stride smooth and assured. She never looked back as the door slid shut with a mechanical sigh.

Tal stood still, gazing at the closed door. The urge to follow was so strong that her body had taken a step before she realized what she was doing. Shaking her head, she turned away and began a warm-up form, a stylized battle that stretched and warmed every muscle. When she had completed two full cycles, she closed her eyes and took herself to her place of serenity. In her mind she was surrounded by a dense forest, the ancient trees flashing past as she ran in glorious solitude. Always this image had soothed her and given her strength, but this time she needed something else. She looked ahead, seeing a figure running on a converging path. Then Salomen was beside her, laughing in pure joy as they dashed through the trees, their footsteps noiseless on the soft duff of the forest floor. They ran without effort, without need for speech, reveling in their freedom and the deep comfort of their companionship.

When she came back to herself, she felt centered and as ready as she would ever be. Though the image of Salomen was gone, her presence was still there, strong and steady.

I am not alone, Tal thought. I will never be alone.

Once it had been an unthinkable burden. Now it was her lifeline.

She pulled her sword grip from the bag, opened the other door, and stepped through.

CHAPTER 57
Fahla's champion

It was the first time in Tal's career as Lancer that a full Council had been utterly quiet upon her entrance. She walked to the edge of the dais and stood looking down at Shantu, who had changed into a red fighting suit and was performing flashy warm-up moves. Vidcams hovered at the edges of the chamber, recording him from every angle.

Overconfident, she thought. It was one point in her favor. She made no gesture to draw his attention, perfectly content to let him tire himself out while attempting to impress their audience.

He twirled around, showing off his fancy footwork, and saw her waiting. With a last flourish, he retracted his sword and stood looking up at her.

She did not move.

The tension rose palpably in the chamber as they stared at each other, each willing the other to give in. But Tal was still Lancer, and she would stand here forever until he gave her the respect her title demanded. It was a small psychological skirmish, but an important one.

Finally, he put his fists against his chest and made the tiniest of bows.

She nodded in return and descended the steps to the floor.

There would be no more grand announcements. The Council was nothing but an audience now, and the chamber no more than a fighting ring. Though Tal was disgusted at the ancient barbarism Shantu had brought to the State House, she had to admire his strategy. By thinking purely as a warrior instead of a politician, he had come up with a nearly foolproof plan, just as he promised Parser. The only thing that might keep it from being completely foolproof was Tal herself, and she was at a disadvantage.

They met in the middle of the floor and stood an arm's length apart. Tal noted that the vidcams remained where they were, coming no closer, and guessed Aldirk had something to do with that. Such technology had not existed the last time a ritual challenge of combat had been fought, so there were no regulations dictating their use. But a ritual challenge was a private fight. Whatever the combatants said to each other had always remained their secret, unless the winner chose to tell.

"You don't have to do this," she said. "There's still time to retract your challenge. Better to live an outcaste than to die a mere tool of a merchant."

Shantu shook his head. "You speak like the coward you've become. In the Battle of Alsea you were a true war leader. I admired you then. You weren't afraid to break Fahla's covenant, and when you found the weakness in the ground pounders' shields, I thought I could put aside our differences and follow you forever. But then you threw it all away. Diplomatic ties to the aliens who left us to die. Asylum for our enemies. And the matter printers—you should have kept them for the warriors. You could have been the greatest caste leader in generations. You could have made Alsea strong. Instead you've weakened us as you've weakened yourself. Really, a producer for a bondmate?"

"You're living in the past, Shantu. I'm bringing Alsea into the future."

"A future where we bow to other races? Where the warriors give up their rightful place among the other castes? No, thank you. Alsea needs stability and strength. You can't provide them, but I will." He smiled at her. "Don't be afraid to die, Lancer Tal. Your Return will put your name in the history books. This will *never* be forgotten."

"Don't you realize that Parser used you? He set up the trap, and you walked right into it. He thinks you're a fool who was easily bought, and I have to agree. You think you'll have any power even if you win? Our caste will oust you before you sit in that chair."

"Let me worry about what happens after I win." He held out his sword grip. "Meet the challenge, Lancer."

She touched her grip to his, sealing the challenge. They stepped back and extended their swords.

The previous night, when Tal arrived at Vellmar's quarters, her Lead Guard had already loaded Shantu's profile on her reader card. Tal had spent the flight to the base listening to Vellmar explain exactly what she was up against. Shantu's weapon was double-edged and longer than Tal's; he would have a greater reach. His training was in the classical style, and he preferred power moves over finesse, but she should not underestimate his speed. Most worrying was his ability to use either hand, which gave him a bigger advantage than anything else. She needed to neutralize that as soon as possible.

Tal assumed her ready stance, drawing into herself and closing down her senses. She could not afford the distraction of the hundreds of minds around her. But Salomen was there, fiercely determined. Her presence kept Tal grounded, allowing her to study Shantu's body language, his facial expressions, any clue she might have to his intentions.

He wove his blade in a series of loops, loosening up his wrist, his left hand held well behind him for balance. "You should have paid more attention to your history lessons. The winner of this challenge takes the State Chair by divine right. The warriors won't go against that." He stepped to the side, and she moved with him.

"Yes, they will. I already have the votes."

"You *had* them. You won't after you're dead."

The sudden tension in his shoulders warned her, and she was ready when an innocuous warm-up loop turned into a vicious cut at her throat. The impact of his blade on hers sent vibrations all the way down her arm—he had put enough strength into that blow to take off her head. She pushed his sword to the side and swung back in for a cut toward his weapon arm, but he parried it and attempted a thrust at her heart. When she knocked that aside, he backed away and smiled.

"I suppose that would have been too easy."

She made no answer, nor did she go on the offensive. He grew increasingly impatient and finally began to circle around her.

"Afraid to move, are you? Perhaps your legs are too shaky from the fear. I always knew you were more of a carefully constructed myth than reality."

She turned in place, staying on the balls of her feet, her legs spread and slightly bent for balance while her right hand was held low at her back. It wasn't the classical stance, but it meant less travel distance when she used that hand for a strike.

"Given your tenuous grasp of reality," she said, "I'm not certain how you could tell the difference."

He lunged at her, testing her defenses with a quick flurry of feints and thrusts, then drew back. "I'm surprised. You've been practicing."

"I knew what you had planned. When it comes to strategy, you've always been two steps behind me."

She had hoped to anger him, but he laughed. "Strategy won't help you now. And it doesn't matter how much you practiced; you never had a chance. You've been playing at being a *producer* for the last moon." He lunged again, and as she parried, she lashed out with a kick at his knee. He dodged in time, her kick landing harmlessly on his thigh.

"Armored shoes, nice touch," he said, and attacked at full speed as she recovered her guard.

Tal let her body respond automatically while she focused on his moves, looking for patterns and any visual cues, anticipating him by one or two strokes. Then he shifted into a higher speed, pressing her so hard that she was forced to give ground as she countered each deadly attack. It was not where she wanted to be, and she looked desperately for a way out. This kind of fighting would kill her before long. He blended explosive thrusts with powerful overhand cuts, using his height to overpower her, and while she had long experience with that strategy, it was still tiring to counter. She let his sword slide off hers again and again, until at last she found enough of an opening to shove his blade to the side and drive her fist into his face, feeling the satisfying crunch of his nose. As his head flew back, she shifted and brought her sword grip straight back in, smashing the weighted pommel against his shoulder joint.

It would have been an excellent move if not for the fact that he had his blade in motion sooner than she could respond, and she was wide open to the blind cut at her side. She saw it coming in time to twist away, but not far enough. The blade tip caught her in the ribs and sent her stumbling, her hand automatically going to the wound. It was deep, the blood already spilling over her fingers. She was too shocked to feel the pain.

Vaguely, she heard the gasps of the audience, but Salomen's distress was much more distracting. She shook her head, forcing her body back into a ready position, and wondered why Shantu had not yet killed her. Then she saw him standing with his sword lowered, the blood running down his face as he held his other hand to his weapon shoulder. She had done more damage than she thought.

With a growl she lunged at him, aiming for his injured side, but he quickly switched hands and met her blade with equal strength. Their swords slid to the crossguards and held as they glared at each other—and she kicked him viciously in the knee.

He howled in pain and rage, coming back at her with such fury that she could barely counter his attacks, the wound in her side tearing a little more every time she parried another violent cut. He was limping and down to one arm, but even with that he was still stronger, still faster at swordplay, still better at anticipating her and making her do the work.

And now he was careful. She had surprised him one time too many, but he would no longer underestimate her. He kept her on the defensive at the edge of his long reach, where she could find no opportunities for damage.

They battled from one end of the chamber to the other, she always moving backward or sideways as he pressed into her. Each time she parried an attack, it took a little more energy from a finite store, and the wound was sapping her as well. She had lost her best chance of ending this fight on her terms and was now reduced to merely staying alive and hoping he would make a mistake.

He did not. His strategy was simple but effective, and she was tiring. It was taking her a fraction of a piptick longer to parry or counter, and the thrusts began to slip through. A shallow cut to the forearm, a deeper one to her thigh... He was going to cut her to pieces until she could no longer raise her blade, and she could do nothing to prevent it. He left her no openings and no time to counterattack.

Again and again she tried to circle into open ground, but every time she turned, his blade was there. He still had the mental space to anticipate her, but she was too busy defending to think ahead. At last she began to accept the inevitable. She would Return, but he had been right about one thing: her death would go down in the history books.

For a moment she allowed herself to think of Salomen's grief, a distraction that was nearly fatal as Shantu came within a hair of taking off her leg. She blocked it at the last piptick, forcing his blade away with a sudden determination. She refused to consider the possibility of losing! Accepting her Return was the first step toward death, and she would *not* go down that path.

She felt more aware now and noticed that Shantu was using fewer overhead blows. In fact, the overall pace of their fighting had slowed; he was tiring as much as she. With new hope she pressed into him, surprising him with a quick parry and riposte. Her blade slipped through and sliced into his side, returning his earlier favor, and he stepped back in shock. She followed it up with a cut toward his sword arm, but he recovered in time.

That was the last opportunity he allowed.

From that moment on, he slowly but surely drove her to the ground. They were both exhausted and bleeding, their swords connecting at a fraction of the pace they had in the beginning, but the damage was no less for the lack of speed. Every blow now seemed to jar her whole body, and though she felt no pain from her wounds, they were draining her as well. Still she fought with all the strength she had, refusing to give in, refusing to think of any option but victory and a long life with Salomen…until the moment came when her tired muscles could not lift the sword high enough, and she failed to fully block the blow to her upper arm. She heard the scrape as his blade bit into bone.

Her sword dropped from useless fingers, hitting the floor with a clatter that echoed through the chamber.

Triumph shone in Shantu's eyes. His body seemed to ripple, and she watched the boot flying toward her, too weak to do anything but wait. The blow caught her square in the chest, sending her crashing onto her back, and she was finished.

He limped up, standing over her with his sword extended as he gasped for breath. "I'll give you your due," he rasped. "You fought well. You had so much potential—but you threw it all away with your weak-minded ideas about caste equality. The castes are not equal. They never have been, and now the warriors will take their rightful place."

She ignored him as she rolled to her left side, putting her good right hand down for leverage and pushing her torso up.

"Don't bother," he said, stepping forward for the killing blow. The point of his sword was almost at her throat when she drew her right leg up and lashed out with her heel, crushing his knee for the second time that morning.

He bellowed in pain, his leg buckling beneath him, and she lashed out again. The second kick caught him in the hip, levering him away from her as he fell. She gathered her legs beneath her and pushed off with her right hand, propelling herself upright with a sudden burst of energy. Two steps brought her within reach of her sword, and she scooped it up. She had little skill with this hand, but if Fahla bore any love for her, she had finally disabled Shantu enough to give her the edge she needed.

When she turned, Shantu was struggling to his feet, balancing on his right leg and bringing up his sword with his left hand. She lunged for him, seeing his blade cross his torso in a late parry. The disengage came without thinking, her blade slipping under the outward arc of his weapon hand and up, inside his guard. The tip plunged into his chest, and with all the momentum of her run she drove it in, feeling the sudden give as the point exited his back.

He folded forward, hunched over her sword. For one moment he hung suspended, a bubbling expulsion of breath carrying red froth from his lungs. Then he toppled, his weight tearing the grip out of her hand as he fell.

"How…?" he whispered.

It was the last word that Prime Warrior Shantu spoke. His front dissolved, revealing utter bewilderment. A pool of blood spread beneath him, creeping toward her across the polished wooden floor. His eyes widened; he stared at her in shock and disbelief, and then he was looking at nothing at all.

Tal swayed on her feet, the exhaustion crashing over her as every wound and muscle began to hurt. With dragging steps she moved to Shantu's side, painfully lifted a foot to his chest, and wrapped her good hand around the grip of her sword. The effort of pulling it out one-handed was almost more than she could muster, but slowly it came free, its normal brilliance dulled by a coating of blood and tissue. She stepped back, bloody sword in hand, and faced the silent Council.

"Alsea!" she cried, raising the sword over her head.

"*Alsea!*" came the answering roar of more than three hundred voices. Even the people in the visitor galleries responded.

"You are all witness!" She dropped the sword to her side, having no strength left to hold it up. "Six cycles ago I was given this title by a vote of the scholar and warrior castes, but today I hold it by the choice of Fahla herself. Fahla has chosen her champion!"

"*For Fahla!*" they shouted. "*For Fahla and Alsea!*"

A rumble sounded as the warrior caste Councilors left their seats, running along the tiers and down the steps to spill onto the chamber floor. A few went to Shantu's body, lifting it up and carrying it out, but most surrounded Tal, catching her as the last shred of energy left. She slumped into a forest of arms that kept her upright, and someone took the sword from her hand, saying something about cleaning it for her. She was carried to the nearest tier, where crafter caste Councilors scrambled to make space as gentle hands pushed her into a seat.

Goddess, it felt good to sit down. Lying down would be even better, but she really didn't want to pass out in front of the entire Council and a worldwide viewing audience.

"Salomen," she said. "Where is Salomen?"

Something was wrong. Their bond had weakened. It felt as if Salomen wasn't quite there, but she was safe in the guest gallery. Wasn't she?

"She's coming," someone said, and there were murmurs of agreement.

Tal rested her head against the back of the seat. "I think I need a healer," she mumbled.

"They're already here," said a woman close by.

Three healers appeared through the crowd, pushing a stretcher and carrying supply packs. Once again she felt herself gathered and lifted by many hands, and then she was lying on a soft surface, her muscles instantly turning to liquid. At last she could rest.

"Let's get these wrapped," said one of the healers. "Cut off the sleeve and leg. I'll get the torso."

Tal closed her eyes as her body was shifted this way and that. Blades hissed through cloth, and her bodysuit was peeled away in several places. Someone lifted her arm, a pressure sack crinkled, and the sudden push on her worst wound made her head swim. She gritted her teeth, waiting for the rest.

Capable hands began wrapping the wound on her thigh. Other hands raised her torso, supporting her while the wound in her side was padded and wrapped. At last they laid her down again, and the pain settled into a pounding ache that was far more tolerable. A skinspray to her wrist lessened even that, and she opened her eyes in relief.

"Thank you," she said.

The healer in her line of vision nodded, and her stretcher began to move.

"There they are," someone said. "Would you look at that?"

"What happened to her?" asked a second voice.

Tal craned her neck, trying to see around the press of bodies. The Councilors in front of her stepped back, giving her a clear sight line down the length of the chamber floor. There were Aldirk and Razine, with Shikal beside them, holding Jaros by the hand. Jaros kept turning to look behind him, and as Tal's stretcher rolled closer, she saw Gehrain and Vellmar towering behind the others. Their expressions were stern, and they were flanking someone who moved slowly.

Lead Guard Ronlin appeared next, bristling with protective menace as he glared around him. Right behind him was Nikin, who cradled Salomen in his arms. Her arms were wrapped around his neck, her head rested on his shoulder, and she seemed barely conscious.

Tal pushed at the people around her, trying to lever herself up, but hands held her back.

"No, Lancer Tal, don't injure yourself," said one of the healers.

She wanted to laugh. Injure herself? Wasn't it a little late for that?

The stretcher kept moving, and Shikal pulled a wide-eyed Jaros to one side to let her pass.

"Stop!" she shouted, though it came out as more of a croak.

When the healers ignored her, she struggled to get free, nearly rolling off the stretcher. They had to stop then, and Nikin stepped up with a white-faced Salomen, who now looked more alert.

"Do not *ever* ignore an order from the Lancer," she said in a tone of absolute authority. "You are in the State House, not the healing center. Show your respect."

The healers stood straight, startled into obedience.

A vidcam swooped in, its operator apparently deciding that since the combat was over, the order regarding distance no longer applied. Before Tal could say a word, Ronlin snatched it out of the air, threw it to the floor, and stomped it into fragments.

"Well done," Vellmar said.

"Salomen…" Tal reached out, needing the contact, and Salomen brought one arm down to clasp her hand.

"I'm all right," she said. "Don't worry. I'm just a little tired."

"What happened?"

"I had faith in you. Just as I said."

Tal was too exhausted for riddles and opened her mouth to say so when she saw the shadows of pain in Salomen's eyes.

I have faith, because you have me, Salomen had said.

She had not fought that combat alone.

Salomen managed a tiny smile and added, "It wasn't exactly regulation."

"Every advantage I had," Tal said. "Even the ones I didn't know about." They stared at each other, absorbing their connection, until Nikin shifted his hold and she realized he had carried her all the way down from the guest gallery.

"Nikin, thank you for being there for her," she said.

"I could be nowhere else. Perhaps someday you'll explain to Father and me what just happened."

"We will. Someday." She patted the space beside her. "Will you put her here?"

"Lancer Tal," a healer protested as Nikin walked to the other side of the stretcher.

Tal held up her hand. "It's wide enough for two, isn't it?"

Nikin bent down to deposit Salomen, who immediately rolled onto her side and brushed her fingers across Tal's cheek. Her voice shook slightly as she said, "I think this might be the only part of you that isn't hurt."

Tal rested her hand atop Salomen's, forgetting all about the other Opahs as the stretcher resumed its motion. Then a suspicion flared and she narrowed her eyes. Pitching her voice low to avoid being overheard, she asked, "You're not still Sharing my pain, are you?"

"No. I couldn't hold it once the fight was over. I think it was my fear that enabled it."

The moment of Shantu's death was the moment Tal had nearly dropped from exhaustion and a sudden awareness of all her wounds. That was when Salomen had let go.

"You held it all," she said, realizing it even as she spoke. "From the very first one, in my side. I thought I was in too much shock to feel it."

"We were both in shock. I felt that sword go in. I was focusing so hard on you, trying to help you in the fight, that I must have set up some sort of link without knowing it. Nikin didn't know what to think when you were cut and I acted like it was me."

"Because it *was* you. Oh, tyrina—you felt every one of them?"

Salomen nodded.

Their stretcher rolled out of the chamber and into the lobby, where several Guards were holding back a noisy crowd. Tal saw a blur of faces, all staring. Some looked horrified, others triumphant. One older man was weeping.

Vellmar and Ronlin followed them into the lift. As Ronlin turned to face outward, he glanced at Salomen and his scowl softened into a look of near worship. Of course, Tal thought. He had been sitting next to her during the fight, and he was a smart man. He knew their secret. Judging by his watchfulness, it had only increased his sense of responsibility. Micah had chosen well.

The lift doors closed, sealing them into a blissful silence. Salomen touched Tal's other arm above the pressure sack and whispered, "That was the worst. I thought I would faint. Actually, I think I did for a moment. The next thing I remember, you were on the floor."

"That was when everything slowed down for me, and I couldn't lift a finger to defend myself when he kicked me onto my back. So you must have woken up again just before I cracked his knee."

"I think so."

The doors opened, ending their quiet moment. They rolled into the soaring ground floor lobby, where more Guards were holding back an even larger crowd that gasped and began calling out as soon as Tal was recognized.

Under cover of the noise, she said, "I had an unbelievable burst of energy after that. A moment before, I just stood there watching him kick me, and then I was bouncing off the floor and racing for my sword. I should have known that was you. Goddess above, Salomen. You're the reason I'm alive. I'm not sure I could have finished him if you hadn't given me your strength—and your will," she added. "That was you, wasn't it? Refusing to let me accept my Return?"

"Visualize your success and achieve it. You and Colonel Micah taught me that. I couldn't let you think about failure."

"You realize that's highly illegal."

"Somehow, I don't think you'll report me." Salomen gave her a tired smile and closed her eyes.

Perhaps she was too weary to realize what she had done. Or perhaps she simply didn't understand the import. But Tal did, and she watched her tyree in increasing wonder.

When Salomen took her pain the night of the assassination attempt, they had been physically connected. This time, she had done it from across the Council chamber while simultaneously using empathic projection to bolster Tal's resilience. The first should not have been possible, and the second was an advanced skill Salomen had never learned.

She remembered sitting in Lanaril's study and understanding for the first time that she shouldn't have been able to save Salomen from that window seat. *You did the impossible for her,* Lanaril had said.

"We did it for each other," she whispered, but Salomen didn't hear her over the calls from the crowd.

They passed through the main entrance and were carried down the stairs to the transport waiting at the bottom, its engines already spun up for instant liftoff. Ronlin and Vellmar climbed in after them, taking seats on the side bench as someone shut the doors from outside.

In the sudden quiet, Vellmar caught Tal's eye and gave her an approving nod. It might have been odd, given their differing ranks, but last night Tal had been her student.

She had passed the test.

One of the healers snapped a restraint bar onto the stretcher and told the pilot to go. As the transport rose into the air, he sat at Tal's side and held a scanner against her wrist.

"You'll be fine, Lancer Tal," he assured her.

She turned her head to look at Salomen, whom Shantu had dismissed as a mere producer—and who had been the one weapon he could not block. Smiling, she said, "I know."

PART FIVE:

INCLUSION

CHAPTER 58
First run

"I thought you were supposed to be getting back into this gradually," Vellmar huffed.

Lancer Tal glanced over, her pace easy and fluid. "Tired already?"

"Not at all. Just concerned about you."

"Don't bother. Salomen takes care of that job."

Vellmar shook her head. Why was she even surprised that the Lancer had insisted on a run only five days after the challenge?

"How is your leg?" she asked.

"Fine. Stop worrying, Vellmar. I said I'd only do a length."

"Yes, but somehow I assumed you meant you'd run it at a more practical pace."

"I needed to blow the spinner's webs out of my mind."

She could understand that. With Shantu's death, Lancer Tal's reputation had gone into orbit. The media labeled her Fahla's Chosen, and public support for her had swelled to such an extent that an entire unit of warriors was called to hold back the crowd from the entrance to Blacksun Healing Center. The air had been thick with the scent of hyacot twigs, broken and left in piles all along the walls as an homage to the woman inside. Blacksun Temple was still ablaze with bowl offerings day and night, as a never-ending stream of Alseans offered thanks to Fahla for her Chosen. It was a near deification, and Lancer Tal was not comfortable with it.

"If it helps," Vellmar offered, "I'm reasonably certain that Fahla's Chosen would never wear a shirt with that many holes in it."

The Lancer laughed as she slowed to a walk. "All right. That's a length." She turned in place and began walking back the way they had come. "Salomen detests this shirt, too. You're in good company."

Vellmar looked around appreciatively, still not quite believing this was considered duty. A trail through a forest was her idea of running perfection, and she had been delighted when the Lancer brought her here for their morning exercise. She wouldn't mind if they did this every day. The forest was old, its massive trees so tall that their tops would vanish when the low clouds of winter came. Birdsong rang all around them, with most of the singers invisible in the heights, though they had startled quite a few lower-dwelling birds during their short run. The crisp air was laden with the scent of damp soil and leaves, and a stream rushed over rocks somewhere behind them. She would bet a nineday's pay that the trail eventually joined it.

Koneza had nothing like this. On top of everything else, it was practically outside her door. Her secondary quarters were only a few hundred paces from the base border and the beginning of the trail.

"What does Raiz Opah think of the base?" she asked.

"She says she understands now why I'd want to bother with two separate sets of quarters only a twenty-tick transport ride apart." Lancer Tal stopped near a knee-high boulder, set her foot atop it, and gently stretched her injured leg. "It was nice to leave the State House behind."

"And the chaos."

"And that."

Vellmar watched her closely, looking for any signs of pain, and unfortunately did not look away in time to avoid being caught.

"Your record never said anything about you being like a winden with a newborn," Lancer Tal said in exasperation. "For the last time, I'm fine. None of the cuts hit anything vital, the muscle and skin sealers are all holding perfectly, and I could probably wrestle you to the ground right now without tearing anything open."

Vellmar raised an eyebrow at that.

"But I wouldn't try," Lancer Tal conceded with a smile.

"Good. Because I know a few more moves than the ones I taught you."

They walked in silence for several ticks, the Lancer deep in thought and Vellmar content to absorb her surroundings with all her senses. This place was beautiful, and she was looking forward to learning every handspan of every trail.

"I never did thank you, did I?" Lancer Tal asked.

"For what?"

"Giving me what I needed. It was almost as if you knew how the fight would end."

Vellmar shrugged. "We both knew he was a better sword fighter. It made sense that at some point you'd be in that position."

They walked a few more paces before Lancer Tal said, "Shantu would be proud to think that it took three people to beat him."

"You think he didn't have moves he learned from someone else? I just gave you the knowledge. And my mothers gave it to me. We're all products of our training."

"And of our character." She shook her head. "I keep thinking about what he said just before I killed him. He truly believed that the matter printers should be kept for the warrior caste. He would have been a terrible Lancer, but at least he wasn't thinking just of himself. He was motivated by a desire to elevate our caste and to keep Alsea strong and independent. But Parser did everything for one man and one man alone. Yet he's alive, and Shantu is dead. There's something very wrong about that."

"Parser is not really alive," Vellmar pointed out.

It was true. The day of the challenge, the Council had reconvened once the Lancer was known to be safe. With the blood still darkening the floor of the chamber, the Councilors listened to Colonel Razine present her evidence. Then they heard Herot Opah's testimony and an unexpected testimony by Councilor Zalringer, one of Shantu's closest allies, who had quickly switched sides when his leader fell.

The judgment of the Council was swift. By unanimous vote, it recommended that both Parser and Shantu be stripped of their caste. Yesterday afternoon the merchant and warrior castes had held their own votes, with conclusive results. Parser was now outcaste, a broken and nameless man who was not likely to survive prison without the protection of his fellow merchants. In fact, they were the ones most likely to kill him, in vengeance for the tremendous dishonor he had brought upon their caste.

For Shantu the result was even more horrifying, at least to Vellmar's way of thinking. He was one of the great heroes of the Battle of Alsea, the commander of the Pallean forces who had beaten back the Voloth in the worst fighting of all. She had been sent from Koneza to Whitesun for that battle and knew just how bad it had been. Shantu was a ferocious warrior and a brilliant commander. Alsea owed much to him.

But all of that was lost. Denied a proper pyre, he was buried like a mere carcass, his body left to be eaten by worms. His name would be erased from the archive rolls, and it would be as if he had never existed. Already this morning's news stories were referring to him as the Challenger. He would be recorded by the history books, but not the way he had planned.

She glanced at her wristcom, the motion not going unnoticed by her sharp-eyed companion.

"Your leave starts in half a hantick, doesn't it? Planning to beat up on Senshalon again?"

Vellmar smiled at the phrasing. "Perhaps later. First I have an appointment at the healing center."

"Good luck with that," Lancer Tal said shortly. She did not make eye contact.

The remainder of their walk passed in silence, with Vellmar cursing herself for ruining what had been a remarkably intimate conversation. Lancer Tal had lost much of her reserve during that frantic night of preparation for a life-or-death moment, and it had carried over into their day-to-day relationship. But since her stay in the healing center, she reacted badly to any mention of Colonel Micah. Vellmar should have known better.

"Enjoy your leave," Lancer Tal said when they reached the base border. She turned toward her own quarters without another glance.

Vellmar stood looking after her. "I will," she said.

CHAPTER 59
The return

ALDIRK WAITED IMPATIENTLY AS THE supercilious desk clerk checked the schedule. "Yes, here you are," the man announced. "You may pass through."

Grumbling to himself, Aldirk went through the archway into the secured area of the healing center. "You'd better appreciate this, Colonel," he said under his breath.

He couldn't believe he was actually doing this. He had signed the schedule in a moment of euphoria right after the Lancer had miraculously avoided death, and now, five days later, he had to make good on his impetuous promise. It was yet another proof that haste never led to anything good. Surely he should have learned that lesson by now.

Colonel Micah's room was full of the scent of hyacot twigs. Lancer Tal had brought a bowl from her own room during her stay here and had asked Aldirk to make sure it remained full for as long as was necessary. It was certainly a far better scent than the acrid stench of narnell root.

The colonel was lying on his side. The healing staff had been turning him regularly to prevent the formation of sores, and Aldirk thought it was just like the man to be in an inconvenient position for a Sharing.

"I suppose it could be worse," he said, shrugging off his rain cloak and hanging it by the door. "You could be on your stomach."

He approached the bed, taking in the pasty skin and the limp facial features, and wondered why the colonel didn't just finish the job. This man had already Returned, for all practical purposes; surely everyone could see that? The Lancer did, he knew. After the challenge, she had spent almost as much time in this room as in her own, and since then she shut down at the mention of his name.

The memory gave him the added impetus to crouch into an extremely uncomfortable position, line up the energy points, and press his forehead against Colonel Micah's.

Many cycles ago, he had Shared with his brother while his older sibling slept. They were discussing what the difference might be between a conscious and an unconscious mind, and like the scholars they were, they decided to experiment. He hadn't liked the feeling then, and he didn't like it now. The darkness was heavy and pressing, and when he emerged above the surface, he found nothing but a distant impression of the man he had argued with so many times.

All right, Colonel. This is the one and only time I will do this. I know you want to Return, and Fahla knows I shouldn't stand in your way, but you are needed here.

Do you hear me? Lancer Tal needs you.

He projected his memories of her, recalling every time she had spoken with him about the colonel since his injury. One by one he retraced the memories, from that first call in the middle of the night, to the day he had spent in Redmoon, to their flight back to Blacksun and the way the Lancer had insisted on accompanying Colonel Micah into this very room. He recalled setting up appointments for the entire Opah family to Share with him, and the look on the Lancer's face four days ago, when she had so clearly given up. Then he went back to the beginning and started over.

After a few repetitions his mind wandered, and thinking about making those appointments for the Opah family led to the memory of Raiz Opah's face on his vidcom unit, calling because the Lancer had disappeared. Because somehow, Lancer Tal had known to prepare for a challenge that no one else had remotely anticipated.

I wonder if you would have caught that one. You're just barbaric enough to have thought of it.

I still watch that recording and shudder. The blood stain won't come out unless the floor is refinished, and the Council voted to let it stay as a reminder. How disgusting.

You would probably approve.

He stayed in the link for several more repetitions, until the vibration of his wristcom broke into his thoughts. He had set it for the end of his time slot, and with considerable relief he ducked back into the darkness, relaxing and letting his mind return to his own body. Groaning, he straightened up and rubbed his aching back.

"Perfect," he grumbled. "I'll have to pick up paincounters on the way out. Probably your idea of a joke."

He plucked his rain cloak from the hook, threw it over his shoulders, and shut the door behind him.

Vellmar waved at the desk clerk as she breezed past. She'd been here often enough that the staff knew her by sight, and no one stopped her as she ducked through the arch into a familiar corridor. She strode along the curving hallway, counting doors out of habit, and walked into the colonel's room.

"Good morning, Colonel Micah," she said as she hung up her rain cloak. "Ready for yet another Sharing?"

He was on his side this time, which made things a great deal more difficult. She walked over to the bed and took a giant straddling step, spreading her legs as far as she could without losing her balance. She knew from prior experience that her back would be killing her if she didn't lower her center of gravity as much as possible when Sharing from this angle.

"If I were you, I'd be desperately tired of this by now," she said, sliding her hands into place. "People coming in at all hanticks, day and night, Sharing with you whether you like it or not. It must be a pain." Shifting her legs a little farther apart, she lowered her head—and stopped in shock as his eyes opened.

They stared at each other for what seemed like half a hantick, with Vellmar so stunned that she could not summon up her powers of speech. At last she cleared her throat and said, "Ah…Colonel Micah? Welcome back."

He made no answer, simply watching her with a furrowed brow. Awkwardly, she pulled herself upright, fetched a chair from the side of the room, and sat next to him. He hadn't moved.

"I don't know if you remember me," she said. "I'm Fianna Vellmar. You promoted me to the Lancer's Lead Guard."

At last he nodded. "I remember you."

His voice was raspy and dry, barely more than a croak. She immediately cursed herself for six kinds of fool and punched the healer's key on the bedside vidcom.

An assistant healer appeared. "Yes?"

"Colonel Micah is awake."

His eyes widened. "We're on our way."

She looked back at the colonel. "There are a *lot* of people who will be happy to see you, Colonel. And one in particular that I need to call right now." She reached for her earcuff, thought better of it, and picked up the vidcom instead.

Lancer Tal answered the call almost instantly, her face tight with fear. "Vellmar? What happened?"

Vellmar could not stop her grin. "There's someone here you need to see." She turned the unit to face the colonel and heard a gasp.

"Micah!"

"Andira," he croaked, and seemed capable of no more than that. Vellmar turned the unit back just in time to witness the most beatific smile she had ever seen. The Lancer was lit from within.

"Tell him I'll be there in fifteen ticks. And tell him to stay out of trouble until I get there."

"I will."

"Salomen!" Lancer Tal shouted, just before the screen went dark.

Vellmar put the unit down and grinned at the colonel. "The base is twenty ticks away. I guess she's in a hurry."

The door flew open, admitting a herd of healers. They swarmed over Colonel Micah, checking his signs and asking questions that he couldn't answer, until finally Vellmar barked at them that the man couldn't speak, for Fahla's sake, and when were they going to give him some water? At that his eyes found hers again and crinkled slightly.

"Don't worry, Colonel Micah," she said. "We'll take care of you."

He nodded just as a cup and straw were thrust under his chin, and closed his eyes in gratitude as he drank.

Ten ticks later, the healers were gone, Colonel Micah was sitting up in bed, and Vellmar could not believe this was the same man who had looked half-dead just a few ticks earlier. He had been given a cup of juice and a piece of fresh bread, and was now brushing his teeth with groans of pleasure and spitting into a bowl she held for him.

"Great Mother," he said, wiping his mouth after polishing off another glass of water. "You have no idea how good that felt."

Vellmar tried to imagine not brushing her teeth for eight days and decided that she never wanted to know what it felt like. "I'm sure Lancer Tal will be grateful for your consideration."

His eyebrows rose. "Getting comfortable in your role already, I see."

Oh, shek. She had gotten too used to speaking with him in familiar terms while he was unconscious. Horrified at her lapse, she lowered her head. "My apologies, Colonel. I didn't mean to offend."

"How many times have you Shared with me?"

She looked up again, feeling no censure from him. "Ah…I'm not certain. Three times in Redmoon, and then two more before the Lancer's challenge, and after that—"

"The Lancer's challenge?" he interrupted.

She hesitated. "You've missed quite a lot, Colonel."

"Then perhaps you should fill me in while we wait for Lancer Tal."

It was an order, not a request, and she tugged her chair closer. "Where do I start?"

"Start with our mission. Was Gehrain hurt? I never found him in the basement."

"Gehrain is fine. He just had a twisted ankle and a minor concussion, and complained about being held for observation to anyone who would listen."

The colonel smiled. "That sounds like him. Anyone else?"

"Not so much as a scratch."

"Good, I'm glad I was the only one."

"Herot Opah was a bit banged up, but nothing serious. He's in custody at Blacksun Base right now."

"Did we complete our mission in time? What happened with Parser?"

"He's finished. But it turned out that the warriors in that house weren't Parser's. They were working for Shantu."

"Shantu!"

"Yes, Parser and Shantu were in it together all along. So Lancer Tal managed to avoid Parser's trap, but she was still caught in Shantu's."

His eyes widened. "You said the Lancer's challenge, didn't you? You couldn't mean…" He trailed off, his poorly fronted alarm jangling her senses.

"Ritual challenge of combat," she confirmed.

He slumped against the stack of pillows. "Spawn of a fantenshekken! Nobody would have anticipated that. I can't believe the Council allowed it."

"They had to. The ritual challenge predates the Council."

"So he caught her by surprise and forced her—oh, Tal," he groaned.

"He didn't surprise her."

His gaze snapped up to hers. "She *knew?*"

Vellmar nodded. "Don't ask me how. She called me in the middle of the night and said she needed to find a way to win a sword fight with a superior opponent. We spent every tick before the Council session practicing. She beat him because he thought losing her sword meant she'd lost the fight. He was thinking like a sword fighter, but she was thinking like a combat fighter. That's what we worked on."

He stared at her for an uncomfortable moment. "She knew, and you helped her."

"Ah...yes," she said hesitantly.

She was warmed by his sudden burst of pride as a broad grin transformed his face. "Trust Tal to see what no one else could. And I am taking full credit for bringing you to our unit. Well done, Vellmar."

"I only did my duty."

"I hope you don't mean that."

At first she was startled. Then she thought back to that night, when she and Lancer Tal had gone to the mat again and again, working out the best moves to disable from both inside and outside the reach of a sword.

"No," she said. "It was more than that."

"Good."

Vellmar cocked her ear toward the door, hearing footsteps pounding down the corridor. She recognized the stride. "I don't think Lancer Tal knows you're not supposed to run in a healing center."

The door opened, and Lancer Tal stepped into the room, her gaze going straight to the bed as she came to a standstill.

"Micah," she whispered.

Lighter footsteps came behind, and Raiz Opah squeezed into the room around the unmoving bulk of the Lancer's body. She also stopped, her head turning as she looked from Colonel Micah to Lancer Tal and back again.

Vellmar stood up. "It was nice to speak with you, Colonel."

He tore his gaze away from the Lancer's and gave her a smile. "Thank you. We'll talk soon."

She nodded, picked up her rain cloak, and scooted sideways to get around the Lancer, who was still doing an excellent imitation of a statue. Closing the door behind her, she looked up to find Nilsinian and Dewar flanking the door while Ronlin stood across the hall.

"Don't let anyone else in unless the Lancer specifically asks," she told them.

"We won't," Dewar said. "He's really all right?"

Vellmar's smile was enormous. "He's really all right."

Micah could not take his eyes off Tal. She looked visibly older than when he had seen her last, and was that just eight days ago? Impossible.

She was still standing there, staring as if she were afraid to get any closer, and he summoned a smile.

"So I hear you beat Shantu in ritual combat."

His words seemed to loosen her limbs, and she closed the distance between them. "I don't want to think about Shantu right now. Micah..."

She clasped both of his palms, then shocked him by kissing his cheek before resting her own against his. It was a gesture of familial affection that she had often given him as a child, but never since her Rite of Ascension. Tentatively, he pulled one hand from their clasp and stroked the back of her head. "I'm all right," he whispered.

"I know." She pulled back, keeping a firm grip on his hand and offering a trembling smile. "I am *so* glad to see you."

He looked at her sadly, feeling much more than that through their touch. "I'm sorry to have worried you."

"Worried is not even the word." She took a sharp breath, her eyes brimming with tears. "Frantic, desperate, so shekking scared that I could hardly function, but I had to, and I had to do it without you." The tears spilled over. "Don't you *ever* do that to me again, do you hear me?"

"I won't," he promised, and her face crumpled.

"I can't believe you're awake," she said in a choked voice. "I can't believe it's finally over."

Salomen came up behind her, and Micah watched with oddly dry eyes as Tal turned, wrapped her arms around her tyree, and made tiny little gasps that broke his heart. Salomen rubbed her back, soothing her with a gentle touch as she looked over at Micah. "It's good to see you, Colonel. You've been more missed than you can ever know."

He nodded, still in shock at seeing Tal like this. It brought back bad memories, and he began to understand what she had been going through.

"I think I know," he said.

Once Tal had herself back under control, she and Salomen pulled up chairs and settled in for a long talk. She told him about everything he'd missed, which was an unbelievable amount, and he filled in the only piece she was missing. She nodded as he described the chase in the basement, her expression showing that he was only confirming what she'd already guessed. When he mentioned the metal control panel, however, her attention sharpened.

"Micah, you were out there in the middle of an open space with no cover anywhere in sight. What possessed you to shoot the panel instead of the warrior?"

He shook his head. "Something just wasn't right about it. It was so shiny and new, and everything else in that house was dusty and old. And that warrior was ignoring disruptor fire…" He stopped and corrected himself. "No, she wasn't ignoring it, because she was running an avoidance pattern. But she wasn't returning fire, and this after she'd already pinned me down several times. It didn't make sense. I had a moving target that I was having a hard time hitting, and a stable target that seemed to be very important to that warrior. And I thought that if it was important enough for her to risk her life to reach it, it was important enough for me to destroy it. But the moment I shot out that panel, she was in a rage. She just held the trigger down and poured it out, and I couldn't roll away fast enough."

"Interesting choice, Micah."

He frowned. "I seem to be making a lot of them lately."

"Let me tell you why that panel was shiny and new," she said. "It had been installed just half a moon earlier. It supplied power to about fifty holes in the basement ceiling. And in those holes were enough explosives to blow the entire house into tiny little pieces, along with everyone in it."

He stared at her, not understanding how she could look…*amused* while she said it.

"The house was a trap?"

She nodded. "It was a trap. Gehrain, Nilsinian, Dewar, Corlander, and Windenal would all be dead right now if you hadn't shot that panel. And you, of course. Six lives saved by an instinctive snap decision under fire. Not bad for an old warrior."

He thought over the whole scenario again, remembering where everyone was and what had been happening, and slowly the truth of it seeped in.

"It was the right decision," he said.

"You're damned right it was. So I hope you'll reconsider that resignation. I know you never really took it off the table, not in your mind. I want it gone. I have need of an old warrior with instincts like yours. You have so much to teach our Guards, Gehrain and Vellmar in particular. Gehrain has done his best to fill in for you, but he needs more seasoning before he can be even half as valuable to me as you are. And Vellmar has all the makings of a future Chief Guardian, but she's young, very young, and she needs a guide who understands how to shape her potential without shutting it down. What do you say?"

"I say you have a lot of nerve, asking hard questions of a man sitting in a healing center."

"Only one question, and is it really that hard?"

He smiled at her. "No. It's not. I want back in."

Her answering smile was brilliant, erasing cycles of age in an instant.

"But we cannot go back to the way it was before," he cautioned, "and I wouldn't want to even if we could. Gehrain is ready to take over the day-to-day duties of running the two units. And I'd like to spend more time training and more time as Salomen's Chief Counselor."

"Done. Good choice, too. I would never have let you walk out of here if you'd said no. Now you can leave whenever the healers clear you."

"So it was blackmail!"

"Of course not. It was a free and clear choice. Unless you made the wrong one."

Salomen laughed. "Colonel Micah, you have no idea how glad I am that you're back. Andira hasn't sounded like this for too long."

"You mean impertinent, demanding, and arrogant?" he asked.

"No," she said, reaching out to caress Tal's cheek. "I mean happy." She shot Micah a stern look. "So I'm going to repeat her earlier order. Don't you ever do that again."

"Only if you two promise never to fight a ritual combat again," he said.

"I think we can safely promise that," said Tal. "Did we tell you that the Council voted not to remove the bloodstains? They wanted them to stay as a reminder, so people will remember the day when barbarism was brought back to the State House and precisely how far it got the challenger. It's already a new stop on the State House tour."

"Really? I can see the warrior caste voting for that, but the whole Council?" He shook his head. "I go away for a few days, and look what happens. The Council actually acquires some sense."

CHAPTER 60
Sentence

MICAH MADE RAPID PROGRESS AT the healing center and was released well in time for the autumn feast at Hol-Opah. The Lancer and Bondlancer Guard units held a feast of their own in celebration, though Salomen commented that the feasts she normally attended featured a great deal of food and some spirits, rather than the other way around.

Tal laughed and asked if she would like another glass.

She spent most of the feast just watching Micah. Not enough time had passed for her to stop thinking of his walking, talking, joking presence as a miracle. He seemed to understand, though they never spoke of it after her loss of control when he first woke. They reverted back to their teasing ways immediately, and the sheer familiarity of it was all she wanted.

Micah moved to the food tables, a glass in one hand and his staff in the other, chatting with various warriors along the way. The staff was a required support for the moment. He would need it for at least another nineday as his new muscles finished their growth and locked themselves into his synthetic hip. Given the way he was already pounding it on the floor to emphasize conversational points, she foresaw it becoming part of his uniform.

Salomen passed him on her way back from refreshing their drinks, and Tal took an unreasonable amount of pleasure in watching her two favorite people spend a moment together, obviously enjoying each other's company. Not too long ago, she had thought Fahla cruel enough to take one from her in exchange for the other. She should have had more faith.

"Trust Micah to turn a walking support into an intimidation factor," she said when Salomen arrived and held out her drink. "He's going to love using that staff during training."

"I'm guessing he'll love thumping it all over Aldirk's office as well."

"Oh, I think he'll be thumping in moderation there. Aldirk will never let him forget that he was the one who woke him."

Salomen smiled as she sipped her spirits. "There were about forty other people Sharing with him."

"Yes, but Aldirk was the last. He's positive that his presence was the one that finally jarred Micah awake. Micah's torn between hating the very thought of it and being grateful to Aldirk for taking part."

"Do you think they'll get along better after this?"

"Of course not."

Two days later, Herot appeared before the adjudicator. Tal sat with the Opahs, her presence causing a stir of anticipation.

The hearing was short; Herot's guilt was not an issue. An officer from the Alsean Investigative Force presented the government testimony, and when the stern-faced adjudicator asked if any wished to add to the government's case, every eye turned to Tal. She remained in her seat, an act that electrified the gallery. She could feel the attending journalists glowing with excitement over this unexpected aspect to their stories.

When the adjudicator asked if any wished to speak on behalf of the criminal, Tal rose and set off such a furious round of exclamations and whispers that the adjudicator threatened to close the entire proceeding if the visitor gallery did not silence itself.

"Please speak, Lancer Tal," she said gravely.

"Thank you, Honored Adjudicator. I am invoking my right to petition for a minimum sentence in the case of Herot Opah."

The adjudicator slammed her palm on her desk, quieting the gasps and murmurs. "For what reason do you make this petition?"

"Herot Opah is a young man who had the misfortune of learning some important life lessons with the whole world watching. He made a mistake. A big one, attributed to pride and anger and selfishness, but others have made similar mistakes with less devastating impacts. We should not judge him by the end result of his mistake, which involved a chain of events beyond his control and several other players with far more sinister intent. We should judge him instead by the cause of it. And for that cause, he has apologized to me and asked my forgiveness. I have given it to him."

The visitor gallery rustled and whispered, but this time the adjudicator didn't seem to hear. She nodded at Tal, her stern expression softening. "I see. That does have weight."

"I would like to add that he understands the full extent of his crime and that he has cooperated in every way possible with the government, including testifying before the Council at my request. These are not the actions of a criminal in need of long-term incarceration. Such a result would not benefit Alsean society, and it certainly would not be my preference. I believe that Herot Opah has done everything possible to make up for his mistake, and to punish him beyond the minimum sentence would serve only to warn others that cooperation and repentance have no impact on a sentence. That is not the message our justice system should send."

"Thank you, Lancer Tal," the adjudicator said as Tal sat down. "Are there any others who wish to speak on behalf of Herot Opah?"

"I do." Salomen stood, and once again the room erupted into whispers and a few too-loud voices. They died down quickly at the adjudicator's glare.

"Very well. Please speak, Raiz Opah."

"Thank you, Honored Adjudicator. Though I do not have the Lancer's right of petition, I speak as a victim of the crime for which this hearing has been convened. As you have heard in the government's testimony, the shot that injured Lancer Tal was actually fired at me. I now live with the knowledge that my own brother directly enabled an attempt on my life. It is not an easy thing to know."

Tal glanced at Herot, sitting in the prisoner's box at the front of the room, and saw him close his eyes at his sister's words.

"Yet I also believe that any sentence other than the minimum would be an inappropriate application of punishment. Herot understands the impact of his actions. He has apologized and asked my forgiveness as well, and I have given it to him. His incarceration, even for the minimum sentence, will tear the fabric of our family. The damage would be far greater should he be ordered to serve a longer sentence."

"It seems to me that the fabric of your family is already torn," the adjudicator said. "Can you tell me why I should not discount your testimony based on your family connection? How can I know that you would not make this request regardless of Herot Opah's repentance or lack thereof?"

"Because if Herot had not apologized, if he had not asked forgiveness from both me and Lancer Tal, neither of us would be attending this hearing. And if his actions had been taken with true intent to kill or cause grievous harm, there would be no family connection at all. I am the head of our family, and I would have retracted the name of Opah. You're welcome to scan me if you wish to confirm the truth of my statement."

Her words ignited the gallery, and Herot stared at his sister in shock. She had never said that to him in her visits—as she had told Tal, there was no point. But it was certainly effective in convincing the adjudicator.

"That will not be necessary," she said. "I believe I can take our future Bondlancer at her word. Thank you."

Salomen nodded and sat down.

"Given that the two individuals most deeply affected by Herot Opah's actions have both petitioned on his behalf, and that he has cooperated with the government in every way regarding his own and another related crime, this court will not presume to impose a justice beyond the minimum called for by our laws. Such an imposition, I am convinced, would not be justice but rather an abuse of it. Herot Opah will serve two cycles and no more." She picked up the small mallet on her desk and struck the bell. "This hearing is adjourned."

Amid the bustle and noise, Herot stood up and leaned against the waist-high bar separating him from the rest of the court. "Salomen!" he called.

Tal caught the eye of the adjudicator, who nodded and gestured to the AIF officer. He came over and saluted, then escorted them out of the guest box and up to the front of the room.

Herot reached for his sister's hand and held it tightly. "Thank you. And thank you, Lancer Tal. This means a lot. I swear that when they release me, I'll spend the rest of my life working to bring honor to the Opah name. I figure it will take about that long to erase the stain I made on it."

"I'll hold you to your word, Herot," said Salomen. "Please be careful. That Opah name may be a hindrance to you in the next two cycles."

"In that case, I'll start working on honoring it that much sooner."

"If your connection with us causes you any trouble, tell us," Tal said. "Just because you're not with us doesn't mean you're not still family. You don't have to fight your battles alone."

"With respect, Lancer Tal, right now I think I do." He leaned over the bar and kissed Salomen on the cheek. "Until the first visit, then."

"Until then. And don't forget to keep your calendar clear for the twenty-third of Rosslin."

"I will." Turning to Tal, he held up his palm. "Take good care of my sister."

Tal touched his palm. "You know I will."

"I know. You're the only person I'd ever trust her with."

Her surprise must have shown on her face, because he actually winked at her before walking away at the side of the AIF officer. Tal stared after him.

"I think he enjoyed that," she said.

Salomen nodded. "And I think you just saw a glimpse of who Herot used to be."

CHAPTER 61
The Chosen

MICAH STRETCHED HIS LEG MORE comfortably and looked over at Tal. "Do you think it will be the same?"

She was watching her control panel as she lifted her personal transport off the State House landing pad. "Do I think what will be the same?"

"Being at Hol-Opah. The last time you saw all of the field workers, you were practically one of them. This time you're Fahla's Chosen."

"If Fahla had truly chosen me, she'd eradicate that name," Tal grumbled. She sat back in her seat, tilting the steering yoke, and Micah watched the domes of Blacksun begin passing beneath them.

"You're the one who gave everyone the idea," he pointed out, enjoying her discomfiture.

Tal had unprecedented public approval, the remaining opposition to the matter printers had dissolved into near nonexistence, the Council was giving her anything she wanted—though he knew that wouldn't last—and yet through it all she muttered and moaned about her new title. He had something new to tease her with.

"That just makes it worse," she said. "And if you keep poking me about it, I'm going to pull your emergency seat release."

He grinned at her, then turned his attention to the view as he rubbed the top of his thigh. The muscles were still growing into his new hip joint, and sometimes they produced an ache that just screamed for him to rub it out. The problem was that the ache was deep inside his leg. He could never reach it, but he was compelled to try.

He turned his head in time to catch Tal watching him with an expression that had become all too familiar. "I'm all right," he said. "Just a little itchy."

"If you were itchy, you'd be scratching. That's rubbing, and that means it hurts."

"It doesn't hurt. It just…throbs. Has anyone ever told you you're like a winden with a newborn?"

It worked; her expression melted into amusement. "Not lately. Though I seem to recall accusing Vellmar of the same thing about half a moon ago."

"And why was that?" He knew he had her.

"Because she was driving me insane worrying about me when there was no need. And don't give me that look. I had a few easily sealed sword cuts. You have new body parts."

"You have a new body part, too."

"A tiny synthetic bone implant hardly counts. They just had to fill in a little chip in my arm. Sorry, but you win this contest. I'm well within my rights to worry about you, and there's not a thing you can do about it." She glanced over, her face serious again. "I earned that right."

That shut him down, and he cast about for a safer topic. "Salomen was certainly distracted this morning. She came by my office to pick up a file clip, and it was the first time I ever felt that she wasn't paying attention. This feast must be quite the production."

Tal nodded. "Over ninety mouths to feed, and that was before we added ten Guards to the mix. And it's a point of pride to produce most of the feast from the holding itself. I cannot believe they used to do this without hiring a cook. Apparently, the whole family has been working in the kitchen dome for the last half nineday. Salomen hasn't said it, but I know she feels guilty about not being there this cycle. Even though she was delighted that Wynsill agreed to take her place."

"Don't you dare let Hol-Opah steal Wynsill from us." The base cook was a favorite among the Guards and for very good reason.

"I already told Salomen that was not an option. Actually, I told her that a moon ago, when she had Wynsill make horten soup for our second date." A wistful smile crossed her face. "We never did get around to a third."

"It *has* been a bit busy. But I suggest you take Salomen out once this feast is over and she's able to concentrate on something else. Otherwise, your bonding ceremony will end up being your third date."

"Good Goddess, what a terrible thought." Tal banked the transport as they exited the Blacksun flight path; now they were making a straight shot over the golden fields and green hills to Hol-Opah. "You're right. I need to make that happen. There's just been so much else going on, especially with the replacement of two caste Primes."

Micah nodded. He had never seen Blacksun so chaotic, but then again, they had never lost one-third of the High Council in a single day. The campaigning among the merchant and warrior castes was ferocious.

"Do you think Ehron has a chance?" he asked.

"Well, he has no established power base and no experience on the more important committees. But this may be the one time that lack is actually an advantage. The warriors are looking for new blood. They want someone as far from Shantu as they can get."

"Ehron certainly fits the description." Micah didn't know much about him, but he had looked up his record while sitting in the healing center, catching up on news. He seemed to be a man of integrity, and right now the Council needed that more than political experience.

"I think the merchant campaign is more clear-cut. There's no question in my mind that Stasinal will get the nod."

"She'll make an excellent Prime Merchant," Micah agreed. "But that would mean no more shouting matches across the chamber floor between the Prime Merchant and the Prime Warrior. What will we do for entertainment?"

"You're not one of those who thinks this peace and mutual goodwill is going to last, are you?"

"Your cynicism is showing, my friend."

"I'm not a cynic. I'm merely a realist."

"And the Chosen," he muttered, just loud enough to be sure she heard it.

CHAPTER 62
Autumn feast

It was almost like old times, Tal thought. Salomen, Shikal, Nikin, and Jaros were all waiting outside as she brought the transport down behind the main house. But now she had no compunction about greeting Salomen with a warmron in front of anyone who wished to see.

"I missed you," she said.

Salomen gave her a quick kiss and pulled back to smile at her. "I only left the State House this morning."

"And it was an emptier place without you."

"You had Colonel Micah."

"Micah almost didn't make it here in one piece." Tal narrowed her eyes at him.

"Colonel." Salomen's voice took on the tone it often did when she spoke to Jaros. "What did you do this time?"

"I merely referred to the Lancer by her new title as an act of respect," he said. "It's not my fault she interprets it otherwise."

"Respect, my backside," said Tal, and Salomen laughed as she stepped over to touch palms with him.

"I am so glad to have you on Opah land again," she said.

"I'm very glad to be here. And ready to eat."

Tal's arms had no time to feel empty, as a small body instantly filled them.

"You're here!" Jaros grinned up at her. "Now the feast can start."

"You were waiting for us?" Tal looked over at Salomen. "You never said anything about delaying the start until we could get here."

Shikal stood behind Jaros and touched Tal's palms over his head. "Believe me, we've started. But this feast takes a long time; we're still on the appetizers. Jaros is just eager for the fantens to be pulled out of the cooking pits."

"Whole fantens," Jaros explained. "Six of them!"

"Speedy," Tal said.

Next in line, Nikin laughed as they clasped hands. "I see you've picked up some new vocabulary."

"Part of my job. Warriors are actually part scholar, you know."

"The good ones, anyway." He grinned and turned toward Micah. "Well met, Colonel. And welcome back to Hol-Opah."

"Thank you. It's a welcome relief after Blacksun, I can tell you."

"A bit busy these days, eh?" Shikal asked. "Perhaps later tonight we can wind down with a bottle of spirits in the parlor."

Micah's face split into an enormous smile. "I've been dreaming about that bottle and a crackling fire for nearly half a moon."

"And the nights are cold enough now for the fire," Shikal said. "I think we can make your dream come true."

As the group moved away, Tal caught Salomen's hand and held her back. "We'll join you in a few ticks," she said, waving them on.

"The kiss wasn't enough?" Salomen asked.

"Never, but that's not why I want you alone. I brought you a gift." Tal opened the rear door of her transport and pulled a small, flat package off the seat. "Micah mentioned our third date, and I know this isn't it, but…it's a special night for you. I wanted to acknowledge that." She held out the package.

"Thank you." Salomen accepted it with a careful touch. "I didn't expect anything tonight."

"It wouldn't be much of a gift if you expected it."

Salomen shot her a quick smile as she broke the seals and lifted the lid off the box. A sudden intake of breath marked her recognition of the contents.

"Oh, Andira…" Reverently, she lifted the tiny bouquet from its cushioned bed. Each flower bore five white, pointed petals and a deep green circle at its center. "Windstars! In autumn? Where did you find them? Glasshouses don't grow these."

"It may be autumn here, but it's spring in southern Pallea."

"You had these flown in from southern Pallea?"

"Mm-hm. I'm afraid they won't last as long as the book you gave me—" Tal's speech was cut off. By the time the kiss ended, all words had fled her head.

"I cannot believe you remembered." Salomen brought the flowers to her nose and closed her eyes, her pleasure washing over Tal's senses with a golden warmth. "They smell like spring. I love this scent."

"I remember everything you told me that morning. It was our first morning together."

"Yes, but it was also right before everything fell apart."

"Your favorite tree is the cinnoralis. Your favorite place on Hol-Opah is right over there." Tal pointed in the direction of the small waterfall on the southern border. "And you love windstars because they're the first flower to bloom in spring, when nothing else can survive."

"You *do* remember it all."

"When you told me that, I thought it was the perfect flower for you."

"Why?" Salomen sniffed the flowers again, a lovely smile bringing out the lines beside her mouth.

"Because it's both beautiful and strong. It blooms when you think it should not. And it's easy to overlook if you only look for the bigger, showier blossoms." Tal ran a fingertip along the edge of one petal, impossibly soft yet able to withstand the last winter winds. "But once you've seen one, and felt it, you cannot forget it."

Salomen was looking at her with her heart in her eyes. "That describes you as well, tyrina. With one exception."

"Which one?"

"You're impossible to overlook."

Tal had no ready answer for that, but a kiss worked just as well. Possibly better.

When they broke apart, Salomen tapped the bouquet clip to activate the molecular grip and pressed it to the lapel of her coat. "Perfect," she said.

It was. Her long coat was a patchwork of autumn colors, reds and tans and black, and the windstars stood out against it like a beacon. Tal thought she might be excused for feeling smug about her success.

Hand in hand, they walked around to the other side of the house, where the land between the front porch and the gates had been transformed into a scene of chaos. The Opahs had rigged up part of a field cover, and beneath it was a forest of tables, chairs, smoking grills, bottle carts, and ninety people milling around and talking so loudly that Tal could already pick out voices she recognized, even at this distance. Though a light mist was beginning to fall, the revelers were dry and comfortable beneath the field cover, and the atmosphere of celebration was almost physically palpable.

She had been nervous about this, dreading the possibility of having to make some sort of speech or otherwise acknowledge her status. Of all places, she did not want to be held apart here. These were her friends and coworkers, and she really just wanted to walk in, pick up a drink, and start chatting with them.

Salomen sensed her reticence and wrapped an arm around her waist. "Don't worry," she said in a low voice. Then she shouted, "Hoi, everyone, look who came for the fanten!"

"Salomen!" Tal would have ducked behind a tree had one been handy.

"Look!" someone cried from the edge of the crowd. "Salomen's brought her bondmate!"

Heads turned and there was a chorus of greetings as Salomen pulled Tal the rest of the way. When they arrived beneath the shelter of the field cover, someone pressed a drink into Tal's hand, someone else was telling her that she had to try the mallowfish before they were all gone, and in moments she had been swallowed into the crowd.

She relaxed as the conversations all seemed to center on Salomen. How was she getting on in the State House? Had she thrown any Councilors out of her office yet? Heads nodded all around as Tal explained Salomen's new policy of independently meeting with every single Councilor and how most of them were, for now at least, completely charmed.

"We knew she'd do just fine," said one.

"As long as they don't make her angry," said another, setting off a round of laughter.

"Aye, Salomen will straighten them out," commented a third, and everyone seemed to agree with that wholeheartedly. Tal raised an eyebrow at her tyree, who gave her a sweet smile and sipped her drink.

It took some time for Tal to understand what was really happening, and when it finally hit, she had to laugh at herself. She had been so wrapped up in the events at Blacksun that she had bought into that Fahla's Chosen concept herself, even while she railed against it. But this wasn't Blacksun. It was Granelle and Hol-Opah, and it was where these people lived out their lives. They hadn't gathered like this since the last day of harvest, and there was a new baby to be talked about, and gossip as to who had been seen dating whom, and discussions about the harvest and the weather and the plantings next moon. To be sure, there was also a great deal of gossip about the arrest of Withernet, Parser's local spy, but even so, they spoke more about the local effect of the arrest than its ties to the greater issues. Parser and Shantu were merely names in the news, distant figures who had caused problems both in Blacksun and to the Opahs. But everyone knew Withernet. His betrayal was personal to them.

And Salomen was personal to them as well. She, not Tal, was the figurehead of this feast.

"I just realized something," Tal said when she found a temporary lull with Micah.

"Me too," said Micah. "I realized that I've never tasted fanten like this before. Can you believe how tender this is?" He took a vast bite and chewed happily.

"Great Goddess, were you raised in a mud puddle? You're eating like Jaros."

His smile was unrepentant, and when he had finally chewed enough to clear his mouth, he said, "I have more sympathy for Jaros these days. So what was your great realization?"

"I'm not the Lancer here. I'm Salomen's bondmate."

"Finally figured that out, eh?" He took another bite.

"Oh, so you already knew? Good of you to share."

He waved a hand. "Some things you have to learn on your own. It has never been my obligation to spoon-feed you."

She glared at him, but there was no heat in it and she soon gave it up. "Not a single person has asked about the ritual combat. I thought they'd be full of questions."

"I think they would consider it rude to ask you about that. You nearly died, and they all saw Salomen being carried down by Nikin because she was too weak to walk. That's not a topic to be explored at an autumn feast. That would be like Varsi coming up to me at our base feast and asking me how I felt when I was shot in the basement."

"I see your point." Tal took a bite of her own fanten and rolled her eyes skyward. "Fahla!"

"Told you," Micah said with satisfaction.

The feast went on until well after dark, the crisp night doing nothing to dampen the spirits of people so full of excellent food and a significant amount of drink. Someone began tapping out a rhythm on a drum, which appeared to be a signal of sorts as everyone rushed to push tables aside and pull out the chairs. Another field worker began playing a windpipe, a third produced a ten-string, and before long most of the crowd was sitting and rocking their heads in time to the music, while those whose stomachs weren't overly full found the energy to twirl and sway in front of the players.

Tal was sitting between Micah and Salomen. As she held Salomen's hand, she thought back to the day when she had first seen Delegate Norsen's impromptu replacement in the State House. Impulsively, she squeezed the hand in hers, then brought it to her lips and planted a soft kiss on it.

Salomen looked over and smiled. "What are you thinking?" she asked, leaning in to be heard over the music.

"About the day we met. And how you looked at me with such disrespect, and I wanted to toss you out of the room, but I couldn't because you turned out to be the most useful delegate in the whole meeting."

"I'm still disrespectful, my Lancer." Salomen leaned farther in and gently bit Tal's earlobe. "When I need to be."

"Salomen!" Tal pulled back and looked around, but Micah was entranced by the music and the dancers, and no one else had noticed. When she turned back, Salomen was laughing.

"Are you afraid people might see me being affectionate toward you?"

"That wasn't affection." Tal shifted uncomfortably, to Salomen's greater amusement.

"Certainly it was. And love, and a little bit of lust, and since when is any of that a problem? Have you noticed what's happening at the edges of the field cover?"

She had, but thought it impolite to look at any of the couples taking advantage of the darkness. "We're sitting in the front."

"And you still think everyone is looking at you?"

For a moment Tal was irritated by the question, but then she shook her head at herself. "I suppose I'm just not used to being one of the crowd."

"I thought that was what you wanted."

Tal looked at her, sensing the honest desire to know. Salomen was doing her best to give Tal what she wished for. It certainly wasn't her fault if Tal herself wasn't clear about those wishes.

"It's exactly what I wanted," she decided, and leaned in to give Salomen a proper kiss. She sensed a small emotional ripple in the people around them; this kiss was not one that was likely to go unnoticed. But when she straightened, all she saw were a few quick smiles as people went back to their conversations or watching the dancers.

"Amazing," she said. "I really am anonymous."

"You most certainly are not. You're my bondmate. That's what Chosen really means, Andira. Fahla chose you for me."

Tal's next kiss was much more difficult for anyone to ignore, but this time she didn't care.

CHAPTER 63
Damage control

By the time the feast wound down and the last guests departed, it was well past Jaros's bedtime, though he was wide awake from all the excitement. Tal and Salomen left the others packing up the food and brought him in to prepare for bed. When he was in his pajamas and had brushed his teeth, Salomen led them down the back stairs to the kitchen and sat him down with a cup of gassy water. "Andira and I will be in the parlor," she told him. "Come find us when you're done. And drink *all* of it."

He nodded and silently began to sip his water.

"Digestive aid," Salomen said as she and Tal walked through the dining room and into the parlor. "He always eats himself sick at these feasts. A little gassy water before bed saves everyone a lot of trouble during the night. Takes him a while to drink it, though. He's never liked the taste." She sat in one of the two armchairs flanking the empty fireplace and looked up. "We need to talk."

Tal took the other chair. "What's wrong?"

Several pipticks of increasingly uncomfortable silence passed as she watched Salomen search for the right words.

"We're going to show Jaros the recording of the ritual combat."

"Wh—" Tal fell back in her chair with a thump, staring at the woman who just two ticks ago had been perfectly sane.

Salomen watched her, waiting.

"All right," Tal said. "I can feel that you're already certain about this, and I know you would not make that decision lightly. So tell me what it is that makes you think this is a good idea, because from where I'm sitting it has disaster written all over it."

"It has disaster written over it from where I'm sitting, too. But I have to agree with Father and Nikin. It's the best thing we can do." She sighed. "Jaros has become obsessed with it. When it happened, he didn't understand why he wasn't allowed to watch, because none of us knew how to explain that you might not survive. So Father took him into the lobby, but of course the chamber proceedings are shown all over the State House. Father managed to find a place where Jaros couldn't see it, but he still heard it. He heard everything."

Tal groaned. "That's my fault. If I'd told you what was going to happen, Jaros would never have been there."

"That's not the issue tonight."

It had certainly been an issue on other nights, and Salomen still hadn't forgiven her. Tal hadn't forgiven herself, either. Not when Salomen's nightmares made her realize how much damage she had done.

And here was one more example.

"So he heard the fight. And of course he saw the aftermath, because he saw Nikin coming out of the guest gallery with you in his arms."

"Yes. And he saw you being taken off to the healing center, when just a hantick earlier you were in full dress uniform, looking like you owned the world. He had a lot of questions, and we've all done our best to answer, but he knows there are details we're not sharing and he's become increasingly obsessed with seeing it for himself."

"But why now? He doesn't have access to it. The broadcasts have never shown the whole thing since the live airing. Let him wait until he's old enough to handle it—like sometime after his Rite of Ascension," she added bitterly. If they waited until Jaros was twenty, it might give her enough time to get used to the idea.

Salomen smiled at that. "I'm afraid that won't work. The recording has become an underground favorite at his school. Father thinks, and I agree, that it's only a matter of time before Jaros gets his hands on it. He's being teased by schoolmates who are delighted that they've seen it and he hasn't, especially since he's your bondbrother. Besides his own personal obsession, now he's obsessed with being able to fight back against the taunts."

"He'll be entering his autumn break in just two ninedays. Surely a moon away from school will put this whole thing to rest?"

"I don't think we have that much time. It's already been two ninedays, and his fascination has risen to alarming levels. Worst of all, I'm sensing a resolve in him that wasn't there before. He knows we don't want him to see it, but he's arrived at the point where he no longer cares."

"I don't suppose forbidding him on pain of permanent banishment from the State House will work."

Salomen shook her head.

"But he's too young!"

"In two moons he'll be ten cycles. And one moon after that, he'll be the same age I was when I defied the testers. He's young, but he has my determination. He'll make it happen. The question is no longer whether or not he sees it; now the question is how he sees it. And I would rather he see it here at home, with you right there to hold him when it's over, than at school or a friend's house with no one around to help him see it in the proper perspective." Compassion warmed her voice as she added, "I know you haven't seen it, and I don't want you to watch it with him. I'd just like for you to be nearby."

Tal rested her head against the back of the chair. "Shek. What a way to end a perfectly wonderful feast. Why did you choose tonight?"

"Because we thought it would be better for him if he spent an entire evening with you beforehand."

"So you had it all planned out. Nice of you to give me some warning."

Salomen's stare singed her ears and brought the guilt rushing to the surface. They both looked away.

"If I'd told you earlier, you would have spent the entire feast worrying about it," Salomen said at last. "I wanted you to be able to enjoy yourself. I'm sorry if that was the wrong choice."

"Salomen...I would do it so differently now—" Tal stopped at the upraised hand.

"Don't. Not tonight. We have to deal with Jaros."

Apologies had limited power, as Tal had recently learned. When the wound was deep enough, all the remorse in the world was not enough to heal it.

"All right," she said. "I'll watch it with him."

"What? Andira, no, I'm not trying to guilt you into that. Take a glass of spirits and go sit on the back porch. I'll come for you as soon as it's over."

"No," Tal said stubbornly. "I'm not going to hide. Besides, I should have watched it before now. What better training vid could there possibly be?"

"Great Mother, you really are a warrior. Can you actually watch it with that in mind?"

"That's probably the only way I can watch it. You realize this will be the end of him idolizing me. I'm going to miss that."

"Don't be too sure." Salomen left her chair and leaned a hip on the wide arm of Tal's. "I still idolize you, and I saw the whole thing."

Jaros came clattering in, happily discussing his impressions of the feast before he was even through the door. Tal watched in silence, worrying herself into such a state that her stomach hurt. She thought wryly that Salomen had been very right not to tell her; she wouldn't have been able to eat a bite at that feast. Now she just wanted to get it over with. Salomen was the one who responded to Jaros, giving all of the appropriate *hm* and *did he?* sounds that kept him engaged.

Soon the others arrived, and Shikal sized up the situation at a glance.

"So she's talked to you?" he asked Tal.

She nodded, then looked at Micah as her senses flooded with his sympathy. "You too? How long have you known?"

"Since this morning. I gave her the file. For what it's worth, I think it's the best thing."

Jaros's chatter faltered. He had picked up on the undercurrents and was gazing from one adult to another.

"Jaros," said Salomen, "now that everyone is here, we're going to have a family council."

"Is this about Herot?" he asked.

"Not this time."

Shikal and Micah sat down while Nikin pressed the control pad in the wall. With a slight hum, the vidscreen lowered from its holder on the ceiling. He slipped a file clip into the pad and took a seat with the others.

"We've decided to show you the recording of Andira's ritual combat." Salomen got no further as Jaros bounced up excitedly.

"Really? Speedy!" He raced over to Tal and grabbed her hand. "Finally! They wouldn't let me see it."

"I know," she said. "For good reason. I haven't seen it either."

"Why not?"

"That was not something I enjoyed. Do you understand that I had to kill a man?"

"I know that! He challenged you to ritual combat, just like in the stories, and you had to stop him. Everyone says you were the better fighter, because even though he cut you more often, you landed more blows."

"Great Goddess, Jaros!" Tal could not remember ever having been this bloodthirsty as a child. She looked beseechingly at Salomen, who raised her eyebrows in a *See what I mean?* expression.

"Jaros," said Shikal, "You seem to have gotten some wrong ideas about that combat. It's not a story. It was very real, and Andira was badly hurt, and she had to do something she did not want to do."

"You mean kill him?" He looked at Tal. "Didn't you want to? He was bad. He was the one who kidnapped Herot."

"No, I didn't want to. I had already arranged his punishment. He was going to lose his title, his freedom, and his caste. There was no greater punishment I could possibly have inflicted."

"Yes, there was," he pointed out. "And you did. He died because he challenged you and lost."

"He died because he forced a situation where my only options were to kill him or die myself!" Tal had no patience left for his ignorant enthusiasm. "And it was close. That's why I didn't want to see it."

He frowned. "You're not watching it with me?"

"I'll watch it. But I don't want to. I'm here because I think I should be."

"But—"

"Jaros, sit down," Salomen said. "You can ask Andira questions afterward, when you know what she's talking about."

He sat grumpily, but his pout turned to excitement when Nikin activated the file. He leaned forward, watching in eager fascination as a black-suited Tal descended the stairs to the chamber floor.

From her perch on the chair arm, Salomen rested a hand on Tal's neck, softly caressing her and keeping her grounded in the here and now.

During the initial feinting and parrying, Jaros leaned forward, his body shifting as he swung his small arm from one side to the other, imitating what he saw on the screen. "Yes!" he cried as Tal kicked Shantu in the leg. "Good one, Lancer Tal!" And when she crushed Shantu's nose and shoulder, he nearly levitated with pride. But a moment later Shantu's sword sliced in, and Jaros went silent as the Tal on screen clutched her side, her hand coming away smeared in blood.

From that point onward, he was increasingly distressed by what he saw. His idol was fighting with all the strength in her body—and losing. When Tal's sword dropped from her badly wounded arm, Jaros let out a small cry of despair. "No," he whispered, caught up in the moment. "Pick it up." Then Shantu kicked her onto her back, and Jaros was so upset that Tal almost left her chair to pull him into a warmron.

It was strange to see herself looking like this. She was long used to seeing her face on vidscreens and other imagery, but only in her public persona. Shantu had a point about her carefully constructed myth. Here, she was exhausted, drenched in sweat, and lying at the feet of an opponent. For Jaros's sake she was grateful for her choice of a black fighting suit. She saw the blood when the wet fabric glinted in the lights, but he didn't know what to look for.

Jaros's relief was vast when Tal rallied, and when she impaled Shantu, he was momentarily gleeful. But he became very somber at the sight of the pooling blood, and even more so when he saw her falling into the arms of the warrior Councilors. They watched the healers treating her and wheeling her toward the doors, and to Tal's relief, Nikin ended the playback there. She had not wanted to see Salomen being carried in. Once was more than enough.

The room was silent as everyone waited for Jaros's reaction.

He turned in his seat and stared at her. Then he stood, walked over, and crawled onto her lap, an act he would normally consider himself far too old for. She wrapped her arms around him as he leaned his head against her shoulder.

"You were hurt," he said.

"Yes, I was. You knew that. You saw me being taken to the healing center."

He nodded. "But it's different."

"You mean, actually seeing it happen?"

Another nod.

"I told you, Jaros. I didn't enjoy it. Now you know why. It was just something I had to do, no matter how much I wished otherwise. Shantu did a bad thing, but he didn't deserve to die."

"But he hurt you." Jaros was fixed on one thing. "They had to carry you."

Tal squeezed his small body. "I'm fine now. It turned out all right."

He snuggled in more closely. "Will you ever have to do that again?"

"No. The Council banned the practice. That was the last ritual challenge that will ever be fought."

"So no other warrior can challenge you?"

"If a warrior doesn't like my leadership now, an old-fashioned caste coup is the only option."

"Good. You should be Lancer forever."

She smiled. "I'll have to retire someday. But it will be a while."

He was quiet then, though his eyes were wide open. Tal wasn't sure what to do next, but the others stirred into activity. Nikin began laying a fire, Shikal fetched a bottle of spirits from the rack, and Micah pulled the glasses from the sideboard. Salomen brushed Jaros's hair away from his face and asked, "Was it what you expected?"

He shook his head.

"What did you expect?"

"I don't know."

Tal did. "Maybe you expected to see me beat Shantu without really being hurt."

He nodded. "Everyone said you were the better fighter. But he almost killed you."

"There were two kinds of fighting happening there," Tal explained. "Shantu was a better sword fighter. But I'm better at hand-to-hand fighting, which is something a warrior is far more likely to use in real-life situations. The problem is that swords cause much more damage. It wasn't glorious and wonderful, Jaros. It hurt, a lot. And those battles and stories you love so much—the people who lived them didn't think it was glorious and wonderful either. They thought it was frightening and painful."

"Were you afraid?" he asked, raising his head to look at her.

"I didn't have time to be afraid during the combat. But I was afraid before it started. Mostly I was afraid of never again seeing the people I love. That's why I didn't enjoy killing Shantu. He had a family, just like you. He had people who loved him, and they'll never see him again."

Jaros settled back against her chest. He had never thought of Shantu having a family, and Tal could feel him turning that concept around in his mind. He was quiet as Shikal and Micah handed out drinks, and Salomen kissed him before leaving to take the chair he had been in. The fire crackled, the adults spoke of everything but the combat, and somewhere in the course of the conversation, Tal sensed that he had fallen asleep. She looked over at Salomen, who set her drink aside and came to take her brother.

"No, that's all right. I'll do it." Tal stood, holding Jaros in her arms. "Lead the way."

The air was noticeably cooler upstairs. While Salomen held up the blankets, Tal carefully lowered Jaros to his bed. He turned to his side, clutching his pillow and frowning as Salomen settled the covers around him.

"He has quite a lot to think about now," Tal said.

"More than I could ever have wished." Salomen stroked his hair, and his frown smoothed out. "But he learned some important lessons, and we controlled the situation. I think it was for the best."

"I agree. Much as I hated the idea at first." Tal followed her out and took her hand as they walked down the curving hallway. "When he's old enough, I look forward to telling him that you fought that combat, too." She pulled Salomen to a halt. "All that concern about me watching it, and you didn't mention that you hadn't seen it either."

"I never wanted to."

Someday, Tal thought, she might stop underestimating Salomen.

"I was afraid," she said. "I thought you were my weakness, and I couldn't afford it. But I made a mistake. You're not my weakness. You're my strength."

"And I know you'll remember that, until the next time you forget."

Tal held Salomen's hand against her heart. "I swear, on my honor as a warrior, that I will never abandon you again."

Salomen's eyes were too shiny in the dim hallway. "The honor you almost died for?"

Muffled sounds of conversation rose from below them, Micah's deep timbre distinctive from the others. Tal remembered the last days before he woke and how angry she had been at him for choosing to die. For leaving her.

"If I leave you, it will not be by choice," she said. "And I would fight Fahla herself to keep it from happening."

Salomen's fingers clenched in her shirt. "I still need time."

"You have it." Tal drew her into a warmron. "And you have me."

"Don't you ever leave like that again," Salomen whispered.

"I won't." Tal had made this promise ten times already, but tonight she felt a difference. Tonight, Salomen was ready to hear it.

CHAPTER 64
Inclusion

Though it was eve-four by the time they landed at Blacksun Base, Tal knew Micah wasn't ready for the night to end. He hesitated only for politeness before agreeing to their invitation for a drink.

She bounced up the stairs to the main entrance, feeling a bit like a pre-Rite child in her intense anticipation. Then she had to stop and wait for Micah, who moved more slowly these days with his staff. Salomen stayed with him, shooting her a castigating look, and after that she was more sober.

When they entered their quarters, Salomen sat down with Micah while Tal bustled around, gathering the glasses and the spirits she had bought for the occasion. Micah's eyebrows nearly crawled off his forehead when he spotted the label on the bottle.

"Valkinon?" He plucked the bottle from the tray. "What are we celebrating?"

"Well, we could celebrate the fact that you're out of the healing center." Tal took the bottle back from him.

"Or the fact that we made it through another feast without any disasters," Salomen said. "Three cycles ago, we tried a supposedly improved technique for the cooking pits. They never got hot enough, and the fanten wasn't done in time. We couldn't start eating it until eve-three."

Tal popped the tab on the bottle and held it up, letting the blue vapor trickle out. "Or we could celebrate the fact that Aldirk didn't have a single sarcastic thing to say about you today. That itself was a minor miracle."

He looked back and forth between them as she poured the spirits. "Something is going on. Tell me now; my heart's too old for this kind of suspense."

"Give it up, Micah, your heart is not old. Besides, we need to make a toast first." She held up her glass. "To family, the thread that holds all of us together."

Salomen made an appreciative sound as she drank. "This is as good as it was in Meadowgreen. Better, I think."

"That's because you're used to drinking better spirits in general. I'm afraid you're developing expensive tastes, tyrina."

"Good thing I chose a very well-paid warrior, then."

"All right!" Micah said. "You're doing this on purpose. I've had my drink; now I want answers."

"Impatient, isn't he?"

"Tal," he growled.

"Don't look at me. Salomen is the one who has something to ask you."

Micah turned to her. "What do you need to ask that requires a set-up like this?"

"Something very important." She set her glass down. "A few ninedays ago, I asked Andira who I could petition for inclusion into her family. She said her only living elder relative was her Aunt Sima."

"But I wouldn't give Aunt Sima the power of granting inclusion," said Tal. "She's family in name only."

"So that left me at a loss. Until I realized that Andira does have real family, someone right here in Blacksun. But then you had to put yourself in the healing center, and there hasn't been a tick since then where it really felt like the right time. We hoped tonight would be the moment. And it is."

Tal's senses were wide open; she was reveling in Micah's dawning comprehension. And when Salomen slid gracefully from her chair to kneel before his, comprehension turned into shock.

"Honored Corozen Lintale Micah, I ask you to hear my petition. Under the eye of Fahla, who sees all, I speak so that all may hear. I love Andira Shaldone Tal. Her happiness is my ambition; her well-being is my purpose. All that is mine I place freely at her disposal, including my heart and my life, which I would gladly lay down to protect hers. This I swear in Fahla's name. I am Salomen Arrin Opah, and I ask this gift of you and all your ancestors: Will you do me the honor of accepting me into your family?"

Micah was speechless as Tal joined her on the floor.

"You *are* my family," she told him. "The only one left whose acceptance I would seek."

Taking Salomen's hand, she recited the petition for the second time in her life. Not until she finished did she realize something was wrong. He was profoundly shocked, more than their petition could possibly explain. And he was…afraid.

"Get up," he croaked. "Please."

Tal and Salomen looked at each other in alarm. Without a word they rose and retook their seats.

Micah passed a trembling hand over his forehead. "Great Mother of us all," he murmured. "After all this time."

By now Tal was frightened as well. She could not imagine what could cause such a reaction. Salomen squeezed her hand, needing some sort of assurance, but Tal had none to give.

At last Micah met her eyes. "Before you make this petition, you need to know something. Something I never imagined telling you. But as much as I want the right to respond to your petition, I don't have it. Not unless you make it knowing the full truth."

He lifted his glass and took a gulp, steadying himself. When he replaced the glass, he nearly tipped it over, barely catching it in time.

"You've asked me many times if I ever gave my heart away," he said. "I always avoided the answer. But you have the right to know. Yes, Andira, I gave my heart away a very long time ago. To your mother."

"What?" she whispered.

"She was like no one I had ever met, nor did I meet her like again. I loved her with all my heart and soul, and she…" He paused, took a deep breath, and finished, "She loved me as well."

Tal sat mute and stunned.

Micah looked at Salomen and added, "She was already bonded to Tal's father. I fell in love with a woman I could never have."

"Oh, no," Salomen murmured.

He gave her a tiny smile before returning his gaze to Tal, who by now had found her voice.

"Did he know?"

"Of course he knew. Do you think I could hold a front against your father? But he never spoke of it."

"He wouldn't," Tal realized. "You were his best friend."

"I don't understand," Salomen said.

"If Father had ever acknowledged it, he would have been obligated to do something about it. By staying silent, he was able to keep Micah's friendship. But that same silence was a tacit condoning of their affair."

"And we took advantage of that," Micah said. "I know I should tell you I'm ashamed, but I'm not. I could not turn my back on her for honor; it would have broken her heart. And I would rather have Returned than caused harm to such a heart."

Tal was almost afraid to skim him, but her need to know was too great. Cautiously, she reached out—and understood that her mother had bonded with two men, though only one had been publicly acknowledged.

Valkinon was meant to be sipped, but she drained half the glass in an effort to steady herself. It still took a moment to form the question.

"Does your blood run in my veins?" she asked.

He smiled at her. "Only in my dreams. You would have been all I could have wished for in a daughter. But no, we never had a creation ceremony. We both loved your father as well, and we could not betray him that way. So please don't think she loved him less for loving me. She had a heart large enough for both of us. It hurt her in so many ways, but it would have hurt her more to give either one of us up."

Tal inhaled deeply, having forgotten to breathe for a moment. "Well, I have to admit, you've surprised me on this one. I don't know what to think."

"Don't think until you've heard the rest of the story." Micah took another drink, his hand steadier now that he had gotten the worst of it out. "Things changed after your mother became pregnant. Not because of her. Fahla, no; her heart never changed. Because of me. I didn't have the same capacity she did to share. I couldn't bear knowing that she was carrying a child I had no part in creating. I knew that child would bury itself in her heart, and I didn't trust her to have a heart large enough for three. I was jealous—young and full of passion and raging with a jealousy I could not control. I envied your father so much that there were times I could barely look at him. He had everything I ever wanted, and even his generosity in sharing that with me just made it worse. So I left. I found a posting in Redmoon, which was as far from Blacksun as I could get and still be on a career path, and I was gone before you were born."

"You left?" Tal frowned. "But there's not a moment in my memory when you weren't in my life."

"Because Fahla saved me from what would have been my greatest mistake. She sent me a vision."

A tingle ran down Tal's spine. "The vision you told me about at Whitemoon. You said…" She searched her memory, trying to recall their conversation on the grounds of the Whitemoon Temple. "You said she showed you that you couldn't avoid loss, but you could gain from it."

"I knew you'd remember. I made an offering to her in Redmoon Temple, begging her to destroy the love in my heart, because living with it seemed so much worse than living without it. And while I stood there, I saw a vision of you."

"Of me!"

"Yes. You were already grown, already in the uniform of a Lead Guard. And you were standing in front of a dual funeral pyre."

Tal tightened her grip on Salomen's hand. "My parents."

"I saw you standing by yourself, several paces apart from a crowd of mourners, with the torch in your hand and not a single tear on your face. I saw a woman who had lost everything and was utterly, completely alone."

"But I wasn't alone. You were there with me."

"I was. But I couldn't approach until you lit the pyre. That right belongs to family, and I wasn't family."

"Great Goddess." Tal stared at him, but it was a younger Micah she was seeing. The Micah who had walked up to her after she had lit the pyre; who had gently taken the torch from her numb fingers and put it back in the stand; who had held her hands, grounding her with his touch as she finally broke down and cried. "I guess Fahla only showed you the part she wanted you to see."

He nodded. "I lost one of my fathers before my Rite of Ascension, and the other not very long after. I knew what it was like to be so alone. You were the daughter of the woman I loved and the man who had been my best friend for half my life. I could not let you face that kind of loss by yourself. And as I stood there in that temple, I felt all my jealousy and pain turn into something different. Suddenly, I was too far away; I had an almost desperate need to get back to all three of you. I resigned my post and was back in Blacksun before you were seven moons old."

"So you knew," Tal said, trying to wrap her brain around it. "You always knew they would die."

"Yes, but Fahla's vision never included any specifics. I didn't know how or when it would happen. There was nothing I could do to protect them. I couldn't even tell them. It wouldn't have helped them prevent it, but it would have condemned them to live with the same kind of fear I felt. I wouldn't have wished that on an enemy, much less the two people I loved. So I focused on being with them whenever I could and on building a relationship with you. It wasn't difficult—you buried yourself in my heart before the end of my first visit with your parents. I understood then why your mother always said she had enough love for all three of us, because it turned out that I had a heart that big as well. I loved you as much as if you were my own daughter. Sometimes I almost convinced myself that you were."

The warmth poured out of him, a love she had felt all her life. At last it made sense.

"You were a true blend of your parents, equal parts scholar and warrior. Your mother was sad to lose you to the warrior caste, but I was able to help her with that. After all, I'd known what your choice would be when you were just a few moons old. And your father nearly burst with pride when you made Lead Guard so young. But the day of your promotion was one of the worst days of my life."

Tal could not imagine it. To live with the knowledge of impending death, but never know when or from which direction it would come; to see it drawing nearer with every milestone of her life—her choice of caste, her decision to join the Alsean Defense Force, the early accomplishments, and then the promotion that gave her the uniform he had seen in his vision. And all the time he had loved her mother the way she loved Salomen, the way Shikal had loved Nashta—but he was never given the right to love openly. Not even at the funeral pyre.

"I'm so sorry, Micah. You lost so much. So much you were never allowed to have."

He smiled at her. "Oh, but you haven't heard the rest of it. I told you that Fahla had also showed me something else: that through loss I could gain. The vision had two parts. And in the second part, I saw you again. Older this time, and not in uniform." He gestured toward the floor. "I saw you on your knees in front of me, and you spoke to me. You said, 'You are my family.'"

"Great Goddess above," said Salomen. "No wonder you were so shocked."

"I didn't know what was happening in that vision. I never dreamed it was part of a petition for inclusion. You weren't in it, Salomen." He met Tal's eyes again. "But I knew that someday you would see me as your family, and that knowledge changed my life. I wasn't alone anymore. I had you. I've always had you, from the very beginning. So don't pity me; I didn't lose what you think I did. I tried to; I tried to throw it away with both hands. But Fahla saved me. And yes, the vision meant I lived with a knowledge I never wanted to have, but it also meant that I cherished every moment with your mother and father. Every single moment. If I hadn't had the vision, I would never have gone back. I would have missed your childhood and all those precious cycles of friendship and love with your parents, and when they Returned, I would have had no right to go to you, no right to comfort you. I lost nothing, but I gained a family."

"But who comforted you?" Salomen asked. "And all this time you never said a word to Andira."

"My relationship with Realta and Andorin was my own," he said. "We made our choices long before Andira was of an age to understand any of them. And by the time she was of age, she and I had our own relationship, separate from what either she or I had with her parents. I never wanted to jeopardize that by telling her a history that could not change the past, but might destroy our future. Even now I was afraid to speak, but your petition made it impossible to keep my secret any longer. I could not give an answer when the question had been asked unknowingly."

"I always thought Father asked you to look after me," Tal said. "That was the only reason I could see for the way you were always there when I needed you, no matter where I was or what was happening."

He shook his head. "Your father knew he never needed to ask. So did your mother. She once told me that if ever a child had three parents, that child was you. They shared you with me in the same way they shared each other. It was a complicated web, but for a man with no family, I was gifted indeed."

"So was I." She was beginning to think more clearly. "I can't deny you've shocked me. This is a whole different view of my parents. I thought I knew them, but…"

His mounting dread made her trail off. He was expecting the worst.

"The end result is, I still have a parent," she said softly. "An unusual one to be sure, but a parent nonetheless. And that is a gift from Fahla."

The hot dread vanished, quenched by a wave of relief. He swallowed hard. "I should have known you would react this way. You have your father's grace and generosity, and your mother's heart and wisdom. You truly are an honor to them."

Her throat constricted. "That means a great deal to me. Thank you."

"I only speak the truth."

There was an awkward pause, until Salomen sat up straight and said, "Well, Colonel, I believe you owe us an answer."

He looked from her to Tal, who nodded.

"She knows what I feel. Our petition stands."

His eyes reddened, and he quickly scrubbed at them before looking up with a beaming smile, the joy practically sitting on his skin. "Then I would be delighted."

Once more they slid to their knees, and he rested a hand on each of their shoulders. Tal smiled as she felt him squeeze.

"Andira, Salomen, I hear your petition. Under the eye of Fahla, who connects our past with our future, and in the name of my..." His voice caught, but he cleared his throat and continued, "...my beloved Realta, my best friend Andorin, and all of our mutual ancestors, I say that Salomen Arrin Opah is now one of our family. May our descendants rejoice in this bond, which enriches our family beyond measure."

"And a unique family it is," Tal said as they stood. "Thank you, Micah."

Salomen took his face in her hands and kissed both of his cheeks. "Thank you. For accepting me, and especially for looking after her."

"It was my pleasure. And if you're going to be a part of my family, you should call me Corozen."

"I would be honored."

"Not me." Tal held up her hands. "Not a chance. I've called you Micah my whole life. I'm too old to change."

"Dokshin. You've changed more in the last two moons than you realize. But since I would probably faint if you called me Corozen, I'm glad you're so firm in your beliefs."

"And what would you like your grandchild to call you?" she asked innocently.

His eyes widened. "You...but..."

Tal sat back in her chair and laughed.

"Don't mind her," Salomen said. "That's a long way in our future. At the very least, there's a little matter of a formal bonding ceremony first."

"Thank Fahla," Micah said, grasping at the arm of his chair as he sat down again. "I'm not ready for that yet."

"Neither am I." Salomen shot Tal a glare.

"A child from the two of you?" He shook his head. "I don't think Alsea is ready."

CHAPTER 65
Flames in the temple II

LANARIL LOOKED OVER THE GLITTERING assemblage and wondered how many generations it had been since Whitemoon Temple had seen anything like it.

Lancers were always bonded in Blacksun Temple, but Andira seemed determined to shake up any number of Alsean traditions. Had she not been Fahla's Chosen, there probably would have been a great deal more grumbling in Blacksun, but all she had to say was "This is the temple where Fahla gave me her sign," and the world spoke of nothing else for days. There were even betting pools on whether Fahla would offer a visible sign at the bonding ceremony. At least, that's what Lanaril's aide told her when he admitted that he had put down two hundred cinteks on "yes." After all, he said, the odds were eleven to one against, and how often did a templar have the chance to simultaneously make money and behave piously? He was just backing up his faith with credit.

Lanaril had secretly slipped him five hundred of her own.

The soaring space of Whitemoon Temple was packed with guests from all over Alsea, a unique combination of the world's most and least influential people. There were the caste Primes, all of the high-powered political, religious, and military figures, a good sprinkling of entertainment stars, the Lancer's and Bondlancer's Guards, warriors and scholars Andira had known for cycles…and a significant number of producers from the tiny town of Granelle, all of whom were bursting with pride as one of their own stepped into a role of such power. There had not been a producer Bondlancer for sixteen generations, but Lanaril knew that Salomen Opah would turn the world's expectations on its collective ear. That woman carried at least three castes in her heart.

Most unusual of all, and a first in Alsean history, was the presence of several representatives of an alien race. Ambassador Solvassen was there, along with Chief Kameha, but what had really set the guests whispering was the entrance of Captain Ekatya Serrado and Doctor Lhyn Rivers.

She had so enjoyed seeing Lhyn and Ekatya again. It hardly seemed possible that a cycle and a quarter had gone by since their departure. When they had arrived in her lodgings the day before, she had greeted them with a joyous palm touch and wondered if Andira had given them warmrons instead. For just a moment, she wished she could do that herself.

Lhyn was exactly the same, breathless with new thoughts and questions, while Ekatya was more measured in her conversation. But their tyree bond had changed. Lanaril could feel its solidity, the difference between a sapling and a tree of twenty cycles. Lhyn said that a great deal had happened, but then the conversation turned to all of the events on Alsea in the past cycle, and Lanaril never did hear any more about her friends' adventures. She was looking forward to seeing them again after the ceremony, when Lhyn had promised to share their tale.

A deep roll of drums brought her attention back to the present, and she drew herself upright at the edge of the wooden platform around the molwyn tree. The bondmates were about to enter.

Every head turned toward the thick wooden doors.

At a final booming note of the drum, the temple doors opened, revealing Andira and Salomen standing motionless in the doorway. A quartet from the Whitemoon Symphony began playing, and Kyrie Razinfin, the most celebrated singer on Alsea, burst into a soaring version of the bonding ballad. Lanaril felt chillbumps rise on her arms. Great Mother, what a voice.

And what a sight. She had the best ticket in the house as the bondmates began their walk to the molwyn.

Andira was resplendent in her all-black embroidered suit, a shining golden breastplate bearing the Seal of the Lancer, and a full-length crimson cape with black embroidery to match the suit. The cape alone must have taken an army of crafters a full moon to finish. Lanaril had never seen anything so beautiful.

Beside her, Salomen was in a suit that matched in every way except that hers was dark green, the color of her caste. She also wore a golden breastplate, a symbol of her obligation to care for the Lancer, though in place of the Seal it bore the tree of the producers. Her cape was a mirror image of Andira's, black with crimson embroidery, and her dark hair swung loose across her shoulders. In contrast, Andira's bright blonde hair was pinned up in an intricate twist. Together they made a glorious sight, and Lanaril thought that Fahla herself must be smiling on this ceremony. Surely she was here, in some way. After all, she had chosen these two herself.

They came toward her, holding hands and smiling broadly, and Lanaril remembered a day a little over a cycle ago, when Andira had fled from her obligations and said she could hardly remember how to laugh.

That had been a different woman. This Andira was Fahla's Chosen, gloriously attired and radiating joy as she approached with her tyree. Lanaril wished she could go back in time and tell that past Andira that her future was brighter than she could imagine.

Then they were in front of her, waiting at the bottom of the steps, and Kyrie Razinfin finished the ballad with her trademark drawn-out final note, lasting far beyond the breath-holding capacity of most Alseans. In the awed silence that followed, Lanaril bowed to the singer, acknowledging the beauty she had brought to this ceremony. Kyrie returned the bow, then shifted and bowed lower to the bondmates.

A swarm of vidcams had followed the couple to the steps and now hovered all around them, recording the ceremony from every possible direction. Lanaril ignored them as she said, "Andira Shaldone Tal, Salomen Arrin Opah, what do you seek in this temple today?"

"We seek Fahla's blessing," Andira said, her voice ringing out and effortlessly filling the space.

"For what purpose?"

"To bless the bond our hearts have made." Salomen's voice was lower but no less powerful.

"Will you show us this bond? And demonstrate with open hearts the love that you share?"

"We will," they said in unison.

"Then please come to the molwyn." Lanaril moved back from the edge of the deck as they mounted the steps, then turned and led them to the heart of the temple. Resting one hand on the ancient molwyn tree, she began the bonding prayer, a call-and-response that involved all of the guests. Several hundred voices murmured the time-honored responses, all of them sharing in the union, though few understood just how extraordinary this bond truly was.

At the end of the prayer, she stepped away from the tree and told the story of Andira and Salomen's bond, how they had met and how they had discovered that their hearts were speaking to each other. It was a tradition she had always loved because every story was different, though this one might be her favorite. The idea of two people fighting so hard not to acknowledge the truth—it was a perfect metaphor for all of those who refused to see the glory of Fahla, though her works shone in the world around them, every day.

But she could not tell all of their story, so she did not speak of the true nature of their bond or the role each had played in saving the other's life. It was difficult to leave out Salomen's heroism in particular, because it spoke so eloquently to the divine gift both of them bore. But even in this moment of celebration, security issues took precedence. When she looked at Salomen, so beautiful in her bonding suit and so untrained in the arts of politics and self-protection, she understood Andira's concerns and felt a protective urge of her own.

The ceremony went by in a blur of song, music, and prayer, until it was time for the great Sharing. Andira and Salomen had long ago worked out the order of the two lines and given the lists to the Whitemoon Templars. The guests were ushered into their places accordingly. Two of the Lancer's Guards, Gehrain and Vellmar, were accorded places of honor very near the bondmates, while some of the more prominent politicians found themselves farther away than they probably felt they deserved. The ultimate places of honor, in direct contact with the bondmates, went to Colonel Micah and Shikal Arrin. Of course everyone understood why Salomen Opah would choose her father, but the Lancer's selection of her Chief Guardian was bound to set tongues wagging. Her positioning of the Gaian captain and her bondmate in the second and third places was equally shocking. Tomorrow's headlines were writing themselves.

Two pairs of attendants removed the capes and breastplates from Andira and Salomen, then unbuttoned their suit jackets and shirts. Lanaril took her place between them, her heart beating faster at the import of what she was about to do. She rarely had the opportunity to officiate at a tyree bonding ceremony, and so far as she knew, no living Alsean had ever officiated at a ceremony for tyrees bearing Fahla's divine spark. She didn't know what to expect. But Andira smiled at her, and she reminded herself that this wasn't just a divine tyree. This was her friend.

She slid her hand inside Andira's open shirt, finding the point where the energy sang through her skin, then did the same for Salomen. When her hand slipped onto the curve of Salomen's breast, the connection sealed itself and the power of it stiffened her spine. It was an order of magnitude stronger than anything she had felt before, and she needed a tick just to get it under control before she could trust herself to send it outward.

When she finally released it, she heard it traveling through the guests. Exclamations, sighs, and murmurs filled the temple as each guest felt the glory and strength of a tyree bond, and Lanaril stood at the very center of it, her body serving as a power converter. Never in her life had she felt so close to Fahla. This, *this* was the divine spark, coursing through her body, electrifying her skin, making her hair crackle and stand away from her scalp.

She could have stood there for eternity, glorying in this connection, and indeed held it longer than normal. But she had a role to play. Many guests made soft sounds of protest when she pulled her hands away, and she took some comfort in knowing she was not the only one to feel bereft.

The attendants refastened the bondmates' shirts and suits, reattached the breastplates and capes, and melted away again as Lanaril turned to the guests for her final pronouncement.

"You have all felt the power of this bond, Shared with open hearts by Andira Shaldone Tal and Salomen Arrin Opah, now Lancer and Bondlancer of Alsea. Every one of you is a witness to their love. From this day forward, none may challenge their status as bondmates, for you have blessed them by your presence, as Fahla has blessed them by hers. I am Lanaril Faramon Satran, Lead Templar of Blacksun, and I say now for all to hear: this bond is sealed by Fahla and can never be broken, except by the will of Fahla or the bondmates themselves."

She turned to Andira and Salomen, who might as well have been alone for all the attention they were paying to her or the ceremony. "Sorry to interrupt," she said.

Laughter swelled through the temple, and they blushed as they straightened and faced her.

"Your guests await your lead," she finished. "Let the celebration begin."

The temple bells rang out in a joyous scale, telling the world that a new Bondlancer had come into her title. A deep boom sounded in response, the first of many fireworks that Whitemoon would be launching as it swung into a citywide party.

Her final words were the cue for the new bondmates to lead their guests out of the temple and into the surrounding grounds for the bonding feast. By tradition, they would thank Fahla for her blessing by resting their hands on her molwyn tree as they passed, though some chose to linger and offer a prayer. As Lanaril waited, listening to the bells, the fireworks, and the beginnings of many conversations among the guests, Andira and Salomen walked to the tree. They lifted their hands to the bark, standing side by side as they prayed.

And Fahla answered.

Lanaril had read about it so many times, and in her heart of hearts she had hoped it would happen tonight, but she had never really believed. She, the Lead Templar of Blacksun, had not had enough faith.

Her jaw dropped when their hands began to glow with a golden flame. They quickly became too bright to look at directly, four tiny suns radiating in the center of the temple. The flame spread to the trunk of the molwyn tree, briefly lighting the area around their hands before it suddenly flashed the length of the trunk and burst into a radiance that sent Lanaril to her knees.

"Fahla, O my Goddess," she murmured. Tears sprang to her eyes as the flame continued outward, traveling along the limbs and branches until it outlined every single leaf. The molwyn tree blazed with a glory that defied understanding, and she wept in gratitude that Fahla truly *had* blessed this bond, that she was here in the temple with them right now, not an abstract idea but a physical presence that no one could deny.

She glanced to the sides and saw every guest on their knees as well, overcome to a person by the power filling the temple—even the Gaians. The only ones still upright were Andira and Salomen, standing calmly at the center of a tower of fire, bearers of Fahla's divine spark who had already been seared by its conflagration and thus were immune to its heat.

The tree burned for several long ticks, its light reflecting off the walls and the glass above, and Lanaril wondered if it was visible from outside, a column of light beaming up into the night sky. At last the flame diminished, retreating from the leaves to the branches, thence to the trunk and finally back into the hands of the tyrees. The temple seemed dull and dim by comparison.

She wiped the tears from her face. Before today, she had only read of miracles. Now she had witnessed one—along with the entire Alsean population, or at least the majority who were watching the live broadcast. How could their lives ever be the same?

Perhaps, as she had once joked to Andira, she would write the next religious text after all. If miracles were still occurring, then wisdom and interpretation still had insights to provide future generations.

Pulling their hands from the now-dark trunk, Andira and Salomen turned back to their guests. In a clear voice, Andira said, "Thank you for sharing this moment with us. We are grateful to Fahla and to you for being here tonight and blessing our bond."

"We invite you now to join us outside for the feast," Salomen added.

They turned and walked out, leaving behind several hundred stunned Alseans who gaped at each other, barely comprehending what they had seen and hardly knowing what to do next.

At last Lanaril said faintly, "Please join the new bondmates in their celebration." It was the traditional end to a ceremony, but after that display of power it seemed ridiculously banal. Still, it was what the guests had needed, and in twos and threes and then groups and streams, they rose and made their way out to the grounds of Whitemoon Temple.

"Oh, my fucking stars," Lhyn whispered as they climbed back to their feet. "I can't believe it. That was *incredible*."

Ekatya rubbed her eyes, still dazzled by the display. "So much for your embellished oral history."

"No kidding. Do you realize what this means? There's a Seeder here. It's the only explanation."

"Well, I'm not quite ready to go that far—"

"Ekatya, really. Maybe you could explain it with technical wizardry today, but that wouldn't apply to the same thing happening a thousand stellar years ago, or two thousand. This has been happening for a long time."

Ambassador Solvassen came up to them, his eyes wide. "What in all the purple planets was *that*?"

"That, Ambassador, was a reminder that neither the Protectorate nor the Voloth hold the greatest power in this corner of the universe." Lanaril had joined them, a serene smile on her face. "And Lhyn, I believe I once told you that if I ever saw this personally, I'd consider it the most fortunate day of my life. Well... here we are."

"I can't wait to see the vids," Lhyn said. "Who do I need to speak to for access?"

"Ready to pick it apart, are you? You and half the secular scholars on Alsea, I imagine, along with all of the templars. It's going to be an interesting few moons watching this play out. And if I were a betting woman"—her smile turned slightly knowing—"I'd lay odds that I'm about to acquire many new worshippers in my temple."

"I might be one of them," said the ambassador. "You really didn't manufacture that?"

"And how would I do that?"

"She didn't," Lhyn said. "Look there, over the main entrance—haven't you ever noticed what the banner of Alsea is showing?"

His eyebrows rose when he saw what she was pointing at. "The tree is in flames. Holy Seeders, no, I never realized it."

"Lanaril, would you like to tell him the story?"

Ekatya left them discussing past and present and made her way out of the temple. Though there was already quite a crowd milling around the brightly lit, elegantly landscaped grounds, she spotted Andira and her tyree in an instant. Not only were they impossible to miss in their bonding suits, but they were also being given a wide berth by guests who apparently did not know how to approach them.

"Didn't you tell me you wanted to keep your true status a secret?" she said when she reached them. "I realize I was ship-lagged and not quite thinking at full speed last night, but I'm pretty sure I remember that."

Andira smiled and shook her head. "We didn't know that would happen."

"Not that it would have stopped us had we known," Salomen said. "I understand Andira's caution, but I'm tired of secrets. Besides, if Fahla meant for us to hide her gift, she wouldn't have advertised it to the whole world."

"That she did," Andira said, drawing her in for a kiss on the cheek.

Once again Ekatya marveled at just how much her friend had changed since their parting two stellar years ago. Some things didn't transmit by quantum com. Andira looked younger, and while some of that could be explained by the smiles and playful humor that so marked her now, there was something else as well, something physical. Lhyn had mentioned it too, commenting that she'd love to run a DNA scan and see whether an Alsean tyree bond had some sort of reverse aging effect. Ekatya had pointed out that she would need a base scan to compare it to, which ended that bit of wishful thinking.

"You've found the perfect match," she said. "Someone who enjoys shaking the tree just as much as you do. Lhyn's in there asking Lanaril for access to the vids so she can analyze the living Hades out of the footage, Ambassador Solvassen is planning his next dispatch even as we speak, Lanaril is already counting her converts, and in the meantime, nobody out here has worked up the courage to come near you."

"Micah was already here," Andira said. "Giving me an earful about advertising to the whole world."

"Just you? I seem to recall two pairs of hands on that tree."

Salomen's smile crinkled her dark eyes and brought out a pair of lovely lines at the sides of her mouth. "Corozen has known Andira all her life. He's known me for a little over three moons. As far as he's concerned, I can do no wrong."

"And you're going to harvest that for as long as you can, aren't you?" Andira asked.

"Of course."

Ekatya laughed. "Just remember that works both ways."

"Oh, yes, I know. Father thinks Andira hung both of our moons, and Jaros thinks she snapped her fingers and the universe came into existence."

"That might be a tiny exaggeration, tyrina."

"Not really." Salomen looked past Ekatya. "Here comes a whole herd of warriors. I guess they got over their awe. Ekatya, will you walk with me?"

"What? You're leaving me alone with them?"

"I doubt I'm the one they want to speak with. Don't worry, I won't go far." Salomen stopped Andira's protest with a kiss, then led Ekatya away from the approaching group. True to her word, she turned at the nearest tree, keeping her bondmate in her line of sight. Ekatya smiled to herself; she recognized this kind of protectiveness.

"I never had a chance to speak with you last night," Salomen said. "At least, not without several sets of ears listening. I wanted to thank you."

"For what?"

"For the gift you gave Andira. You saw through her front. It had been a very long time since anyone besides Corozen treated her like a person, and not a rank or title."

Ekatya nodded. "At a certain level, we start to forget how to separate ourselves from the rank. It's what we need our friends and family for."

"Were you forgetting yours?"

Looking at her, Ekatya had the feeling that Salomen understood everything, despite not being there or really knowing her. No wonder this woman had captured Andira's heart.

"I was," she said. "Worse, I was forgetting why I joined Fleet in the first place and what I wanted my life to stand for. That was the gift Andira gave me. Well, one of them. You owe me no thanks, Bondlancer. I think I'm still in debt."

"Salomen, please. I'm still not ready for the walls that title is going to raise."

"Just making sure I didn't start a diplomatic incident. Speaking of which, did Andira ever tell you the story of when our friendship really began?"

"She told me that she liked you from the start, but no, she hasn't mentioned any specific moment." Salomen looked intrigued. "It involved a diplomatic incident?"

"A fistfight, actually…"

The feast was sumptuous, offering specialty dishes and drinks from all over Alsea, and the entire Whitemoon Symphony played at the far edge of the grounds, its music drifting over the revelers as they gradually loosened up.

Vellmar needed a full glass of spirits before the chills stopped, and a second before she could begin to relax. After that, she happily stuffed herself with some of the best food she'd ever tasted while wandering about the grounds and chatting with the guests. Every conversation naturally started with the same topic, but after a hantick, even that had been sufficiently reviewed and people reverted to their normal gossip, debates, and discussions.

But when she came around a curve in the garden path and found herself facing her oath holders, she was too awed to speak normally.

"Lancer Tal, Bondlancer Opah. Congratulations on a, ah, memorable ceremony."

"Thank you." Lancer Tal indicated the glass in her hand. "Nice to know you can drink all you want and not have to run with me tomorrow, isn't it?"

Vellmar's hand twitched, almost spilling her drink. "No! I mean, ah, yes? The feast is fantastic, I've never even had Valkinon before, but I'd run with you if you wanted…" She trailed off, her face heating as they smiled at her.

"Don't tell me that after all these ninedays the Fahla's Chosen thing finally got to you, too?"

"Well, no…but…" She gestured toward the temple. "I might be a few cycles behind in my offerings to Fahla."

"And you're telling me this why? I'm not a templar."

"You made a molwyn tree glow," Vellmar said bluntly. "That's a miracle."

"A little credit here, please," the Bondlancer said. "She didn't do it by herself."

Vellmar looked from one to the other, not knowing what to say without digging herself in deeper.

Lancer Tal leaned closer. "Don't let it get to you. It shocked the shek out of us, too."

Vellmar's eyes widened at the casual profanity. They were on temple grounds, on the night of a miracle, and Lancer Tal was just…

…acting like normal. Or at least normal when they were alone, training or exercising.

The laugh bubbled up out of nowhere. "It shocked two sheks out of me. I was remembering all the times I've hit you in our sparring sessions and wondering when the temple floor was going to crack open and swallow me."

"Don't even think about going easy on her after this," Opah said. "I know what those sessions do for her. She'll never get that kind of relaxation if she's not battling for it."

"Salomen is a fast learner." Lancer Tal winked at her.

"Hard not to be, when I'm feeling what you feel."

"What did Colonel Micah think about it?" Vellmar asked curiously.

"He asked if we could for once make his life easier instead of harder."

She nodded, understanding exactly how he felt. "Well, I suppose it was going to come out sooner or later. And Ronlin is prepared for it." Besides her professional interactions with Salomen's Lead Guard, she saw him quite a bit on their off duty time since their quarters were adjoining in both the State House and the base. They had struck up a friendship, and she respected Ronlin as a highly—but appropriately—paranoid man.

"I'm beginning to wonder if Ronlin isn't gifted with the forward sight," Opah said. "He told me he was preparing for imminent exposure because all the world would be watching today. I thought he was just being…" She gestured at them.

"A warrior?" Lancer Tal asked with a raised eyebrow.

"Yes. And can we talk about something else besides security? There *are* other topics of interest, you know."

"Such as?"

The Bondlancer pointed up. "That."

Micah was done with crowds. He had mingled and conversed and enjoyed it, but after two hanticks, he needed some time alone.

He found the stone steps in the northeast corner of the temple grounds. A moon ago, climbing them would have required effort and his walking stick, but tonight he walked up easily. As he stood atop the park wall, looking out over the city and the vast bay beyond, he sent a thought of gratitude to the Redmoon healers who had done such excellent work on him.

It wasn't often that a man owed his life to so many. When he had first seen the schedule for his Sharings, with nearly every time slot filled in for eight days *and* nights, he had broken down and wept. Then he determined that he would thank every one of those people for what they had done.

Even Aldirk.

It took nearly two moons, because one did not start such a conversation out of nothing. But he had just one left, and he could finish on the bonding break.

A soft breeze brushed his face, bringing with it the scent of the sea, and he lifted his eyes to the moons. He had been watching them all evening. Sonalia was the first to rise, full and brilliant, her light enhancing the natural glow of the temple dome. The largest and most distant of their moons, she moved with the stately grace befitting the eldest. Eusaltin was the impatient younger sister, rising later but catching up quickly as she dashed across the sky.

And now she was there, riding the trailing edge of her sister's larger disc. Behind him, Micah heard the symphony play a fanfare as most of the feast lights went out. The hum of conversation and laughter ceased, and the temple grounds fell silent as every head turned skyward.

He settled himself on the wall, his legs dangling over the edge while he watched the moons begin their slide into the shadow of Alsea. Slowly, their brilliance was quenched. The stars blazed in the now-dark sky, and behind him, the glow of the temple dome seemed twice as bright.

The dark moons glided onward, almost invisible, until first Sonalia and then Eusaltin began to return to life—but not with their former silver light. This was an otherworldly red glow, as they reflected the light from Alsea's atmosphere rather than the sun. Eusaltin began her passage across Sonalia, and gradually, the two moons merged into one.

"There," he whispered, entranced. For the next half hantick, Alsea would have one moon only—a red moon. It happened only once or twice each cycle, and since the earliest days of Alsean history, it had been associated with the unfathomable power of Fahla. Later scientific explanations did not lessen the instinctive awe the spectacle induced, and it seemed to him that a red moon shining on Andira and Salomen's bonding feast was the perfect counterpoint to the flame of the molwyn tree. In every possible way, this bonding was blessed.

And so was he. He had carried his secret for so long that when he finally released it, he hardly knew what to feel. For Andira to know and accept it so easily…at times, it seemed like a miracle. Other times he was ashamed for ever thinking she would react otherwise. After all, she had been raised by Realta and Andorin—and himself.

Love feeds love, Realta had often told him. It was why she had no trouble finding room in her heart for both him and Andorin. He had never understood that until Fahla gave him the vision in Redmoon. Now he had a family of his own, and his heart seemed made of elastic for the ease with which it expanded to include its new members. Best of all, he had the freedom to speak of his great love as well as his great friend. He had always been afraid to bring up Realta too often, for fear of raising suspicion. In a way, telling his secret had brought her back to him.

"You would be so proud of her," he murmured to the sky. "I think not even your dreams encompassed what she's become." Smiling broadly, he added, "But mine did."

GLOSSARY

UNITS OF TIME

piptick: one 100th of a tick (about half a second).

tick: about a minute (50 seconds).

tentick: ten ticks.

hantick: 10 tenticks, just shy of 1.5 hours (83.33 minutes). One Alsean day is 20 hanticks (27.7 hours) or 1.15 days.

moon: a basic unit of Alsean time, similar to our month but 36 days long. Each moon is divided into four parts called **ninedays**. One Alsean moon equals 41.55 stellar (Earth) days.

cycle: the length of time it takes the Alsean planet to revolve around their sun (13 moons or approximately 17 stellar months).

Alsean days are divided into quarters, each five hanticks long, which reset at the end of the eve quarter. The quarters are: **night, morn, mid, and eve**. A specific hantick can be expressed in one of two ways: its place in the quarter or its exact number. Thus **morn-three** would be three hanticks into the morning quarter, which can also be expressed as hantick eight (the five hanticks of the night quarter plus three of the morning). In the summer, the long days result in sunrise around morn-one (hantick six), lunch or midmeal at mid-one (hantick eleven), dinner or evenmeal at eve-one (hantick sixteen), and sunset around eve-five (hantick twenty).

UNITS OF MEASUREMENT

pace: half a stride.

stride: the distance of a normal adult's stride at a fast walk (about a meter).

length: a standard of distance equalling one thousand strides (about a kilometer).

GENERAL TERMS

ADF: Alsean Defense Force.

AIF: Alsean Investigative Force.

artisan: honorific for a crafter.

ba: short name for bondparent (either bondmother or bondfather).

bai: short name for birthparent (either birthmother or birthfather).

bondmate: a life partner.

boren: deer-like grazing animals.

cintek: the Alsean monetary unit.

deme: honorific for a secular scholar.

dokker: a farm animal similar to a cow. Slow moving and rather stupid, but with a hell of a kick when it's angry or frightened.

dokshin: vulgar term for dokker feces.

Eusaltin: the smaller and nearer moon of Alsea.

evenmeal: dinner.

Fahla: the goddess of the Alseans, also called Mother.

fanten: a farm animal similar to a pig, used for meat.

front: a mental protection that prevents one's emotions from being sensed by another.

gender-locked: an Alsean who is unable to temporarily shift genders for the purposes of reproduction. Considered a grave handicap, denying the individual the full blessing of Fahla.

grainbird: a small black and red seed-eating bird common in agricultural fields. It is known for singing even at night, leading to an old perception of the birds as lacking in intelligence—hence "grainbird" is also a slang term for an idiot.

grainstem powder: powder derived from crushed stems of a particular grain, which yields a sweet taste. Commonly used in cooking; also used to sprinkle over fresh bread.

Great Belt: the equator.

holcat: a small domesticated feline.

horten: an Alsean delicacy, often used in soup. It comes from a plant that, once harvested, stays fresh for a very short time and must be processed immediately. Due to that short window of time, fresh horten is very expensive and usually served only in the nicer restaurants.

hornstalk: a very fast-growing weed.

hyacot: a tree whose twigs, when snapped, provide a pleasant and long-lasting scent. Used in fine restaurants and as a room freshener.

joining: sexual relations. Joining is considered less significant than Sharing between lovers. The two acts can take place simultaneously, though this would only occur in a serious relationship.

kiral: honorific for a warrior serving in neither the Guards nor the Mariners.

kyne: honorific for a builder.

magtran: a form of public transport consisting of a chain of cylindrical passenger carriers accelerated by magnetic fields through transparent tubes.

marmello: a sweet, orange fruit.

midmeal: lunch.

molwine: the curved apex of the pelvic ridges on both male and female Alseans. A very sensitive sexual organ.

molwyn: Fahla's sacred tree. It has a black trunk and leaves with silver undersides. A molwyn grows at the center of every temple of decent size.

mornmeal: breakfast.

mountzar: a carnivorous animal that lives at high elevations and hibernates during the winter.

panfruit: a common breakfast or dessert fruit.

probe: to push beyond the front and read emotions that are not available for a surface skim. Probing without permission is a violation of Alsean law.

raiz: honorific for a producer.

reese: honorific for a merchant.

Return: the passage after death, in which an Alsean returns to Fahla and embarks on the next plane of existence.

Rite of Ascension: the formal ceremony in which a child becomes a legal and social adult. The Rite takes place at twenty cycles, after which one's choice of caste cannot be changed.

shannel: a traditional hot drink, used for energy and freshening one's breath. Made from the dried leaves (and sometimes flowers) of the shannel plant.

skim: to sense any emotions that an Alsean is not specifically holding behind her or his front.

Sharing: the act of physically connecting the emotional centers between two or more Alseans, resulting in unshielded emotions that can be fully accessed by anyone in the Sharing link. It is most frequently done between lovers or bondmates but is also part of a bonding ceremony (in which all guests take part in a one-time Sharing with the two new bondmates). It can also be done between friends, family, or for medical purposes.

shek: vulgar slang for penetrative sex. Usually used as a profanity.

Sonalia: the larger and more distant moon of Alsea.

sonsales: one who is empathically blind.

thantane: a potent pain reliever, on a level with morphine.

tyrees: Alseans whose empathic centers share a rare compatibility, which has physiological consequences. Tyrees can sense each other's emotions at greater distances than normal, have difficulty being physically apart, and are ferociously protective of each other. Tyrees are always bonded, usually for life.

warmron: an embrace. Warmrons are shared only between lovers, or parents and children—and only until the child reaches the Rite of Ascension. A warmron is too close to a Sharing for it to be used at any other time.

weeper: a soap opera.

winden: a large six-toed mammal, adapted to an alpine environment. It is wary, able to climb nearly sheer walls, and the fastest animal on Alsea. Winden travel in herds and are rarely seen.

wristcom: wrist-mounted communication device, often used in conjunction with an earcuff.

zalren: a venomous snake.

THE STORY DOESN'T HAVE TO END ON THE LAST PAGE

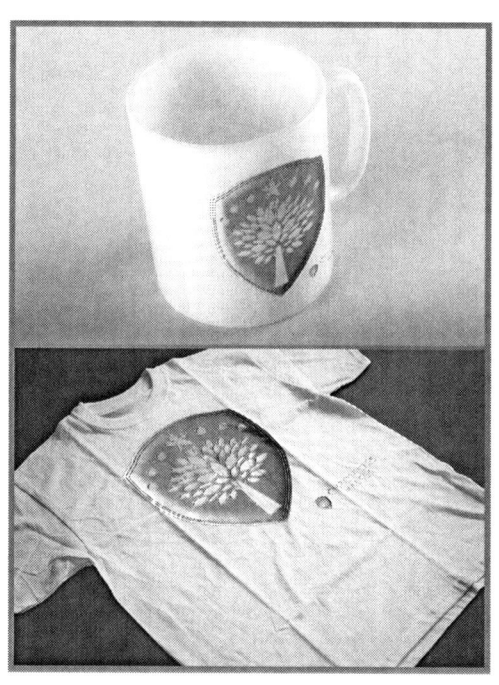

Take it with you—on a shirt, a phone case, a mug and so much more. Choose your caste, or give a caste gift to a friend. That way, Alsea will always be there.

HTTP://WWW.CAFEPRESS.COM/CHRONICLESOFALSEA

ABOUT FLETCHER DELANCEY

Fletcher DeLancey spent her early career as a science educator, which was the perfect combination of her two great loves: language and science. These days she combines them while writing science fiction.

She is an Oregon expatriate who left her beloved state when she met a Portuguese woman and had to choose between home and heart. She chose heart. Now she lives with her wife and son in the beautiful sunny Algarve, where she writes full-time, teaches Pilates, tries to learn the local birds and plants, and samples every regional Portuguese dish she can get her hands on. (There are many. It's going to take a while.)

She is best known for her geeky romance *Mac vs. PC* and her science fiction series, *Chronicles of Alsea*. Currently, she is working on the next books in the *Chronicles of Alsea* and as an editor for Ylva Publishing.

CONNECT WITH THIS AUTHOR:
Website: http://www.chroniclesofalsea.com
Blog: http://www.chroniclesofalsea.com/blog
E-mail: fletcher@mailhaven.com
Twitter: @AlseaAuthor

OTHER BOOKS FROM YLVA PUBLISHING

www.ylva-publishing.com

THE CAPHENON

(Chronicles of Alsea – Book #1)

Fletcher DeLancey

ISBN: 978-3-95533-253-2
Length: 374 pages (165,000 words)

An emergency call to Lancer Andira Tal has shocking news: there is other intelligent life in the universe, and it's landing on the planet right now. The aliens sacrificed their ship to save Alsea—temporarily.

Alsea is now a prize to be bought and sold in galactic politics. But Lancer Tal is not one to accept a fate imposed by aliens, and she'll do whatever it takes to save her world.

WITHOUT A FRONT: THE PRODUCER'S CHALLENGE

(Chronicles of Alsea – Book #2)

Fletcher DeLancey

ISBN: 978-3-95533-436-9
Length: 340 pages (140,000 words)

In the aftermath of war, Andira Tal, Lancer of Alsea, is working nonstop to heal her world and bring it into the future. The producer caste—and one producer in particular—stands in her way. Tal's solution leads to an unexpected sanctuary and the kind of love she always dreamed of...but her enemies are watching, and now she has more to lose.

THE TEA MACHINE

Gill McKnight

ISBN: 978-3-95533-432-1
Length: 346 pages (97,000 words)

Spinster by choice, Millicent Aberly has managed to catapult herself from her lovely Victorian mews house into a strange future full of giant space squid, Roman empires, and a most annoying centurion to whom she owes her life.

Decanus Sangfroid was just doing her job rescuing the weird little scientist chick from a squid attack. Now she finds herself in London, 1862, and it's not a good fit.

BANSHEE'S HONOR

Shaylynn Rose

ISBN: 978-3-95533-103-0
Length: 379 pages (153,000 words)

Warleader—in Y'Dan, this is a title of pride, of honor, and of joy. Oathbreaker—a word branded only on those whose crimes are so heinous, all must know of their crime. Both of these names have been given to Azhani Rhu'len. Only one of them is right.

Without a Front: The Warrior's Challenge
© 2015 by Fletcher DeLancey

ISBN: 978-3-95533-440-6

Also available as e-book.

Published by Ylva Publishing, legal entity of Ylva Verlag, e.Kfr.

Ylva Verlag, e.Kfr.
Owner: Astrid Ohletz
Am Kirschgarten 2
65830 Kriftel
Germany

www.ylva-publishing.com

First edition: November 2015

No part of this book may be reproduced, scanned, or distributed in any printed or electronic form without permission. Please do not participate in or encourage piracy of copyrighted materials in violation of the author's rights. Thank you for respecting the hard work of this author.

This is a work of fiction. Names, characters, places, and incidents either are a product of the author's imagination or are used fictitiously, and any resemblance to locales, events, business establishments, or actual persons—living or dead—is entirely coincidental.

Credits
Edited by Sandra Gerth & Cheri Fuller
Proofread by Lisa Shaw
Cover Design & Print Layout by Streetlight Graphics

CPSIA information can be obtained at www.ICGtesting.com
Printed in the USA
LVOW08s0113140716

496237LV00001B/70/P